DORSAI

< < < < < < < < < < < < < < < < <

SPIRIT

Tor Books by Gordon R. Dickson

Novels

Alien Art
The Alien Way
Arcturus Landing
The Far Call
Gremlins, Go Home! (with Ben Bova)
Hoka! (with Poul Anderson)
Home from the Shore
The Last Master
Masters of Everon
Mission to Universe
Naked to the Stars
On the Run
Other
Outposter
Planet Run (with Keith Laumer)
The Pritcher Mass
Pro
Secrets of the Deep
Sleepwalker's World
The Space Swimmers
The Space Winners
Spacepaw
Spacial Delivery
Way of the Pilgrim
Wolf and Iron

The Dorsai Series

Necromancer
Tactics of Mistake
Lost Dorsai: The New Dorsai
Companion
Soldier, Ask Not
The Spirit of Dorsai
Dorsai!
Young Bleys
The Final Encyclopedia,
vol. 1 (rev. ed.)
The Final Encyclopedia,
vol. 2 (rev. ed.)
The Chantry Guild
Dorsai Spirit

The Dragon Series

The Dragon Knight
The Dragon and the Gnarly King
The Dragon in Lyonesse
The Dragon and
the Fair Maid of Kent

Collections

Beyond the Dar al-Harb
Guided Tour
Love Not Human
The Man from Earth
The Man the Worlds Rejected
Steel Brother
Stranger

Gordon R. Dickson

DORSAI

SPIRIT

DORSAI!

and

THE SPIRIT OF DORSAI

A Tom Doherty Associates Book
New York

DORSAI SPIRIT

A Tor Book
Published by Tom Doherty Associates, LLC
175 Fifth Avenue
New York, NY 10010

www.tor.com

Tor® is a registered trademark of Tom Doherty Associates, LLC.

ISBN 0-312-87764-1

First Edition: June 2002

Printed in the United States of America

0 9 8 7 6 5 4 3 2 1

CONTENTS

INTRODUCTION

by David Drake

I don't insist that you believe *Dorsai!* is the best novel of military SF ever written: one could make a pretty good case for Heinlein's *Starship Troopers*. I will, however, insist that those two novels (first published within weeks of one another in 1959) are in combination the standard against which the subgenre of military SF must be judged.

Everybody who's attempted a complex task knows that there are more ways to go wrong than there are to do the job right. *Dorsai!* and *Starship Troopers* are a useful illustration of the diversity nonetheless possible between first-class works, even within a category as narrow as military SF. Heinlein's novel focused on the individual soldier and the social forces that molded him. *Dorsai!* is an investigation of the problems of high command and the qualities that produce the ideal commander.

The differences in approach aren't so much apples and oranges but rather the drive and driven plates of a clutch: both command and execution are necessary for a military system to work. In my opinion, Dickson and Heinlein have explored these segments of the system not only as well as anybody in the field has done, but as well as anybody is likely ever to do.

Dorsai! is an exposition of what Basil Liddell-Hart termed the Strategy of Indirection. (I do not imply a necessarily direct connection.) Instead of overwhelming one's opponent by brute force, the exponent of indirection maneuvers so that his opponent has to attack or (better yet) is checkmated without a battle.

Liddell-Hart developed his theories as a reaction to the blood-drenched killing grounds of World War One, a conflict that was as perfect an example of the brute force approach and its limitations as one could find. The brute force technique as refined to its quintessential form by Field Marshal Haig involved silencing hostile machine guns by attacking with more infantry than the machine gunners had bullets. (I wish I were exaggerating, but read the accounts.)

Liddell-Hart went further back in history and examined the campaigns of Hannibal, Sherman, and particularly the Byzantine general Belisarius to find an alternative strategy. To defeat an entrenched enemy, maneuver around him and force him to leave his fortifications in order to protect his rear areas. Instead of attacking an enemy, destroy his supplies so that he has to retreat. Move into a position that the enemy *must* take (ideally for reasons of perceived honor rather than pragmatic need) and let him waste his strength against your fortifications—until you move out and leave him with a useless shell.

These are the sorts of campaigns that Donal Graeme, the hero of *Dorsai!*, fights. Anyone who has had the fortune to be involved in the other sort of war will wish that more real-life officers had considered the responsibilities of command as clearly as Dickson did.

Dorsai! is and was conceived as a self-standing novel. Because of the strength of its conception, however, it has become the foundation of one of science fiction's most ambitious and far-ranging constructs, the Childe Cycle. The Cycle is a vast structure, spanning a millennium from the historical fourteenth century to a fictional future in which the triune aspects of humanity will be united again in a form both superhuman and super-humane.

Much of the Cycle remained to be written when Dickson

died more than forty years after the original publication of *Dorsai!*, though further pieces of the interlocking whole continued to appear throughout his lifetime, each excellent in its own right. It is a tribute to the structure of the original novel that the conception shown here in microcosm remain valid despite the weight of detail accreting in the later novels.

I've discussed *Dorsai!* as paradigm: for fiction writers in general, for military professionals, and for Dickson himself in his later work. None of the above could have touched me when I first read the novel at age fifteen. (Well, I read *The Genetic General*; which is not quite the same thing, but almost.)

What struck me and caused me to reread the novel a number of times was that this is one heck of a good story. It's a model of clean prose, seamless structure, and fast action. In this too, *Dorsai!* is a paradigm—for other writers. But that doesn't have to matter to readers, whether first-timers or (like me the other day) for the umpteenth time.

Dive in and have fun!

> > DORSAI! < <

Cadet

The boy was odd.

This much he knew for himself. This much he had heard his seniors—his mother, his father, his uncles, the officers at the Academy—mention to each other, nodding their heads confidentially, not once but many times during his short eighteen years of life, leading up to this day. Now, apart, wandering the empty rec fields in this long, amber twilight before returning to his home and the graduation supper awaiting him there, he admitted to the oddness—whether truly in himself, or only in what others thought of him.

"An odd boy," he had overheard the Commandant at the Academy saying once to the Mathematics Officer, "you never know which way he'll jump."

Back at home right now, the family would be waiting his return—unsure of which way he would jump. They would be half expecting him to refuse his Outgoing. Why? He had never given them any cause to doubt. He was Dorsai of the Dorsai, his mother a Kenwick, his father a Graeme, names so very old their origin was buried in the prehistory of the Mother Planet. His courage was unquestioned, his word unblemished. He had headed his class. His very blood and bones were the heritage of a long line of great professional soldiers. No blot of dishonor had ever marred that roll of warriors, no home had ever been burnt, its inhabitants scattered and hiding their family shame under new names, because of some failure on the part of one of the family's sons. And yet, they doubted.

He came to the fence that marked off the high hurdles from

the jump pits, and leaned on it with both elbows, the tunic of a Senior Cadet pulled tight across his shoulders. In what way was he odd? he wondered into the wide glow of the sunset. How was he different?

He put himself apart from him in his mind's eye, and considered himself. A slim young man of eighteen years—tall, but not tall by Dorsai standards, strong, but not strong by Dorsai standards. His face was the face of his father, sharp and angular, straightnosed; but without his father's massiveness of bones. His coloring was the dark coloring of the Dorsai, hair straight and black and a little coarse. Only his eyes—those indeterminate eyes that were no definite color but went from gray to green to blue with his shifting moods—were not to be found elsewhere on his family trees. But surely eyes alone could not account for a reputation of oddness?

There was, of course, his temper. He had inherited, in full measure, those cold, sudden, utterly murderous Dorsai rages which had made his people such that no sane man cared to cross one of them without good reason. But that was a common trait; and if the Dorsai thought of Donal Graeme as odd, it could not be for that alone.

Was it, he wondered now, gazing into the sunset, that even in his rages he was a little too calculating—a little too controlled and remote? And as he thought that thought, all his strangeness, all his oddness came on him with a rush, together with that weird sense of disembodiment that had afflicted him, now and again, ever since his birth.

It came always at moments like this, riding the shoulders of fatigue and some great emotion. He remembered it as a very young boy in the Academy chapel at evening service, half-faint with hunger after the long day of hard military exercises and harder lessons. The sunset, as now, came slanting in through the high windows on the bare, highly polished walls and the solidographs of famous battles inset in them. He stood among

the rows of his classmates between the hard, low benches, the
ranked male voices, from the youngest cadet to the deep man-
voices of the officers in the rear, riding the deep, solemn notes
of the Recessional—that which was known as the Dorsai Hymn
now, wherever man had gone, and which a man named Kipling
had written the words of, over four centuries before.

> . . . Far called, our navies melt away,
> On dune and headland sinks the fire.
> Lo! All our pomp of yesterday,
> Is one with Nineveh, and Tyre . . .

As he had remembered it being sung at the burial service when
his youngest uncle's ashes had been brought back from the
slagged battlefield of Donneswort, on Freiland, third planet circling the star of Sirius.

> . . . For heathen heart that puts her trust
> In reeking tube and iron shard,
> All valiant dust, that builds on dust
> And guarding, calls not thee to guard . . .

And he had sung with the rest, feeling then, as now, the final
words in the innermost recesses of his heart.

> . . . For frantic boast and foolish word—
> *Thy Mercy on Thy People, Lord!*

A chill shiver ran down his back. The enchantment was complete. Far and wide about him the red and dying light flooded
the level land. In the farther sky the black dot of a hawk circled.
But here by the fence and the high hurdles, he stood removed
and detached, enclosed by some clear, transparent wall that set
him apart from all the universe, alone, untouchable and enrap-

tured. The inhabited worlds and their suns sank and dwindled in his mind's eye; and he felt the siren, deadly pull of that ocean of some great, hidden purpose that promised him at once fulfillment and a final dissolution. He stood on its brink and its waves lapped at his feet; and, as always, he strove to lift his foot and step forward into its depths and be lost forever; but some small part of him cried out against the self-destruction and held him back.

Then suddenly—as suddenly as it had come—the spell was broken. He turned toward the craft that would take him home.

As he came to the front entrance, he found his father waiting for him, in the half-shadow leaning with his wide shoulders spread above the slim metal shaft of his cane.

"Be welcome to this house," said his father and straightened up. "You'd better get out of that uniform and into some man's clothes. Dinner will be ready in half an hour."

Man

The men of the household of Eachan Khan Graeme sat around the long, shimmering slab of the dining board in the long and shadowy room, at their drinking after the women and children had retired. They were not all present, nor—short of a minor miracle—was it ever likely that they would be, in this life. Of sixteen adult males, nine were off at the wars among the stars, one was undergoing reconstructive surgery at the hospital in Omalu, and the eldest, Donal's granduncle, Kamal, was quietly dying in his own room at the back of the household with an oxygen tube up his nose and the faint scent of the bay lilac to remind him of his Maran wife, now forty years dead. Sitting at the table were five—of which, since three o'clock this afternoon—Donal was one.

Those others who were present to welcome him to his adulthood were Eachan, his father; Mor, his elder brother, who was home on leave from the Friendlies; and his twin uncles Ian and Kensie, who had been next in age above that James who had died at Donneswort. They sat grouped around the high end of the table, Eachan at its head, with his two sons on his right and his two younger twin brothers on his left.

"They had good officers when I was there," Eachan was saying. He leaned over to fill Donal's glass, and Donal took it up automatically, listening with both ears.

"Freilanders all," said Ian, the grimmer of the two dark twins. "They run to stiffness of organization without combat to shake them up. Kensie says Mara or Kultis, and I say why not?"

"They have full companies of Dorsai there, I hear," said Mor, at Donal's right. The deep voice of Eachan answered from his left.

"They're show guards. I know of those. Why make a cake of nothing but icing? The Bond of Kultis likes to think of having an unmatched bodyguard; but they'd be farmed out to the troops fast enough in case of real trouble between the stars."

"And meanwhile," put in Kensie, with a sudden smile that split his dark face, "no action. Peacetime soldiering goes sour. The outfits split up into little cliques, the cake-fighters move in and an actual man—a Dorsai—becomes an ornament."

"Good," said Eachan, nodding. Donal swallowed absently from his glass and the unaccustomed whiskey burned fiercely at the back of his nose and throat. Little pricklings of sweat popped out on his forehead; but he ignored them, concentrating on what was being said. This talk was all for his benefit, he knew. He was a man now, and could no longer be told what to do. The choice was his, about where he would go to take service, and they were helping him with what knowledge they had, of the eight systems and their ways.

". . . I was never great for garrison duty myself," Eachan was continuing. "A mercenary's job is to train, maintain and fight; but when all's said and done, the fighting's the thing. Not that everyone's of my mind. There are Dorsai and Dorsai—and not all Dorsai are Graemes."

"The Friendlies, now—" said Mor, and stopped with a glance at his father, afraid that he had interrupted.

"Go on," said Eachan, nodding.

"I was just about to point out," said Mor, "there's plenty of action on Association—and Harmony, too, I hear. The sects will always be fighting against each other. And there's body-guard work—"

"Catch us being personal gunmen," said Ian, who—being closer in age to Mor than Mor's father—did not feel the need to be quite so polite. "That's no job for a soldier."

"I didn't mean to suggest it," said Mor, turning to his uncle. "But the psalm-singers rate it high among themselves, and that takes some of their best talent. It leaves the field posts open for mercenaries."

"True enough," said Kensie, equably. "And if they had less fanatics and more officers, those two worlds would be putting strong forces out between the stars. But a priest-soldier is only troublesome when he's more soldier than priest."

"I'll back that," said Mor. "This last skirmish I was in on Association, an elder came down the line after we'd taken one little town and wanted five of my men for hangmen."

"What did you do?" asked Kensie.

"Referred him to my Commandant—and then got to the old man first and told him that if he could find five men in my force who actually wanted such a job, he could transfer them out the next day."

Ian nodded.

"Nothing spoils a man for battle like playing butcher," he said.

"The old man got that," said Mor. "They got their hangmen, I heard—but not from me."

"The lusts are vampires," said Eachan, heavily, from the head of the table. "Soldiering is a pure art. A man with a taste for blood, money or women was one I never trusted."

"The women are fine on Mara and Kultis," grinned Mor. "I hear."

"I'll not deny it," said Kensie, merrily. "But you've got to come home, some day."

"God grant that you all may," said Eachan, somberly. "I am a Dorsai and a Graeme, but if this little world of ours had something else to trade for the contracts of out-world professionals besides the blood of our best fighting men, I'd be more pleased."

"Would *you* have stayed home, Eachan," said Mor, "when you were young and had two good legs?"

"No, Mor," said Eachan, heavily. "But there are other arts, beside the art of war—even for a Dorsai." He looked at his eldest son. "When our forefathers settled this world less than a hundred and fifty years ago, it wasn't with the intention of providing gun-fodder for the other eight systems. They only wanted a world where no man could bend the destinies of another man against that second man's will."

"And that we have," said Ian, bleakly.

"And that we have," echoed Eachan. "The Dorsai is a free world where any man can do as he likes as long as he respects the rights of his neighbor. Not all the other eight systems combined would like to try their luck with this one world. But the price—the price—" He shook his head and refilled his glass.

"Now those are heavy words for a son who's just going out," said Kensie. "There's a lot of good in life just the way she is now. Beside, it's economic pressures we're under today, not military. Who'd want the Dorsai, anyway, besides us? We're all nut here, and very little kernel. Take one of the rich new worlds—like Ceta under Tau Ceti—or one of the richer, older worlds like Freiland, or Newton—or even old Venus herself. They've got cause to worry. They're the ones that are at each other's throats for the best scientists, the best technicians, the top artists and doctors. And the more work for us and the better life for us, because of it."

"Eachan's right though, Kensie," growled Ian. "They still dream of squeezing our free people up into one lump and then negotiating with that lump for the force to get the whip hand over all the other worlds." He leaned forward across the table toward Eachan and in the muted light of the dining room Donal saw the sudden white flash of the seared scar that coiled up his forearm like a snake and was lost in the loose sleeve of his short, undress tunic. "That's the danger we'll never be free of."

"As long as the cantons remain independent of the Council," said Eachan, "and the families remain independent of the cantons, there'll be no success for them, Ian." He nodded at all about the table. "That's my end of the job here at home. You can go out to the wars with easy consciences. I promise you your children will grow up free in this house—free of any man's will—or the house will no longer stand."

"I trust you," said Ian. His eyes were gleaming pale as the scar in the dimness and he was very close to that Dorsai violence of emotion that was at once so cold and so deadly. "I have two boys now under this roof. But remember no men are perfect—even the Dorsai. There was Mahub Van Ghent only five years back, who dreamed about a little kingdom among the Dorsai in the Midland South—only five years ago, Eachan!"

"He was on the other side of the world," said Eachan. "And he's dead now, at the hand of one of the Benali, his closest neighbor. His home is burnt and no man acknowledges himself a Van Ghent any more. What more do you want?"

"He should have been stopped sooner."

"Each man has a right to his own destiny," said Eachan, softly. "Until he crosses the line into another man's. His family has suffered enough."

"Yes," said Ian. He was calming down. He poured himself another drink. "That's true—that's true. They're not to blame."

"About the Exotics—" said Mor, gently.

"Oh, yes," answered Kensie, as if the twin brother that was so much a part of himself had never gotten excited at all. "Mara and Kultis—interesting worlds. Don't mistake them if you ever go there, Mor—or you either, Donal. They're sharp enough, for all their art and robes and trappings. They won't fight themselves, but they know how to hire good men. There's things being done on Mara and Kultis—and not only in the arts. Meet one of their psychologists, one time."

"They're honest," said Eachan.

"That, too," said Kensie. "But what catches at me is the fact they're going some place, in their own way. If I had to pick one of the other worlds to be born on—"

"I would always be a soldier," said Mor.

"You think so now," said Kensie, and drank. "You think so now. But it's a wild civilization we have nowadays, with its personality split a dozen different ways by a dozen different cultures. Less than five hundred years ago the average man never dreamed of getting his feet off the ground. And the farther we go the faster. And the faster the farther."

"It's the Venus group forcing that, isn't it?" asked Donal, his youthful reticence all burnt away in the hot fumes of the whiskey.

"Don't you think it," said Kensie. "Science is only one road to the future. Old Venus, Old Mars—Cassida, Newton—maybe they've had their day. Project Blaine's a rich and powerful old man, but he doesn't know all the new tricks they're dreaming up on Mara and Kultis, or the Friendlies—or Ceta, for that matter. Make it a point to take two good looks at things when you get out among the stars, you two young ones, because nine times out of ten that first glance will leave you fooled."

"Listen to him, boys," said Eachan from the top of the table. "Your uncle Kensie's a man and a half above the shoulders. I just wish I had as good advice to give you. Tell them, Kensie."

"Nothing stands still," said Kensie—and with those three words, the whiskey seemed to go to Donal's head in a rush, the table and the dark harsh-boned faces before him seemed to swim in the dimness of the dining room, and Kensie's voice came roaring at him as if from a great distance. "Everything changes, and that's what you must bear in mind. What was true yesterday about something may not be true today. So remember that and take no man's word about something without reservation, even mine. We have multiplied like the biblical locusts and spread out among the stars, splitting into different groups with different ways. Now, while we still seem to be rushing forward to where I have no idea, at a terrific rate, increasing all the time, I have this feeling—as if we are all poised, hanging on the brink of something, something great and different and maybe terrible. It's a time to walk cautious, it is indeed."

"I'll be the greatest general that ever was!" cried Donal, and was startled as the rest to hear the words leap, stumbling and thick-tongued, but loud, from within him. "They'll see—I'll show them what a Dorsai can be!"

He was aware of them looking at him, though all their faces were blurred, except—by some trick of vision—that of Kensie, diagonally across the table from him. Kensie was considering him with somber, reading eyes. Donal was conscious of his father's hand on his shoulder.

"Time to turn in," said his father.

"You'll see—" said Donal, thickly. But they were all rising, picking up their glasses and turning to his father, who held his own glass up.

"May we all meet again," said his father. And they drank, standing. The remains of the whiskey in his glass flowed tasteless as water down Donal's tongue and throat—and for a second everything cleared and he saw these tall men standing around him. Big, even for Dorsai, they were; even his brother Mor topping him by half a head, so that he stood like a half-grown boy among them. But at that same instant of vision he was suddenly wrung with a terrible tenderness and pity for them, as if he was the grown one, and they the children to be protected. He opened his mouth to say, for once in his life, how much he loved them, and how always he would be there to take care of them—and then the fog closed down again; and he was only aware of Mor leading him stumblingly to his room.

Later, he opened his eyes in the darkness to become aware of a dim figure drawing the curtains of his room against the bright new light of the double moon, just risen. It was his mother; and with a sudden, reflexive action he rolled off his bed and lurched to her and put his hands on her shoulders.

"Mother—" he said.

She looked up at him with a pale face softened by the moonlight.

"Donal," she said tenderly, putting her arms around him. "You'll catch cold, Donal."

"Mother—" he said, thickly. "If you ever need me . . . to take care of you—"

"Oh, my boy," she said, holding his hard young body tightly to her, "take care of yourself; my boy . . . my boy—"

Mercenary

Donal shrugged his shoulders in the tight civilian half-jacket and considered its fit as reflected in the mirror of his tiny, box-like cabin. The mirror gave him back the image of someone almost a stranger. So much difference had three short weeks brought about in him, already. Not that he was so different, but his own appraisal of himself had changed; so that it was not merely the Spanish-style jacket, the skintight under-tunic, and the narrow trousers that disappeared into boots as black as all the rest of the costume, that made him unfamiliar to himself—but the body within. Association with the men of other worlds had done this to his point of view. Their relative shortness had made him tall, their softness had made him hard, their untrained bodies had made his balanced and sure. Outbound from the Dorsai to Alpha Centauri and surrounded by other Dorsai passengers, he had not noticed the gradual change. Only in the vast terminal on Newton, surrounded by their noisy thousands, had it come on him, all at once. And now, transhipped and outbound for the Friendlies, facing his first dinner on board a luxury-class liner where there would probably be no others from his world, he gazed at himself in the mirror and felt himself as suddenly come of age.

He went out through the door of his cabin, letting it latch quietly behind him, and turned right in the tightly narrow, metal-walled corridor faintly stale with the smell of dust from the carpet underfoot. He walked down its silence toward the main lounge and pushed through a heavy sealing door that sucked shut behind him, into the corridor of the next section.

He stepped into the intersection of the little cross corridor that led right and left to the washrooms of the section ahead—and almost strode directly into a slim, tall girl in an ankle-length, blue dress of severe and conservative cut, who stood by the water fountain at the point of the intersection. She moved hastily back out of his way with a little intake of breath, backing into the corridor to the women's washroom. They stared at each other, halted, for a second.

"Forgive me," said Donal, and took two steps onward—but between these and a third, some sudden swift prompting made him change his mind without warning; and he turned back.

"If you don't mind—" he said.

"Oh, excuse me." She moved back again from the water fountain. He bent to drink; and when he raised his head from the fountain, he looked her full in the face again and recognized what had brought him back. The girl was frightened; and that strange, dark ocean of feeling that lay at the back of his oddness had stirred to the gust of her palpable fear.

He saw her now, clearly and at once; at close range. She was older than he had thought at first—at least in her early twenties. But there was a clear-eyed immaturity about her—a hint that her full beauty would come later in life, and much later than that of the usual woman. Now, she was not yet beautiful; merely wholesome-looking. Her hair was a light brown, verging into chestnut, her eyes wide-spaced and so clearly green that, opening as she felt the full interest of his close gaze, they drove all the other color about her from his mind. Her nose was slim and straight, her mouth a little wide, her chin firm; and the whole of her face so perfectly in balance, the left side with the right, that it approached the artificiality of some sculptor's creation.

"Yes?" she said, on a little gasping intake of breath—and he saw, suddenly, that she was shrinking from him and his close survey of her.

He frowned at her. His thoughts were galloping ahead with

the situation, so that when he spoke, it was unconsciously in the middle of the conversation he had in mind, rather than at the beginning.

"Tell me about it," said Donal.

"You?" she said. Her hand went to her throat above the high collar of her dress. Then, before he could speak again, it fell to her side and some of the tightness leaked out of her. "Oh," she said. "I see."

"See what?" said Donal, a little sharply; for unconsciously he had fallen into the tone he would have used to a junior cadet these last few years, if he had discovered one of them in some difficulty. "You'll have to tell me what your trouble is, if I'm going to be any help to you."

"Tell you—?" she looked desperately around her, as if expecting someone to come upon them at any moment. "How do I know you're what you say you are?"

For the first time Donal check-reined the horses of his galloping estimate of the situation; and, looking back, discovered a possible misconception on her part.

"I didn't say I was anybody," he answered. "And in fact—I'm not. I just happened to be passing by and saw you seemed upset about something. I offered to help."

"Help?" Her eyes widened again and her face suddenly paled. "Oh, no—" she murmured, and tried to go around him. "Please let me go. Please!"

He stood his ground.

"You were ready to accept help from someone like me, if he could only provide proofs of identity, a second ago," said Donal. "You might as well tell me the rest of it."

That stopped her efforts to escape. She stiffened, facing him.

"I haven't told you anything."

"Only," said Donal, ironically, "that you were waiting here

for someone. That you did not know that someone by sight, but
expected him to be a man. And that you were not sure of his
bona fides, but very much afraid of missing him." He heard the
hard edge in his own voice and forced it to be more gentle.
"Also that you're very frightened and not very experienced at
what you're doing. Logic could take it further."

But she had herself under control now.

"Will you move out of the way and let me by?" she said
evenly.

"Logic might make it that what you're engaged in is something illegal," he replied.

She sagged under the impact of his last word as if it had been
a blow; and, turning her face blindly to the wall, she leaned
against it.

"What are you?" she said brokenly. "Did they send you to
trap me?"

"I tell you," said Donal, with just a hint of exasperation, "I'm
nothing but a passer-by who thought maybe I could help."

"Oh, I don't believe you!" she said, twisting her face away
from him. "If you're really nobody . . . if nobody sent you . . .
you'll let me go. And forget you ever saw me."

"Small sense in that," said Donal. "You need help evidently.
I'm equipped to give it. I'm a professional soldier. A Dorsai."

"Oh," she said. The tension drained from her. She stood
straighter and met his eyes with a look in which he thought he
read some contempt. "One of those."

"Yes," he said. Then frowned. "What do you mean *one of
those?*"

"I understand," she answered. "You're a mercenary."

"I prefer the term professional soldier," he said—a little stiffly
in his turn.

"The point is," she said, "you're for hire."

He felt himself growing cold and angry. He inclined his head to her and stepped back, leaving her way clear. "My mistake," he said, and turned to leave her.

"No, wait a minute," she said. "Now that I know what you really are, there's no reason why I can't use you."

"None at all, of course," said Donal.

She reached in through a slit in her tight gown and produced a small, thick folding of some printed matter, which she pushed into his hand.

"You see this is destroyed," she said. "I'll pay you—whatever the usual rates are." Her eyes widened suddenly as she saw him unfold what he held and start to read it. "What are you doing? You aren't supposed to read that! How dare you!"

She grabbed for the sheet, but he pushed her back absently with one hand. His gaze was busily running down the form she had given him, his own eyes widening at the sight of the facsimile portrait on it, which was that of the girl herself.

"Anea Marlivana," he said. "Select of Kultis."

"Well, what if I am?" she blazed. "What about it?"

"Only," said Donal, "that I expected your genes to imply intelligence."

Her mouth fell open.

"What do you mean by that?"

"Only that you're one of the worst fools I've had the bad fortune to meet." He put the sheet into his pocket. "I'll take care of it."

"You will?" Her face lit up. A second later it was twisted in wrath. "Oh, I don't like you!" she cried. "I don't like you at all!"

He looked at her a little sadly.

"You will," he said, "if you live long enough." He turned about and pushed open the door through which he had come just a few minutes ago.

"But wait a minute—" her voice leaped after him. "Where will I see you after you've got rid of it? How much do I have to pay—"

He let the door, sucking to behind him, be the period to that question of hers—and his answer to it.

He went back through the section he had just traversed to his own cabin. There, with the door locked he considered the sheet she had given him, a little more closely. It was nothing more— and nothing less—than a five-year employment contract, a social contract, for her services as companion in the entourage of William, Prince, and Chairman of the Board of that very commercial planet Ceta which was the only habitable world circling the sun Tau Ceti. And a very liberal social contract it was, requiring no more than that she accompany William wherever he wished to go and supply her presence at such public and polite social functions as he might require. It was not the liberalness of the contract that surprised him so much—a Select of Kultis would hardly be contracted to perform any but the most delicately moral and ethical of duties—but the fact that she had asked him to destroy it. Theft of contract from her employer was bad enough, breach of contract infinitely worse— calling for complete rehabilitation—but destruction of contract required the death penalty wherever any kind of government operated. The girl, he thought, must be insane.

But—and here the fine finger of irony intruded into the situation—being the Select of Kultis she could not possibly be insane, any more than an ape could be an elephant. On the extreme contrary, being the product of a number of the most carefully culled forebearers on that planet where careful genetic culling and wizardry of psychological techniques was commonplace, she must be eminently sane. True, she had impressed Donal on first acquaintance as possessing nothing much out of the ordinary except a suicidal foolishness. But this was one instance where you had to go by the record books. And the record books implied that if anything about this business was abnormal, it was the situation itself, and not the girl involved in it.

Thoughtfully, Donal fingered the contract. Anea had clearly had no conception at all of what she was requesting when she so blithely required him to destroy it. The single sheet he held, and even the words and signatures upon it, were all integral parts of a single giant molecule which in itself was well-nigh indestructible and could not be in any way altered or tampered with short of outright destruction. As for destruction itself— Donal was quite sure that there was nothing aboard this ship that could in any way burn, shred, dissolve, or in any other fashion obliterate it. And the mere possession of it by anyone but William, its rightful owner, was as good as an order of sentence.

A soft chime quivered on the air of his cabin, announcing the serving of a meal in the main lounge. It chimed twice more to indicate that this was the third of the four meals interspersed throughout the ship "day." Contract in hand, Donal half-turned toward the little orifice of the disposal slot that led down to the central incinerator. The incinerator, of course, was not capable of disposing of the contract—but it might be that it could lie unnoticed there until the ship had reached its destination and its passengers had dispersed. Later, it would be difficult for William to discover how it had reached the incinerator in the first place.

Then he shook his head, and replaced the contract in his pocket. His motives for doing so were not entirely clear to himself. It was that oddness of his at work again, he thought. Also, he told himself that it seemed a sloppy way of handling the situation this girl had got him into. Quite typically, he had already forgotten that his participation in the matter was all of his own contriving.

He straightened his half-jacket and went out of his cabin and down the long corridor through various sections to the main lounge. A slight crowding of likewise dinner-bound passengers in the narrow entrance to the lounge delayed him momentarily; and, in that moment, looking over the heads of those before him, he caught sight of the long captain's table at the far end of the lounge and of the girl, Anea Marlivana, amongst those seated at it.

The others seated with her appeared to consist of a strikingly handsome young officer of field rank—a Freilander, by the look of him—a rather untidy, large young man almost as big as the Freilander, but possessing just the opposite of the other's military bearing; in fact, he appeared to half-slouch in his seat as if he were drunk. And a spare, pleasant-looking man in early middle age with iron-gray hair. The fifth person at the table was quite obviously a Dorsai—a massive, older man in the uniform of a Freiland marshal. The sight of this last individual moved Donal to sudden action. He pushed abruptly through the little knot of people barring the entrance and strode openly across the room to the high table. He extended his fist across it to the Dorsai marshal.

"How do you do, sir," he said. "I was supposed to look you up before the ship lifted; but I didn't have time. I've got a letter for you from my father, Eachan Khan Graeme. I'm his second son, Donal."

Blue Dorsai eyes as cold as river water lifted under thick gray brows to consider him. For part of a second the situation trembled on the balance-point of Dorsai pride with the older man's curiosity weighed against the bare-faced impudence of Donal's claim to acquaintance. Then the marshal took Donal's fist in a hard grip.

"So he remembered Hendrik Galt, did he?" the marshal smiled. "I haven't heard from Eachan for years."

Donal felt a slight, cold shiver of excitement course down his spine. Of all people, he had chosen one of the ranking Dorsai soldiers of his day to bluff acquaintance with. Hendrik Galt, First Marshal of Freiland.

"He sends you his regards, sir," said Donal, "and . . . but perhaps I can bring you the letter after dinner and you can read it for yourself."

"To be sure," said the marshal. "I'm in Stateroom Nineteen."

Donal was still standing. The occasion could hardly be prolonged further. But rescue came—as something in Donal had more than half-expected it would—from farther down the table.

"Perhaps," said the gray-haired man in a soft and pleasant voice, "your young friend would enjoy eating with us before you take him back to your stateroom, Hendrik?"

"I'd be honored," said Donal, with glib promptness. He pulled out the empty float before him and sat down upon it, nodding courteously to the rest of the company at the table as he did so. The eyes of the girl met him from the table's far end. They were as hard and still as emeralds caught in the rock.

Mercenary II

"Anea Marlivana," said Hendrik Galt, introducing Donal around the table. "And the gentleman who was pleased to invite you—William of Ceta, Prince and Chairman of the Board."

"Greatly honored," murmured Donal, inclining his head toward them.

". . . The Unit Commandant, here, my adjutant . . . Hugh Killien—"

Donal and the Commandant Freilander nodded to each other.

". . . And ArDell Montor, of Newton." The loose-limbed young man slumping in his float, lifted a careless, half-drunken hand in a slight wave of acknowledgment. His eyes—so dark as to appear almost black under the light eyebrows that matched his rather heavy, blond hair, cleared for a disconcerting fraction of a second to stare sharply at Donal, then faded back to indifference. "ArDell," said Galt, humorlessly, "set a new high score for the competitive exams on Newton. His field was social dynamics."

"Indeed," muttered the Newtonian, with something between a snort and a laugh. "Indeed, was. Was, indeed." He lifted a heavy tumbler from the table before him and buried his nose in its light golden contents.

"ArDell—" said the gray-haired William, gently reproving. ArDell lifted his drink-pale face and stared at the older man, snorted again, on laughter, and lifted the tumbler again to his lips.

"Are you enlisted somewhere at the moment, Graeme?" asked the Freilander, turning to Donal.

"I've a tentative contract for the Friendlies," said Donal. "I thought I'd pick between the Sects when I got there and had a chance to look over the opportunities for action."

"Very Dorsai of you," said William, smiling, from the far end of the table, next to Anea. "Always the urge to battle."

"You over-compliment me, sir," said Donal. "It merely happens that promotion comes more quickly on a battlefield than in a garrison, under ordinary conditions."

"You're too modest," said William.

"Yes, indeed," put in Anea, suddenly. "Far too modest."

William turned about to gaze quizzically at the girl.

"Now, Anea," he said. "You mustn't let your Exotic contempt for violence breed a wholly unjustified contempt for this fine young man. I'm sure both Hendrik and Hugh agree with him."

"Oh, they would—of course," said Anea, flashing a look at the other two men. "Of course, they would!"

"Well," said William, laughing, "we must make allowances for a Select, of course. As for myself, I must admit to being male enough, and unreconstructed enough, to like the thought of action, myself. I . . . ah, here comes the food."

Brimming soup plates were rising above the surface of the table in front of everybody but Donal.

"You'd better get your order in now," said William. And, while Donal pressed the communicator key before him and attended to this necessary duty, the rest of them lifted their spoons and began their meal.

". . . Donal's father was a classmate of yours, was he, Hendrik?" inquired William, as the fish course was being served.

"Merely a close friend," said the marshal, dryly.

"Ah," said William, delicately lifting a portion of the white, delicate flesh on a fork. "I envy you Dorsai for things like that. Your professions allow you to keep friendship and emotional connections unrelated to your work. In the Commercial area"—

he gestured with a slim, tanned hand—"a convention of general friendliness obscures the deeper feelings."

"Maybe it's what the man is to begin with," answered the marshal. "Not all Dorsai are soldiers, Prince, and not all Cetans are entrepreneurs."

"I recognize that," said William. His eyes strayed to Donal. "What would you say, Donal? Are you a simple mercenary soldier, only, or do you find yourself complicated by other desires?"

The question was as blunt as it was obliquely put. Donal concluded that ingenuousness overlaid with a touch of venality was perhaps the most proper response.

"Naturally, I'd like to be famous," he said—and laughed a trifle self-consciously, "and rich."

He caught the hint of a darkening cloud on the brow of Galt. But he could not be concerned with that now. He had other fish to fry. There would, he hoped, be a chance to clear up the marshal's contempt for him at some later time. For the present he must seem self-seeking enough to arouse William's interest.

"Very interesting," said William, pleasantly. "How do you plan to go about becoming these pleasant things?"

"I was hoping," said Donal, "maybe to learn something of the worlds by being out among them—something I might be able to use to my own advantage, as well as others."

"Good Lord, is *that* all?" said the Freilander, and laughed in a way that invited the rest of the table to join in with him.

William, however, did not laugh—although Anea joined her own clear amusement to that of the commandant, and ArDell's snorted chuckle.

"No need to be unkind, Hugh," he said. "I like Donal's attitude. I had the same sort of notion myself once—when I was younger." He smiled in a kindly fashion on Donal. "You must come talk to me, too," he said, "after you've had your chat with Hendrik. I like young men with ambition."

ArDell snorted with laughter again. William turned to look sadly at him.

"You should try to eat, ArDell," he said. "We'll be making a phase shift in four hours or so; and if you don't have something solid on your stomach—"

"My stomach?" said the young man, drunkenly. "And what if my stomach should reach universal dimensions, out of phase? What if *I* should reach universal dimensions; and be everywhere and never come back to point position again?" He grinned at William. "What a waste of good food."

Anea had paled to a sickly color.

"If you'll excuse me—" she murmured, rising hastily.

"I don't blame you a bit!" said William sharply. "ArDell, that was in inexcusable bad taste. Hugh, help Anea to her stateroom."

"I don't want him!" flared Anea. "He's just like all the rest of you—"

But the Freilander was already on his feet, looking almost like a recruiting poster in his trim uniform and coming around the table to take her arm. She jerked away from him, turned, and went unsteadily out of the lounge, Hugh following closely behind her. They passed through the doorway into the corridor, but as they turned to move out of sight, Donal saw her turn to the tall soldier and lean into the protection of his arm, just before they disappeared.

William was continuing to speak calm and acid words of disapprobation to ArDell, who made no retort, but gazed drunkenly and steadily back at him out of his black, unmoving eyes. During the rest of the meal the talk turned to military affairs, in particular field strategy, in which triologue—ArDell pointedly excluded—Donal was able to win back some of the per-

sonal credit which his earlier remark about fame and riches had
cost him—in the marshal's eyes.

". . . Remember," William said, as they parted in the corridor
outside the lounge, after the meal. "Come in and see me after
you've finished with Hendrik, Donal. I'll be glad to help you if
I can." And with a smile, and a nod, he turned away.

Donal and Galt went off down the narrow corridor that forced
them to walk one behind the other. Following the thick shoulders of the older man, Donal was surprised to hear him ask:
"Well, what do you think of them?"

"Sir?" said Donal. Hesitating, he chose what he took to be
the safest subject. "I'm a little surprised about the girl."

"Anea?" said Galt, stopping before a door marked with the
number nineteen.

"I thought a Select of Kultis would be—" Donal stopped,
honestly at a loss, "more . . . more in control of herself."

"She's very healthy, very normal, very intelligent—but those
are only potentialities," retorted the marshal, almost gruffly.
"What did you expect?"

He threw open the door, ushered them both in, and closed
the door firmly behind them. When he turned around, there
was a harder, more formal note to his voice.

"All right now," he said, sharply, "what's all this about a
letter?"

Donal took a deep breath. He had tried hard to read Galt's
character during the course of the dinner—and he staked everything now in the honesty of his answer, on what he thought he
had seen there.

"No letter, sir," he said. "To the best of my knowledge, my
father never met you in his life."

"Thought as much," said Galt. "All right—what's it all about, then?" He crossed to a desk on the other side of the room, took something from a drawer, and when he turned about Donal was astonished to find him filling an antique pipe with tobacco.

"That Anea, sir," he said. "I never met such a fool in my life." And he told, fully and completely, the story of the episode in the corridor. Galt half-sat on the edge of the desk, the pipe in his mouth now, and alight, puffing little clouds of white smoke which the ventilating system whisked away the second they were formed.

"I see," he said, when Donal had finished. "I'm inclined to agree with you. She is a fool. And just what sort of insane idiot do you consider yourself?"

"I, sir?" Donal was honestly astonished.

"I mean you, boy," said Galt, taking the pipe out of his mouth. "Here you are, still damp from school, and sticking your nose into a situation a full planetary government'd hesitate at." He stared in frank amazement at Donal. "Just what did you think— what did you figure . . . hell, boy, what did you *plan* to get out of it?"

"Why, nothing," said Donal. "I was only interested in seeing a ridiculous and possibly dangerous situation smoothed out as neatly as possible. I admit I hadn't any notion of the part William played in the matter—he's apparently an absolute devil."

The pipe rattled in Galt's suddenly unclenched jaws and he had to grab it quickly with one thick hand to keep it from falling. He took it from his lips and stared in amazement at Donal.

"Who told you that?" he demanded.

"No one," said Donal. "It's obvious, isn't it?" Galt laid his pipe down on the table and stood up.

"Not to ninety-nine per cent of the civilized worlds, it isn't," he retorted. "What made it so obvious to you?"

"Certainly," said Donal, "any man can be judged by the character and actions of the people with which he surrounds himself.

And this William has an entourage of thwarted and ruined people."

The marshal stiffened.

"You mean me?" he demanded.

"Naturally not," said Donal. "After all—you're a Dorsai." The stiffness went out of Galt. He grinned a little sourly and, reaching back for his pipe, retrieved and relit it.

"Your faith in our common origin is . . . quite refreshing," he said. "Go on. On this piece of evidence you read William's character, do you?"

"Oh, not just that," said Donal. "Stop and think of the fact that a Select of Kultis finds herself at odds with him. And the good instincts of a Select are inbred. Also, he seems to be an almost frighteningly brilliant sort of man, in that he can dominate personalities like Anea, and this fellow Montor, from Newton—who must be a rather high-level mind himself to have rated as he did on his tests."

"And someone that brilliant must be a devil?" queried Galt, dryly.

"Not at all," explained Donal, patiently. "But having such intellectual capabilities, a man must show proportionately greater inclinations toward either good or evil than lesser people. If he tends toward evil, he may mask it in himself—he may even mask its effect on the people with which he surrounds himself. But he has no way of producing the reflections of good which would ordinarily be reflected from his lieutenants and initiates—and which, if he was truly good—he would have no reason to try and hide. And by that lack, you can read him."

Galt took the pipe from his mouth and gave a long, slow whistle. He stared at Donal.

"You weren't brought up on one of the Exotics, by any chance, were you?" he asked.

"No, sir," said Donal. "My father's mother was a Maran, though. And my mother's mother was Maran."

"This," Galt paused and tamped thoughtfully in the bowl of his pipe—it had gone out—with one thick forefinger, "business of reading character—did you get this from your mother, or your grandmother—or is it your own idea?"

"Why, I imagine I must have heard it somewhere," replied Donal. "But surely it stands to reason—anyone would arrive at it as a conclusion, with a few minutes' thought."

"Possibly the majority of us don't think," said Galt, with the same dryness. "Sit down, Donal. And I'll join you."

They took a couple of armchair floats facing each other. Galt put his pipe away.

"Now, listen to me," he said, in a low and sober voice. "You're one of the oddest young fish I can remember meeting. I don't know quite what to do with you. If you were my son, I'd pack you up in quarantine and ship you home for ten more years seasoning before I let you out among the stars—all right—" he interrupted himself abruptly, raising a silencing hand as Donal's mouth opened. "I know you're a man now and couldn't be shipped anywhere against your will. But the way you strike me now is that you've got perhaps one chance in a thousand of becoming something remarkable, and about nine hundred and ninety-nine chances of being quietly put out of the way before the year's out. Look, boy, what do you know about the worlds, outside the Dorsai?"

"Well," said Donal. "There are fourteen planetary governments not counting the anarchic setups on Dunnin's World and Coby—"

"Governments, my rear echelon!" interrupted Galt, rudely. "Forget your civics lessons! Governments in this twenty-fourth century are mere machinery. It's the men who control them who count. Project Blaine, on Venus; Sven Holman, on Earth; Eldest Bright on Harmony, the very planet we're headed for—

and Sayona the Bond on Kultis, for the Exotics."

"General Kamal—" began Donal.

"Is nothing!" said Galt, sharply. "How can the Elector of the Dorsai be anything when every little canton hangs to its independence with tooth and nail? No, I'm talking about the men who pull the strings between the stars. The ones I mentioned, and others." He took a deep breath. "Now, how do you suppose our Merchant Prince and Chairman of the Board on Ceta ranks with those I mentioned?"

"You'd say he's their equal?"

"At least," said Galt. "At least. Don't be led astray by the fact that you see him traveling like this, on a commercial ship, with only the girl and Montor with him. Chances are he owns the ship, the crew and officers—and half the passengers."

"And you and the commandant?" asked Donal, perhaps more bluntly than was necessary. Galt's features started to harden; and then he relaxed.

"A fair question," he rumbled. "I'm trying to get you to question most of the things you've taken for granted. I suppose it's natural you'd include myself. No—to answer your question—I am First Marshal of Freiland, still a Dorsai, and with my professional services for hire, and nothing more. We've just hired out five light divisions to the First Dissident Church, on Harmony, and I'm coming along to observe that they operate as contracted for. It's a complicated deal—like they are all—involving a batch of contract credits belonging to Ceta. Therefore William."

"And the commandant?" persisted Donal.

"What about him?" replied Galt. "He's a Freilander, a professional, and a good one. He'll take over one of the three-Force commands for a short test period when we get to Harmony, for demonstration purposes."

"Have you had him with you long?"

"Oh, about two standard years," said Galt.

"And he's good, professionally?"

"He's damn good," said Galt. "Why do you think he's my adjutant? What're you driving at, anyway?"

"A doubt," said Donal, "and a suspicion." He hesitated for a second. "Neither of which I'm ready to voice yet."

Galt laughed.

"Save that Maran character-sniffing of yours for civilians," he said. "You'll be seeing a snake under every bush. Take my word for it, Hugh's a good, honest soldier—a bit flashy, perhaps—but that's all."

"I'm hardly in a position to argue with you," murmured Donal, stepping aside gracefully. "You were about to say something about William, when I interrupted you?"

"Oh yes," said Galt. He frowned. "It adds up to this—and I'll make it short and clear. The girl's none of your business; and William's deadly medicine. Leave them both alone. And if I can help you to the kind of post you're after—"

"Thank you very much," said Donal. "But I believe William will be offering me something."

Galt blinked and stared.

"Hell's breeches, boy!" he exploded after half a second. "What gives you that idea?"

Donal smiled a little sadly.

"Another one of my suspicions," he said. "Based on what you call that Maran character-sniffing of mine, no doubt." He stood up. "I appreciate your trying to warn me, sir." He extended his fist. "If I could talk to you again, sometime?"

Galt stood up himself, taking the proffered fist, mechanically.

"Any time," he said. "Damned if I understand you."

Donal peered at him, suddenly struck by a thought.

"Tell me, sir," he asked. "Would you say I was—odd?"

"Odd!" Galt almost exploded on the word. "Odd as—" his imagination failed him. "What makes you ask that?"

"I just wondered," said Donal. "I've been called that so often. Maybe they were right."

He withdrew his fist from the marshal's grasp. And on that note, he took his leave.

Mercenary III

Returning again up the corridor toward the bow of the ship, Donal allowed himself to wonder, a little wistfully, about this succubus of his own strange difference from other people. He had thought to leave it behind with his cadet uniform. Instead, it seemed, it continued to ride with him, still perched on his shoulders. Always it had been this way. What seemed so plain, and simple and straightforward to himself, had always struck others as veiled, torturous, and involved. Always he had been like a stranger passing through a town, the ways of whose people were different, and who looked on him with a lack of understanding amounting to suspicion. Their language failed on the doorstep of his motives and could not enter the lonely mansion of his mind. They said "enemy" and "friend"; they said "strong" and "weak"—"them" and "us". They set up a thousand arbitrary classifications and distinctions which he could not comprehend, convinced as he was that all people were only people—and there was very little to choose between them. Only, you dealt with them as individuals, one by one; and always remembering to be patient. And if you did this successfully, then the larger, group things all came out right.

Turning again into the entrance of the lounge, he discovered—as he had half-expected to—the young Newtonian ArDell Montor, slumped in a float by one end of the bar that had made its appearance as soon as the dinner tables had been taken up into the walls. A couple of other small, drinking groups sparsely completed the inhabitants of the lounge—but none of these were having anything to do with Montor. Donal walked directly to him; and Montor, without moving, lifted the gaze of his dark eyes to watch Donal approach.

"Join you?" said Donal.

"Honored," replied the other—not so much thickly as slowly, from the drink inside him. "Thought I might like to talk to you." His fingers crept out over the buttons on the bar-pad next to him. "Drink?"

"Dorsai whiskey," said Donal. Montor pressed. A second later a small transparent goblet, full, rose to the bartop. Donal took it and sipped cautiously. The drinking the night he had attained his majority had acquainted him with the manner in which alcohol affected him; and he had made a private determination never to find himself drunk again. It is a typical matter of record with him, that he never did. Raising his eyes from the glass, he found the Newtonian staring steadily at him with his eyes unnaturally clear, lost, and penetrating.

"You're younger than I," said ArDell. "Even if I don't look it. How old do you think I am?"

Donal looked him over curiously. Montor's face, for all its lines of weariness and dissipation, was the scarcely mature visage of a late adolescent—a situation to which his shock of uncombed hair and the loose-limbed way he sprawled in his float, contributed.

"A quarter of a standard century," said Donal.

"Thirty-three years absolute," said ArDell. "I was a schoolchild, a monk, until I was twenty-nine. Do you think I drink too much?"

"I think there's no doubt about it," answered Donal.

"I agree with you," said ArDell, with one of his sudden snorts of laughter. "I agree with you. There's no doubt about it—one of the few things in this God-abandoned universe about which there is no doubt. But that's not what I was hoping to talk to you about."

"What was that?" Donal tasted his glass of whiskey again.

"Courage," said ArDell, looking at him with an empty, penetrating glance. "Have you got courage?"

"It's a necessary item for a soldier," said Donal. "Why do you ask?"

"And no doubts? No doubts?" ArDell swirled the golden drink in his tall tumbler and took a swallow from it. "No secret fears that when the moment comes your legs will weaken, your heart will pound, you'll turn and run?"

"I will not, of course, turn and run," said Donal. "After all, I'm a Dorsai. As for how I'll feel—all I can say is, I've never felt the way you describe. And even if I did—"

Above their heads a single mellow chime sounded, interrupting.

"Phase shift in one standard hour and twenty minutes," announced a voice. "Phase shift in one standard hour and twenty minutes. Passengers are advised to take their medication now and accomplish the shift while asleep, for their greatest convenience."

"Have you swallowed a pill yet?" asked ArDell.

"Not yet," said Donal.

"But you will?"

"Of course." Donal examined him with interest. "Why not?"

"Doesn't taking medication to avoid the discomfort of a phase shift strike you as a form of cowardice?" asked ArDell. "Doesn't it?"

"That's foolish," said Donal. "Like saying it's cowardly to wear clothes to keep you warm and comfortable, or to eat, to keep from starving. One is a matter of convenience; the other is a matter of"—he thought for a second—"duty."

"Courage is doing your duty?"

". . . In spite of what you personally might want. Yes," said Donal.

"Yes," said ArDell, thoughtfully. "Yes." He replaced his

empty glass on the bar and pressed for a refill. "I *thought* you had courage," he said, musingly, watching the glass sink, fill, and begin to reemerge.

"I am a Dorsai," said Donal.

"Oh, spare me the glories of careful breeding!" said ArDell, harshly, picking up his now-full glass. As he turned back to face Donal, Donal saw the man's face was tortured. "There's more to courage than that. If it was only in your genes—" he broke off suddenly, and leaned toward Donal. "Listen to me," he almost whispered. "I'm a coward."

"Are you sure?" said Donal, levelly. "How do you know?"

"I'm frightened sick," whispered ArDell. "Sick-frightened of the universe. What do you know about the mathematics of social dynamics?"

"It's a predicative system of mathematics, isn't it?" said Donal. "My education didn't lie in that direction."

"No, no!" said ArDell, almost fretfully. "I'm talking about the statistics of social analysis, and their extrapolation along lines of population increase and development." He lowered his voice even further. "They approach a parallel with the statistics of random chance!"

"I'm sorry," said Donal. "That means nothing to me."

ArDell gripped Donal's arm suddenly with one surprisingly strong hand.

"Don't you understand?" he murmured. "Random chance provides for every possibility—including dissolution. It must come, because the chance is there. As our social statistics grow into larger figures, we, too, entertain the possibility. In the end, it must come. We must destroy ourselves. There is no other alternative. And all because the universe is too big a suit of clothes for us to wear. It gives us room to grow too much, too fast. We will reach a statistically critical mass—and then," he snapped his fingers, "the end!"

"Well, that's a problem for the future," said Donal. But then, because he could not help reacting to the way the other man was feeling, he added, more gently, "Why does it bother you, so much?"

"Why, don't you see?" said ArDell. "If it's all to go—just like that—as if it never has been, then what was the use of it all? What's to show for our existence? I don't mean things we built—they decay fast enough. Or knowledge. That's just a copying down from an open book into our own language. It has to be those things that the universe didn't have to begin with and that we brought to it. Things like love, and kindness—and courage."

"If that's the way you feel," said Donal, gently withdrawing his arm from the other's grasp, "why drink this way?"

"Because I *am* a coward," said ArDell. "I feel it out there, all the time, this enormousness that is the universe. Drinking helps me shut it out—that God-awful knowledge of what it can do to us. That's why I drink. To take the courage I need out of a bottle, to do the little things like passing through phase shift without medication."

"Why," said Donal, almost tempted to smile. "What good would that do?"

"It's facing it, in a little way," ArDell fixed him with his dark and pleading eyes. "It's saying, in one little instance—go ahead, rip me to the smallest shreds you can manage, spread me over your widest limits. I can take it."

Donal shook his head.

"You don't understand," said ArDell, sinking back in his float. "If I could work, I wouldn't need the alcohol. But I'm walled away from work nowadays. It's not that way with you. You've got your job to do; and you've got courage—the real kind. I thought maybe I could . . . well, never mind. Courage wouldn't be transferable, anyway."

"Are you going to Harmony?" asked Donal.

"Whither my Prince goes, there go I," said ArDell, and

snorted his laugh again. "You should read my contract, sometime." He turned back to the bar. "Another whiskey?"

"No," said Donal, standing up. "If you'll excuse me—"

"I'll see you again," muttered ArDell, keying for another drink. "I'll be seeing you."

"Yes," said Donal. "Until then."

"Until then," ArDell lifted his newly filled glass from the bar. The chime sounded again overhead, and the voice reminded them that only seventy-odd minutes remained before shift-time. Donal went out.

Half an hour later, after he had gone back to his own room for one more careful rereading and study of Anea's contract, Donal pressed the button on the door of the stateroom of William, Prince and Chairman of the Board, on Ceta. He waited.

"Yes?" said the voice of William, over his head.

"Donal Graeme, sir," said Donal. "If you aren't busy—"

"Oh, of course—Donal. Come in!" The door swung open before him and Donal entered.

William was sitting on a plain float before a small deskboard holding a pile of papers and a tiny portable secretary. A single light glowed directly above him and the deskboard, silvering his gray hair. Donal hesitated, hearing the door click to behind him.

"Find a seat somewhere," said William, without looking up from his papers. His fingers flickered over the keys of the secretary. "I have some things to do."

Donal turned about in the gloom outside the pool of light, found an armchair float and sat down in it. William continued for some minutes, scanning through his papers, and making notes on the secretary.

After a while he shoved the remaining papers aside and the deskboard, released, drifted with its burden to over against a farther wall. The single overhead light faded and a general illumination flooded the cabin.

Donal blinked at the sudden light. William smiled.

"And now," he said, "what's the nature of your business with me?"

Donal blinked, stared, and blinked again.

"Sir?" he said.

"I think we can avoid wasting time by ignoring pretenses," said William, still in his pleasant voice. "You pushed yourself on us at the table because you wanted to meet someone there. It was hardly the marshal—your Dorsai manners could have found a better way than that. It was certainly not Hugh, and most unlikely to be ArDell. That leaves Anea; and she's pretty enough, and you're both young enough to do something that foolish . . . but, I think not, under the conditions." William folded his lean fingers together, and smiled. "That leaves me."

"Sir, I—" Donal started to stand up, with the stiffness of outraged dignity.

"No, no," said William, gesturing him back. "Now it'd be foolish to leave, after going to all this trouble to get here, wouldn't it?" His voice sharpened. "Sit down!"

Donal sat.

"Why did you want to see me?" asked William.

Donal squared his shoulders.

"All right," he said. "If you want me to put it bluntly . . . I think I might be useful to you."

"By which," said William, "you think you might be useful to yourself, by tapping the till, as it were, of my position and authority—go on."

"It so happened," said Donal, "that I came into possession of something belonging to you."

William extended his hand, without a word. After a second's hesitation, Donal extracted Anea's contract from his pocket and passed it over. William took it, unfolded it, and glanced over it. He laid it carelessly down on a little table beside him.

"She wanted me to get rid of it for her," said Donal. "She wanted to hire me to dispose of it for her. Evidently she didn't know how hard it is to destroy a sheet of the material contracts are made on."

"But you took the job," said William.

"I made no promises," said Donal, painfully.

"But from the start, you intended to bring it straight to me."

"I believe," said Donal, "it's your property."

"Oh, of course," said William. He smiled at Donal for a long moment. "You realize, of course," he said, finally, "that I needn't believe a word of what you've said. I only need to assume that you stole it yourself and later got cold feet about disposing of it—and dreamed up this cock-and-bull story in an attempt to sell it back to me. The captain of this ship would be glad to put you under arrest at my word and hold you for trial as soon as we reach Harmony."

A slight, cold, galvanic shiver ran down Donal's spine.

"A Select of Kultis won't lie under oath," he said. "She—"

"I see no reason to involve Anea in this," said William. "It could be all handled very conveniently without her. My statement against yours."

Donal said nothing. William smiled again.

"You see," said William, "the point I'm laboring to bring home to you. You happen not only to be venal, but a fool."

"*Sir!*" the word shot from Donal's lips. William waved a disinterested hand.

"Save your Dorsai rages for someone who'll be impressed by them. I know as well as you do, you've no intention of attacking me. Possibly, if you were a different sort of Dorsai—but you're not. You are as I say, both venal and a fool. Accept these statements for the obvious facts they are; and we can get down to business."

He looked at Donal. Donal said nothing.

"Very well, then," went on William. "You came to me, hoping I could find you of some use. As it happens, I can. Anea is, of course, just a foolish young girl—but for her benefit, as well as my own, being her employer, we'll have to see she doesn't get into serious trouble. Now, she had confided in you once. She may again. If she does so—by no means discourage her. And to keep you available for such confidences," William smiled again, quite good humoredly, this time, "I believe I can find you a commission as Force-Leader, under Commandant Hugh Killien, when we touch down on Harmony. There is no reason why a military career shouldn't go hand in hand with whatever other uses I can find for you."

"Thank you, sir," said Donal.

"Not at all—" A chime sounded over some hidden wall speaker. "Ah—phase shift in five minutes." William picked up a small silver box from a table near his feet, and sprung it open. "Have you taken your medication, yet? Help yourself."

He extended to Donal.

"Thank you, sir," said Donal carefully. "I have."

"Then," said William, helping himself to a white tablet, and replacing the box. "I believe that is all."

"I believe so, sir," said Donal.

Donal inclined his head and went out. Stopping outside the stateroom door only long enough to take one of his own phase shift sedatives, he headed back toward his own stateroom. On the way, he stopped by the ship's library to check out an information spool on the First Dissident Church, of Harmony; and this delayed him sufficiently so that he was passing down one of the long sectional corridors when the phase shift occurred.

He had been prudently asleep during those previous shifts he had gone through while outbound from Dorsai; and, of course, he had learned years ago what to expect. In addition, he was fully medicated; and the shift itself was over before it was really begun. In fact, it took place in no time, in no conceivable interval at all. Yet it *had* happened; and some inextinguishable recognizing part of him *knew* and remembered that he had been torn apart, down to the most fractional elements of his being, and spread to the wide universe and caught and collected and reassembled at some arbitrary point light-years from his destruction. And it was this memory, not the shift itself, that made him falter, for one short step, before he took up again his steady march back to his stateroom. And the memory would stay with him.

He continued on down the corridor; but he was far from having run his gauntlet for the day. As he reached the end of one section, Anea stepped out from the cross-bar corridor there that was the exact duplicate of the one, several sections down, where he had first met her. Her green eyes were afire.

"You've been seeing him!" she snapped, barring his way.

"Seeing . . . oh, William," he said.

"Don't deny it."

"Why should I?" Donal looked at her almost with wonder. "Surely, it's nothing to make a secret about?"

She stared at him.

"Oh!" she cried. "You just don't care for anything, do you? What did you do . . . about what I gave you?"

"I gave it back to its owner, of course," said Donal. "There was no other sensible thing I could do."

She turned suddenly so white that he almost reached out to catch her, certain she was about to faint. But she did no such womanish thing. Her eyes, as she stared at him, were shocked to enormity.

"Oh!" she breathed. "You . . . you traitor. You *cheat*!" and before he could make a move or say a word to stop her, she had whirled about and was running off down the corridor back in the direction from which she had come.

With a certain wry unhappiness—for, in spite of his rather low opinion of her common sense, he had really expected her to listen to his explanation—he took up his solitary walk to his stateroom. He traveled the rest of the way without meeting anyone. The corridors, in the aftermath of the phase shift were deserted by prudent passengers.

Only, passing a certain stateroom, he heard sounds of sickness from within; and, looking up, recognized the number on its door as one he had looked up just now on his recent trip to the library.

It was the stateroom of ArDell Montor; and that would be the man himself inside it now, unmedicated and racked by the passing of the phase shift, fighting his own long battle with the universe.

Force-Leader

"All right, gentlemen," said Hugh Killien.

He stood, confident and impressive in his chameleon battle-dress, with the fingertips of his right hand resting on the gently domed surface of the mapviewer before him.

"If you'll gather around the viewer, here—" he said. The five Force-Leaders moved in until all six men stood thickly clustered around the meter-square area of the viewer. The illumination from the blackout shell enclosing them beat down and met the internal upward illumination of the viewer, so that Donal, glancing around at his fellow-officers, was irresistibly reminded of men caught between wrath and wrath, in some small package section of that hell their First Dissident Church Liaison-Elder had been so eloquent about, only a few hours since at the before-battle service.

". . . Our position is here," Hugh was saying. "As your commandant I make you the customary assurance that it is a perfectly tenable position and that the contemplated advance in no way violates the Mercenaries Code. Now—" he went on more briskly, "as you can see, we occupy an area five kilometers in front and three kilometers in depth, between these two ridges. Second Command of Battle Unit 176 to our right, Fourth Command of Battles to our left.

"The contemplated action calls for the Second and Fourth Commands to hold fast in full strength on both our flanks, while we move forward at sixty per cent of strength and capture a small town called Faith Will Succour, which is *here*—"

His index finger stabbed down and rested upon the domed image of the map.

". . . At approximately four kilometers of distance from our present position. We will use three of our five Forces, Skuak's, White's and Graeme's; and each Force will make its separate way to the objective. You will each have your individual maps. There are woods for the first twelve hundred meters. After that, you will have to cross the river, which is about forty meters in width, but which Intelligence assures us is fordable at the present time with a maximum depth of a hundred and twenty centimeters. On the other side it will be woods again, thinning out gradually right up to the edge of the town. We leave in twenty minutes. It'll be dawn in an hour and I want all three Forces across that river before full daylight. Any questions?"

"What about enemy activity in the area?" asked Skuak. He was a short, stocky Cassidan, who looked Mongoloid, but was actually Eskimo in ancestry. "What kind of opposition can we expect?"

"Intelligence says nothing but patrols. Possibly a small Force holding the town, itself. Nothing more." Hugh looked around the circle of faces. "This should be bread and butter. Any more questions?"

"Yes," said Donal. He had been studying the map. "What sort of military incompetent decided to send us at only sixty per cent of strength?"

The atmosphere in the shell froze suddenly and sharply. Donal looked up to find Hugh Killien's eyes on his across the viewer.

"As it happened," said the commandant, a slight edge to his words, "it was *my* suggestion to Staff, Graeme. Perhaps you've forgotten—I'm sure none of the other Force-Leaders have—but this is a demonstration campaign to show the First Dissident Church we're worthy of our hire."

"That hardly includes gambling the lives of four hundred and fifty men," retorted Donal, unmoved.

"Graeme," said Hugh, "you're junior officer here; and I'm

commandant. You ought to know I don't have to explain tactics to you. But just to set your mind at rest, Intelligence has given a clear green on enemy activity in the area."

"Still," persisted Donal, "why take unnecessary chances?"

Hugh sighed in exasperation.

"I certainly shouldn't have to give you lessons in strategy," he said bitingly. "I think you abuse the right the code gives you to question Staff decisions. But to put an end to this—there's a good reason why we'll be using the minimum number of men. Our main thrust at the enemy is to come through this area. If we moved forward in strength, the United Orthodox forces would immediately begin to strengthen defenses. But doing it this way, it should appear we're merely moving to take up a natural vacuum along the front. Once we have the town tied down, the Second and Fourth Commands can filter in to reinforce us and we are in position to mount a full-scale attack at the plains below. Does that answer you?"

"Only partially," said Donal. "I—"

"Give me patience!" snapped the Freilander. "I have five campaigns to my credit, Force-Leader. I'd hardly stick my own neck in a noose. But I'll be taking over White's Force and leaving him in command back here in the Area. You, I and Skuak will make the assay. *Now*, are you satisfied?"

There was, of course, no reply to be made to that. Donal bowed his head in submission and the meeting broke up. Walking back to his Force area, however, alongside Skuak, Donal remained unreconstructed enough to put an extra question to the Cassidan.

"Do *you* think I'm starting at shadows?" asked Donal.

"Huh!" grunted Skuak. "It's his responsibility. He ought to know what he's doing." And, on that note, they parted; each to marshal his own men.

*   *   *

Back in his own Force area, Donal found that his Groupmen had already assembled his command. They stood under arms, drawn up in three lines of fifty men each, with a senior and junior Groupman at the head of each line. The ranking senior Groupman, a tall, thin Cetan veteran named Morphy, accompanied him as he made his rounds of the ranks, inspecting the men.

They were a good unit, Donal thought, as he paced down between the rows. Well-trained men, battle-seasoned, although in no sense elite troops, since they had been picked at random by the Elders of the First Dissident Church—William having stipulated only his choice of officers for the demonstration Battle Unit. Each man carried a handgun and knife in addition to his regular armament; but they were infantry, spring-rifle men. Weapon for weapon, any thug in the back alley of a large city had more, and more modern firepower; but the trick with modern warfare was not to outgun the enemy, but carry weapons he could not gimmick. Chemical and radiation armament was too easily put out of action from a distance. Therefore, the spring-rifle with its five thousand-sliver magazine and its tiny, compact, nonmetallic mechanism which could put a sliver in a man-sized target at a thousand meters time after time with unvarying accuracy.

Yet, thought Donal, pacing between the silent men in the faint darkness of pre-dawn, even the spring-rifle would be gimmickable one of these days. Eventually, the infantryman would be back to the knife and short sword. And the emphasis would weigh yet again more heavily on the skill of the individual soldier. For sooner or later, no matter what fantastic long-range weapons you mounted, the ground itself had to be taken—and for that there had never been anything but the man in the ranks.

Donal finished his inspection and went back to stand in front of them.

"Rest, men," he said. "But hold your ranks. All Groupmen over here with me."

He walked off out of earshot of the men in ranks and the Groupmen followed him. They squatted in a circle and he passed on to them the orders of the Staff he had just received from Hugh, handing out maps to each of them.

"Any questions?" he asked, as Hugh had asked his Force-Leaders.

There were none. They waited for him to go on. He, in turn looked slowly around the circle, assessing these men on whom his command would depend.

He had had a chance to get to know them in the three weeks previous to this early morning. The six who faced him represented, in miniature, the varying reactions his appointment as Force-Leader had produced in the Force as a whole. Of the hundred and fifty men under him, a few were doubtful of him because of his youth and lack of battle experience. A larger number were unequivocally glad to have him over them because of the Dorsai reputation. A few, a very few, were of that class of men who bristle automatically, as man to man, whenever they find themselves in contact with another individual who is touted as better than they. The instinctive giant-killers. Of this type was the Senior Groupman of the Third Group, an ex-Coby miner named Lee. Even squatting now in this circle, on the brink of action, he met Donal's eye with a faint air of challenge, his brush of dark hair stiffly upright in the gloom, his bony jaw set. Such men were troublemakers unless they had responsibility to hold them down. Donal revised his original intention to travel, himself, with the Third Group.

"We'll split up into patrol-sized units of twenty-five men each," he said. "There'll be a Senior or Junior Groupman to each unit.

You'll move separately as units, and if you encounter an enemy patrol, you'll fight as a unit. I don't want any unit going to the rescue of another. Is that clear?"

They nodded. It was clear.

"Morphy," said Donal, turning to the thin Senior Groupman. "I want you to go with the Junior unit of Lee's Group, which will have the rearguard position. Lee will take his own half-group directly in front of you. Chassen"—he looked at the Senior Groupman of the Second Group—"you and Zolta will take positions third and fourth from the rear. I want you personally in fourth position. Suki, as Junior of the First Group, you'll be ahead of Chassen and right behind me. I'll take the upper half of the First Group in advance position."

"Force," said Lee. "How about communications?"

"Hand-signal. Voice. And that's all. And I don't want any of you closing up to make communication easier. Twenty-meter minimum interval between units." Donal looked around the circle again. "Our job here is to penetrate to the little town as quickly and quietly as we can. Fight only if you're forced into it; and break away as quickly as you can."

"The word is it's supposed to be a Sunday walk," commented Lee.

"I don't operate by back-camp rumor," said Donal flatly, his eyes seeking out the ex-miner. "We'll take all precautions. You Groupmen will be responsible for seeing that your men are fully equipped with everything, including medication."

Lee yawned. It was not a gesture of insolence—not quite.

"All right," said Donal. "Back to your Groups."

The meeting broke up.

A few minutes later the almost inaudible peep of a whistle was carried from Force to Force; and they began to move out. Dawn was not yet in the sky, but the low overcast above the treetops was beginning to lighten at their backs.

The first twelve hundred meters through the woods, though

they covered it cautiously enough, turned out to be just what Lee had called it—a Sunday walk. It was when Donal, in the lead with the first half-Group, came out on the edge of the river that things began to tighten up.

"Scouts out!" he said. Two of the men from the Group sloshed into the smoothly flowing water, and, rifles held high, waded across its gray expanse to the far side. The glint of their rifles, waved in a circle, signaled the all clear and Donal led the rest of the men into the water and across.

Arrived on the far side, he threw out scouts in three directions—ahead, and along the bank each way—and waited until Suki and his men appeared on the far side of the river. Then, his scouts having returned with no sight of the enemy, Donal spread his men out in light skirmish order and went forward.

The day was growing rapidly. They proceeded by fifty meter jumps, sending the scouts out ahead, then moving the rest of the men up when the signal came back that the ground was clear ahead. Jump succeeded jump and there was no contact with the enemy. A little over an hour later, with the large orange disk of E. Eridani standing clear of the horizon, Donal looked out through a screen of bushes at a small, battle-torn village that was silent as the grave.

Forty minutes later, the three Forces of the Third Command, Battle Unit 176 were united and dug in about the small town of Faith Will Succour. They had uncovered no local inhabitants.

They had had no encounter with the enemy.

Force-Leader II

The name of Force-Leader Graeme was mud.

The Third Command, or at least that portion of it that was dug in around the village, made no great attempt to hide the fact from him. If he had shown at all that he was sensitive to their opinion of him, they would have made even less. But there was something about his complete indifference to their attitude that put a check to their obvious contempt. Nevertheless, the hundred and fifty men that had been forced by him to make their approach on the village under full equipment and maximum security effort, and the three hundred other men who had made a much more casual and easy approach, and were congratulating themselves on being out from under such an officer, agreed in an opinion of Donal that had reached its nadir! There is only one thing that veterans hate worse than being made to sweat unnecessarily in garrison; and that is being made to sweat unnecessarily in the field. The word had gone out that the day's work was to be a Sunday walk. And it *had* been a Sunday walk, except for those serving under a green young Dorsai officer, name of Graeme. The men were not happy.

Along about twilight, as the sunset was fading through the bushy-limbed trees that were the local mutant variform of the Earthly conifer that had been imported when this planet was terraformed, a runner came from Hugh at Command HQ, just outside the enemy end of the village. He found Donal seated astride a fallen log, studying a map of the local area.

"Signal from Battles," said the runner, squatting beside the log.

"Stand up," said Donal, quietly. The runner stood. "Now, what's the signal?"

"Second and Third Commands won't be moving up until tomorrow morning," said the runner, sulkily.

"Signal acknowledged," said Donal, waving him off. The runner turned and hurried away with another instance of the new officer's wax-and-braid to relate to the other enlisted men back at HQ.

Left to himself, Donal continued to study the map as long as the light lasted. When it was completely gone, he put the map away, produced a small black whistle from his pocket and peeped for his ranking Senior Groupman.

A moment later a thin body loomed up against the faintly discernible sky beyond the treetops.

"Morphy, sir. Reporting," came a voice of the Senior Groupman.

"Yes—" said Donal. "Sentries all posted, Groupman?"

"Yes, sir." The quality of Morphy's tone was completely without inflection.

"Good. I want them alert at all times. Now, Morphy—"

"Yes, sir?"

"Who do we have in the Force that has a good sense of smell?"

"Smell, sir?"

Donal merely waited.

"Well, sir," said Morphy, finally and slowly. "There's Lee, he practically grew up in the mines, where you have to have a good sense of smell. That's the mines on Coby, Force-Leader."

"I assumed those were the mines you meant," said Donal, dryly. "Get Lee over here, will you?"

Morphy took out his own whistle and blew for the Senior Groupman, Third Group. They waited.

"He's about the camp isn't he?" said Donal, after a moment. "I want all the men within whistle sound that aren't on sentry duty."

"Yes, sir," said Morphy. "He'll be here in a moment. He knows it's me. Everybody sounds a little different on these whistles and you get to know them like voices after a while, sir."

"Groupman," said Donal. "I'd be obliged if you didn't feel the need to keep telling me things I already know."

"Yes, sir," said Morphy, subsiding.

Another shadow loomed up out of the darkness.

"What is it, Morphy?" said the voice of Lee.

"I wanted to see you," spoke up Donal, before the Senior Groupman had a chance to answer. "Morphy tells me you have a good sense of smell."

"I do pretty well," said Lee.

"*Sir!*"

"I do pretty well, sir."

"All right," said Donal. "Both of you take a look at the map here. Look sharp. I'm going to make a light," He flicked on a little flash, shielded by his hand. The map was revealed, spread out on the log before them. "Look here," said Donal, pointing. "Three kilometers off this way. Do you know what that is?"

"Small valley," said Morphy. "It's way outside our sentry posts."

"We're going there," Donal said. The light went out and he got up from the log.

"Us? Us, sir?" the voice of Lee came at him.

"The three of us," said Donal. "Come along." And he led the way surefootedly out into the darkness.

Going through the woods, he was pleased to discover the two Groupmen were almost as sure-footed in the blackness as himself. They went slowly but carefully for something over a mile; and then they felt the ground beginning to slope upward under their feet.

"All right. Down and easy," said Donal quietly. The three

men dropped to their bellies and began in skilled silence to work
their way up to the crest of the slope. It took them a good half-
hour; but at the end of that time they lay side by side just under
the skyline of a ridge, looking over into a well of blackness that
was a small, hidden valley below. Donal tapped Lee on the
shoulder and when the other turned his face toward him in
the gloom, Donal touched his own nose, pointed down into the
valley and made sniffing motions. Lee turned his face back to
the valley and lay in that position for several minutes, apparently doing nothing at all. However, at the end of that time,
he turned toward Donal again, and nodded. Donal motioned
them all back down the slope.

Donal asked no questions and the two Groupmen volunteered nothing until they were once more back safely within
the lines of their own sentry posts. Then Donal turned toward
Lee.

"Well, Groupman," he said. "What did you smell?"

Lee hesitated. His voice, when he answered, had a note of
puzzlement in it.

"I don't know, sir," he answered. "Something—sour, sort of.
I could just barely smell it."

"That's the best you can do?" inquired Donal. "Something
sour?"

"I don't know, sir," said Lee. "I've got a pretty good nose,
Force—in fact," a note of belligerence crept into his voice. "I've
got a damned good nose. I never smelled anything like this
before. I'd remember."

"Have either of you men ever contracted on this planet before?"

"No," said Lee.

"No, sir," answered Morphy.

"I see," said Donal. They had reached the same log from
which they had started a little less than three hours before.
"Well, that'll be all. Thank you, Groupmen."

He sat down on the log again. The other two hesitated a moment; and then went off together.

Left alone, Donal consulted the map again; and sat thinking for a while. Then he rose, and hunting up Morphy, told him to take over the Force, and stay awake. Donal himself was going to Command HQ. Then he took off.

Command HQ was a blackout shell containing a sleepy orderly, a map viewer and Skuak.

"The commandant around?" asked Donal, as he came in.

"Been asleep three hours," said Skuak. "What're you doing up? I wouldn't be if I didn't have the duty."

"Where's he sleeping?"

"About ten meters off in the bush, at eleven o'clock," said Skuak. "What's it all about? You aren't going to wake him, are you?"

"Maybe he'll still be awake," said Donal; and went out.

Outside the shell, and the little cleared space of the HQ area, he cat-footed around to the location Skuak had mentioned. A battle hammock was there, slung between two trees, with a form mounding its climate cover. But when Donal reached in to put his hand on the form's shoulder, it closed only on the soft material of a rolled-up battle jacket.

Donal breathed out and turned about. He went back the way he had come, past the Command HQ area, and was stopped by a sentry as he approached the village.

"Sorry, Force," said the sentry. "Commandant's order. No one to go into the village area. Not even himself, he says. Booby traps."

"Oh, yes—thank you, sentry," said Donal; and, turning about, went off into the darkness.

As soon as he was safely out of sight, however, he turned again, and worked his way back past the sentry lines and in among the houses of the village. The small but very bright moon which the Harmonites called The Eye of the Lord was just rising, and throwing, through the ruined walls, alternate patches of tricky silver and black. Slipping in and out of the black places, he began patiently to search the place, house by house, and building by building.

It was a slow and arduous process, carried out the way he was doing it, in complete silence. And the moon mounted in the sky. It was nearly four hours later that he came upon what he was searching for.

In the moonlit center of a small building's roofless shell stood Hugh Killien, looking very tall and efficient in his chameleon battle-dress. And close to him—almost close enough to be in his arms—was Anea, the Select of Kultis. Beyond them both, blurred by action of the polarizer that had undoubtedly been the means of allowing it to carry her invisibly to this spot, was a small flying platform.

". . . Sweet," Hugh was saying, his resonant voice pitched so low it barely carried to the ears of Donal, shrouded in shadow outside the broken wall, "Sweet, you must trust me. Together we can stop him; but you must let me handle it. His power is tremendous—"

"I know, I know!" she interrupted, fiercely, all but wringing her hands. "But every day we wait makes it more dangerous for you, Hugh. Poor Hugh—" gently she raised her hand to touch his cheek, "what I've dragged you into."

"Dragged? Me?" Hugh laughed, low and confidently. "I went into this with my eyes open." He reached out for her. "For you—"

But she slipped away from him.

"Now's not the time for that," she said. "Anyway, it's not me you're doing this for. It's Kultis. He's not going to use me," she said fiercely, "to get *my* world under his thumb!"

"Of course, it's for Kultis," said Hugh. "But you *are* Kultis, Anea. You're everything I love about the Exotics. But don't you see; all we have to work on are your suspicions. You *think* he's planning against the Bond, against Sayona, himself. But that's not enough for us to go to Kultis with."

"But what can I do?" she cried. "I can't use his own methods against him. I can't lie, or cheat, or set agents on him while he still holds my contract. I . . . I just *can't*. That's what being Select means!" She clenched her fists. "I'm trapped by my own mind, my own body." She turned on him suddenly. "You said when I first spoke to you, two months ago you said you had evidence!"

"I was mistaken," Hugh's tone was soothing. "Something came to my attention—at any rate I was wrong. I have my own built-in moral system, too, Anea. It may not reach the level of psychological blockage like yours," he drew himself up, looking very martial in the moonlight. "But I know what's honorable and right."

"Oh, I know. I know, Hugh—" she was all contrition, "But I get so desperate. You don't know—"

"If he had only made some move against you personally—"

"Me?" She stiffened. "He wouldn't dare! A Select of Kultis— and besides," she added with more of a touch of common sense than Donal had heretofore given her credit for possessing, "that'd be foolish. He'd have nothing to gain; and Kultis would be alerted against him."

"I don't know," Hugh scowled in the moonlight. "He's a man like anyone else. If I thought—"

"Oh, Hugh!" she giggled suddenly, like any schoolgirl. "Don't be absolutely ridiculous!"

"Ridiculous!" His tone rang with wounded feelings.

"Oh, now—I didn't mean that. Hugh, now stop looking like an elephant that just had his trunk stung by a bee. There's no point in making things up. He's far too intelligent to—" she giggled again, then sobered. "No, it's his head we have to worry about; not his heart."

"Do you worry about my heart?" he asked in a low voice.

She looked down at the ground.

"Hugh—I do like you," she said. "But you don't understand. A Select is a . . . a symbol."

"If you mean you can't—"

"No, no, not that—" she looked up quickly. "I've no block against love, Hugh. But if I was involved in something . . . something small, and mean, it's what it would do to those back on Kultis to whom a Select means something—You *do* understand?"

"I understand that I'm a soldier," he said. "And that I never know whether I'll have a tomorrow or not."

"I know," she said. "And they send you out on things like this, dangerous things."

"My dear little Anea," he said, tenderly. "How little you understand what it is to be a soldier. I volunteered for this job."

"Volunteered?" She stared at him.

"To go look for danger—to go look for opportunities to prove myself!" he said, fiercely. "To make myself a name, so that the stars will believe I'm the kind of man a Select of Kultis could want and belong with!"

"Oh, Hugh!" she cried on a note of enthusiasm. "If you only could! If only something would make you famous. Then we could really fight him!"

He checked, staring at her in the moonlight with such a sandbagged expression that Donal, in the shadows, nearly chuckled.

"Must you always be talking about politics?" he cried.

* * *

But Donal had already turned away from the two of them. There was no point in listening further. He moved silently out of earshot; but after that he went quickly, not caring about noise. His search for Hugh had taken him clear across the village, so that what was closest to him now was his own Force area. The short night of Harmony's northern continent was already beginning to gray toward dawn. He headed toward his own men, one of his odd certainties chilling him.

"Halt!" cried one of his own sentries, as Donal broke clear of the houses. "Halt and give—sir!"

"Come with me!" snapped Donal. "Where's the Third Group Area from here?"

"This way, sir," said the man; and led the way, trotting to keep up with Donal's long strides.

They burst into the Third Group area. Donal put his whistle to his lips and blew for Lee.

"What—?" mumbled a sleepy voice from half a dozen meters' distance. A hammock heaved and disgorged the bony figure of the ex-miner. "What the hell . . . sir?"

Donal strode up to him and with both hands swung him about so that he faced toward the enemy territory from which the dawn breeze was coming. "Smell!" he ordered.

Lee blinked, scrubbed his nose with one knotty fist, and stifled a yawn. He took a couple of deep breaths filling his lungs, his nostrils spread—and suddenly he snapped into complete awakedness.

"Same thing, sir," he said, turning to Donal. "Stronger."

"All right!" Donal wheeled about on the sentry. "Take a signal to Senior Groupmen, First and Second Groups. Get their men into trees, high up in trees, and get themselves up, too."

"Trees, sir?"

"Get going! I want every man in this Force a dozen meters off the ground in ten minutes—*with* their weapons!" The sentry turned to make off. "If you've got time after making that signal, try to get through to Command HQ with it. If you see you can't, climb a tree yourself. Got that?"

"Yes, sir."

"Then get going!"

Donal wheeled about and started himself on the business of getting the sleeping Third Group soldiers out of their hammocks and up the trunks of tall trees. It was not done in ten minutes. It was closer to twenty by the time they were all off the ground. A group of Dorsai schoolboys would have made it in a quarter of the time, from the sounder sleep of youth. But on the whole, thought Donal, pulling himself at last up into a tree, they had been in time; and that was what counted.

He did not stop as the others had, at a height of a dozen meters. Automatically, as he hurried the others out of their hammocks, he had marked the tallest tree in the area; and this he continued to climb until he had a view out over the tops of the lesser vegetation of the area. He shaded his eyes against the new-rising sun, peering off toward enemy territory, and between the trees.

"Now, what d'we do?" floated up an aggrieved voice from below and off to one side of his own lofty perch. Donal took his palm from his eyes and tilted his head downward.

"Senior Groupman Lee," he said in a low, but carrying voice. "You will shoot the next man who opens his mouth without being spoken to first by either you, or myself. That is a direct order."

He raised his head again, amid a new silence, and again peered off under his palm through the trees.

The secret of observation is patience. He saw nothing, but he continued to sit, looking at nothing in particular, and everything in general; and after four slow minutes he was rewarded by a slight flicker of movement that registered on his gaze. He made no effort to search it out again, but continued to observe in the same general area; and gradually, as if they were figures developing on a film out of some tangled background, he became aware of men slipping from cover to cover, a host of men, approaching the camp.

He leaned down again through the branches.

"No firing until I blow my whistle," he said, in an even lower voice than before. "Pass the word—quietly."

He heard, like the murmur of wind in those same branches, the order being relayed on to the last man in the Third Group and—he hoped—to the Second and First Groups as well.

The small, chameleon-clad figures continued to advance. Squinting at them through the occulting leaves and limbs, he made out a small black cross sewn to the right shoulder of each battle-dress. These were no mercenaries. These were native elite troops of the United Orthodox Church itself, superb soldiers and wild fanatics both. And even as the recognition confirmed itself in his mind, the advancing men broke into a charge upon the camp, bursting forth all at once in the red-gray dawnlight into full-throated yips and howls, underlaid a second later by the high-pitched singing of their spring-gun slivers as they ripped air and wood and flesh.

They were not yet among the trees where Donal's force was hiding. But his men were mercenaries, and had friends in the camp the Orthodox elite were attacking. He held them as long as he could, and a couple of seconds longer; and then, putting his whistle to lips, he blew with the damper completely off—a blast that echoed from one end of the camp to the other.

Savagely, his own men opened up from the trees. And for several moments wild confusion reigned on the ground. It is not easy to tell all at once from which direction a sliver gun is being fired at you. For perhaps five minutes, the attacking Orthodox soldiers labored under the delusion that the guns cutting them

down were concealed in some groundlevel ambush. They killed
ruthlessly, everything they could see on their own eye-level;
and, by the time they had discovered their mistake, it was too
late. On their dwindled numbers was concentrated the fire of a
hundred and fifty-one rifles; and if the marksmanship of only
one of these was up to Dorsai standards, that of the rest was
adequate to the task. In less than forty minutes from the moment in which Donal had begun to harry his sleep-drugged men
up into the trees, the combat was over.

The Third Group slid down out of their trees and one of the
first down—a soldier named Kennedy—calmly lifted his rifle to
his shoulder and sent a sliver through the throat of an Orthodox
that was writhing on the ground, nearby.

"None of that!" cried Donal, sharply and clearly; and his
voice carried out over the sea. A mercenary hates wanton killing, it not being his business to slaughter men, but to win battles. But not another shot was fired. The fact said something
about a significant change in the attitude of the men of the
Third Command toward a certain new officer by the name of
Graeme.

Under Donal's orders, the wounded on both sides were collected and those with serious wounds medicated. The attacking
soldiery had been wiped out almost to a man. But it had not
been completely one-sided. Of the three hundred-odd men who
had been on the ground at the time of the attack, all but forty-
three—and that included Force-Leader Skuak—were casualties.

"Prepare to retreat," ordered Donal—and, at that moment,
the man facing him turned his head to look past at something
behind Donal. Donal turned about. Pounding out of the ruined
village, hand gun in his fist, was Commandant Killien.

In silence, not moving, the surviving soldiers of the Command watched him race up to him. He checked at their stare;
and his eyes swung about to focus on Donal. He dropped to a

walk and strode up to within a few meters of the younger officer.

"Well, Force-Leader!" he snapped. "What happened? Report?"

Donal did not answer him directly. He raised his hand and pointed to Hugh; and spoke to two of the enlisted men standing by.

"Soldiers," he said. "Arrest that man. And hold him for immediate trial under Article Four of the Mercenaries Code."

Veteran

Directly after getting into the city, with his canceled contract stiff in his pocket, and cleaning up in his hotel room, Donal went down two flights to pay his visit to Marshal Hendrik Galt. He found him in, and concluded certain business with him before leaving to pay his second call at a different hotel across the city.

In spite of himself, he felt a certain weakness in the knees as he announced his presence to the doorbot. It was a weakness most men would have excused him. William, Prince of Ceta, was someone few persons would have cared to beard in his own den; and Donal, in spite of what he had just experienced, was still a young—a very young—man. However, the doorbot invited him in, and summoning up his calmest expression, Donal strode into the suite.

William was, as the last time Donal had seen him, busy at his desk. This was no affectation on William's part, as a good many people between the stars could testify. Seldom has one individual accomplished in a single day what William accomplished in the way of business, daily, as a matter of routine. Donal walked up to the desk and nodded his greeting. William looked up at him.

"I'm amazed to see you," he said.

"Are you, sir?" said Donal.

William considered him in silence for perhaps half a minute.

"It's not often I make mistakes," he said. "Perhaps I can console myself with the thought that when I do they turn out to be on the same order of magnitude as my successes. What inhuman kind of armor are you wearing, young man, that leads you to trust yourself in my presence, again?"

"Possibly the armor of public opinion," replied Donal. "I've been in the public eye, recently. I have something of a name, nowadays."

"Yes," said William. "I know that type of armor from personal experience, myself."

"And then," said Donal, "you did send for me."

"Yes." And then, without warning, William's face underwent a change to an expression of such savagery as Donal had never seen before. "How dare you!" snarled the older man, viciously. "How dare you!"

"Sir," said Donal, wooden-faced, "I had no alternative."

"No alternative! You come to me and have the effrontery to say—no alternative?"

"Yes, sir," said Donal.

William rose in swift and lithe motion. He stalked around the desk to stand face to face, his eyes uptilted a little to bore into the eyes of this tall young Dorsai.

"I took you on to follow my orders, nothing else!" he said icily. "And you—grandstand hero that you are—wreck everything."

"Sir?"

"Yes—'sir'. You backwoods moron! You imbecile. Who told you to interfere with Hugh Killien? Who told you to take any action about him?"

"Sir," said Donal. "I had no choice."

"No choice? How—no choice?"

"My command was a command of mercenaries," answered Donal, without moving a muscle. "Commandant Killien had given his assurance in accordance with the Mercenaries Code. Not only had his assurance proved false, he himself had neglected his command while in the field and in enemy territory.

Indirectly, he had been responsible for the death of over half his men. As ranking field officer present, I had no choice but to arrest him and hold him for trial."

"A trial held on the spot?"

"It is the code, sir," said Donal. He paused. "I regret it was necessary to shoot him. The court-martial left me no alternative."

"Again!" said William. "No alternative! Graeme, the space between the stars does not go to men who can find *no alternatives!*" He turned about abruptly, walked back around his desk and sat down.

"All right," he said coldly but with all the passion gone, "get out of here." Donal turned and walked toward the door as William picked up a paper from before him. "Leave your address with my doorbot," said William. "I'll find some kind of a post for you on some other world."

"I regret, sir—" said Donal.

William looked up.

"It didn't occur to me that you would have any further need of me. Marshal Galt has already found me another post."

William continued to look at him for a long moment. His eyes were as cold as the eyes of a basilisk.

"I see," he said at last, slowly. "Well, Graeme, perhaps we shall have something to do with each other in the future."

"I'll hope we will," said Donal. He went out. But, even after he had closed the door behind him, he thought he could feel William's eyes still coming at him through all the thickness of its panel.

He had yet one more call to make, before his duty on this world was done. He checked the directory out in the corridor and went down a flight.

*   *   *

The doorbot invited him in; and ArDell Montor, as large and untidy as ever, with his eyes only slightly blurred from drink, met him halfway to the entrance.

"You!" said ArDell, when Donal explained what it was he wanted. "She won't see *you.*" He hunched his heavy shoulders, looking at Donal; and for a second his eyes cleared. Something sad and kind looked out of them, to be replaced with bitter humor. "But the old fox won't like it. I'll ask her."

"Tell her it's about something she needs to know," said Donal.

"I'll do that. Wait here," ArDell went out the door.

He returned in some fifteen minutes.

"You're to go up," he said. "Suite 1890." Donal turned toward the door. "I don't suppose," said the Newtonian, almost wistfully, "I'll be seeing you again."

"Why, we may meet," answered Donal.

"Yes," said ArDell. He stared at Donal penetratingly. "We may at that. We may at that."

Donal went out and up to Suite 1890. The doorbot let him in. Anea was waiting for him, slim and rigid in one of her high-collared, long dresses of blue.

"Well?" she said. Donal considered her almost sorrowfully.

"You really hate me, don't you?" he said.

"You killed him!" she blazed.

"Oh, of course." In spite of himself, the exasperation she was always so capable of tapping in him rose to the surface. "I had to—for your own good."

"For my good!"

He reached into his tunic pocket and withdrew a small tell-tale. But it was unlighted. For a wonder this apartment was unbugged. And then he thought—*of course, I keep forgetting who she is.*

"Listen to me," he said. "You've been beautifully equipped by gene selection and training to be a Select—but not to be anything else. Why can't you understand that interstellar intrigue isn't your dish?"

"Interstellar . . . what're you talking about?" she demanded.

"Oh, climb down for a moment," he said wearily—and more youngly than he had said anything since leaving home. "William is your enemy. You understand that much; but you don't understand why or how, although you think you do. And neither do I," he confessed, "although I've got a notion. But the way for you to confound William isn't by playing his game. Play your own. Be the Select of Kultis. As the Select, you're untouchable."

"If," she said, "you've nothing more to say than that—"

"All right," he took a step toward her. "Listen, then. William was making an attempt to compromise you. Killien was his tool—"

"How dare you?" she erupted.

"How dare I?" he echoed wearily. "Is there anyone in this interstellar community of madmen and madwomen who doesn't know that phrase and use it to me on sight? I dare because it's the truth."

"Hugh," she stormed at him, "was a fine, honest man. A soldier and a gentleman! Not a . . . a—"

"Mercenary?" he inquired. "But he was."

"He was a career officer," she replied haughtily. "There's a difference."

"No difference." He shook his head. "But you wouldn't understand that. Mercenary isn't necessarily the dirty word somebody taught you it is. Never mind. Hugh Killien was worse than any name you might be mistaken enough to call me. He was a fool."

"Oh!" she whirled about.

He took her by one elbow and turned her around. She came

about in shocked surprise. Somehow, it had never occurred to her to imagine how strong he was. Now, the sudden realization of her physical helplessness in his hands shocked her into abrupt and unusual silence.

"Listen to the truth, then," he said. "William dangled you like an expensive prize before Killien's eyes. He fed him full of the foolish hope that he could have *you*—the Select of Kultis. He made it possible for you to visit Hugh that night at Faith Will Succour—yes," he said, at her gasp, "I know about that. I saw you there with him. He also made sure Hugh would meet you, just as he made sure that the Orthodox soldiers would attack."

"I don't believe it—" she managed.

"Don't you be a fool, too," Donal said, roughly. "How else do you think an overwhelming force of Orthodox elite troops happened to move in on the encampment at just the proper time? What other men than fanatic Orthodox soldiery could be counted on to make sure none of the men in our unit escaped alive? There was supposed to be only one man to escape from that affair—Hugh Killien, who would be in a position then to make a hero's claim on you. You see how much your good opinion is worth?"

"Hugh wouldn't—"

"Hugh didn't," interrupted Donal. "As I said, he was a fool. A fool but a good soldier. Nothing more was needed for William. He knew Hugh would be fool enough to go and meet you, and good soldier enough not to throw his life away when he saw his command was destroyed. As I say, he would have come back alone—and a hero."

"But you saw through this!" she snapped. "What's your secret? A pipeline to the Orthodox camp?"

"Surely it was obvious from the situation; a command exposed, a commandant foolishly making a love-tryst in a battleground, that something like the attack was inevitable. I simply asked myself what kind of troops would be used and how they might be detected. Orthodox troops eat nothing but native herbs, cooked in the native fashion. The odor of their cooking permeates their clothing. Any veteran of a Harmony campaign would be able to recognize their presence the same way."

"If his nose was sensitive enough. If he knew where to look for them—"

"There was only one logical spot—"

"Anyway," she said coldly. "This is beside the point. The point is"—suddenly she fired up before him—"Hugh wasn't guilty. You said it yourself. He was, even according to you, only a fool! And you had him murdered!"

He sighed in weariness.

"The crime," he said, "for which Commandant Killien was executed was that of misleading his men and abandoning them in enemy territory. It was *that* he paid with his life for."

"Murderer!" she said. "Get out!"

"But," he said, staring bafficdly at her, "I've just explained."

"You've explained nothing," she said, coldly, and from a distance. "I've heard nothing but a mountain of lies, lies about a man whose boots you aren't fit to clean. Now, will you get out, or do I have to call the hotel guard?"

"You don't believe—?" He stared at her, wide-eyed.

"Get out." She turned her back on him. Like a man in a daze, he turned himself and walked blindly to the door and numbly out into the corridor. Still walking, he shook his head, like a person who finds himself in a bad dream and unable to wake up.

What was this curse upon him? She had not been lying—she was not capable of doing so successfully. She had really heard his explanation and—it had meant nothing to her. It was all so obvious, so plain—the machinations of William, the stupidity of Killien. And she had not seen it when Donal pointed it out to her. *She,* of all people, a Select of Kultis!

Why? Why? Why?

Scourged by the devils of self-doubt and loneliness, Donal moved off down the corridor, back in the direction of Galt's hotel.

Aide-de-camp

They met in the office of Marshal Galt, in his Freiland home; and the enormous expanse of floor and the high vaulted ceiling dwarfed them as they stood three men around a bare desk.

"Captain Lludrow, this is my Aide, Commandant Donal Graeme," said Galt, brusquely. "Donal, this is Russ Lludrow, Patrol Chief of my Blue Patrol."

"Honored, sir," said Donal, inclining his head.

"Pleased to meet you, Graeme," answered Lludrow. He was a fairly short, compact man in his early forties, very dark of skin and eye.

"You'll trust Donal with all staff information," said Galt. "Now, what's your reconnaissance and intelligence picture?"

"There's no doubt about it, they're planning an expeditionary landing on Oriente." Lludrow turned toward the desk and pressed buttons on the map keyboard. The top of the desk cleared to transparency and they looked through at a non-scale map of the Sirian system. "Here we are," he said, stabbing his finger at the world of Freiland, "here's New Earth"—his finger moved to Freiland's sister planet—"and here's Oriente"—his finger skipped to a smaller world inward toward the sun—"in the positions they'll be in, relative to one another twelve days from now. You see, we'll have the sun between the two of us and also almost between each of our worlds and Oriente. They couldn't have picked a more favorable tactical position."

Galt grunted, examining the map. Donal was watching Lludrow with quiet curiosity. The man's accent betrayed him for a New Earthman, but here he was high up on the Staff of Frei-

land's fighting forces. Of course, the two Sirian worlds were
natural allies, being on the same side as Old Earth against the
Venus-Newton-Cassida group; but simply because they were so
close, there was a natural rivalry in some things, and a career
officer from one of them usually did best on his home world.

"Don't like it," said Galt, finally. "It's a fool stunt from what
I can see. The men they land will have to wear respirators; and
what the devil do they expect to do with their beachhead when
they establish it? Oriente's too close to the sun for terraforming,
or we would have done it from here long ago."

"It's possible," said Lludrow, calmly, "they could intend to
mount an offensive from there against our two planets here."

"No, no," Galt's voice was harsh and almost irritable. His
heavy face loomed above the map. "That's as wild a notion as
terraforming Oriente. They couldn't keep a base there supplied,
let alone using it to attack two large planets with fully established population and industry. Besides, you don't conquer civilized worlds. That's a maxim."

"Maxims can become worn out, though," put in Donal.

"What?" demanded Galt, looking up. "Oh—Donal. Don't in-
terrupt us now. From the looks of it," he went on to Lludrow,
"it strikes me as nothing so much as a live exercise—you know
what I mean."

Lludrow nodded—as did Donal unconsciously. Live exercises
were something that no planetary Chief of Staff admitted to,
but every military man recognized. They were actual small battles provoked with a handy enemy either for the purpose of
putting a final edge on troops in training, or to keep that edge
on troops that had been too long on a standby basis. Galt, almost alone among the Planetary Commanders of his time, was
firmly set against this action, not only in theory, but in practice.
He believed it more honest to hire his troops out, as in the
recent situation on Harmony, when they showed signs of going
stale. Donal privately agreed with him; although there was al-

ways the danger that when you hired troops out, they lost the sense of belonging to you, in particular, and were sometimes spoiled through mismanagement.

"What do you think?" Galt was asking his Patrol chief.

"I don't know, sir," Lludrow answered. "It seems the only sensible interpretation."

"The thing," interrupted Donal, again, "would be to go over some of the nonsensible interpretations as well, to see if one of them doesn't constitute a possible danger. And from that—"

"Donal," broke in Galt, dryly, "you are my aide, not my Battle Op."

"Still—" Donal was persisting, when the marshal cut him off in a tone of definite command.

"That will be all!"

"Yes, sir," said Donal, subsiding.

"Then," said Galt, turning back to Lludrow, "we'll regard this as a heaven-sent opportunity to cut an arm or two off the fighting strength of the Newton Cassidan fleet and field force. Go back to your Patrol. I'll send orders."

Lludrow inclined his head and was just about to turn and go when there was an interruption—the faint swish of air from one of the big office doors sliding back, and the tap of feminine heels approaching over the polished floor. They turned to see a tall, dazzlingly beautiful woman with red hair coming at them across the office.

"Elvine!" said Galt.

"Not interrupting anything, am I?" she called, even before she came up to them. "Didn't know you had a visitor."

"Russ," said Galt. "You know my sister-in-law's daughter, The Elvine Rhy? Elvine, this is my Blue Patrol Chief, Russ Lludrow."

"Very deeply honored," said Lludrow, bowing.

"Oh, we've met—or at least I've seen you before." She gave him her hand briefly, then turned to Donal. "Donal, come fishing with me."

"I'm sorry," said Donal. "I'm on duty."

"No, no," Galt waved him off with a large hand. "There's nothing more at the moment. Run along, if you want."

"At your service, then," said Donal.

"But what a cold acceptance!" she turned on Lludrow. "I'm sure the Patrol chief wouldn't have hesitated like that."

Lludrow bowed again.

"I'd never hesitate where the Rhy was concerned."

"There!" she said. "There's your model, Donal. You should practice manners—and speeches like that."

"If you suggest it," said Donal.

"Oh, Donal." She tossed her head. "You're hopeless. But come along, anyway." She turned and left; and he followed her.

They crossed the great central hall and emerged into the garden terrace above the blue-green bay of the shallow, inland sea that touched the edges of Galt's home. He expected her to continue down to the docks, but instead she whirled about in a small arbor, and stood facing him.

"Why do you treat me like this?" she threw at him. "Why?"

"Treat you?" He looked down at her.

"Oh, you wooden man!" Her lips skinned back over her perfect teeth. "What're you afraid of—that I'll eat you up?"

"Wouldn't you?" he asked her quite seriously—and she checked at his answer.

"Come on. Let's go fishing!" she cried, and whirled about and ran down toward the dock.

So, they went fishing. But even slicing through the water in pursuit of a twisting fish at sixty fathoms depth, Donal's mind was not on the sport. He let the small jet unit on his shoulders push him whither the chase led him; and, in the privacy of his helmet, condemned himself darkly for his own ignorance. For it was this crime of ignorance which he abhorred above all else—in this case his ignorance of the ways of women—that had led him to believe he could allow himself the luxury of a casual and friendly acquaintanceship with a woman who wanted him badly, but whom he, himself, did not want at all.

She had been living here, in this household, when Galt had brought him here as a personal aide. She was, by some intricate convolution of Freiland inheritance laws, the marshal's responsibility; in spite of the distance of their relationships and the fact that her own mother and some other relatives were still living. She was some five years older than Donal, although in her wild energy and violence of emotion, this difference was lost. He had found her excitements interesting, at first; and her company a balm to what—though he would not admit it to himself in so many words—was a recently bruised and very tender portion of his ego. That had been at first.

"You know," she had said to him in one of her peculiar flashes of directness. "Anybody would want me."

"Anybody would," he admitted, considering her beauty. It was not until later that he discovered, to his dismay, that he had accepted an invitation he had not even suspected was there.

For four months now, he had been established at the marshal's estate, learning some of the elements of Freilander Staff Control; and learning also, to his increasing dismay, some of the intricacies of a woman's mind. And, in addition to it all, he found himself puzzled as to why he did not want her. Certainly he liked Elvine Rhy. Her company was enjoyable, her attractiveness was undeniable, and a certain brightness and hunger in her personality matched similar traits in his own. Yet, he did not want her. No, not the least bit, not at all.

They gave up their fishing after several hours. Elvine had caught four, averaging a good seven or eight kilograms. He had caught none.

"Elvine—" he began, as he went up the steps of the terrace with her. But, before he could finish his carefully thought out speech, an annunciator hidden in a rosebush chimed softly.

"Commandant," said the rosebush, gently, "the doorbot announces a Senior Groupman Tage Lee to see you. Do you wish to see him?"

"Lee—" murmured Donal. He raised his voice. "From Coby?"

"He says he is from Coby," answered the rosebush.

"I'll see him," said Donal, striding quickly toward the house. He heard the sound of running feet behind him and Elvine caught at his arm.

"Donal—" she said.

"This'll just take a minute," he answered. "I'll see you in the library in a few minutes."

"All right—" She let go and fell behind him. He went in and to the entrance hall.

Lee, the same Lee who had commanded his Third Group, was waiting for him.

"Well, Groupman," said Donal, shaking hands. "What brings you here?"

"You do, sir," said Lee. He looked Donal in the eye with something of the challenge Donal had marked the first time Donal had seen him. "Could you use a personal orderly?"

Donal considered him.

"Why?"

"I've been carrying my contract around since they let us all go after that business with Killien," said Lee. "If you want to know, I've been on a bat. That's my cross. Out of uniform I'm an alcoholic. In uniform, it's better, but sooner or later I get into a hassle with somebody. I've been putting off signing up again because I couldn't make up my mind what I wanted. Finally, it came to me. I wanted to work for you."

"You look sober enough now," said Donal.

"I can do anything for a few days—even stop drinking. If I'd come up here with the shakes, you'd never have taken me."

Donal nodded.

"I'm not expensive," said Lee. "Take a look at my contract. If you can't afford me yourself, I'll sign up as a line soldier and you pull strings to get me assigned to you. I don't drink if I've got something to do; and I can make myself useful. Look here—"

He extended his hand in a friendly manner, as if to shake hands again, and suddenly there was a knife in it.

"That's a back-alley, hired killer trick," said Donal. "Do you think it'd work with me?"

"With you—no." Lee made the knife vanish again. "That's why I want to work for you. I'm a funny character, commandant. I need something to hang to. I need it the way ordinary people need food and drink and home and friends. It's all there in the psychological index number on my contract, if you want to copy it down and check on me."

"I'll take your word for it, for now," said Donal. "What *is* wrong with you?"

"I'm borderline psycho," Lee answered, his lean face expressionless. "Not correctable. I was born with a deficiency. What they tell me is, I've got no sense of right or wrong; and I can't manage just by abstract rules. The way the doctors put it when I first got my contract, I need my own, personal, living god in front of me all the time. You take me on and tell me to cut the throat of all the kids under five I meet, and that's fine. Tell me to cut my own throat—the same thing. Everything's all right, then."

"You don't make yourself sound very attractive."

"I'm telling you the truth. I can't tell *you* anything else. I'm like a bayonet that's been going around all my life looking for a rifle to fit on to; and now I've found it. So, don't trust me. Take me on probation for five years, ten years—the rest of my life. But don't shut me out." Lee half-turned and pointed one bony finger at the door behind him. "Out there is hell for me, commandant. Anything inside here is heaven."

"I don't know," said Donal, slowly. "I don't know that I'd want the responsibility."

"No responsibility." Lee's eyes were shining; and it struck home to Donal suddenly that the man was terrified: terrified of being refused. "Just tell me. Try me, now. Tell me to get down and bark like a dog. Tell me to cut my left hand off at the wrist. As soon as they've grown me a new one I'll be back to do whatever you want me to do." The knife was suddenly back in his hand. "Want to see?"

"Put that away!" snapped Donal. The knife disappeared. "All right, I'll buy your contract personally. My suit of rooms are third door to the right, the head of the stairs. Go up there and wait for me."

Lee nodded. He offered no word of thanks. He only turned and went.

Donal shook himself mentally as if the emotional charge that had crackled in the air about him the last few seconds was a thing of physical mass draped heavily upon his shoulders. He turned and went to the library.

Elvine was standing looking out the great expanse of open wall at the ocean, as he came in. She turned quickly, at the sound of his steps and came to meet him.

"What was it?" she asked.

"One of my soldiers from the Harmony business," he said. "I've taken him on as my personal orderly." He looked down at her. "Ev—"

Instantly, she drew a little away from him. She looked out the wall, one hand falling down to play with a silver half-statuette that sat on a low table beside her.

"Yes?" she said.

He found it very hard to get the words out.

"Ev, you know I've been around here a long time," he said.

"A long time?" At that, she turned to face him with a slight look of startlement. "Four months? It seems like hours, only."

"Perhaps," he said, doggedly. "But it *has* been a long time. So perhaps it's just as well I'm leaving."

"Leaving?" Her eyes shot wide; hazel eyes, staring at him. "Who said you were leaving?"

"I have to, of course," he said. "But I thought I ought to clear something up before I go. I've liked you a great deal, Ev—"

But she was too quick for him.

"Liked me?" she cried. "I should think you should! Why, I haven't hardly had a minute to myself for entertaining you. I swear I hardly know what it looks like any more outside of this place! Liked me! You certainly ought to like me after the way I've put myself out for you!"

He gazed at her furious features for a long moment and then he smiled ruefully.

"You're quite right," he said. "I've put you to a great deal of trouble. Pardon me for being so dense as not to notice it." He bent his head to her. "I'll be going now."

He turned and walked away. But he had hardly taken a dozen steps across the sunlit library before she called his name.

"Donal!"

He turned and saw her staring after him, her face stiff, her fists clenched at her side.

"Donal, you . . . you can't go," she said, tightly.

"I beg your pardon?" He stared at her.

"You can't go," she repeated. "Your duty is here. You're assigned here."

"No." He shook his head. "You don't understand, Ev. This business of Oriente's come up. I'm going to ask the marshal to assign me to one of the ships."

"You can't." Her voice was brittle. "He isn't here. He's gone down to the Spaceyard."

"Well, then, I'll go there and ask him."

"You can't. I've already asked him to leave you here. He promised."

"You *what?*" The words exploded from his lips in a tone more suited to the field than to this quiet mansion.

"I asked him to leave you here."

He turned and stalked away from her.

"Donal!" He heard her voice crying despairingly after him, but there was nothing she, or anyone in that house could have done, to stop him then.

He found Galt examining the new experimental model of a two-man anti-personnel craft. The older man looked up in surprise as Donal came up.

"What is it?" he asked.

"Could I see you alone for a minute, sir?" said Donal. "A private and urgent matter."

Galt shot him a keen glance, but motioned aside with his head and they stepped over into the privacy of a tool control booth.

"What is it?" asked Galt.

"Sir," said Donal. "I understand Elvine asked you if I couldn't continue to be assigned to your household during the upcoming business we talked about with Patrol Chief Lludrow earlier today."

"That's right. She did."

"I did not know of it," said Donal, meeting the older man's eyes. "It was not my wish."

"Not your wish?"

"No, sir."

"Oh," said Galt. He drew a long breath and rubbed his chin with one thick hand. Turning his head aside, he gazed out through the screen of the control booth at the experimental ship. "I see," he said. "I didn't realize."

"No reason why you should," Donal felt a sudden twist of

emotion inside him at the expression on the older man's face. "I should have spoken to you before sir."

"No, no," Galt brushed the matter aside with a wave of his hand. "The responsibility's mine. I've never had children. No experience. She has to get herself settled in life one of these days; and . . . well, I have a high opinion of you, Donal."

"You've been too kind to me already, sir," Donal said miserably.

"No, no . . . well, mistakes will happen. I'll see you have a place with the combat forces right away, of course."

"Thank you," said Donal.

"Don't thank me, boy." Abruptly, Galt looked old. "I should have remembered. You're a Dorsai."

Staff Liaison

"Welcome aboard," said a pleasant-faced Junior Captain, as Donal strode through the gas barrier of the inner lock. The Junior Captain was in his early twenties, a black-haired, square-faced young man who looked as if he had gone in much for athletics. "I'm J. C. Allmin Clay Andresen."

"Donal Graeme." They saluted each other. Then they shook hands.

"Had any ship experience?" asked Andresen.

"Eighteen months of summer training cruises in the Dorsai," answered Donal. "Command and armament—no technical posts."

"Command and armament," said Andresen, "are plenty good enough on a Class 4J ship. Particularly Command. You'll be senior officer after me—if anything happens." He made the little ritual gesture, reaching out to touch a close, white, carbon-plastic wall beside him. "Not that I'm suggesting you take over in such a case. My First can handle things all right. But you may be able to give him a hand, if it should happen."

"Be honored," said Donal.

"Care to look over the ship?"

"I'm looking forward to it."

"Right. Step into the lounge, then." Andresen led the way across the small reception room, and through a sliding bulkhead to a corridor that curved off ahead of them to right and left. They went through another door in the wall of the corridor directly in front of them, down a small passage, and emerged through a final door into a large, pleasantly decorated, circular room.

"Lounge," said Andresen. "Control center's right under our feet; reversed gravity." He pressed a stud on the wall and a section of the floor slid back. "You'll have to flip," he warned, and did a head-first dive into the hole.

Donal, who knew what to expect, followed the J. C.'s example. The momentum of his dive shot him through and into another circular chamber of the same size as the lounge, in which everything would have been upside down and nailed to the ceiling, except for the small fact that here the gravity was reversed; and what had been down, was up, and up was down instead.

"Here," said Andresen, as Donal landed lightly on the floor at one side of the opening, "is our Control Eye. As you probably saw when you were moving in to come aboard, the Class 4J is a ball-and-hammer ship." He pressed several studs and in the large globe floating in the center of the floor, that which he had referred to as the Control Eye, a view formed of their craft, as seen from some little distance outside the ship. Half-framed against the star-pricked backdrop of space, and with just a sliver of the curved edge of Freiland showing at the edge of the scene, she floated. A sphere thirty meters in diameter, connected by two slim shafts a hundred meters each in length to a rhomboid-shape that was the ship's thrust unit, some five meters in diameter at its thickest and looking like a large child's spinning top, pivoted on two wires that clamped it at the middle. This was the "hammer." The ship, proper, was the "ball."

"No phase-shift equipment?" asked Donal. He was thinking of the traditional cylinder shape of the big ships that moved between the stars.

"Don't fool yourself," answered Andresen. "The grid's there. We just hope the enemy doesn't see it, or doesn't hit it. We can't protect it, so we try to make it invisible." His finger stabbed out to indicate the apparently bare shafts. "There's a covering

grid running the full length of the ship, from thrust to nose.
Painted black."

Donal nodded thoughtfully.

"Too bad a polarizer won't work in the absence of atmosphere," he said.

"You can say that," agreed Andresen. He flicked off the Eye.
"Let's look around the rest of the ship by hand."

He led out a door and down a passage similar to the one by
which they had entered the lounge. They came out into a corridor that was the duplicate of the curving one they had passed
in the other half of the ship.

"Crew's quarters, mess hall, on the other one," explained Andresen. "Officer's quarters, storage and suppliers, repair section,
on this one." He pushed open a door in the corridor wall opposite them and they stepped into a section roughly the size of
a small hotel room, bounded on its farther side by the curving
outer shell of the ship, proper. The shell in this section was, at
the moment, on transparent; and the complicated "dentist's
chair" facing the bank of controls at the foot of the transparency
was occupied; although the figure in it was dressed in coveralls
only.

"My First," said Andresen. The figure looked up over the
headrest of the chair. It was a woman in her early forties.

"Hi, All," she said. "Just checking the override." Andresen
made a wry grimace at Donal.

"Antipersonnel weapons," he explained. "Nobody likes to
shoot the poor helpless characters out of the sky as they fall in
for an assault—so it's an officer's job. I usually take it over myself
if I'm not tied up with something else at the moment. Staff
Liaison Donal Graeme—First Officer Coa Benn."

Donal and she shook hands.

"Well, shall we get on?" asked Andresen. They toured the rest of the ship and ended up before the door of Donal's stateroom in Officer's Country.

"Sorry," said Andresen. "But we're short of bunk space. Full complement under battle conditions. So we had to put your orderly in with you. If you've no objection—"

"Not at all," said Donal.

"Good," Andresen looked relieved. "That's why I like the Dorsai. They're so sensible." He clapped Donal on the shoulder, and went hurriedly off back to his duties of getting his ship and crew ready for action.

Entering his stateroom, Donal found Lee had already set up both their gear, including a harness hammock for himself to supplement the single bunk that would be Donal's.

"All set?" asked Donal.

"All set," answered Lee. He still chronically forgot the "sir"; but Donal, having already had some experience with the fanatic literal-mindedness with which the man carried out any command given him, had refrained from making an issue of it. "You settle my contract, yet?"

"I haven't had time," said Donal. "It can't be done in a day. You knew that, didn't you?"

"No," said Lee. "All I ever did was hand it over. And then, later on when I was through my term of service they gave it back to me; and the money I had coming."

"Well, it usually takes a number of weeks or months," Donal said. He explained what it had never occurred to him that anyone should fail to know, that the contracts are owned entirely by the individual's home community or world, and that a contract agreement was a matter for settlement between the employer and the employee's home government. The object was not to provide the individual so much with a job and a living wage, as to provide the home government with favorable monetary and "contractual" balances which would enable them to hire, in their turn, the trained specialists *they* needed. In the case of Lee's contract, since Donal was a private employer and had money to offer, but no contractual credits, the matter of Lee's employment had to be cleared with the Dorsai authorities, as well as the authorities on Coby, where Lee came from.

"That's more of a formality than anything else, though," Donal assured him. "I'm allowed an orderly, since I've been commandant rank. And the intent to hire's been registered. That means your home government won't draft you for any special service some place else."

Lee nodded, which was almost his utmost expression of relief.

". . . Signal!" chimed the annunciator in the stateroom wall by the door, suddenly. "Signal for Staff Liaison Graeme. Report to Flagship, immediately. Staff Liaison Graeme report to Flagship immediately."

Donal cautioned Lee to keep from under the feet of the ship's regular crew; and left.

The Flagship of the Battle made up by the Red and Green Patrols of the Freilander Space Force was, like the Class 4J Donal had just left, already in temporary loose orbit around Oriente. It took him some forty minutes to reach her; and when he entered her lock reception room and gave his name and rank, he was assigned a guide who took him to a briefing room in the ship's interior.

The room was filled by some twenty-odd other Staff Liaisons.

They ranged in rank from Warrant Couriers to a Sub-Patrol Chief in his fifties. They were already seated facing a platform; and, as Donal entered—he was, apparently, the last to arrive—a Senior Captain of flag rank entered, followed closely by Blue Patrol Chief Lludrow.

"All right, gentlemen," said the Senior Captain; and the room came to order. "Here's the situation." He waved a hand and the wall behind him dissolved to reveal an artist's extrapolation of the coming battle. Oriente floated in black space, surrounded by a number of ships in various patterns. The size of the ships had been grossly exaggerated in order to make them visible in comparison with the planet which was roughly two-thirds the diameter of Mars. The largest of these, the Patrol Class—long cylindrical interstellar warships—were in varying orbit eighty to five hundred kilometers above the planet's surface, so that the integration of their pattern enclosed Oriente in a web of shifting movement. A cloud of smaller craft, C4Js, A (subclass) 9s, courier ships, firing platforms, and individual and two-man gnat class boats, held position out beyond and planetward of them, right down into the atmosphere.

"We think," said the Senior Captain, "that the enemy, at effective speed and already braking, will come into phase about here—" a cloud of assault ships winked into existence abruptly, a half million kilometers sunward of Oriente, and in the sun's eye. They fell rapidly toward the planet, swelling visibly in size. As they approached, they swung into a circular landing orbit about the planet. The smaller craft closed in, and the two fleets came together in a myriad of patterns whose individual motions the eye could not follow all at once. Then the attacking fleet emerged below the mass of the defenders, spewing a sudden cloud of tiny objects that were the assault troops. These drifted down, attacked by the smaller craft, while the majority of the assault ships from Newton and Cassida began to disappear like blown-out candles as they sought safety in a phase shift that would place them light-years from the scene of battle.

To Donal's fine-trained professional mind it was both beautifully thrilling—and completely false. No battle since time began had ever gone off with such ballet grace and balance and none ever would. This was only an imaginative guess at how the battle would take place, and it had no place in it for the inevitable issuance of wrong orders, the individual hesitations, the underestimation of an opponent, the navigational errors that resulted in collisions, or firing upon a sister ship. These all remained for the actual event, like harpies roosting upon the yet-unblasted limbs of a tree, as dawn steals like some gray thief onto the field where men are going to fight. In the coming action off Oriente there would be good actions and bad, wise decisions, and stupid ones—and none of them would matter. Only their total at the end of the day.

". . . Well, gentlemen," the Senior Captain was saying, "there you have it as Staff sees it. Your job—yours personally, as Staff Liaisons—is to observe. We want to know anything you can see, anything you can discover, anything you can, or think you can, deduce. And of course"—he hesitated, with a wry smile— "there's nothing we'd appreciate quite so much as a prisoner."

There was a ripple of general laughter at this, as all men there knew the fantastic odds against being able to scoop up a man from an already broken-open enemy ship under the velocities and other conditions of a space battle—and find him still alive, even if you succeeded.

"That's all," said the Senior Captain. The Staff Liaisons rose and began to crowd out the door.

"Just a minute, Graeme!"

Donal turned. The voice was the voice of Lludrow. The Patrol Chief had come down from the platform and was approaching him. Donal turned back to meet him.

"I'd like to speak to you for a moment," said Lludrow. "Wait until the others are out of the room." They stood together in silence until the last of the Staff Liaisons had left, and the Senior Captain had disappeared.

"Yes, sir?" said Donal.

"I'm interested in something you said—or maybe were about to say the other day—when I met you at Marshal Galt's in the process of assessing this Oriente business. You said something that seemed to imply doubt about the conclusions we came to. But I never did hear what it was you had in mind. Care to tell me now?"

"Why, nothing, sir," said Donal. "Staff and the marshal undoubtedly know what they're doing."

"It isn't possible, then, you saw something in the situation that we didn't?" Donal hesitated.

"No, sir. I don't know any more about enemy intentions and plans than the rest of you. Only—" Donal looked down into the dark face below his, wavering on the verge of speaking his mind. Since the affair with Anea he had been careful to keep his flights of mental perception to himself. "Possibly I'm just suspicious, sir."

"So are all of us, man!" said Lludrow, with a hint of impatience. "What about it? In our shoes what would *you* be doing?"

"In your shoes," said Donal, throwing discretion to the winds, "I'd attack Newton."

Lludrow's jaw fell. He stared at Donal.

"By heaven," he said, after a moment. "You're not shy about expedients, are you? Don't you know a civilized world can't be conquered?"

Donal allowed himself the luxury of a small sigh. He made an effort to explain himself, once again, in terms others could understand.

"I remember the marshal saying that," he said. "I'm not so sanguine, myself. In fact, that's a particular maxim I'd like to try to disprove some day. However—that's not what I meant. I didn't mean to suggest we attempt to *take* Newton; but that we *attack* it. I suspect the Newtonians are as maxim-ridden as ourselves. Seeing us try the impossible, they're very like to conclude we've suddenly discovered some way to make it possible. From their reactions to such a conclusion we might learn a lot—including about the Oriente affair."

Lludrow's look of amazement was tightening into a frown.

"Any force attacking Newton would suffer fantastic losses," he began.

"Only if they intended to carry the attack through," interrupted Donal, eagerly. "It could be a feint—nothing more than that. The point wouldn't be to do real damage, but to upset the thinking of the enemy strategy by introducing an unexpected factor."

"Still," said Lludrow, "to make their feint effective, the attacking force would have to run the risk of being wiped out."

"Give me a dozen ships—" Donal was beginning; when Lludrow started and blinked like a man waking up from a dream.

"Give you—" he said; and smiled. "No, no, commandant, we were speaking theoretically. Staff would never agree to such a wild, unplanned gamble; and I've no authority to order it on my own. And if I did—how could I justify giving command of such a force to a young man with only field experience, who's never held command in a ship in his life?" He shook his head. "No, Graeme—but I will admit your idea's interesting. And I wish one of us at least had thought of it."

"Would it hurt to mention it—"

"It wouldn't do any good—to argue with a plan Staff has already had in operation for over a week, now." He was smiling broadly. "In fact, my reputation would find itself cut rather severely. But it was a good idea, Graeme. You've got the makings of a strategist. I'll mention the fact in my report to the marshal."

"Thank you, sir," said Donal.

"Back to your ship, then," said Lludrow.

"Good-by, sir."

Donal saluted and left. Behind him, Lludrow frowned for just a moment more over what had just been said—before he turned his mind to other things.

Acting Captain

Space battles, mused Donal, are said to be held only by mutual consent. It was one of those maxims he distrusted; and which he had privately determined to disprove whenever he should get the chance. However—as he stood now by the screen of the Control Eye in the main control room of the C4J, watching the enemy ships appearing to swell with the speed of their approach—he was forced to admit that in this instance, it was true. Or true at least to the extent that mutual consent is involved when you attack an enemy point that you know that enemy will defend.

But what if he should not defend it after all? What if he should do the entirely unexpected—

"Contact in sixty seconds. Contact in sixty seconds!" announced the speaker over his head.

"Fasten all," said Andresen, calmly into the talker before him. He sat, with his First and Second Officers duplicating him on either side, in a "dentist's chair" across the room—"seeing" the situation not in actual images as Donal was doing, but from the readings of his instruments. And his knowledge was therefore the more complete one. Cumbersome in his survival battle suit, Donal climbed slowly into the similar chair that had been rigged for him before the Eye, and connected himself to the chair. In case the ship should be broken apart, he and it would remain together as long as possible. With luck, the two of them would be able to make it to a survival ship in orbit around Oriente in forty or fifty hours—if none of some dozens of factors intervened.

He had time to settle himself before the Eye before contact was made. In those last few seconds, he glanced around him; finding it a little wonderful in spite of all he knew, that this white and quiet room, undisturbed by the slightest tremor, should be perched on the brink of savage combat and its own quite possible destruction. Then there was no more time for thinking. Contact with the enemy had been made and he had to keep his eyes on the scene.

Orders had been to harry the enemy, rather than close with him. Estimates had been twenty per cent casualties for the enemy, five per cent for the defending forces. But such figures, without meaning to be, are misleading. To the man in the battle, twenty per cent, or even five per cent casualties do not mean that he will be twenty per cent or five per cent wounded. Nor, in a space battle, does it mean that one man out of five, or one man out of twenty will be a casualty. It means one *ship* out of five, or one *ship* out of twenty—and every living soul aboard her; for, in space, one hundred per cent casualties mean ninety-eight per cent dead.

There were three lines of defense. The first were the light craft that were meant to slow down the oncoming ships so that the larger, more ponderous craft, could try to match velocities well enough to get to work with heavy weapons. Then there were the large craft themselves in their present orbits. Lastly, there were the second line of smaller craft that were essentially antipersonnel, as the attackers dropped their space-suited assault troops. Donal in a C4J was in the first line.

There was no warning. There was no full moment of battle. At the last second before contact, the gun crews of the C4J had opened fire. Then—

It was all over.

Donal blinked and opened his eyes, trying to remember what had happened. He was never to remember. The room in which he lay, fastened to his chair, had been split as if by a giant hatchet. Through the badly-lit gap, he could see a portion of an officer's stateroom. A red, self-contained flare was burning somewhere luridly overhead, a signal that the control room was without air. The Control Eye was slightly askew, but still operating. Through the transparency of his helmet, Donal could see the dwindling lights that marked the enemy's departure on toward Oriente. He struggled upright in his chair and turned his head toward the Control panel.

Two were quite dead. Whatever had split the room open had touched them, too. The Second officer was dead, Andresen was undeniably dead. Coa Benn still lived, but from the feeble movements she was making in the chair, she was badly hurt. And there was nothing anyone could do for her now that they were without air and all prisoners in their suits.

Donal's soldier-trained body began to react before his mind had quite caught up to it. He found himself breaking loose the fastenings that connected him to his chair. Unsteadily, he staggered across the room, pushed the lolling head of Andresen out of the way, and thumbed the intership button.

"C4J One-twenty-nine," he said. "C4J One-twenty-nine—" he continued to repeat the cabalistic numbers until the screen before him lit up with a helmeted face as bloodless as that of the dead man in the chair underneath him.

"KL," said the face. "A-twenty-three?" Which was code for: *"Can you still navigate?"*

Donal looked over the panel. For a wonder, it had been touched by what had split the room—but barely. Its instruments were all reading.

"A-twenty-nine," he replied affirmatively.

"M-forty," said the other, and signed off. Donal let the intership button slip from beneath his finger. M-forty was—*Proceed as ordered.*

* * *

Proceed as ordered, for the C4J One-twenty-nine, the ship Donal was in, meant—get in close to Oriente and pick off as many assault troops as you can. Donal set about the unhappy business of removing his dead and dying from their control chairs.

Coa, he noted, as he removed her, more gently than the others, seemed dazed and unknowing. There were no broken bones about her, but she appeared to have been pinched, or crushed on one side by just a touch of what had killed the others. Her suit was tight and intact. He thought she might make it, after all.

Seating himself in the captain's chair, he called the gun stations and other crew posts.

"Report," he ordered.

Gun stations One and Five through Eight answered.

"We're going in planetward," he said. "All able men abandon the weapon stations for now and form a working crew to seal ship and pump some air back in here. Those not sealed off, assemble in lounge. Senior surviving crewman to take charge."

There was a slight pause. Then a voice spoke back to him.

"Gun Maintenanceman Ordovya," it said. "I seem to be surviving Senior, sir. Is this the captain?"

"Staff Liaison Graeme, Acting Captain. Your officers are dead. As ranking man here, I've taken command. You have your orders, Maintenanceman."

"Yes, sir." The voice signed off.

Donal set himself about the task of remembering his ship training. He got the C4J underway toward Oriente and checked all instruments. After a while, the flare went out abruptly overhead and a slow, hissing noise registered on his eardrums—at first faintly, then scaling rapidly up in volume and tone to a shriek. His suit lost some of its drum-tightness.

A few moments later, a hand tapped him on his shoulder.

He turned around to look at a blond-headed crewman with his helmet tilted back.

"Ship tight, sir," said the crewman. "I'm Ordovya."

Donal loosened his own helmet and flipped it back, inhaling the room air gratefully.

"See to the First Officer," he ordered. "Do we have anything in the way of a medic aboard?"

"No live medic, sir. We're too small to rate one. Freeze unit, though."

"Freeze her, then. And get the men back to their posts. We'll be on top of the action again in another twenty minutes."

Ordovya went off. Donal sat at his controls, taking the C4J in cautiously and with the greatest possible margins of safety. In principle, he knew how to operate the craft he was seated in; but no one knew better than he what a far cry he was from being an experienced pilot and captain. He could handle this craft the way someone who has taken half a dozen riding lessons can handle a horse—that is, he knew what to do, but he did none of it instinctively. Where Andresen had taken in the readings of all his instruments at a glance and reacted immediately, Donal concentrated on the half dozen main telltales and debated with himself before acting.

So it was that they came late to the action on the edges of Oriente's atmosphere; but not so late that the assault troops were already safely down out of range. Donal searched the panel for the override button on the antipersonnel guns and found it.

"Override on the spray guns," he announced into the mike before him. He looked at the instruments, but he saw in his imagination the dark and tumbling spacesuited bodies of the assault troops, and he thought of the several million tiny slivers of carbon steel that would go sleeting among them at the touch of his finger. There was a slight pause before answering; and then the voice of Ordovya came back.

"Sir . . . if you like, the gunmen say they're used to handling the weapons—"

"Maintenanceman!" snapped Donal. "You heard the order. Override!"

"Override, sir."

Donal looked at his scope. The computer had his targets in the gunsights. He pressed the button, and held it down.

Two hours later, the C4J, then in standby orbit, was ordered to return to rendezvous and its captain to report to his Sub-Patrol chief. At the same time came a signal for all Staff Liaisons to report to the flagship; and one for Staff Liaison Donal Graeme to report personally to Blue Patrol Chief Lludrow. Considering the three commands, Donal called Ordovya on the ship's phone and directed him to take care of the first errand. He himself, he decided, could take care of the other two, which might—or might not—be connected.

Arriving at the flagship, he explained his situation to the Reception Officer, who made a signal both to the Staff Liaison people and to the Blue Patrol chief.

"You're to go directly to Lludrow," he informed Donal; and assigned him a guide.

Donal found Lludrow in a private office on the flagship that was not much bigger than Donal's stateroom in the C4J.

"Good!" said Lludrow, getting up behind a desk as Donal came in and coming briskly around it. He waited until the guide had left, and then he put a dark hand on Donal's arm.

"How'd your ship come through?" he asked.

"Navigating," said Donal. "There was a direct hit on the control room though. All officers casualties."

"All officers?" Lludrow peered sharply at him. "And you?"

"I took command, of course. There was nothing left, though, but antipersonnel mop-up."

"Doesn't matter," said Lludrow. "You were Acting Captain for part of the action?"

"Yes."

"Fine. That's better than I hoped for. Now," said Lludrow, "tell me something. Do you feel like sticking your neck out?"

"For any cause I can approve of, certainly," answered Donal. He considered the smaller, rather ugly man; and found himself suddenly liking the Blue Patrol chief. Directness like this had been a rare experience for him, since he had left the Dorsai.

"All right. If you agree, we'll both stick our necks out." Lludrow looked at the door of the office, but it was firmly closed. "I'm going to violate top security and enlist you in an action contrary to Staff orders, if you don't mind."

"Top security?" echoed Donal, feeling a sudden coolness at the back of his neck.

"Yes. We've discovered what was behind this Newton-Cassida landing on Oriente . . . you know Oriente?"

"I've studied it, of course," said Donal. "At school—and recently when I signed with Freiland. Temperatures up to seventy-eight degrees centigrade, rock, desert, and a sort of native vine and cactus jungle. No large bodies of water worth mentioning and too much carbon dioxide in the atmosphere."

"Right. Well," said Lludrow, "the important point is, it's big enough to hide in. They're down there now and we can't root them out in a hurry—and not at all unless we go down there after them. We thought they were making the landing as a live exercise and we could expect them to run the gauntlet back out in a few days or weeks. We were wrong."

"Wrong?"

"We've discovered their reason for making the landing on Oriente. It wasn't what we thought at all."

"That's fast work," said Donal. "What's it been . . . four hours since the landing?"

"*They* made fast work of it," said Lludrow. "The news is being sat on; but they are firing bursts of a new kind of radiation from projectors that fire once, move, and fire again from some new hiding place—a large number of projectors. And the bursts they fire hit old Sirius himself. We're getting increased sunspot activity." He paused and looked keenly at Donal, as if waiting for comment. Donal took his time, considering the situation.

"Weather difficulties?" he said at last.

"That's it!" said Lludrow, energetically, as though Donal had been a star pupil who had just shone again. "Meteorological opinion says it can be serious, the way they're going about it. And we've already heard their price for calling it off. It seems there's a trade commission of theirs on New Earth right now. No official connection—but the Commission's got the word across."

Donal nodded. He was not at all surprised to hear that trade negotiations were going on in normal fashion between worlds who were at the same time actively fighting each other. That was the normal course of existence between the stars. The ebb and flow of trained personnel on a contractual basis was the lifeblood of civilization. A world who tried to go it on its own would be left behind within a matter of years, to wither on the vine—or at last buy the mere necessities of existence at ruinous cost to itself. Competition meant the trading of skilled minds, and that meant contracts, and contracts meant continuing negotiations.

"They want a reciprocal brokerage agreement," Lludrow said.

Donal looked at him sharply. The open market trading of contracts had been abandoned between the worlds for nearly fifty years. It amounted to speculating in human lives. It removed the last shreds of dignity and security from the individual and treated him as so much livestock or hardware to be traded for no other reason than the greatest possible gain. The Dorsai, along with the Exotics, Mara and Kultis, had led the fight against it. There was another angle as well. On "tight" worlds

such as those of the Venus Group—which included Newton
and Cassida—and the Friendlies, the open market became one
more tool of the ruling group; while on "loose" worlds like Freiland, it became a spot of vulnerability where foreign credits
could take advantage of local situations.

"I see," said Donal.

"We've got three choices," Lludrow said. "Give in—accept
the agreement. Suffer the weather effects over a period of
months while we clean out Oriente by orthodox military means.
Or pay a prohibitive price in casualties by a crash campaign to
clean up Oriente in a hurry. We'd lose as many lives to the
conditions down there as we would to the enemy in a crash
campaign. So, it's my notion that it's a time to gamble—my
notion, by the way, not Staff's. They don't know anything about
this; and wouldn't stand for it if they did. Care to try your idea
of throwing a scare into Newton, after all?"

"With pleasure!" said Donal, quickly, his eyes glowing.

"Save your enthusiasm until you hear what you're going to
have to do it with," replied Lludrow, dryly. "Newton maintains
a steady screen of ninety ships of the first class, in defensive
orbit around it. I can give you five."

Sub-Patrol Chief

"Five!" said Donal. He felt a small crawling sensation down his spine. He had, before Lludrow turned him down the first time, worked out rather carefully what could be done with Newton and how a man might go about it. His plan had called for a lean and compact little fighting force of thirty first-class ships in a triangular organization of three sub-patrols, ten ships to each.

"You see," Lludrow was explaining, "it's not what craft I have available—even with what losses we've just suffered, my Blue Patrol counts over seventy ships of the first class, alone. It's what ships I can trust to you on a job where at least the officers and probably the men as well will realize that it's a mission that should be completely volunteer and that's being sneaked off when Staff's back is turned. The captains of these ships are all strongly loyal to me, personally, or I couldn't have picked them." He looked at Donal. "All right," he said. "I know it's impossible. Just agree with me and we can forget the matter."

"Can I count on obedience?" asked Donal.

"That," said Lludrow, "is the one thing I can guarantee you."

"I'll have to improvise," said Donal. "I'll go in with them, look at the situation, and see what can be done."

"Fair enough. It's decided then."

"It's decided," said Donal.

"Then come along." Lludrow turned and led him out of the office and through corridors to a lock. They passed through the lock to a small courier ship, empty and waiting for them there; and took it to a ship of the first class, some fifteen minutes off.

Ushered into the ship's large and complex main control

room, Donal found five senior captains waiting for him. Lludrow accepted a salute from a gray-haired powerful-looking man, who by saluting revealed himself as captain of this particular ship.

"Captain Bannerman," said Lludrow, introducing him to Donal, "Captain Graeme." Donal concealed a start well. In the general process of his thinking, he had forgotten that a promotion for himself would be necessary. You could hardly put a Staff Liaison with a field rank of commandant over men captaining ships of the first class.

"Gentlemen," said Lludrow, turning to the other executive officers. "I've been forced to form your five ships rather hastily into a new Sub-Patrol unit. Captain Graeme will be your new chief. You'll form a reconnaissance outfit to do certain work near the very center of the enemy space area; and I want to emphasize the point that Captain Graeme's command is absolute. You will obey any and all of his orders without question. Now, are there any questions any of you would like to ask before he assumes command?"

The five captains were silent.

"Fine, then." Lludrow led Donal down the line. "Captain Graeme, this is Captain Aseini."

"Honored," said Donal, shaking hands.

"Captain Sukaya-Mendez."

"At your service, captain."

"Captain El Man."

"Honored," said Donal. A scarred Dorsai face nearing forty looked at him. "I believe I know your family name, captain. High Island, isn't it?"

"Sir, near Bridgehead," answered El Man. "I've heard of the Graemes." Donal moved on.

"And Captain Ruoul."

"Honored."

"Well, then," said Lludrow, stepping back briskly. "I'll leave the command in your hands, Captain Graeme. Anything in the way of special supplies?"

"Torpedoes, sir," answered Donal.

"I'll have Armaments Supply contact you," said Lludrow. And left.

Five hours later, with several hundred extra torpedoes loaded, the five-ship Sub-Patrol moved out for deep space. It was Donal's wish that they get clear of the home base as soon as possible and off where the nature of their expedition could not be discovered and countermanded. With the torpedoes, Lee had come aboard; Donal having remembered that his orderly had been left aboard the C4J. Lee had come through the battle very well, being strapped in his hammock harness throughout in a section of the ship that was undamaged by the hit that had pierced to the control room. Now, Donal had definite instructions for him.

"I want you with me, this time," he said. "You'll stay by me. I doubt very much I might need you; but if I do, I want you in sight."

"I'll be there," said Lee, unemotionally.

They had been talking in the Patrol chief's stateroom, which had been opened to Donal. Now, Donal headed for the main control room, Lee following behind. When Donal reached that nerve center of the ship, he found all three of the ship's officers engaged in calculating the phase shift, with Bannerman overseeing.

"Sir!" said Bannerman as Donal came up. Looking at him, Donal was reminded of his mathematics instructor at school; and he was suddenly and painfully reminded of his own youth.

"About ready to shift?" asked Donal.

"In about two minutes. Since you specified no particular conclusion point, the computer run was a short one. We've merely been making the usual checks to make sure there's no danger of collision with any object. A four light-year jump, sir."

"Good," said Donal. "Come here with me, Bannerman."

He led the way over to the larger and rather more elaborate Control Eye that occupied the center of this control room; and pressed keys. A scene from the library file of the ship filled the globe. It showed a green-white planet with two moons floating in space and lit by the illumination from a G2 type sun.

"The orange and the two pips," said Bannerman, revealing a moonless Freilander's dislikes for natural planetary satellites.

"Yes," said Donal. "Newton." He looked at Bannerman. "How close can we hit it?"

"Sir?" said Bannerman, looking around at him. Donal waited, holding his eyes steady on the older man. Bannerman's gaze shifted and dropped back to the scene in the Eye.

"We can come out as close as you want, sir," he answered. "See, in deep space jumps, we have to stop to make observations and establish our location precisely. But the precise location of any civilized planet's already established. To come out at a safe distance from their defenses, I'd say, sir—"

"I didn't ask you for a safe distance from their defenses," said Donal, quietly. "I said—how close?"

Bannerman looked up again. His face had not paled; but there was now a set quality about it. He looked at Donal for several seconds.

"How close?" he echoed. "Two planetary diameters."

"Thank you, captain," said Donal.

"Shift in ten seconds," announced the First Officer's voice; and began to count down. "Nine seconds—eight—seven—six— five—four—three—two—*shift!*" They shifted.

"Yes," said Donal, as if the shift itself had never interrupted what he was about to say, "out here where it's nice and empty, we're going to set up a maneuver, and I want all the ships to practice it. If you'll call a captain's conference, captain."

Bannerman walked over to the control board and put in the

call. Fifteen minutes later, with all junior officers dismissed, they gathered in the privacy of the control room of Bannerman's ship and Donal explained what he had in mind.

"In theory," he said, "our Patrol is just engaged in reconnaissance. In actuality, we're going to try to simulate an attacking force making an assault on the planet Newton."

He waited a minute to allow the weight of his words to register on their minds; and then went on to explain his intentions.

They were to set up a simulated planet on their ship's instruments. They would approach this planet, which was to represent Newton, according to a random pattern and from different directions, first a single ship, then two together, then a series of single ships—and so on. They would, theoretically, appear into phase just before the planet, fire one or more torpedoes, complete their run past the planet and immediately go out of phase again. The intention would be to simulate the laying of a pattern of explosions covering the general surface of the planet.

There was, however, to be one main difference. Their torpedoes were to be exploded well without the outer ring of Newton's orbits of defense, as if the torpedoes were merely intended as a means to release some radiation or material which was planned to fall in toward the planet, spreading as it went.

And, one other thing, the runs were to be so timed that the five-ship force, by rotation, could appear to be a large fleet engaged in continuous bombardment.

". . . Any suggestions or comments?" asked Donal, winding it up. Beyond the group facing him, he could see Lee, lounging against the control room wall and watching the captains with a colorless gaze.

There was no immediate response; and then Bannerman spoke up slowly, as if he felt it had devolved upon him, the unwelcome duty of being spokesman for the group.

"Sir," he said, "what about the chances of collision?"

"They'll be high, I know," said Donal. "Especially with the

defending ships. But we'll just have to take our chances."

"May I ask how many runs we'll be making?"

"As many," said Donal, "as we can." He looked deliberately around the group. "I want you gentlemen to understand. We're going to make every possible attempt to avoid open battle or accidental casualties. But these things may not be avoidable considering the necessarily high number of runs."

"How many runs did you have in mind, captain?" asked Sukaya-Mendez.

"I don't see," replied Donal, "how we can effectively present the illusion of a large fleet engaged in saturation bombardment of a world in under a full two hours of continuous runs."

"Two hours!" said Bannerman. There was an instinctive murmur from the group. "Sir," continued Bannerman. "Even at five minutes a run, that amounts with five ships to better than two runs an hour. If we double up, or if there's casualties it could run as high as four. That's eight phase shifts to an hour—sixteen in a two-hour period. Sir, even doped to the ears, the men on our ships can't take that."

"Do you know of anyone who ever tried, captain?" inquired Donal.

"No, sir—" began Bannerman.

"Then how do we know it can't be done?" Donal did not wait for an answer. "The point is, it must be done. You're being required only to navigate your ships and fire possibly two torpedoes. That doesn't require the manpower it would to fight your ships under ordinary conditions. If some of your men become unfit for duty, make shift with the ones you have left."

"*Shai Dorsai!*" murmured the scarred El Man; and Donal glanced toward him, as grateful for the support as for the compliment.

"Anyone want out?" Donal asked crisply.

There was a slow, but emphatic, mutter of negation from all of them.

"Right." Donal took a step back from them. "Then let's get about our practice runs. Dismissed, gentlemen."

He watched the four from other ships leave the control room.

"Better feed and rest the crews," Donal said, turning to Bannerman. "And get some rest yourself. I intend to. Have a couple of meals sent to my quarters."

"Sir," acknowledged Bannerman. Donal turned and left the control room, followed by Lee as by a shadow. The Cobyman was silent until they were in the stateroom; then he growled: "What did that scarface mean by calling you shy?"

"Shy?" Donal turned about in surprise.

"Shaey, shy—something like that."

"Oh," Donal smiled at the expression on the other's face. "That wasn't an insult, Lee. It was a pat on the back. *Shai* was what he said. It means something like—true, pure, the actual."

Lee grunted. Then he nodded.

"I guess you can figure on him," he said.

The food came, a tray for each of them. Donal ate lightly and stretched himself out on the couch. It seemed he dropped instantly into sleep; and when he awoke at the touch of Lee's hand on his shoulder he knew he had been dreaming—but of what, he could not remember. He remembered only a movement of shapes in obscurity, as of some complex physics problem resolving itself in terms of direction and mass, somehow given substance.

"Practice about to start," said Lee.

"Thank you, orderly," he said automatically. He got to his feet and headed toward the control room, shedding the druggedness of his sleep as he went. Lee had followed him, but he was not aware of this until the Cobyman pushed a couple of small white tablets into his hand.

"Medication," said Lee. Donal swallowed them automatically. Bannerman, over by the control board, had seen him come in, and now turned and came across the floor.

"Ready for the first practice run, sir," he said. "Where would you like to observe—controls, or Eye?"

Donal looked and saw they had a chair set up for him in both locations.

"Eye," he said. "Lee, you can take the other chair, as long as there does not seem to be one for you."

"Captain, you—"

"I know, Bannerman," said Donal, "I should have mentioned the fact I meant to have my orderly up here. I'm sorry."

"Not at all, sir." Bannerman went over and fitted himself into his own chair, followed by Lee. Donal turned his attention to the Eye.

The five ships were in line, in deep space, at thousand-kilometer intervals. He looked at their neat Indian file and stepped up the magnification slightly so that in spite of the distance that should have made even the nearest invisible, they appeared in detail, in-lighted by the Eye.

"Sir," said Bannerman; and his quiet voice carried easily across the room. "I've arranged a key-in. When we make our phase shift, that library tape will replace the image in the Eye, so you can see what our approach will actually look like."

"Thank you, captain."

"Phase shift in ten seconds—"

The count-down ticked off like the voice of a clock. Then, there was the sensation of a phase shift; and abruptly Donal was sweeping closely over a planet, barely fifty thousand kilometers distance from its surface. "Fire—" and "Fire—" spoke the speaker in the control room ceiling. Again, the indescribable destruction and rebuilding of the body. The world was gone and they were again in deep space.

Donal looked at the four other ships in line. Abruptly the leading one disappeared. The rest continued, seemingly, to hang there, without motion. There was no sound in the control room about him. The seconds crept by, became minutes. The minutes crawled. Suddenly—a ship appeared in front of Bannerman's craft.

Donal looked back at the three behind. Now, there were only two.

The run continued until all the ships had made their pass.

"Again," ordered Donal.

They did it again; and it went off without a hitch.

"Rest," said Donal, getting out of the chair. "Captain, pass the word for all ships to give their personnel a break of half an hour. Make sure everyone is fed, rested, and supplied with medication. Also supply every person with extra medication to be taken as needed. Then, I'd like to talk to you, personally."

When Bannerman had accomplished these orders and approached Donal, Donal took him aside.

"How about the reactions of the men?" he asked.

"Fine, captain," Bannerman said; and Donal was surprised to read a true enthusiasm in his voice. "We've got good crews, here. High level-ratings, and experience."

"I'm glad to hear it," said Donal, thankfully. "Now . . . about the time interval—"

"Five minutes exactly, sir." Bannerman looked at him inquiringly. "We can shorten slightly, or lengthen as much as you want."

"No," said Donal. "I just wanted to know. Do you have battle dress for me and my orderly?"

"It's coming up from stores."

The half hour slid by quickly. As it approached its end and they prepared to tie into their chairs, Donal noticed the chronometer on the control room wall. It stood at 23:10 and the half hour would be up at 23:12.

"Make that start at 23:15," he directed Bannerman. The word was passed to the other ships. Everyone was in battle dress in their chairs and at their posts, waiting. Donal felt a strange metallic taste in his mouth and the slow sweat began to work out on the surface of his skin.

"Give me an all-ship hookup," he said. There was a few seconds pause, and then a Third Officer spoke from the control panel.

"You're hooked in, sir."

"Men," said Donal. "This is Captain Graeme." He paused. He had no idea what he had intended to say. He had asked for the hookup on impulse, and to break the strain of the last few moments which must be weighing on all the rest as much as him. "I'll tell you one thing. This is something Newton's never going to forget. Good luck to all of you. That's all."

He wigwagged to the Third Officer to cut him off; and looked up at the clock. A chime sounded softly through the ship.

It was 23:15.

Sub-Patrol Chief II

Newton was not to forget.

To a world second only to Venus in its technical accomplishments—and some said not even second—to a world rich in material wealth, haughty with its knowledge, and complacent in the contemplation of its lavish fighting forces, came the shadow of the invader. One moment its natives were secure as they had always been behind the ringing strength of their ninety ships in orbit—and then enemy craft were upon them, making runs across the skies of their planet, bombing them with—*what?*

No, Newton was never to forget. But that came afterward.

To the men in the five ships, it was the here and now that counted. Their first run across the rich world below them seemed hardly more than another exercise. The ninety ships were there—as well as a host of other spacecraft. They—or as many of them as were not occluded by the body of the planet—registered on the instruments of the Freilander ships. But that was all. Even the second run was almost without incident. But by the time Donal's leading ship came through for the start of the third run, Newton was beginning to buzz like a nest of hornets, aroused.

The sweat was running freely down Donal's face as they broke into the space surrounding the planet; and it was not tension alone that was causing it. The psychic shocks of five phase shifts were taking their toll. Halfway in their run there was a sudden sharp tremor that shook their small white-walled world that was the control room, but the ship continued as if unhurt, released its second torpedo and plunged into the safety of its sixth phase shift.

"Damage?" called Donal—and was surprised to hear his voice issue on an odd croaking note. He swallowed and asked again, in a more normal, controlled tone. "Damage?"

"No damage—" called an officer sharply, from the control panel. "Close burst."

Donal turned his eyes almost fiercely back onto the scene in the Eye. The second ship appeared. Then the third. The fourth. The fifth.

"Double up this time!" ordered Donal harshly. There was a short minute or two of rest and then the sickening wrench of the phase shift again.

In the Eye, its magnification jumping suddenly, Donal caught sight of two Newtonian ships, one planetward, the other in a plane and at approximately two o'clock to the line of the bombing run they had begun.

"Defensive—" began Donal; but the gun crews had waited for no order. Their tracking had been laid and the computers were warm. As he watched, the Newtonian ship which was ahead and in their plane opened out like a burst balloon in slow motion and seemed to fall away from them.

—Another phase shift.

The room swam for a second in Donal's blurred eyes. He felt a momentary surge of nausea; and, on the heels of it, heard someone over at the panel, retching. He blazed up inside, forcing an anger to fight the threatening sickness.

It's in your mind—it's all in your mind—he slapped the thought at himself like a curse. The room steadied; the sickness retreated a little way.

"Time—" It was Bannerman, calling in a half-gasping voice from the panel. Donal blinked and tried to focus on the scene in the Eye. The rank odor of his own sweat was harsh in his nostrils—or was it simply that the room was permeated with the stink of all their sweating?

In the Eye he could make out that four ships had come through on this last run. As he watched, the fifth winked into existence.

"Once more!" he called, hoarsely. "In at a lower level, this time." There was a choked, sobbing-like sound from the direction of the panel; but he deliberately did not turn his head to see who it was.

Again the phase shift.

Blur of planet below. A sharp shock. Another.

Again the phase shift.

The control room—full of mist? No—his own eyes. Blink them. Don't be sick.

"Damage?"

No answer.

"Damage!"

"—Light hit. Aft. Sealed—"

"Once more."

"Captain—" Bannerman's voice, "we can't make it again. One of our ships—"

Check in the Eye. Images dancing and wavering—yes, only four ships.

"Which one?"

"I think—" Bannerman, gasping, "Mendez."

"Once more."

"Captain, you can't ask—"

"Give me a hookup then." Pause. "You hear me? Give me a hookup."

"Hookup—" some officer's voice. "You're hooked up, captain."

"All right, this is Captain Graeme." Croak and squeak. Was that *his* voice speaking? "I'm calling for volunteers—one more run. Volunteers only. Speak up, anyone who'll go."

Long pause.

"*Shai Dorsai!*"

"*Shai El Man!*—any others?"

"Sir—" Bannerman—"The other two ships aren't receiving."

Blink at Eye. Focus. True. Two of three ships there yawning out of line.

"Just the two of us then. Bannerman?"

"At"—croaking—"your orders, sir."

"Make the run."

Pause . . .

Phase shift!

Planet, whirling—shock—dark space. Can't black out now—

"Pull her out of it!" Pause. "*Bannerman!*"

Weakly responding: "Yes sir—"

PHASE SHIFT

—Darkness . . .

"—Up!"

It was a snarling, harsh, bitter whisper in Donal's ear. He wondered, eyes-closed, where it was coming from. He heard it again, and once again. Slowly it dawned on him that he was saying it to himself.

He fought his eyes open.

The control room was still as death. In the depths of the eye before him three small tiny shapes of ships could be seen, at full magnification, far-flung from each other. He fumbled with dead fingers at the ties on his suit, that bound him to his chair. One by one they came free. He pushed himself out of the chair and fell to his knees on the floor.

Swaying, staggering, he got to his feet. He turned himself toward the five chairs at the control panel, and staggered to them.

In four of the chairs, Bannerman and his three officers sagged unconscious. The Third Officer seemed more than unconscious. His face was milkish white and he did not seem to be breathing. All four men had been sick.

In the fifth chair, Lee hung twisted in his ties. He was not unconscious. His eyes were wide on Donal as he approached, and a streak of blood had run down from one corner of the orderly's mouth. He had apparently tried to break his ties by main strength, like a mindless animal, and go directly to Donal. And yet his eyes were not insane, merely steady with an unnatural fixity of purpose. As Donal reached him Lee tried to speak; but all he was able to manage for a second was a throttled sound, and a little more blood came out of the corner of his mouth.

"Y'arright?" he mumbled, finally.

"Yes," husked Donal. "Get you loose in a minute. What happened to your mouth?"

"Bit tongue—" mumbled Lee thickly. "M'arright."

Donal unfastened the last of the ties and, reaching up, opened Lee's mouth with his hands. He had to use real strength to do so. A little more blood came out, but he was able to see in. One edge of Lee's tongue, halfway back from the tip, had been bitten entirely through.

"Don't talk," directed Donal. "Don't use that tongue at all until you can get it fixed."

Lee nodded, with no mark of emotion, and began painfully to work out of the chair.

By the time he was out, Donal had managed to get the ties loose on the still form of the Third Officer. He pulled the man out of the chair and laid him on the floor. There was no perceptible heartbeat. Donal stretched him out and attempted to begin artificial respiration; but at the first effort his head swam dizzily and he was forced to stop. Slowly he pulled himself erect and began to break loose the ties on Bannerman.

"Get the Second, if you feel up to it," he told Lee. The Co-byman staggered stiffly around to the Second Officer and began work on his ties.

Between the two of them, they got the three Freilanders stretched out on the floor and their helmets off. Bannerman and the Second Officer began to show signs of regaining conscious-ness and Donal left them to make another attempt at respiration with the Third Officer. But he found the body, when he touched it, was already beginning to cool.

He turned back and began work on the First Officer, who was still laxly unconscious. After a while the First Officer began to breathe deeply and more steadily; and his eyes opened. But it was apparent from his gaze that he did not see the rest of them, or know where he was. He stared at the control panel with blank eyes like a man in a heavily drugged condition.

"How're you feeling?" Donal asked Bannerman. The Freiland captain grunted, and made an effort to raise himself up on one elbow. Donal helped, and between the two of them they got him, first sitting up, then to his knees, and finally—with the help of the back of a chair to pull him up—to his feet.

Bannerman's eyes had gone directly to the control panel, from the first moment they had opened. Now, without a word, he pulled himself painfully back into his chair and began clum-sily to finger studs.

"All ship sections," he croaked into the grille before him. "Report."

There was no answer.

"Report!" he said. His forefinger came down on a button and an alarm bell rang metallically loud through the ship. It ceased and a faint voice came from the speaker overhead.

"Fourth Gun Section reporting as ordered, sir—"

The battle of Newton was over.

Hero

Sirius himself had just set; and the small bright disk of that white dwarf companion that the Freilanders and the New Earthmen had a number of uncomplimentary names for was just beginning to show strongly through the wall of Donal's bedroom. Donal sat, bathed in the in-between light, dressed in only a pair of sport trunks, sorting through some of the interesting messages that had come his way, recently—since the matter of the raid on Newton.

So engrossed was he that he paid no attention until Lee tapped him on one brown-tanned shoulder.

"Time to dress for the party," said the Cobyman. He had a gray dress uniform of jacket and trousers, cut in the long-line Freiland style, over one arm. It was fashionably free of any insignia of rank. "I've got a couple of pieces of news for you. First, *she* was here again."

Donal frowned, getting into the uniform. Elvine had conceived the idea of nursing him after his return from the short hospital stay that had followed the Newton affair. It was her convenient conclusion that he was still suffering from the psychological damage of the overdose of phase-shifting they had all gone through. Medical opinion and Donal's to the contrary, she had insisted on attaching herself to him with a constancy which lately had led him to wonder if perhaps he would not have preferred the phase shifting itself. The frown now vanished, however.

"I think I see an end to that," he said. "What else?"

"This William of Ceta you're so interested in," answered Lee. "He's here for the party."

Donal turned his head to look sharply at the man. But Lee was merely delivering a report. The bony face was empty of even those small signs of expression which Donal had come to be able to read, in these past weeks of association.

"Who told you I was interested in William?" he demanded.

"You listen when people talk about him," said Lee. "Shouldn't I mention him?"

"No, that's all right," Donal said. "I want you to tell me whenever you find out anything about him you think I might not know. I just didn't know you observed that closely."

Lee shrugged. He held the jacket for Donal to slide his arms into.

"Where'd he come from?" asked Donal.

"Venus," said Lee. "He's got a Newton man with him—big young drunk named Montor. And a girl—one of those special people from the Exotics."

"The Select of Kultis?"

"That's right."

"What're they doing here?"

"He's top-level," said Lee. "Who is on Freiland and not here for your party?"

Donal frowned again. He had almost managed to forget that it was in his honor these several hundred well-known people would be gathered here tonight. Oh—not that he would be expected to place himself on show. The social rules of the day and this particular world made lionizing impolite. Direct lionizing, that is. You honored a man by accepting his hospitality, that was the theory. And since Donal had little in the way of means to provide hospitality for the offering, the marshal had stepped into the breach. Nevertheless, this was the sort of occasion that went against Donal's instinctive grain.

He put that matter aside and returned to that of William. If the man happened to be visiting Freiland it would be unthinkable that he should not be invited, and hardly thinkable that he should decline to come. It could be just that. Perhaps, thought Donal with a weariness beyond his years, I'm starting at shadows. But even as his mind framed the thought, he knew it was not true. It was that oddness in him, now more pronounced than ever since the psychic shaking-up of the Newtonian battle, with its multiple phase shifts. Things seen only dimly before were now beginning to take on shape and substance for him. A pattern was beginning to form, with William as its center, and Donal did not like what he saw of the pattern.

"Let me know what you can find out about William," he said.

"Right," replied Lee. "And the Newton man?"

"And the girl from the Exotics." Donal finished dressing and took a back slipway down to the marshal's office. Elvine was there, and with her and the marshal, as guests, were William and Anea.

"Come in, Donal!" called Galt, as Donal hesitated in the entrance. "You remember William and Anea, here!"

"I'd be unlikely to forget." Donal came in and shook hands. William's smile was warm, his hand-clasp firm; but the hand of Anea was cool and quickly withdrawn from Donal's grasp, and her smile perfunctory. Donal caught Elvine watching them closely; and a faint finger of warning stirred the surface of Donal's mind.

"I've looked forward to seeing you again," said William. "I owe you an apology, Donal. Indeed I do. I've underestimated your genius considerably."

"Not genius," said Donal.

"Genius," insisted William. "Modesty's for little men." He smiled frankly. "Surely you realize this affair with Newton's made you the newest nova on our military horizon?"

"I'll have to watch out your flattery doesn't go to my head, Prince." Donal could deal in double meaning, too. William's first remark had put him almost at his ease. It was not the wolves among people who embarrassed and confused him; but the sheep dogs gone wrong. Those, in fact, who were equipped by nature and instinct to be one thing and through chance and wrongheadedness found themselves acting contrary to their own natures. Possibly, he had thought, that was the reason he found men so much easier to deal with than women—they were less prone to self-deception. Now, however, a small intake of breath drew his attention to Anea.

"You're modest," she said; but two touches of color high on the cheek-bones of her otherwise slightly pale face, and her unfriendly eyes, did not agree with her.

"Maybe," he said, as lightly as he could, "that's because I don't really believe I've got anything to be modest about. Anyone could have done what I did above Newton—and, in fact, several hundred other men did. Those that were there with me."

"Oh, but it was your idea," put in Elvine.

Donal laughed.

"All right," he said. "For the idea, I'll take credit."

"Please do," said Anea.

"Well," put in Galt, seeing that things were getting out of hand. "We were just about to go in and join the party, Donal. Will you come along?"

"I'm looking forward to it," answered Donal, smoothly.

They proceeded, a small knot of people, out through the big doors of the office and into the main hall of the mansion. It was already full of guests interspersed with drifting floats laden with food and drinks. Into this larger body of people, their small group melted like one drop of coloring matter into a glass of water. Their individual members were recognized, captured and dispersed by other guests; and in a few seconds they were all separated—all but Donal and Elvine, who had taken his arm possessively, as they had come out of the office.

She pulled him into the privacy of a small alcove.

"So that's what you've been mooning over!" she said fiercely.
"It's her!"

"Her?" he pulled his arm loose. "What's wrong with you, Ev?"

"You know who I mean!" she snapped. "That Select girl. It's
her you're after—though why, I don't know. She's certainly
nothing special to look at. And she's hardly even grown up yet."

He chilled suddenly. And she—abruptly realizing that this
time she had gone too far, took a sudden, frightened step back
from him. He fought to control himself; but this was the au-
thentic article, one of the real Dorsai rages that was his by inheritance. His limbs were cold, he saw everything with an
unwonted clarity, and his mind ticked away like some detached
machine in the far depths of his being. There was murder in
him at the moment. He hung balanced on the knife edge of it.

"Good-by, Ev," he said. She took another, stiff-legged step
back from him, then another, and then she turned and fled. He
turned about to see the shocked faces of those nearby upon him.

His glance went among them like a scythe, and they fell away
before it. He walked forward through them and out of the hall
as if he had been alone in the room.

He was pacing back and forth in the bare isolation of the marshal's office, walking off the charge of adrenalin that had surged
through him on the heels of his emotion, when the door opened.
He turned like a wolf; but it was only Lee.

"You need me?" asked Lee.

The three words broke the spell. The tension in him snapped
suddenly; and he burst out laughing. He laughed so long and
loud that the Cobyman's eyes became shadowed first with puzzlement, and then with a sort of fear.

"No . . . no . . . it's all right," he gasped at last. He had a fas-
tidiousness about casually touching people; but now he clapped
Lee on the shoulder to reassure him, so unhappy did the lean

man look. "See if you can find me a drink—some Dorsai whisky."

Lee turned and left the room. He was back in seconds with a tulip-shaped glass holding perhaps a deciliter of the bronze whisky. Donal drank it down, grateful for the burn in his throat.

"Learn anything about William?" He handed the glass back to Lee.

Lee shook his head.

"Not surprised," murmured Donal. He frowned. "Have you seen ArDell Montor around—that Newtonian that came with William?"

Lee nodded.

"Can you show me where I can find him?"

Lee nodded again. He led Donal out onto the terrace, down a short distance, and in through an open wall to the library. There, in one of the little separate reading cubicles, he found ArDell alone with a bottle and some books.

"Thanks, Lee," said Donal. Lee vanished. Donal came forward and sat down at the small table in the cubicle opposite ArDell and his bottle.

"Greetings," said ArDell, looking up. He was not more than slightly drunk by his own standards. "Hoping to talk to you."

"Why didn't you come up to my room?" asked Donal.

"Not done," ArDell refilled his glass, glanced about the table for another and saw only a vase with some small native variform lilies in it. He dumped these on the floor, filled the vase and passed it politely to Donal.

"No thanks," said Donal.

"Hold it anyway," ArDell said. "Makes me uncomfortable, drinking with a man who won't drink. No, besides, better to just bump into each other." He looked at Donal suddenly with one of his unexpected flashes of soberness and shrewdness. "He's at it again."

"William?"

"Who else?" ArDell drank. "But what would he be going with Project Blaine?" ArDell shook his head. "*There's* a man. And a scientist. Make two of any of the rest of us. Can't see *him* leading Blaine around by the nose—but still . . ."

"Unfortunately," said Donal, "we are all tied to the business end of our existence by the red tape in our contracts. And it's in business William shines."

"But he doesn't make sense!" ArDell twisted the glass in his hands. "Take me. Why would he want to ruin me? But he does." He chuckled suddenly. "I've got him scared now."

"You have?" asked Donal. "How?"

ArDell tapped the bottle with one forefinger.

"This. He's afraid I may kill myself. Evidently he doesn't want that."

"Will you?" asked Donal, bluntly.

ArDell shook his head.

"I don't know. Could I come out of it, now? It's been five years. I started it deliberately to spite him—didn't even like the stuff, like you. Now, I wonder. I'll tell you"—he leaned forward over the table—"they can cure me, of course. But would I be any good now, if they did? Math—it's a beautiful thing. Beautiful like art. That's the way I remember it; but I'm not sure. Not sure at all any more." He shook his head again. "When the time comes to dump this," he pointed again at the bottle, "you need something that means more to you. I don't know if work does, any more."

"How about William?" asked Donal.

"Yes," said ArDell slowly, "there is him. That would do it. One of these days I'm going to find out why he did this to me. Then—"

"What does he seem to be after?" asked Donal. "I mean, in general?"

"Who knows?" ArDell threw up his hands. "Business. More business. Contracts—more contracts. Agreements with every government, a finger in every honey-pot. That's our William."

"Yes," said Donal. He pushed back his float and stood up.

"Sit down," said ArDell. "Stop and talk. You never sit still for more than a second or two. For the love of peace, you're the only man between the stars I can talk to, and you won't sit still."

"I'm sorry," Donal said. "But there're things I have to do. A day'll come, maybe, when we can sit down and talk."

"I doubt it," muttered ArDell. "I doubt it very much."

Donal left him there, staring at his bottle.

He went in search of the marshal; but it was Anea he encountered first, standing upon a small balcony, deserted except for herself; and gazing out over the hall, directly below, with an expression at the same time so tired and so longing that he was suddenly and deeply moved by the sight of it.

He approached her, and she turned at the sound of his footsteps. At the sight of him, her expression changed.

"You again," she said, in no particularly welcome tone.

"Yes," said Donal, brusquely. "I meant to search you out later, but this is too good a chance to pass up."

"Too good."

"I mean you're alone . . . I mean I can talk to you privately," said Donal, impatiently.

She shook her head.

"We've got nothing to talk about," she said.

"Don't talk nonsense," said Donal. "Of course we have— unless you've given over your campaign against William."

"Well!" The word leaped from her lips and her eyes flashed their green fire at him. "Who do you think you are!" she cried furiously. "Who ever gave you the right to have any say about what I do?"

"I'm part Maran through both my grandmothers," he said. "Maybe that's why I feel a sense of responsibility to you."

"I don't believe it!" she snapped. "About you being part
Maran, that is. You couldn't be part Maran, someone like you,
a—" she checked, fumbling for words.

"Well?" He smiled a little grimly at her. "A what?"

"A . . . *mercenary!*" she cried triumphantly, finding at last the
word that would hurt him the most, in her misinterpretation
of it.

He *was* hurt, and angered; but he managed to conceal it. This
girl had the ability to get through his defenses on the most
childish level, where a man like William could not.

"Never mind that," he said. "My question was about you and
William. I told you not to try intriguing against him the last
time I saw you. Have you followed that advice?"

"Well, I certainly don't have to answer that question," she
blazed directly at him. "And I won't."

"Then," he said, finding suddenly an insight into her that was
possibly a natural compensation for her unusual perceptiveness
where he was concerned. "You have. I'm glad to know that."
He turned to go. "I'll leave you now."

"Wait a minute," she cried. He turned back to her. "I didn't
do it because of you!"

"Didn't you?"

Surprisingly, her eyes wavered and fell.

"All right!" she said. "It just happened your ideas coincided
with mine."

"Or, that what I said was common sense," he retorted, "and
being the person you are, you couldn't help seeing it."

She looked fiercely up at him again.

"So he just goes on . . . and I'm chained to him for another
ten years with options—"

"Leave that part to me," said Donal.

Her mouth opened.

"You!" she said; and her astonishment was so great that the
word came out in a tone of honest weakness.

"I'll take care of it."

"*You!*" she cried. And the word was entirely different this time. "*You* put yourself in opposition to a man like William—" she broke off suddenly, turning away. "Oh!" she said angrily, "I don't know why I keep listening to you as if you were actually telling the truth—when I know what kind of person you are."

"You don't know anything at all about what kind of a person I am!" he snapped, nettled again. "I've done a few things since you first saw me."

"Oh, yes," she said, "you've had a man shot, and pretended to bomb a planet."

"Good-by," he said, wearily, turning away. He went out through the little balcony entrance, abruptly leaving her standing there; and unaware that he had left her, not filled with the glow of righteous indignation and triumph she had expected, but oddly disconcerted and dismayed.

He searched throughout the rest of the mansion and finally located the marshal back in his office, and alone.

"May I come in, sir?" he said from the doorway.

"Of course, of course—" Galt looked up from his desk. "Lock the door behind you. I've had nothing but people drifting in, thinking this was an extra lounge. Why'd they think I had it set up without any comfortable floats or cushions in the first place?"

Donal locked the door behind him and came across the wide floor to the desk.

"What is it, boy?" asked the marshal. He raised his heavy head and regarded Donal intently. "Something up?"

"A number of things," agreed Donal. He took the bare float beside the desk that Galt motioned him into. "May I ask if William came here tonight with the intention of transacting any business with you?"

"You may ask," answered Galt, putting both his massive forearms on the desk, "but I don't know why I should answer you."

"Of course you needn't," said Donal. "Assuming he did, how-ever, I'd like to say that in my opinion it would be exceedingly unwise to do any business with Ceta at this time—and partic-ularly William of Ceta."

"And what causes this to be your opinion?" asked Galt, with a noticeable trace of irony. Donal hesitated.

"Sir," he said, after a second. "I'd like to remind you that I was right on Harmony, and right about Newton; and that I may be right here, as well."

It was a large pill of impertinence for the marshal to swallow; since, in effect, it pointed out that if Donal had twice been right, Galt had been twice wrong—first about his assessment of Hugh Killien as a responsible officer, and second about his assessment of the reasons behind the Newtonian move on Oriente. But if he was Dorsai enough to be touchy about his pride, he was also Dorsai enough to be honest when he had to.

"All right," he said. "William did come around with a prop-osition. He wants to take over a large number of our excess land forces, not for any specific campaign, but for re-leasing to other employers. They'd remain our troops. I was against it, on the grounds that we'd be competing against ourselves when it came to offering troops to outside markets, but he proved to me the guarantee he's willing to pay would more than make up for any losses we might have. I also didn't see how he intended to make his own profit out of it, but evidently he intends training the men to finer specializations than a single planet can afford to do, and maintain a balanced force. And God knows Ceta's big enough to train all he wants, and that its slightly lower gravity doesn't hurt either—for our troops, that is."

He got his pipe out of a compartment in the desk and began to fill it.

"What's your objection?" he asked.

"Can you be sure the troops won't be leased to someone who might use them against you?" Donal asked.

Galt's thick fingers ceased suddenly to fill his pipe. "We can insist on guarantees."

"But how much good are guarantees in a case like that?" asked Donal. "The man who gives you the guarantee—William—isn't the man who might move the troops against you. If Freilander leased troops were suddenly found attacking Freilander soil, you might gain the guarantee, but lose the soil."

Galt frowned.

"I still don't see," he said, "how that could work out to William's advantage."

"It might," said Donal, "in a situation where what he stood to gain by Freilander fighting Freilander was worth more than the guarantee."

"How could that be?"

Donal hesitated on the verge of those private suspicions of his own. Then he decided that they were not yet solid enough to voice to the marshal; and might, indeed, even weaken his argument.

"I don't know," he replied. "However, I think it'd be wise not to take the chance."

"Hah!" Galt snorted and his fingers went back to work, filling the pipe. "*You* don't have to turn the man down—and justify your refusal to Staff and Government."

"I don't propose that you turn him down outright," said Donal. "I suggest you only hesitate. Say that in your considered opinion the interstellar situation right now doesn't justify your leaving Freiland shorthanded of combat troops. Your military reputation is good enough to establish such an answer beyond question."

"Yes"—Galt put the pipe in his mouth and lit it thoughtfully—"I think I may just act on that recommendation of yours. You know, Donal, I think from now on you better remain as

my aide, where I can have the benefit of your opinions handy
when I need them."

Donal winced.

"I'm sorry, sir," he said. "But I was thinking of moving on—if
you'll release me."

Galt's eyebrows abruptly drew together in a thicket of dense
hair. He took the pipe from his mouth.

"Oh," he said, somewhat flatly. "Ambitious, eh?"

"Partly," said Donal. "But partly—I'll find it easier to oppose
William as a free agent." Galt bent a long, steady look upon
him.

"By heaven," he said, "what is this personal vendetta of yours
against William?"

"I'm afraid of him," answered Donal.

"Leave him alone and he'll certainly leave you alone. He's
got bigger fish to fry—" Galt broke off, jammed his pipe into
his mouth and bit hard on the stem.

"I'm afraid," said Donal, sadly, "there are some men between
the stars that are just not meant to leave each other alone." He
straightened in his chair. "You'll release my contract, then?"

"I won't hold any man against his will," growled the marshal.
"Except in an emergency. Where were you thinking of going?"

"I've had a number of offers," said Donal. "But I was thinking
of accepting one from the Joint Church Council of Harmony
and Association. Their Chief Elder's offered me the position of
War Chief for both the Friendlies."

"Eldest Bright? He's driven every commander with a spark of
independence away from him."

"I know," said Donal. "And just for that reason I expect to
shine the more brightly. It should help build my reputation."

"By—" Galt swore softly. "Always thinking, aren't you?"

"I suppose you're right," said Donal, a trifle unhappily. "It comes
of being born with a certain type of mind."

War Chief

The heels of his black boots clicking against the gray floor of the wide office of the Defense Headquarters on Harmony, the aide approached Donal's desk, which had been his home for three years now.

"Special, urgent and private, sir." He placed a signal tape in the blue shell of ordinary communications on the desk pad.

"Thank you," said Donal, and waved him off. He broke the seal on the tape, placed it in his desk unit, and—waiting until the aide had left the room—pressed the button that would start it.

His father's voice came from the speaker, deep-toned.

"Donal, my son—

"We were glad to get your last tape; and to hear of your successes. No one in this family has done so well in such a short time, in the last five generations. We are all happy for you here, and pray for you and wait to hear from you again.

"But I am speaking to you now on an unhappy occasion. Your uncle, Kensie, was assassinated shortly over a month ago in the back streets of the city of Blauvain, on Ste. Marie, by a local terrorist group in opposition to the government there. Ian, who was, of course, an officer in the same unit, later somehow managed to discover the headquarters of the group in some alley or other and killed the three men he found there with his hands. However, this does not bring Kensie back. He was a favorite of us all; and we are all hard hit, here at home, by his death.

"It is Ian, however, who is presently the cause of our chief concern. He brought Kensie's body home, refusing burial on Ste.

Marie, and has been here now several weeks. You know he was always the dark-natured of the twins, just as it seemed that Kensie had twice the brightness and joy in life that is the usual portion of the normal man. Your mother says it is now as if Ian had lost his good angel, and is abandoned to the forces of darkness which have always had such a grip on him.

"She does not say it in just that way, of course. It is the woman and the Maran in her, speaking—but I have not lived with her twenty-seven years without realizing that she can see further into the soul of a man or woman than I can. You have in some measure inherited this same gift, Donal; so maybe you will understand better what she means. At any rate, it is at her urging that I am sending you this signal; although I would have been speaking to you about Kensie's death, in any case.

"As you know, it has always been my belief that members of the same immediate family should not serve too closely together in field or garrison—in order that family feelings should not be tempted to influence military responsibilities. But it is your mother's belief that Ian should not now be allowed to sit in his dark silence about the place, as he has been doing; but that he should be once more in action. And she asks me to ask you if you could find a place for him on your staff, where you can keep your eye on him. I know it will be difficult for both of you to have him filling a duty post in a position subordinate to you; but your mother feels it would be preferable to the present situation.

"Ian has expressed no wish to return to an active life; but if I speak to him as head of the family, he will go. Your brother Mor is doing well on Venus and has recently been promoted to commandant. Your mother urges you to write him, whether he has written you or not, since he may be hesitant to write you without reason, you having done so well in so short a time, although he is the older.

"All our love. Eachan."

The spool, seen through the little transparent cover, stopped turning. The echoes of Eachan Khan Graeme's voice died against the gray walls of the office. Donal sat still at his desk, his eyes fixed on nothing, remembering Kensie.

It seemed odd to him, as he sat there, to discover that he could remember so few specific incidents. Thinking back, his early life seemed to be filled with his smiling uncle—and yet Kensie had not been home much. He would have thought that it would be the separate occasions of Kensie's going and coming that would be remembered—but instead it was more as if some general presence, some light about the house, had been extinguished.

Donal sighed. It seemed he was accumulating people at a steady rate. First Lee. Then the scarfaced El Man had asked to accompany him, when he left Freiland. And now Ian. Well, Ian was a good officer, aside from whatever crippling the death of his twin brother had caused him now. It would be more than easy for Donal to find a place for him. In fact, Donal could use him handily.

Donal punched a stud and turned his mouth to the little grille of the desk's signal unit.

"Eachan Khan Graeme, Graeme-house, South District, Foralie Canton, the Dorsai," he said. "Very glad to hear from you, although I imagine you know how I feel about Kensie. Please ask Ian to come right along. I will be honored to have him on my staff; and, to tell the truth, I have a real need for someone like him here. Most of the ranking officers I inherited as War Chief have been browbeaten by these Elders into a state of poor usefulness. I know I won't have to worry about Ian on that score. If he would take over supervision of my training program, he would be worth his weight in diamonds—natural ones. And I could give him an action post either on my personal staff, or as Patrol Chief. Tell Mother I'll write Mor but that the letter may be a bit sketchy right at present. I am up to my ears in work at the moment. These are good officers and men; but they have been so beaten about the ears at every wrong move that they will not blow their nose without a direct order. My love to all at home. Donal."

He pressed the button again, ending the recording and sealing it ready for delivery with the rest of the outgoing signals his office sent daily on their way. A soft chime from his desk reminded him that it was time for him to speak once more with Eldest Bright. He got up and went out.

The ranking elder of the joint government of the Friendly Worlds of Harmony and Association maintained his own suite of offices in Government Center, not more than half a hundred meters from the military nerve center. This was not fortuitous. Eldest Bright was a Militant, and liked to keep his eye on the fighting arm of God's True Churches. He was at work at his desk, but rose as Donal came in.

He advanced to meet Donal, a tall, lean man, dressed entirely in black, with the shoulders of a back-alley scrapper and the eyes of a Torquemada, that light of the Inquisition in ancient Spain.

"God be with you," he said. "Who authorized this requisition order for sheathing for the phase shift grids on the sub-class ships?"

"I did," said Donal.

"You spend credit like water." Bright's hard, middle-aged face leaned toward Donal. "A tithe on the churches, a tithe of a tithe on the church members of our two poor planets is all we have to support the business of government. How much of this do you think we can afford to spend on whims and fancies?"

"War, sir," said Donal, "is hardly a matter of whims and fancies."

"Then why shield the grids?" snapped Bright. "Are they liable to rust in the dampness of space? Will a wind come along between the stars and blow them apart?"

"Sheathe, not shield," replied Donal. "The point is to change their appearance; from the ball-and-hammer to the cylindrical. I'm taking all ships of the first three classes through with me. When they come out before the Exotics, I want them all looking like ships of the first class."

"For what reason?"

"Our attack on Zombri cannot be a complete surprise," explained Donal, patiently. "Mara and Kultis are as aware as anyone else that from a military standpoint it is vulnerable to such action. If you'll permit me—" He walked past Bright to the latter's desk and pressed certain keys there. A schematic of the Procyon system sprang into existence on one of the large gray walls of the office, the star itself in outline to the left. Pointing, Donal read off the planets in their order, moving off to the right. "Mara—Kultis—Ste. Marie—Coby. As close a group of habitable planets as we're likely to discover in the next ten generations. And simply because they are habitable—and close, therefore—we have this escaped moon, Zombri, in its own eccentric orbit lying largely between Coby and Ste. Marie—"

"Are you lecturing me?" interrupted Bright's harsh voice.

"I am," said Donal. "It's been my experience that the things people tend to overlook are those they learned earliest and believe they know best. Zombri is not habitable and too small for terraforming. Yet it exists like the Trojan horse, lacking only its complement of latter-day Acheans to threaten the Procyon peace—"

"We've discussed this before," broke in Bright.

"And we'll continue to discuss it," continued Donal, pleasantly, "whenever you wish to ask for the reason behind any individual order of mine. As I was saying—Zombri is the Trojan horse of the Procyon city. Unfortunately, in this day and age, we can hardly smuggle men onto it. We can, however, make a sudden landing in force and attempt to set up defenses before the Exotics are alerted. Our effort, then, must be to make our landing as quickly and effectively as possible. To do that best is to land virtually unopposed in spite of the fact that the Exotics will undoubtedly have a regular force keeping its eye on Zombri. The best way to achieve that is to appear in overwhelming strength, so that the local commanders will realize it is foolish to attempt to interfere with our landing. And the best way to put on a show of strength is to appear to have three times the ships of the first class that we do have. Therefore the sheathing."

Donal stopped talking, walked back across to the desk, and pressed the keys. The schematic disappeared.

"Very well," said Bright. The tone of his voice showed no trace of defeat or loss of arrogance. "I will authorize the order."

"Perhaps," said Donal, "you'll also authorize another order to remove the Conscience Guardians from my ships and units."

"Heretics—" began Bright.

"Are no concern of mine," said Donal. "My job is to get these people ready to mount an assault. But I've got over sixty per cent native troops of yours under me; and their morale is hardly being improved, on an average of three trials for heresy a week."

"This is a church matter," said Bright. "Is there anything else you wished to ask me, War Chief?"

"Yes," said Donal. "I ordered mining equipment. It hasn't arrived."

"The order was excessive," said Bright. "There should be no need to dig in anything but the command posts, on Zombri."

Donal looked at the black-clad man for a long moment. His white face and white hands—the only uncovered part of him— seemed rather the false part than the real, as if they were mask and gloves attached to some black and alien creature.

"Let's understand each other," said Donal. "Aside from the

fact that I don't order men into exposed positions where they'll be killed—whether they're mercenaries or your own suicide-happy troops, just what do you want to accomplish by this move against the Exotics?"

"They threaten us," answered Bright. "They are worse than the heretics. They are Satan's own legion—the deniers of God." The man's eyes glittered like ice in the sunlight. "We must establish a watchtower over them that they may not threaten us without warning; and we may live in safety."

"All right," said Donal. "That's settled then. I'll get you your watchtower. And you get me the men and equipment I order without question and without delay. Already, these hesitations of your government mean I'll be going into Zombri ten to fifteen per cent understrength."

"What?" Bright's dark brows drew together. "You've got two months yet until Target Date."

"Target Dates," said Donal, "are for the benefit of enemy intelligence. We'll be jumping off in two weeks."

"Two weeks!" Bright stared at him. "You can't be ready in two weeks."

"I earnestly hope Colmain and his General Staff for Mara and Kultis agrees with you," replied Donal. "They've the best land and space forces between the stars."

"How?" Bright's face paled with anger. "You dare to say that our own organization's inferior?"

"Facing facts is definitely preferable to facing defeat," said Donal, a little tiredly. "Yes, Eldest, our forces are definitely in-ferior. Which is why I'm depending on surprise rather than prep-aration."

"The Soldiers of the Church are the bravest in the universe!" cried Bright. "They wear the armor of righteousness and never retreat."

"Which explains their high casualty rate, regular necessity for green replacements, and general lower level of training,"

Donal reminded him. "A willingness to die in battle is not necessarily the best trait in a soldier. Your mercenary units, where
you've kept them free of native replacements, are decidedly
more combat-ready at the moment. Do I have your backing from
now on, for anything I feel I need?"

Bright hesitated. The tension of fanaticism relaxed out of his
face, to be replaced by one of thoughtfulness. When he spoke
again his voice was cold and businesslike.

"On everything but the Conscience Guardians," he answered. "They have authority, after all, only over our own Members of the Churches." He turned and walked around once more
behind his desk. "Also," he said, a trifle grimly, "you may have
noticed that there are sometimes small differences of opinion
concerning dogma between members of differing Churches. The
presence of the Conscience Guardians among them makes them
less prone to dispute, one with the other—and this you'll grant,
I'm sure, is an aid to military discipline."

"It's effective," said Donal, shortly. He turned himself to go.
"Oh, by the way, Eldest," he said. "That true Target Date of two
weeks from today. It's essential it remain secret; so I've made
sure it's known only to two men and will remain their knowledge exclusively until an hour or so before jump-off."

Bright's head came up.

"Who's the other?" he demanded sharply.

"You, sir," said Donal. "I just made my decision about the
true date a minute ago."

They locked eyes for a long minute.

"May God be with you," said Bright, in cold, even tones.

Donal went out.

War Chief II

Genève bar-Colmain was, as Donal had said, commander of the best land-and-space forces between the stars. This because the Exotics of Mara and Kultis, though they would do no violence in their own proper persons, were wise enough to hire the best available in the way of military strength. Colmain, himself, was one of the top military minds of his time, along with Galt on Freiland, Kamal on the Dorsai, Isaac on Venus, and that occasional worker of military miracles—Dom Yen, Supreme Commander on the single world of Ceta where William had his home office. Colmain had his troubles (including a young wife who no longer cared for him) and his faults (he was a gambler—in a military as well as a monetary sense) but there was nothing wrong with either the intelligence that had its home in his skull, or the Intelligence that made its headquarters in his Command Base, on Mara.

Consequently, he was aware that the Friendly Worlds were preparing for a landing on Zombri within three weeks of the time when the decision to do so had become an accomplished fact. His spies adequately informed him of the Target Date that had been established for that landing; and he himself set about certain plans of his own for welcoming the invaders when they came.

The primary of these was the excavation of strong points on Zombri, itself. The assault troops would find they had jumped into a hornet's nest. The ships of the Exotic fleet would meanwhile be on alert not too far off. As soon as action had joined on the surface of Zombri, they would move in and drive the space forces of the invasion inward. The attackers would be caught between two fires; their assault troops lacking the chance to dig in and their ships lacking the support from below that entrenched ground forces could supply with moon-based heavy weapons.

The work on the strong points was well under way one day as, at the Command Base, back on Mara, Colmain was laying out a final development of strategy with his General Staff. An interruption occurred in the shape of an aide who came hurrying into the conference room without even the formality of asking permission first.

"What's this?" growled Colmain, looking up from the submitted plans before him with a scowl on his swarthy face, which at sixty was still handsome enough to provide him compensation in the way of other female companionship for his wife's lack of interest.

"Sir," said the aide, "Zombri's attacked—"

"*What?*" Colmain was suddenly on his feet; and the rest of the heads of the General Staff with him.

"Over two hundred ships, sir. We just got the signal." The aide's voice cracked a little—he was still in his early twenties. "Our men on Zombri are fighting with what they have—"

"Fighting?" Colmain took a sudden step toward the aide almost as if he would hold the man personally responsible. "They've started to land assault troops?"

"They've landed, sir—"

"How many?"

"We don't know sir—"

"Knucklehead! How many ships went in to drop men?"

"None, sir," gasped the aide. "They didn't drop any men. They all landed."

"Landed?"

*   *   *

For the fraction of a second, there was no sound at all in the long conference room.

"Do you mean to tell me—" shouted Colmain. "They landed two hundred ships of the first class on Zombri?"

"Yes, sir," the aide's voice had thinned almost to a squeak: "They're cleaning out our forces there and digging in—"

He had no chance to finish. Colmain swung about on his Battle Ops and Patrol Chiefs.

"Hell and damnation!" he roared. "Intelligence!"

"Sir?" answered a Freilander officer halfway down the length of the table.

"What's the meaning of this?"

"Sir—" stammered the officer. "I don't know how it happened. The latest reports I had from Harmony, three days ago—"

"Damn the latest reports. I want every ship and every man we can get into space in five hours! I want every patrol ship of any class to rendezvous with everything we can muster here, off Zombri in ten hours. Move!"

The General Staff of the Exotics moved.

It was a tribute to the kind of fighting force that Colmain commanded that they were able to respond at all in so short a time as ten hours to such orders. The fact that they accomplished the rendezvous with nearly four hundred craft of all classes, all carrying near their full complement of crews and assault troops, was on the order of a minor miracle.

Colmain and his chief officers, aboard the flagship, regarded the moon, swimming below them in the Control Eye of the ship. There had been reports of fighting down there up until three hours ago. Now there was a silence that spoke eloquently of captured troops. In addition, Observation reported—in addition to the works instigated by the Exotic forces—another hundred and fifty newly mined entrances in the crust of the moon.

"They're in there," said Colmain, "ships and all." Now that
the first shock of discovery had passed, he was once more a cool
and capable commander of forces. He had even found time to
make a mental note to get together with this Dorsai, Graeme.
Supreme command was always sweet bait to a brilliant youngster; but he would find the Council of United Churches a difficult employer in time—and the drawback of a subordinate
position under Colmain himself could be compensated for by
the kind of salary the Exotics were always willing to pay. Concerning the outcome of the actual situation before him, Colmain saw no real need for fear, only for haste. It was fairly
obvious now that Graeme had risked everything on one bold
swoop. He had counted on surprise to get him onto the moon
and so firmly entrenched there that the cost of rooting him out
would be prohibitive—before reinforcements could arrive.

He had erred only—and Colmain gave him full credit for all
but that single error—in underestimating the time it would take
for Colmain to gather his strength to retaliate. And even that
error was forgiveable. There was no other force on the known
worlds that could have been gotten battle-ready in under three
times the time.

"We'll go in," said Colmain. "All of us—and fight it out on
the moon." He looked around his officers. "Any comment?"

"Sir," said his Blue Patrol chief, "maybe we could wait them
out up here?"

"Don't you think it," said Colmain, good-humoredly. "They
would not come and dig in, in our own system, without being
fully supplied for long enough to establish an outpost we can't
take back." He shook his head. "The time to operate is now,
gentlemen, before the infection has a chance to get its hold.
All ships down—even the ones without assault troops. We'll
fight them as if they were ground emplacements."

His staff saluted and went off to execute his orders.

* * *

The Exotic fleet descended on the moon of Zombri like locusts upon an orchard. Colmain, pacing the floor of the control room in the flagship—which had gone in with the rest—grinned as the reports began to flood in of strong points quickly cleaned of the Friendly troops that had occupied them—or dug in ships quickly surrendering and beginning to dig themselves out of the deep shafts their mining equipment had provided for them. The invading troops were collapsing like cardboard soldiers; and Colmain's opinion of their commander—which had risen sharply with the first news of the attack—began to slip decidedly. It was one thing to gamble boldly; it was quite another to gamble foolishly. It appeared from the morale and quality of the Friendly troops that there had, after all, been little chance of the surprise attack succeeding. This Graeme should have devoted a little more time to training his men and less to dreaming up dramatic actions. It was, Colmain thought, very much what you might expect of a young commander in supreme authority for the first time in his life.

He was enjoying the roseate glow of anticipated victory when it was suddenly all rudely shattered. There was a sudden ping from the deep-space communicator and suddenly two officers at the board spoke at once.

"Sir, unidentified call from—"

"Sir, ships above us—"

Colmain, who had been watching the Zombri surface through his Control Eye, jabbed suddenly at his buttons and the seeker circuit on it swung him dizzily upward and toward the stars, coming to rest abruptly, on full magnification, on a ship of the first class which unmistakably bore the mark of Friendly design and manufacture. Incredulously, he widened his scope, and in one swift survey, picked out more than twenty such ships in orbit around Zombri, within the limited range of his ground-restricted Eye, alone.

"Who is it?" he shouted, turning on the officer who had reported a call.

"Sir—" the officer's voice was hesitantly incredulous, "he says he's the Commander of the Friendlies."

"What?" Colmain's fist came down on a stud beside the controls of the Eye. A wall screen lit up and a lean young Dorsai with odd, indefinite-colored eyes looked out at him.

"Graeme!" roared Colmain. "What kind of an imitation fleet are you trying to bluff me with?"

"Look again, commander," answered the young man. "The imitation are digging their way out down there on the surface by you. They're my sub-class ships. Why'd you think they would be taken so easily? These are my ships of the first class—one hundred and eighty-three of them."

Colmain jammed down the button and blanked the screen. He turned on his officers at the control panel.

"Report!"

But the officers had already been busy. Confirmations were flooding in. The first of the attacking ships had been dug out and proved to be sub-class ships with sheathing around their phase-shift grids, little weapons, and less armor. Colmain swung back to the screen again, activated it, and found Donal in the same position, waiting for him.

"We'll be up to see you in ten minutes," he promised, between his teeth.

"You've got more sense than that, commander," replied Donal, from the screen. "Your ships aren't even dug in. They're sitting ducks as they are; and in no kind of formation to cover each other as they try to jump off. We can annihilate you if you try to climb up here, and lying as you are we can pound you to pieces on the ground. You're not equipped from the standpoint of supplies to dig in there; and I'm well enough informed about your total strength to know you've got no force left at large that's strong enough to do us any damage." He paused. "I suggest you come up here yourself in a single ship and discuss terms of surrender."

Colmain stood, glaring at the screen. But there was, in fact, no alternative to surrender. He would not have been a commander of the caliber he was, if he had not recognized the fact. He nodded, finally, grudgingly.

"Coming up," he said; and blanked the screen. Shoulders a little humped, he went off to take the little courier boat that was attached to the flagship for his own personal use.

"By heaven," were the words with which he greeted Donal, when he at last came face to face with him aboard the Friendly flagship, "you've ruined me. I'll be lucky to get the command of five C-class and a tender, on Dunnin's World, after this."

It was not far from the truth.

Donal returned to Harmony two days later, and was cheered in triumph even by the sourest of that world's fanatics, as he rode through the streets to Government Center. A different sort of reception awaited him there, however, when he arrived and went alone to report to Eldest Bright.

The head of the United Council of Churches for the worlds of Harmony and Association looked up grimly as Donal came in, still wearing the coverall of his battle dress under a barrel-cut jacket he had thrown on hastily for the ride from the spaceport. The platform on which he had ridden had been open for the admiration of the crowds along the way; and Harmony was in the chill fall of its short year.

"Evening, gentlemen," said Donal, taking in not only Bright in the greeting, but two other members of the Council who sat alongside him at his desk. These two did not answer. Donal had hardly expected them to. Bright was in charge here. Bright nod-

ded at three armed soldiers of the native elite guard that had
been holding post by the door and they went out, closing the
door behind them.

"So you've come back," said Bright.

Donal smiled.

"Did you expect me to go some place else?" he asked.

"This is no time for humor!" Bright's large hand came down
with a crack on the top of the desk. "What kind of an explanation have you got for us, for this outrageous conduct of yours?"

"If you don't mind, Eldest!" Donal's voice rang against the
gray walls of the room, with a slight cutting edge the three had
never heard before and hardly expected on this occasion. "I
believe in politeness and good manners for myself; and see no
reason why others shouldn't reciprocate in kind. What're you
talking about?"

Bright rose. Standing wide-legged and shoulder-bent above
the smooth, almost reflective surface of the gray desk, the re-
semblance to the back-alley scrapper for the moment out-
weighed the Torquemada in his appearance.

"You come back to us," he said, slowly and harshly, "and
pretend not to know how you betrayed us?"

"Betrayed you?" Donal considered him with a quietness that
was almost ominous. "How—betrayed you?"

"We sent you out to do a job."

"I believe I did it," said Donal dryly. "You wanted a watchtower over the Godless. You wanted a permanent installation
on Zombri to spot any buildup on the part of the Exotics to
attack you. You remember I asked you to set out in plain terms
what you were after, a few days back. You were quite explicit
about that being just what you wanted. Well—you've got it!"

"You limb of Satan!" blared Bright, suddenly losing control.
"Do you pretend to believe that you thought that was all we
wanted? Did you think the anointed of the Lord would hesitate
on the threshold of the Godless?" He turned and stalked sud-

denly around the desk to stand face to face with Donal. "You had them in your power and you asked them only for an unarmed observation station on a barren moon. You had them by the throat and you slew none of them when you should have wiped them from the face of the stars, to the last ship—to the last man!"

He paused and Donal could hear his teeth gritting in the sudden silence.

"How much did they pay you?" Bright snarled.

Donal stood in an unnatural stillness.

"I will pretend," he said, after a moment, "that I didn't hear that last remark. As for your questions as to why I asked only for the observation station, that was all you had said you wanted. As to why I did not wipe them out—wanton killing is not my trade. Nor the needless expenditure of my own men in the pursuit of wanton killing." He looked coldly into Bright's eyes. "I suggest you could have been a little more honest with me, Eldest, about what you wanted. It was the destruction of the Exotic power, wasn't it?"

"It was," gritted Bright.

"I thought as much," said Donal. "But it never occurred to you that I would be a good enough commander to find myself in the position to accomplish that. I think," said Donal, letting his eyes stray to the other two black-clad elders as well, "you are hoist by your own petard, gentlemen." He relaxed; and smiling slightly, turned back to Bright. "There are reasons," he said, "why it would be very unwise tactically for the Friendly Worlds to break the back of Mara and Kultis. If you'll allow me to give you a small lesson in power dis—"

"You'll come up with better answers than you have!" burst out Bright. "Unless you want to be tried for betrayal of your employer!"

"Oh, come now!" Donal laughed out loud.

* * *

Bright whirled away from him and strode across the gray room. Flinging wide the door by which Donal had entered, and they had exited, he revealed the three elite guard soldiers. He whirled about, arm outstretched to its full length, finger quivering.

"Arrest that traitor!" he cried.

The guards took a step toward Donal—and in that same moment, before they had any of them moved their own length's-worth of distance toward him—three faint blue beams traced their way through the intervening space past Bright, leaving a sharp scent of ionized air behind them. And the three dropped.

Like a man stunned by a blow from behind, Bright stared down at the bodies of his three guards. He swayed about to see Donal reholstering his handgun.

"Did you think I was fool enough to come here unarmed?" asked Donal, a little sadly. "And did you think I'd submit to arrest?" He shook his head. "You should have wit enough to see now I've just saved you from yourselves."

He looked at their disbelieving faces.

"Oh, yes," he said. He gestured to the open wall at the far end of the office. Sounds of celebration from the city outside drifted lightly in on the evening breeze. "The better forty per cent of your fighting forces are out there. Mercenaries. Mercenaries who appreciate a commander who can give them a victory at the cost of next to no casualties at all. What do you suppose their reaction would be if you tried me for betrayal, and found me guilty, and had me executed?" He paused to let the thought sink in. "Consider it, gentlemen."

He pinched his jacket shut and looked grimly at the three dead elite guards; and then turned back to the elders, again.

"I consider this sufficient grounds for breach of contract," he said. "You can find yourself another War Chief."

He turned and walked toward the door. As he passed through it, Bright shouted after him.

"Go to them, then! Go to the Godless on Mara and Kultis!"

Donal paused and turned. He inclined his head gravely.

"Thank you, gentlemen," he said. "Remember—The suggestion was yours."

Part-Maran

There remained the interview with Sayona the Bond. Going up
some wide and shallow steps into the establishment—it could
not be called merely a building, or group of buildings—that
housed the most important individual of the two Exotic planets,
Donal found cause for amusement in the manner of his approach.

Farther out, among some shrubbery at the entrance to the—
estate?—he had encountered a tall, gray-eyed woman; and explained his presence.

"Go right ahead," the woman had said, waving him onward.
"You'll find him." The odd part of it was, Donal had no doubt
that he would. And the unreasonable certainty of it tickled his
own strange sense of humor.

He wandered on by a sunlit corridor that broadened imper-
ceptibly into a roofless garden, past paintings, and pools of water
with colorful fish in them—through a house that was not a
house, in rooms and out until he came to a small sunken patio,
half-roofed over; and at the far end of it, under the shade of the
half-roof, was a tall bald man of indeterminate age, wrapped in
a blue robe and seated on a little patch of captive turf, surrounded by a low, stone wall.

Donal went down three stone steps, across the patio, and up
the three stone steps at the far side until he stood over the tall,
seated man.

"Sir," said Donal. "I'm Donal Graeme."

The tall man waved him down on the turf.

"Unless you'd rather sit on the wall, of course," he smiled.

"Sitting cross-legged doesn't agree with everyone."

"Not at all, sir," answered Donal, and sat down cross-legged himself.

"Good," said the tall man; and apparently lost himself in thought, gazing out over the patio.

Donal also relaxed, waiting. A certain peace had crept into him in the way through this place. It seemed to beckon to meditation; and—Donal had no doubt—was probably cleverly constructed and designed for just that purpose. He sat, comfortably now, and let his mind wander where it chose; and it happened— not so oddly at all—to choose to wander in the direction of the man beside him.

Sayona the Bond, Donal had learned as a boy in school, was one of the human institutions peculiar to the Exotics. The Exotics were two planetsful of strange people, judged by the standards of the rest of the human race—some of whom went so far as to wonder if the inhabitants of Mara and Kultis had developed wholly and uniquely out of the human race, after all. This, however, was speculation half in humor and half in superstition. In truth, they were human enough.

They had, however, developed their own forms of wizardry. Particularly in the fields of psychology and its related branches, and in that other field which you could call gene selection or planned breeding depending on whether you approved or disapproved of it. Along with this went a certain sort of general mysticism. The Exotics worshiped no god, overtly, and laid claim to no religion. On the other hand they were nearly all— they claimed, by individual choice—vegetarians and adherents of nonviolence on the ancient Hindu order. In addition, however, they held to another cardinal nonprinciple; and this one was the principle of noninterference. The ultimate violence, they believed, was for one person to urge a point of view on another—in any fashion of urging. Yet, all these traits had not destroyed their ability to take care of themselves. If it was their creed to do violence to no man, it was another readily admitted part of their same creed that no one should therefore be wantonly permitted to do violence to them. In war and business, through mercenaries and middlemen, they more than held their own.

But, thought Donal—to get back to Sayona the Bond, and his place in Exotic culture. He was one of the compensations peculiar to the Exotic peoples, for their different way of life. He was—in some way that only an Exotic fully understood—a certain part of their emotional life made manifest in the person of a living human being. Like Anea, who—devastatingly normal and female as she was—was, to an Exotic, *literally* one of the select of Kultis. She was their best selected qualities made actual—like a living work of art that they worshiped. It did not matter that she was not always joyful, that indeed, her life must bear as much or more of the normal human sorrow of situation and existence. That was where most people's appreciation of the matter went astray. No, what was important was the capabilities they had bred and trained into her. It was the capacity in her for living, not the life she actually led, that pleasured them. The actual achievement was up to her, and was her own personal reward. They appreciated the fact that—if she chose, and was lucky—she could appreciate life.

Similarly, Sayona the Bond. Again, only in a sense that an Exotic would understand, Sayona was the actual bond between their two worlds made manifest in flesh and blood. In him was the capability for common understanding, for reconciliation, for an expression of the community of feeling between people . . .

Donal awoke suddenly to the fact that Sayona was speaking to him. The older man had been speaking some time, in a calm, even voice, and Donal had been letting the words run through his mind like water of a stream through his fingers. Now, something that had been said had jogged him to a full awareness.

". . . Why, no," answered Donal, "I thought this was standard procedure for any commander before you hired him."

Sayona chuckled.

"Put every new commander through all that testing and trouble?" he said. "No, no. The word would get around and we'd never be able to hire the men we wanted."

"I rather enjoy taking tests," said Donal, idly.

"I know you do," Sayona nodded. "A test is a form of competition, after all; and you're a competitor by nature. No, normally when we want a military man we look for military proofs like everyone else—and that's as far as we go."

"Why the difference with me, then?" asked Donal, turning to look at him. Sayona returned his gaze with pale brown eyes holding just a hint of humor in the wrinkles at their corners.

"Well, we weren't just interested in you as a commander," answered Sayona. "There's the matter of your ancestors, you know. You're actually part-Maran; and those genes, even when outmatched, are of interest to us. Then there's the matter of you, yourself. You have astonishing potentials."

"Potentials for what?"

"A number of rather large things," said Sayona soberly. "We only glimpse them, of course, in the results of our tests."

"Can I ask what those large things are?" asked Donal, curiously.

"I'm sorry, no. I can't answer that for you," said Sayona. "The answers would be meaningless to you personally, anyway—for the reason you can't explain anything in terms of itself. That's why I thought I'd have this talk with you. I'm interested in your philosophy."

"Philosophy!" Donal laughed. "I'm a Dorsai."

"Everyone, even Dorsai, every living thing has its own philosophy—a blade of grass, a bird, a baby. An individual philosophy is a necessary thing, the touchstone by which we judge our own existence. Also—you're only part Dorsai. What does the other part say?"

Donal frowned.

"I'm not sure the other part says anything," he said. "I'm a soldier. A mercenary. I have a job to do; and I intend to do it—always—in the best way I know how."

"But beyond this—" urged Sayona.

"Why, beyond this—" Donal fell silent, still frowning. "I suppose I would want to see things go well."

"You said want to see things go well—rather than *like* to see things go well." Sayona was watching him. "Don't you see any significance in that?"

"Want? Oh—" Donal laughed. "I suppose that's an unconscious slip on my part. I suppose I was thinking of *making* them go well."

"Yes," said Sayona, but in a tone that Donal could not be sure was meant as agreement or not. "You're a doer, aren't you?"

"Someone has to be," said Donal. "Take the civilized worlds now—" he broke off suddenly.

"Go on," said Sayona.

"I meant to say—take civilization. Think how short a time it's been since the first balloon went up back on Earth. Four hundred years? Five hundred years? Something like that. And look how we've spread out and split up since then."

"What about it?"

"I don't like it," said Donal. "Aside from the inefficiency, it strikes me as unhealthy. What's the point of technological development if we just split in that many more factions—everyone hunting up his own type of aberrant mind and hiving with it? That's no progress."

"You subscribe to progress?"

Donal looked at him.

"Don't you?"

"I suppose," said Sayona. "A certain type of progress. My kind of progress. What's yours?"

Donal smiled.

"You want to hear that, do you? You're right. I guess I do have a philosophy after all. You want to hear it?"

"Please," said Sayona.

"All right," said Donal. He looked out over the little sunken garden. "It goes like this—each man is a tool in his own hands. Mankind is a tool in *its* own hands. Our greatest satisfaction doesn't come from the rewards of our work, but from the working itself; and our greatest responsibility is to sharpen, and improve the tool that is ourselves so as to make it capable of tackling bigger jobs." He looked at Sayona. "What do you think of it?"

"I'd have to think about it," answered Sayona. "My own point of view is somewhat different, of course. I see Man not so much as an achieving mechanism, but as a perceptive link in the order of things. I would say the individual's role isn't so much to *do* as it is to *be*. To realize to the fullest extent the truth already and inherently in him—if I make myself clear."

"Nirvana as opposed to Valhalla, eh?" said Donal, smiling a little grimly. "Thanks, I prefer Valhalla."

"Are you sure?" asked Sayona. "Are you quite sure you've no use for Nirvana?"

"Quite sure," said Donal.

"You make me sad," said Sayona, somberly. "We had had hopes."

"Hopes?"

"There is," said Sayona, lifting one finger, "this possibility in you—this great possibility. It may be exercised in only one direction—that direction you choose. But you have freedom of choice. There's room for you here."

"With you?"

"The other worlds don't know," said Sayona, "what we've begun to open up here in the last hundred years. We are just beginning to work with the butterfly implicit in the matter-bound worm that is the present human species. There are great opportunities for anyone with the potentialities for this work."

"And I," said Donal, "have these potentialities?"

"Yes," answered Sayona. "Partly as a result of a lucky genetic accident that is beyond our knowledge to understand, now. Of course—you would have to be retrained. That other part of your character that rules you now would have to be readjusted to a harmonious integration with the other part *we* consider more valuable."

Donal shook his head.

"There would be compensations," said Sayona, in a sad, almost whimsical tone, "things would become possible to you—do you know that you, personally, are the sort of man who, for example, could walk on air if only you believed you could?"

Donal laughed.

"I am quite serious," said Sayona. "Try believing it some time."

"I can hardly try believing what I instinctively disbelieve," said Donal. "Besides, that's beside the point. I am a soldier."

"But what a strange soldier," murmured Sayona. "A soldier full of compassion, of whimsical fancies and wild daydreams. A man of loneliness who wants to be like everyone else; but who finds the human race a conglomeration of strange alien creatures whose twisted ways he cannot understand—while still he understands them too well for their own comfort."

He turned his eyes calmly onto Donal's face, which had gone set and hard.

"Your tests *are* quite effective, aren't they?" Donal said.

"They are," said Sayona. "But there's no need to look at me

like that. We can't use them as a weapon, to make you do what we would like to have you do. That would be an action so self-crippling as to destroy all its benefits. We can only make the offer to you." He paused. "I can tell you that on the basis of our knowledge we can assure you with better than fair certainty that you'll be happy if you take our path."

"And if not?" Donal had not relaxed.

Sayona sighed.

"You are a strong man," he said: "Strength leads to responsibility, and responsibility pays little heed to happiness."

"I can't say I like the picture of myself going through life grubbing after happiness." Donal stood up. "Thanks for the offer, anyway. I appreciate the compliment it implies."

"There is no compliment in telling a butterfly he is a butterfly and need not crawl along the ground," said Sayona.

Donal inclined his head politely.

"Good-by," he said. He turned about and walked the few steps to the head of the shallow steps leading down into the sunken garden and across it to the way he had come in.

"Donal—" The voice of Sayona stopped him. He turned back and saw the Bond regarding him with an expression almost impish. "I believe you can walk on air," said Sayona.

Donal stared; but the expression of the other did not alter. Swinging about, Donal stepped out as if onto level ground—and to his unutterable astonishment his foot met solidity on a level, unsupported, eight inches above the next step down. Hardly thinking why he did it, Donal brought his other foot forward into nothingness. He took another step—and another. Unsupported on the thin air, he walked across above the sunken garden to the top of the steps on the far side.

Striding once more onto solidity, he turned about and looked across the short distance. Sayona still regarded him; but his expression now was unreadable. Donal swung about and left the garden.

* * *

Very thoughtful, he returned to his own quarters in the city of Portsmouth, which was the Maran city holding the Command Base of the Exotics. The tropical Maran night had swiftly enfolded the city by the time he reached his room, yet the soft illumination that had come on automatically about and inside all the buildings by some clever trick of design failed to white-out the overhead view of the stars. These shone down through the open wall of Donal's bedroom.

Standing in the center of the bedroom, about to change for the meal which would be his first of the day—he had again forgotten to eat during the earlier hours—Donal paused and frowned. He gazed up at the gently domed roof of the room, which reached its highest point some twelve feet above his head. He frowned again and searched about through his writing desk until he found a self-sealing signal-tape capsule. Then, with this in one hand, he turned toward the ceiling and took one rather awkward step off the ground.

His foot caught and held in air. He lifted himself off the floor. Slowly, step by step he walked up through nothingness to the high point of the ceiling. Opening the capsule, he pressed its self-sealing edges against the ceiling, where they clung. He hung there a second in air, staring at them.

"Ridiculous!" he said suddenly—and, just as suddenly, he was falling. He gathered himself with the instinct of long training in the second of drop and, landing on hands and feet, rolled over and came to his feet like a gymnast against a far wall. He got up, brushing himself off, unhurt—and turned to look up at the ceiling. The capsule still clung there.

He lifted the little appliance that was strapped to his wrist and keyed its phone circuit in.

"Lee," he said.

He dropped his wrist and waited. Less than a minute later,

Lee came into the room. Donal pointed toward the capsule on the ceiling. "What's that?" he asked.

Lee looked.

"Tape capsule," he said. "Want me to get it down?"

"Never mind," answered Donal. "How do you suppose it got up there?"

"Some joker with a float," answered Lee. "Want me to find out who?"

"No—never mind," said Donal. "That'll be all."

Bending his head at the dismissal, Lee went out of the room. Donal took one more look at the capsule, then turned and wandered over to the open wall of his room, and looked out. Below him lay the bright carpet of the city. Overhead hung the stars. For longer than a minute he considered them.

Suddenly he laughed, cheerfully and out loud.

"No, no," he said to the empty room. "I'm a Dorsai!"

He turned his back on the view and went swiftly to work at dressing for dinner. He was surprised to discover how hungry he actually was.

Protector

Battle Commander of Field Forces Ian Ten Graeme, that cold, dark man, strode through the outer offices of the Protector of Procyon with a *private-and-secret* signal in his large fist. In the three outer offices, no one got in his way. But at the entrance to the Protector's private office, a private secretary in the green-and-gold of a staff uniform ventured to murmur that the Protector had left orders to be undisturbed. Ian merely looked at her, placed one palm flat against the lock of the inner office door—and strode through.

Within, he discovered Donal standing by an open wall, caught by a full shaft of Procyon's white-gold sunlight, gazing out over Portsmouth and apparently deep in thought. It was a position in which he was to be discovered often, these later days. He looked up now at the sound of Ian's measured tread approaching.

Six years of military and political successes had laid their inescapable marks upon Donal's face, marks plain to be seen in the sunlight. At a casual glance he appeared hardly older than the young man who had left the Dorsai half a dozen years before. But a closer inspection showed him to be slightly heavier of build now—even a little taller. Only this extra weight, slight increase as it was, had not served to soften the clear lines of his features. Rather these same features had grown more pronounced, more hard of line. His eyes seemed a little deeper set now; and the habit of command—command extended to the point where it became unconscious—had cast an invisible shadow upon his brows, so that it had become a face men obeyed without thinking, as if it was the natural thing to do.

"Well?" he said, as Ian came up.

"They've got New Earth," his uncle answered; and handed over the signal tape. "Private-and-secret to you from Galt."

Donal took the tape automatically, that deeper, more hidden part of him immediately taking over his mind. If the six years had wrought changes upon his person and manner, they had worked to even greater ends below the surface of his being. Six years of command, six years of estimate and decision had beaten broad the path between his upper mind and that dark, oceanic part of him, the depthless waters of which lapped on all known shores and many yet unknown. He had come—you could not say to terms—but to truce with the source of his oddness; hiding it well from others, but accepting it to himself for the sake of the tool it placed in his hands. Now, this information Ian had just brought him was like one more stirring of the shadowy depths, a rippled vibration spreading out to affect all, integrate with all—and make even more clear the vast and shadowy ballet of purpose and counter-purpose that was behind all living action; and—for himself—a call to action.

As Protector of Procyon, now responsible not only for the defense of the Exotics, but of the two smaller inhabited planets in that system—Ste. Marie, and Coby—that action was required of him. But even more; as himself, it was required of him. So that what it now implied was not something he was eager to avoid. Rather, it was due, and welcome. Indeed, it was almost too welcome—fortuitous, even.

"I see—" he murmured. Then, lifting his face to his uncle, "Galt'll need help. Get me some figures on available strength, will you Ian?"

Ian nodded and went out, as coldly and martially as he had entered.

*　*　*

Left alone, Donal did not break open the signal tape immediately. He could not now remember what he had been musing about when Ian entered, but the sight of his uncle had initiated a new train of thought. Ian seemed well, these days—or at least as well as could be expected. It did not matter that he lived a solitary life, had little to do with the other commanders of his own rank, and refused to go home to the Dorsai, even for a trip to see his family. He devoted himself to his duties of training field troops—and did it well. Aside from that, he went his own way.

The Maran psychiatrists had explained to Donal that no more than this could be expected of Ian. Gently, they had explained it. A normal mind, gone sick, they could cure. The unfortunate thing was that—at least in so far as his attachment to his twin had been—Ian was not normal. Nothing in this universe could replace the part of him that had died with Kensie—had, indeed, *been* Kensie—for the peculiar psychological make-up of the twins had made them two halves of a whole.

"Your uncle continued to live," the psychiatrists had explained to Donal, "because of an unconscious desire to punish himself for letting his brother die. He is, in fact, seeking death—but it must be a peculiar sort of death which will include the destruction of all that matters to him. 'If thy right hand offend thee, cut if off.' To his unconscious, the Ian-Kensie gestalt holds the Ian part of it to blame for what happened and is hunting a punishment to fit the crime. That is why he continues to practice the—for him—morbid abnormality of staying alive. The normal thing for such a personality would be to die, or get himself killed.

"And that is why," they had concluded, "he refuses to see or have anything to do with his wife or children. His unconscious recognizes the danger of pulling them down to destruction with him. We would advise against his being urged to visit them against his will."

Donal sighed. Thinking about it now, it seemed to him strange that the people who had come to group around him had none of them come—really—because of the fame he had won or the positions he could offer them. There was Ian, who had come because the family had sent him. Lee, who had found the supply of that which his own faulty personality lacked—and would have followed if Donal had been Protector of nothing, instead of being Protector of Procyon. There was Lludrow, Donal's now assistant Chief of Staff, who had come to him not under his own free will, but under the prodding of his wife. For Lludrow had ended up marrying "the" Elvine Rhy, Galt's niece, who had not let even marriage impose a barrier to her interest in Donal. There was Genève bar-Colmain, who was on Donal's staff because Donal had been kind; and because he had no place else to go that was worthy of his abilities. And, lastly, there was Galt, himself, whose friendship was not a military matter, but the rather wistful affection of a man who had never had a son, and saw its image in Donal—though it was not really fair to count Galt, who was apart, as still Marshal of Freiland.

And—in contradistinction to all the rest—there was Mor, the one Donal would have most liked to have at his side; but whose pride had driven him to place himself as far from his successful younger brother as possible. Mor had finally taken service with Venus, where in the open market that flourished on that technological planet, he had had his contract sold to Ceta; and now found himself in the pay of Donal's enemy, which would put them on opposite sides if conflict finally came.

Donal shook himself abruptly. These fits of depression that took him lately were becoming more frequent—possibly as a result of the long hours of work he found himself putting in. Brusquely, he broke open the signal from Galt.

Donal:
The news about New Earth will have reached you

by this time. The *coup d'état* that put the Kyerly government in control of the planet was engineered with troops furnished by Ceta. I have never ceased to be grateful to you for your advice against leasing out units to William. But the pattern here is a bad one. We will be facing the same sort of internal attack here through the local proponents of an open exchange for the buying and selling of contracts. One by one, the worlds are falling into the hands of manipulators, not the least of which is William himself. Please furnish us with as many field units as you can conveniently spare.

There is to be a General Planetary Discussion, meeting on Venus to discuss recognition of the new government on New Earth. They would be wise not to invite you; so come anyway. I, myself, must be there; and I need you, even if no other reason impels you to come.

Hendrik Galt
Marshal, Freiland.

Donal nodded to himself. But he did not spring immediately into action. Where Galt was reacting against the shock of a sudden discovery, Donal, in the situation on New Earth, recognized only the revelation of something he had been expecting for a long time.

The sixteen inhabited worlds of the eight stellar systems from Sol to Altair survived within a complex of traded skills. The truth of the matter was that present day civilization had progressed too far for each planet to maintain its own training systems and keep up with progress in the many necessary fields. Why support a thousand mediocre school systems when it was possible to have fifty superb ones and trade the graduates for the skilled people you needed in other areas of learning? The overhead of such systems was tremendous, the number of top men in each field necessarily limited; moreover, progress was more effective if all the workers in one area of knowledge were kept closely in touch with each other.

The system seemed highly practical. Donal was one of the few men of his time to see the trouble inherent in it.

The joker to such an arrangement comes built in to the question—how much is a skilled worker an individual in his own right, and how much is he a piece of property belonging to whoever at the moment owns his contract? If he is too much an individual, barter between worlds breaks down to a series of individual negotiations; and society nowadays could not exist except on the basis of community needs. If he is too much a piece of property, then the field is opened for the manipulators—the buyers and sellers of flesh, those who would corner the manpower market and treat humanity like cattle for their own gain.

Among the worlds between the stars, this question still hung in argument. "Tight" societies, like the technological worlds of the so-called Venus group—Venus herself, Newton and Cassida—and the fanatic worlds of Harmony and Association, and Coby, which was ruled by what amounted to a criminal secret society—had always favored the piece of property view more strongly than the individual one. "Loose" societies, like the republican worlds of Old Earth, and Mars, the Exotics—Mara and Kultis—and the violently individualistic society of the Dorsai, held to the individual side of the question. In between were the middling worlds—the ones with strong central governments like Freiland and New Earth, the merchandising world of Ceta, the democratic theocracy of Ste. Marie, and the pioneer, underpopulated fisher-planet of Dunnin's World, ruled by the cooperative society known as the Corbel.

Among the "tight" societies, the contract exchange mart had been in existence for many years. On these worlds, unless your contract was written with a specific forbidding clause, you might find yourself sold on no notice at all to a very different employer—possibly on a completely different world. The advantages of such a mart were obvious to an autocratic government, since the government itself was in a position to control the market through its own vast needs and resources, which no individual could hope to match. On a "loose" world, where the government was hampered by its own built in system of checks from taking advantage of opposing individual employers, the field was open for the sharp practices not only of individuals, but of other governments.

Thus, an agreement between two worlds for the establishment of a reciprocal open market worked all to the advantage of the "tighter" of the two governments—and must inevitably end in the tighter government gaining the lion's share of the talent available on the two worlds.

This, then, was the background for the inevitable conflict that had been shaping up now for fifty years between two essentially different systems of controlling what was essentially the lifeblood of the human race—its skilled minds. In fact, thought Donal, standing by the open wall—the conflict was here, and now. It had already been under way that day he had stepped aboard the ship on which he was to meet Galt, and William, and Anea, the Select of Kultis. Behind the scenes, the build-up for a final battle had been already begun, and his own role in that battle, ready and waiting for him.

He went over to his desk and pressed a stud, speaking into a grille.

"I want all Chiefs of Staff here immediately," he said. "For a top-level conference."

He took his finger from the stud and sat down at the desk. There was a great deal to be done.

Protector II

Arriving at Holmstead the capital city of Venus five days later, Donal went immediately to a conference with Galt in the latter's suite of rooms at Government Hotel.

"There were things to take care of," he said, shaking hands with the older man and sitting down, "or I'd have been here sooner." He examined Galt. "You're looking tired."

The Marshal of Freiland had indeed lost weight. The skin of his face sagged a little on the massive bones, and his eyes were darkened with fatigue.

"Politics—politics—" answered Galt. "Not my line at all. It wears a man down. Drink?"

"No thanks," said Donal.

"Don't care for one myself," Galt said. "I'll just light my pipe . . . you don't mind?"

"I never did before. And," said Donal, "you never asked me before."

"Heh . . . no," Galt gave vent to something halfway between a cough and a chuckle; and, getting out his pipe, began to fill it with fingers that trembled a little. "Damned tired, that's all. In fact I'm ready to retire—but how can a man quit just when all hell's popping? You got my message—how many field units can you let me have?"

"A couple and some odds and ends. Say twenty thousand of first-line troops—" Galt's head came up. "Don't worry," Donal smiled. "They will be moved in by small, clumsy stages to give the impression I'm letting you have five times that number, but the procedure's a little fouled up in getting them actually transferred."

Galt grunted.

"I might've known you'd think of something," he said. "We can use that mind of yours here, at the main Conference. Officially, we're gathered here just to agree on a common attitude to the new government on New Earth—but you know what's really on the fire, don't you?"

"I can guess," said Donal. "The open market."

"Right." Galt got his pipe alight; and puffed on it gratefully. "The split's right down the middle, now that New Earth's in the Venus Group's camp and we—Freiland, that is—are clear over on the nonmarket side by way of reaction. We're in fair enough strength counting heads as we sit around the table; but that's not the problem. They've got William—and that white-haired devil Blaine." He looked sharply over at Donal. "You know Project Blaine, don't you?"

"I've never met him. This is my first trip to Venus," said Donal.

"There's a shark," said Galt with feeling. "I'd like to see him and William lock horns on something. Maybe they'd chew each other up and improve the universe. Well . . . about your status here—"

"Officially I'm sent by Sayona the Bond as an observer."

"Well, that's no problem then. We can easily get you invited to step from observer to delegate status. In fact, I've already passed the word. We were just waiting for you to arrive." Galt blew a large cloud of smoke and squinted at Donal through it. "But how about it, Donal? I trust that insight of yours. What's really in the wind here at the Conference?"

"I'm not sure," answered Donal. "It's my belief somebody made a mistake."

"A mistake?"

"New Earth," explained Donal. "It was a fool's trick to overthrow the government there right now—and by force, at that. Which is why I believe we'll be getting it back."

Galt sat up sharply, taking his pipe from his mouth.

"Getting it back? You mean—the old government returned to power?" He stared at Donal. "Who'd give it back to us?"

"William for one, I'd imagine," said Donal. "This isn't *his* way of doing things—piecemeal. But you can bet as long as he's about returning it, he'll exact a price for it."

Galt shook his head.

"I don't follow you," he said.

"William finds himself working with the Venus group right now," Donal pointed out. "But he's hardly out to do them a kindness. His own aims are what concerns him—and it's those he'll be after in the long run. In fact, if you look, I'll bet you see two kinds of negotiations going on at this Conference. The short range, and the long range. The short range is likely to be this matter of an open market. The long range will be William's game."

Galt sucked on his pipe again.

"I don't know," he said, heavily. "I don't hold any more of a brief for William than you do—but you seem to lay everything at his doorstep. Are you sure you aren't a little overboard where the subject of him is concerned?"

"How can anyone be sure?" confessed Donal, wryly. "I think what I think about William, because—" he hesitated, "if I were in his shoes, I'd be doing these things I suspect him of." He paused. "William's weight on our side could swing the conference into putting enough pressure on New Earth to get the old government back in power, couldn't it?"

"Why—of course."

"Well, then." Donal shrugged. "What could be better than William setting forth a compromise solution that at one and the same time puts him in the opposite camp and conceals as well as requires a development in the situation he desires?"

"Well—I can follow that," said Galt, slowly. "But if that's the case, what's he after? What is it he'll want?"

Donal shook his head.

"I'm not sure," he said carefully. "I don't know."

On that rather inconclusive note, they ended their own private talk and Galt took Donal off to meet with some of the other delegates.

The meeting developed, as these things do, into a cocktail gathering in the lounges of the suite belonging to Project Blaine of Venus. Blaine himself, Donal was interested to discover, was a heavy, calm-looking white-haired man who showed no surface evidences of the character Galt had implied to him.

"Well, what do you think of him?" Galt murmured, as they left Blaine and his wife in the process of circulating around the other guests.

"Brilliant," said Donal. "But I hardly think someone to be afraid of." He met Galt's raised eyebrows with a smile. "He seems too immersed in his own point of view. I'd consider him predictable."

"As opposed to William?" asked Galt, in a low voice.

"As opposed to William," agreed Donal. "Who is not—or, not so much."

They had all this time been approaching William, who was seated facing them at one end of the lounge and talking to a tall slim woman whose back was to them. As Galt and Donal came up, William's gaze went past her.

"Well, Marshal!" he said, smiling. "Protector!" The woman turned around; and Donal found himself face to face with Anea.

If six years had made a difference in the outward form of Donal, they had made much more in that of Anea. She was in her late twenties now, and past the last stages of that delayed adolescence of hers. She had begun now to reveal that rare beauty that would deepen with age and experience and never completely leave her, even in extreme old age. She was more developed now, than the last time Donal had seen her, more fully woman-formed and more poised. Her green eyes met

Donal's indeterminate ones across mere centimeters of distance.

"Honored to see you again," said Donal, inclining his head.

"The honor is mine." Her voice, like the rest of her, had matured. Donal looked past her to William. "Prince!" he said.

William stood up and shook hands, both with Donal and with Galt.

"Honored to have you with us, Protector," he said cheerfully to Donal. "I understand the marshal's proposing you for delegate. You can count on me."

"That's good of you," answered Donal.

"It's good for me," said William. "I like open minds around the Conference table and young minds—no offense, Hendrik— are generally open minds."

"I don't pretend to be anything but a soldier," growled Galt.

"And it's precisely that that makes you dangerous in negotiations," replied William. "Politicians and businessmen always feel more at home with someone who they know doesn't mean what he says. Honest men always have been a curse laid upon the sharpshooter."

"A pity," put in Anea, "that there aren't enough honest men, then, to curse them all." She was looking at Donal.

William laughed.

"The Select of Kultis could hardly be anything else but savage upon us underhanded characters, could you, Anea?" he said.

"You can ship me back to the Exotics, any time I wear too heavily on you," she retorted.

"No, no." William wagged his head, humorously. "Being the sort of man I am, I survive only by surrounding myself with good people like yourself. I'm enmeshed in the world of hard reality— it's my life and I wouldn't have it any other way—but for vacation, for a spiritual rest, I like to glance occasionally over the wall of a cloister to where the greatest tragedy is a blighted rose."

"One should not underestimate roses," said Donal. "Men have died over a difference in their color."

"Come now," said William turning on him. "The Wars of the Roses—ancient England? I can't believe such a statement from you, Donal. That conflict, like everything else, was over practical and property disputes. Wars never get fought for abstract reasons."

"On the contrary," Donal said. "Wars invariably get fought for abstract reasons. Wars may be instigated by the middle aged and the elderly; but they're fought by youth. And youth needs more than a practical motive for tempting the tragedy of all tragedies—the end of the universe—which is dying, when you're young."

"What a refreshing attitude from a professional soldier!" laughed William. "Which reminds me—I may have some business to discuss with you. I understand you emphasize the importance of field troops over everything else in a world's armed forces—and I hear you've been achieving some remarkable things in the training of them. That's information right down my alley, of course, since Ceta's gone in for this leasing of troops. What's your secret, Protector? Do you permit observers?"

"No secret," said Donal. "And you're welcome to send observers to our training program any time, Prince. The reason behind our successful training methods is the man in charge— my uncle, Field Commander Ian Graeme."

"Ah—your uncle," said William. "I hardly imagine I could buy him away from you if he's a relative."

"I'm afraid not," answered Donal.

"Well, well—we'll have to talk, anyway. By heaven—my glass seems to have got itself empty. Anyone else care for another?"

"No thank you," said Anea.

"Nor I," said Donal.

"Well, I will," Galt said.

"Well, in that case, come along marshal," William turned to Galt. "You and I'll make our own way to the bar." They went

off together across the lounge. Donal and Anea were left facing
each other.

"So," said Donal, "you haven't changed your mind about me."

"No."

"So much for the fair-mindedness of a Select of Kultis," he
said ironically.

"I'm not superhuman, you know!" she flashed, with a touch
of her younger spirit. "No," she said, more calmly, "there's probably millions as bad as you—or worse—but you've got ability.
And you're a self-seeker. It's that I can't forgive you."

"William's corrupted your point of view," he said.

"At least he makes no bones about being the kind of man
he is!"

"Why should there be some sort of virtue always attributed
to a frank admission of vice?" wondered Donal. "Besides, you're
mistaken. William"—he lowered his voice—"sets himself up as
a common sort of devil to blind you to the fact that he is what
he actually is. Those who have anything to do with him recognize the fact that he's evil; and think that in recognizing this,
they've plumbed the depths of the man."

"Oh?" Her voice was scornful. "What *are* his depths, then?"

"Something more than personal aggrandizement. You, who
are so close to him, miss what the general mass of people who
see him from a distance recognize quite clearly. He lives like a
monk—he gets no personal profit out of what he does and his
long hours of work. And he does not care what's thought of
him."

"Any more than you do."

"Me?" Caught by an unexpected amount of truth in this
charge, Donal could still protest. "I care for the opinion of the
people whose opinion I care for."

"Such as?" she said.

"Well, you," he answered, "for one. Though I don't know why."

About to say something, and hardly waiting for him to finish so she could say it, she checked suddenly; and stared at him, her eyes widening.

"Oh," she gasped, "don't try to tell me that!"

"I hardly know why I try to tell you anything," he said, suddenly very bitter; and went off, leaving her where she stood.

He went directly out from the cocktail gathering and back to his own suite, where he immersed himself in work that kept him at his desk until the small hours of the morning. Even then, when he at last got to bed, he did not sleep well—a condition he laid to a walking hangover from the drinks at the cocktail gathering.

His mind would have examined this excuse further—but he would not let it.

Protector III

"... A typical impasse," said William, Prince of Ceta. "Have some more of this Moselle."

"Thank you, no," answered Donal. The Conference was in its second week and he had accepted William's invitation to lunch with him in William's suite, following a morning session. The fish was excellent, the wine was imported—and Donal was curious, although so far they had spoken of nothing of real importance.

"You disappoint me," William said, replacing the decanter on the small table between them. "I'm not very strong in the food and drink department myself—but I do enjoy watching others enjoy them." He raised his eyebrows at Donal. "But your early training on the Dorsai is rather Spartan?"

"In some respects, yes," answered Donal. "Spartan and possibly a little provincial. I'm finding myself sliding into Hendrik Galt's impatience with the lack of progress in our talks."

"Well, there you have it," said William. "The soldier loves action, the politician the sound of his own voice. But there's a better explanation than that, of course. You've realized by now, no doubt, that the things that concern a Conference aren't settled at the Conference table"—he gestured with his hand at the food before him—"but at small tete-a-tetes like these."

"I'd guess then that the tete-a-tetes haven't been too productive of agreements so far." Donal sipped at the wine left in his glass.

"Quite right," said William cheerfully. "Nobody really wants to interfere in local affairs on a world; and nobody really wants to impose an institution on it from the outside, such as the open market, against the will of some of its people." He shook his head at Donal's smile. "No, no—I'm being quite truthful. Most of the delegates here would just as soon the problem of an open market had never come up at all on New Earth, so that they could tend to their own styles of knitting without being bothered."

"I'll still reserve my judgment on that," said Donal. "But in any case, now we're here, we've got to come to some decision. Either for or against the current government; and for or against the market."

"Do we?" asked William. "Why not a compromise solution?"

"What sort of compromise?"

"Well that, of course," said William, in a frank tone, "is why I asked you to lunch. I feel very humble about you, Donal—I really do. I was entirely wrong in my estimate of you, five years ago. I did you an injustice."

Donal lifted his right hand in a small gesture of deprecation.

"No . . . no," said William. "I insist on apologizing. I'm not a kind man, Donal. I'm interested only in buying what others have to sell—and if a man has ability, I'll buy it. If not—" He let the sentence hang significantly. "But you *have* ability. You had it five years ago, and I was too concerned with the situation to recognize it. The truth of the matter is, Hugh Killien was a fool."

"On that, I can agree with you," Donal said.

"Attempting to carry on with Anea under my nose—I don't blame the girl. She was still a child then, for all her size. That's the way these Exotic hothouse people are—slow growing. But I should have seen it and expected it. In fact, I'm grateful to you for what you did, when I think back on it."

"Thank you," murmured Donal.

"No, I mean that absolutely. Not that I'm talking to you now out of a sense of gratitude alone—I wouldn't insult your credulity with such a suggestion. But I am pleased to be able to find things working out in such a way that my own profit combines with the chance to pay you a small debt of gratitude."

"At any rate, I appreciate it," said Donal.

"Not at all. Now, the point is this," said William, leaning forward over the table, "personally, of course, I favor the open market. I'm a businessman, after all, and there're business advantages to perfectly free trading. But more than open markets, it's important to business to have peace between the stars; and peace comes only from a stable situation."

"Go on," said Donal.

"Well, there are after all only two ways of imposing peace on a community—from the inside or from the outside. We don't seem to be able to do it to ourselves from the inside; so why not try imposing it from the outside?"

"And how would you go about that?"

"Quite simply," said William, leaning back in his float. "Let *all* the worlds have open markets, but appoint a separate, individual supraplanetary authority to police the markets. Equip it with sufficient force to back up its authority against even individual governments if need be—and appoint a responsible individual in charge whom governments will think twice about tangling with." He raised his eyes calmly to Donal across the table and paused to let expectation build to its proper peak in this young man. "How would you like the job?" he asked.

"I?"

Donal stared at him. William's eyes were shrewd upon him. Donal hesitated; and the muscles of his throat worked, once.

"I?" he said. "Why, the man who commanded a force like that would be—" the word faltered and died, unspoken.

"He would, indeed," said William, softly. Across from him Donal seemed to come slowly back to himself. He turned narrowed eyes on William. "Why come to me with an offer like this?" he demanded. "There are older commanders. Men with bigger names."

"And that is just precisely why I come to you, Donal," replied William, without hesitation. "Their stars are fading. Yours is rising. Where will these older men be twenty years from now? On the other hand, you—" he waved a self-explanatory hand.

"I!" said Donal. He seemed to be dazzled. "Commander—"

"Call it Commander in Chief," said William. "The job will be there; and you're the man for the job. I'm prepared, in the name of Ceta, to set up a tax on interplanetary transactions which, because of our volume of trade, we will bear the most heavily. The tax would pay for your forces, and yourself. All we want in exchange is a place on a three-man commission which will act as final authority over you." He smiled. "We could hardly put such power in your hands and turn you loose under no authority."

"I suppose—" Donal was hesitant. "I'd have to give up my position around Procyon—"

"I'm afraid so," said William, frankly. "You'd have to remove any suspicion of conflicting interests."

"I don't know." Donal's voice was hesitant. "I might lose this new post at any time—"

"There's no need to worry about that," said William. "Ceta should effectively control the commission—since we will be paying the lion's share. Besides, a force like that, once established, isn't easy to disband. And if they're loyal to their commander—and your troops, I hear, usually are very much so—you would be in a position to defend your own position, if it came to that."

"Still—" Donal still demurred. "Taking a post like that I'd inevitably make enemies. If something *should* go wrong, I'd have no place to turn, no one would hire me—"

"Frankly," said William, sharply, "I'm disappointed in you, Donal. Are you completely lacking in foresight?" His tone took on a little impatience. "Can't you see that we're inevitably tending toward a single government for all the worlds? It may not come tomorrow, or even in the next decade; but any supraplanetary organization must inevitably grow into the ultimate, central authority."

"In which case," said Donal, "I'd still be nothing but a hired hand. What I want"—his eyes burned a little more brightly—"is to own something. A world . . . why not? I'm equipped to control a world; and defend it." He turned on William. "You'll have *your* position," he said.

William's eyes were hard and bright as two cut stones. He laughed shortly.

"You don't mince words," he said.

"I'm not that kind of man," said Donal, with a slight swagger in his tone. "You should have expected me to see through this scheme of yours. You want supreme authority. Very well. Give me one of the worlds—under you."

"And if I was to give you a world," said William. "Which one?"

"Any fair size world." Donal licked his lips. "Well, why not New Earth?"

William laughed. Donal stiffened.

"We're getting nowhere," said Donal. He stood up. "Thank you for the lunch." He turned and headed for the exit from the lounge.

"Wait!"

He turned to the sound of William's voice. The other man was also on his feet; and he came toward Donal.

"I've underestimated you again," said William. "Forgive me." He placed a detaining hand on Donal's arm. "The truth is, you've only anticipated me. Indeed, I'd intended you to be something more than a hired soldier. But . . . all this is in the future," he shrugged. "I can hardly do more than promise you what you want."

"Oh," said Donal. "Something more than a promise. You could give me a contract, confirming me as the supreme authority on New Earth."

William stared at him and this time he did laugh, loudly and long.

"Donal!" he said. "Excuse me . . . but what good would a contract like that be?" He spread his arms wide. "Some day New Earth may be mine to write you a contract for. But now—?"

"Still, you could write it. It would serve as a guarantee that you mean what you say."

William stopped laughing. His eyes narrowed.

"Put my name to a piece of writing like that?" he said. "What kind of a fool do you take me for?"

Donal wilted a little under the angry contempt in the older man's voice.

"Well . . . at least draw up such a contract," he said. "I suppose I couldn't expect you to sign it. But . . . at least I'd have something."

"You have something that could possibly cause me some slight embarrassment," said William. "I hope you realize it'd do nothing more than that—in the face of my denial of ever having discussed the matter with you."

"I'd feel more secure if the terms were laid out ahead of time," said Donal, almost humbly. William shrugged, not without a touch of scorn.

"Come on then," he said; and led the way across the room to a desk. He pressed a stud on it and indicated a grille. "Dictate," he said.

*   *   *

Later, leaving William's suite of rooms with the unsigned contract in his pocket, Donal came out into the general hotel corridor outside so swiftly that he almost trod upon the heels of Anea, who seemed also to be leaving.

"Where away?" he said. She turned on him.

"None of your business!" she snapped; but an expression which the inescapable honesty of her face would not permit her to hide, aroused his sudden suspicions. He reached out swiftly and caught up her right hand, which was clenched into a fist. She struggled, but he lifted the fingers easily back. Tucked into the nest of her palm was a tiny contact snooper mike.

"You *will* continue to be a fool," he said, wearily, dropping her hand with the mike still in it. "How much did you hear?"

"Enough to confirm my opinion of *you*!" she hissed.

"Bring that opinion to the next session of the Conference, if you can get in," he said. And went off. She stared after him, shaken with a fury, and a sudden pain of betrayal for which she could find no ready or sensible explanation.

She had, she told herself through that afternoon and the evening that followed, no intention of watching the next session personally. Early the next morning, however, she found herself asking Galt if he would get her a visitor's pass to the Conference room.

The marshal was obliged to inform her that at William's request, this session of the Conference was to be a closed one. He promised, however, to bring her what news he could; and she was forced to rest uneasily content with that.

As for Galt, himself, he went on to the Conference, arriving some few minutes late and discovering that the session had already started. William himself had begun the proposal of a plan that made the Dorsai Marshal of Freiland stiffen to attention, even as he was sitting down on his float at the Conference table.

"... To be established by a vote of this body," William was

saying. "Naturally," he smiled, "our individual governments will have to ratify later, but we all know that to be pretty much a formality. A supraplanetary controlling body—having jurisdiction over trade and contracts, only—in conjunction with a general establishment of the open market, satisfies the requirements of all our members. Also, once this is out of the way, there should be no reason why we should not call upon the present insurgent government of New Earth to resign in favor of the previous, regular government. And I expect that if we call with a united voice, the present heads of state there will yield to our wishes." He smiled around the table. "I'm open for questions and objections, gentlemen."

"You said," spoke up Project Blaine, in his soft, precise voice, "something about a supranational armed force which would enforce the rulings of this controlling body. Such an armed force is, of course, contrary to our principles of individual worldrights. I would like to say right now that I hardly think we would care to support such a force and allow it such freedom if a commander inimical to our interests was at its head. In short—"

"We have no intention of subscribing to a commander other than one with a thorough understanding of our own principles and rights," interrupted Arjean, of Ste. Marie, all but glaring at the Venusian. Galt's shaggy brows shot together in a scowl.

There was something entirely too pat about the way these two had horned in. He started to look over at Donal for confirmation of this suspicion but William's voice drew his attention back to the Cetan.

"I understand, of course," said William. "However, I think I have the answer to all of your objections." He smiled impersonally at all of them. "The top commanders, as you know, are few. Each one has various associations which might make him objectionable to some one or more of the delegates here. In the main, I would say nothing more than a professional soldier. The prime examples of this, of course, are our Dorsai—"

The glances around the table swung quickly in on Galt, who scowled back to hide his astonishment.

". . . The Marshal of Freiland would, therefore, because of his position in his profession and between the stars, be our natural choice. But—" William barely got the word out in time to stifle objections that had begun to voice themselves from several points around the table, "Ceta recognizes that because of the marshal's long association with Freiland, some of you may not welcome him in such a position. We're therefore proposing another man entirely—equally a Dorsai, but one who is young enough and recently enough on the scene to be considered free of political prejudice—I refer to the Protector of Procyon, Donal Graeme."

He gestured at Donal and sat down.

A babble of voices broke out all at once, but Donal was on his feet, looking tall, and slim, and remarkably young amongst the group of them. He stood, waiting, and the voices finally died down.

"I won't keep you for more than a minute," said Donal, looking around at them. "I agree thoroughly with Prince William's compromise solution to the problem of this Conference; because I most heartily believe the worlds *do* need a watchdog over them to prevent what's just now taken place, from happening." He paused, and looked around the table again. "You see, honored as I am by Prince William's nomination, I can't accept because of something which just recently came into my hands. It names no names, but it promises things which will be a revelation to all of us. I also will name no names, but I would guess however that if this is a sample of what's going on, there are probably half a dozen other such writings being traded around."

He paused to let this sink in.

"So, I hereby refuse the nomination. And, further, I'm now withdrawing as a Delegate from this Conference in protest against being approached in this manner. I could not accept such a post or such a responsibility except with perfectly clean hands and no strings attached. Good-by, gentlemen."

He nodded to them and stepped back from their stunned silence. About to turn toward the exit, he stopped and pulled from his pocket the unsigned and nameless contract he had received from William the previous day. "Oh, by the way," he said. "This is the matter I was talking about. Perhaps you'd all like to look it over."

He threw it onto the table in their midst and strode out. As he left the lounge behind him, a sudden eruption of voices reached to his ears.

He did not go directly back to his own suite, but turned instead to Galt's. The doorbot admitted him; and he made his way to the main lounge of the suite, striding in with the confidence of one who expects to find it empty.

It was not, however. He had made half a dozen long strides into the room before he discovered another person seated alone at a chess board on a little table, and looking up at his entrance with startled eyes.

It was Anea.

He checked and inclined his head to her.

"Excuse me," he said. "I was going to wait for Hendrik. I'll take one of the other lounges."

"No," she had risen to her feet. Her face was a little pale, but controlled. "I'm waiting for him, too. Is the session over?"

"Not yet," he replied.

"Then let's wait together." She sat down at the table again. She waved a hand at the pieces, presently set up in the form of a knights-castles problem. "You play?"

"Yes," he said.

"Then join me." It was almost an order the way she said it. Donal showed no reaction, however, but crossed the lounge and took a seat opposite her. She began to set out the pieces.

If she expected to win, she was mistaken. Donal won three swift games; but oddly without showing any particular flair or brilliance. Consistently he seemed able to take advantage of opportunities she had overlooked, but which had been there before her in perfect obviousness all the time. The games seemed more a tribute to her obtuseness, than his perception. She said as much. He shrugged.

"You were playing me," he said. "And you should rather have been playing my pieces."

She frowned; but before she had a chance to sort this answer out in her mind, there was the sound of steps outside the lounge, and Galt entered, striding along, fast and excitedly.

Donal and she both rose.

"What happened?" she cried.

"Eh? What?" Galt's attention had been all for Donal. Now the older man swung on her. "Didn't he tell you what happened up to the time he left?"

"No!" She flashed a look at Donal, but his face was impassive.

Quickly, Galt told her. Her face paled and became shadowed by bewilderment. Again, she turned to Donal; but before she could frame the question in her mind, Donal was questioning Galt.

"And after I left?"

"You should have seen it!" the older man's voice held a fierce glee. "Each one was at the throat of everybody else in the room before you were out of sight. I swear the last forty years of behind-the-scenes deals, and the crosses and the double-crosses came home to roost in the next five minutes. Nobody trusted anybody, everybody suspected everybody else! What a bomb-shell to throw in their laps!" Galt chuckled. "I feel forty years younger just for seeing it. Who was it that actually approached you, boy? It was William, wasn't it?"

"I'd rather not say," said Donal.

"Well, well—never mind that. For all practical purposes it could have been any of them. But guess what happened! Guess how it all ended up—"

"They voted me in as commander in chief after all?" said Donal.

"They—" Galt checked suddenly, his face dropping into an expression of amazement. "How'd you know?"

Donal smiled a little mirthlessly. But before he could answer, a sharp intake of breath made both men turn their heads. Anea was standing off a little distance from them, her face white and stiff.

"I might have suspected," she said in a low, hard voice to Donal. "I might have known."

"Known? Known what?" demanded Galt, staring from one to the other. But her eyes did not waver from Donal.

"So this was what you meant when you told me to bring my opinion to today's session," she went on in the same low, hate-filled voice. "Did you think that this . . . this sort of double-dealing would change it?"

For a second pain shadowed Donal's normally enigmatic eyes.

"I should have known better, I suppose," he said, quietly. "I assumed you might look beyond the necessities of this present action to—"

"Thank you," she broke in icily. "Ankle deep into the mud is far enough." She turned on Galt. "I'll see you another time, Hendrik." And she stalked out of the room.

The two men watched her go in silence. Then Galt slowly turned back to look at the younger man.

"What's between you two, boy?" he asked.

Donal shook his head.

"Half of heaven and all of hell, I do believe," he said; and that was the most illuminating answer the marshal was able to get out of him.

Commander in Chief

Under the common market system, controlled by the United Planetary Forces under Commander in Chief Donal Graeme, the civilized worlds rested in a highly unusual state of almost perfect peace for two years, nine months, and three days absolute time. Early on the morning of the fourth day, however, Donal woke to find his shoulder being shaken.

"What?" he said, coming automatically awake.

"Sir—" It was the voice of Lee. "Special Courier here to see you. He says his message won't wait."

"Right." Groggily, but decisively, Donal swung his legs over the edge of his sleeping float and reached for his trunks on the ordinary float beside him. He gathered them in, brushing something to the floor as he did so.

"Light," he said to Lee. The light went on, revealing that what he had knocked down was his wrist appliance. He picked it up and stared at it with blurry eyes. "March ninth," he murmured. "That right, Lee?"

"That's right," responded the voice of Lee, from across the room. Donal chuckled, a little huskily.

"Not yet the ides of March," he murmured. "But close. Close."

"Sir?"

"Nothing. Where's the courier, Lee?"

"The garden lounge."

Donal pulled on the trunks and—on a second's impulse—followed them with trousers, tunic and jacket, complete outerwear. He followed Lee through the pre-dawn darkness of his suite in Tomblecity, Cassida, and into the garden lounge. The courier, a slim, small, middle-aged man in civilian clothes, was waiting for him.

"Commander—" the courier squinted at him. "I've got a message for you. I don't know what it means myself—"

"Never mind," interrupted Donal. "What is it?"

"I was to say to you 'the gray rat has come out of the black maze and pressed the white lever.' "

"I see," said Donal. "Thank you." The courier lingered.

"Any message or orders, commander?"

"None, thank you. Good morning," said Donal.

"Good morning, sir," said the courier; and went out, escorted by Lee. When Lee returned, he found Donal already joined by his uncle Ian Graeme, fully dressed and armed. Donal was securing a weapons belt around his own waist. In the new glare of the artificial light after the room's darkness, and beside his dark and giant uncle, the paring-down effect of the last months showed plainly on Donal. He was not so much thinned down as stretched drum-tight over the hard skeleton of his own body. He seemed all harsh angles and tense muscle. And his eyes were hollowed and dark with fatigue.

Looking at him, it would be hard not to assume that here was a man either on the verge of psychological and nervous breakdown, or someone of fanatic purpose who had already pushed himself beyond the bounds of ordinary human endurance. There was something of the fanatic's translucency about him—in which the light of the consuming will shows through the frailer vessel of the body. Except that Donal was not really translucent, but glowed, body and all, like one fine solid bar of tempered steel with the white, ashy heat of his consuming but all-unconsumable will.

"Arm yourself, Lee," he said, pointing to a weapons belt. "We've got two hours before sun-up and things begin to pop. After that, I'll be a proscribed criminal on any world but the

Dorsai—and you two with me." It did not occur to him to ask either of the other men whether they wished to throw themselves into the holocaust that was about to kindle about him; and it did not occur to the others to wonder that he did not. "Ian, did you make a signal to Lludrow?"

"I did," said Ian. "He's in deep space with all units, and he'll hold them there a week if need be, he says—incommunicado."

"Good. Come on."

As they left the building for the platform awaiting them on the landing pad outside; and later, as the platform slipped them silently through the pre-dawn darkness to a landing field not far from the residence, Donal was silent, calculating what could be done in seven days time, absolute. On the eighth day, Lludrow would have to open his communication channels again, and the orders that would reach him when he did so would be far different from the sealed orders Donal had left him and which he would be opening right now. Seven days—

They landed at the field. The ship, a space-and-atmosphere courier N4J, was lying waiting for them, its ground lights gleaming dimly on steady-ready. The forward lock on the great shadowy cylinder swung open as they approached; and a scar-faced senior captain stepped out.

"Sir," he said, saluting Donal, and standing aside to let them enter. They went in and the lock closed behind them.

"Coby, captain," said Donal.

"Yes, sir." The captain stepped to a grille in the wall. "Control room. Coby," he said. He turned from the grille. "Can I show you to the lounge, commander?"

"For the time being," said Donal. "And get us some coffee."

They went on into the courier's lounge, which was fixed up like the main room on a private yacht. And presently coffee was forthcoming on a small autocart from the galley, which scooted in the door by itself and parked itself in the midst of their floats.

"Sit down with us, Cor," said Donal. "Lee, this is Captain Coruna El Man, Cor, my uncle Ian Graeme."

"Dorsai!" said Ian, shaking hands.

"Dorsai!" responded El Man. They smiled slightly at each other, two grimly-carved professional warriors.

"We have met," Ian said.

"Right," said Donal. "Now that introductions are over—how long will it take us to make it to Coby?"

"We can make our first jump immediately we get outside atmosphere," answered El Man, in his rather harsh, grating voice. "We've been running a steady calculation on a standby basis. After the first jump, it'll take a minimum of four hours to calculate the next. We'll be within a light-year of Coby then, and each phase shift will take progressively less calculation as we zero in. Still—five more calculation periods at an average of two hours a period. Ten hours, plus the original four makes fourteen, straight drive and landing in on Coby another three to four hours. Call it eighteen hours—minimum."

"All right," said Donal. "I'll want ten of your men for an assault party. And a good officer."

"Myself," said El Man.

"Captain, I . . . very well," said Donal. "You and ten men. Now." He produced an architectural plan from inside his jacket. "If you'll all look here; this is the job we have to do."

The plan was that of an underground residence on Coby, that planet which had grown into a community from a collection of mines and never been properly terraformed. Indeed, there was a question whether, even with modern methods, it could be. Coby was just too far out from hospitable Procyon, and formed of the wrong materials.

The plan itself showed a residence of the middle size, comprising possibly eighteen rooms, surrounded by gardens and courtyards. The differences, which only began to appear as Donal proceeded to point them out, from an above-ground residence of the ordinary type on other planets, lay in the fakery involved. As far as appearances went, someone in the house, or in one of the gardens, would imagine he was surface-dwelling on at least a terraformed world. But eight-tenths of that impression would be sheer illusion. Actually, the person in question would have ultimate rock in all directions—rock ten meters overhead at the furthest, rock underfoot, and rock surrounding.

For the assault party, this situation effected certain drawbacks, but also certain definite advantages. A drawback was, that after securing their objective—who was a man Donal did not trouble himself to identify—withdrawal would not be managed as easily as it might on the surface, where it was simply a matter of bundling everyone into the nearby ship and jumping off. A great advantage, however, which all but offset the drawback mentioned, was the fact that in this type of residence, the rock walls surrounding were honeycombed with equipment rooms and tunnels which maintained the above-ground illusion—a situation allowing easy ingress and surprise.

As soon as the four with him had been briefed, Donal turned the plans over to El Man, who went off to inform his assault party, and suggested to Lee and Ian that they join him in getting what sleep they could. He took himself to his own cabin, undressed and fell into the bunk there. For a few minutes his mind, tight-tuned by exhaustion, threatened to wander off into speculations about what would be taking place on the various worlds while he slept. Unfortunately, no one had yet solved the problems involved in receiving a news broadcast in deep space. Which was why, of course, all interstellar messages were taped and sent by ship. It was the swiftest and, when you came right down to it, the only practical way to get them there.

However, twenty years of rigid training slowly gained control of Donal's nerves. He slept.

He woke some twelve hours later, feeling more rested than he had in over a year. After eating, he went down to the ship's gym; which, cramped and tiny as it was, was still a luxurious accessory on a deep-space vessel. He found Ian methodically working out in the Dorsai fashion—a procedure the large dark man went through every morning when conditions did not prohibit it, as conscientiously and as nearly without thought as most men shave and brush their teeth. For several minutes Donal watched Ian on the single bar, doing arm twists and stands; and when his uncle dropped to the mat, his wide torso gleaming with perspiration and the reek of it strong in Donal's nostrils, Donal took him on at grips-and-holds.

The results were a little shocking to Ian. That Ian was stronger than he was only to be expected. His uncle was the bigger man. But Donal should have had a clear edge in speed, both because of age and because of his own natural reflexes, which were unusually good. The past year's strain and physical idleness, however, had taken their toll. He broke three holds of his uncle's with barely a fraction of a second to spare; and when he did, at last, throw the older man, it was by the use of a feint he would have scorned to use his senior year at school back on the Dorsai, a feint that took sneaking advantage of a slight stiffness he knew to be the result of an old wound in his uncle's deep-scarred left arm.

Ian could hardly have failed to recognize the situation and the reason behind the slightly unfair maneuver that had downed him. But nothing seemed to matter to him these days. He said nothing, but showered and dressed with Donal; and they went in to the lounge.

*   *   *

Shortly after they sat down there, there was the medication warning, and—a few minutes later—the shock of a phase shift. On the heels of it, El Man came walking into the lounge.

"We're in range, commander," he said. "If you want the news—"

"Please," said Donal.

El Man touched one of the walls and it thinned into transparency through which they could see the three-dimensional image of a Cobyman seated at a desk.

". . . Has been spreading," came the voice of the man at the desk, "following quickly upon the charges brought by the Commission for the Common Market System against Commander in Chief Graeme of the United Planetary Forces. The Com Chief himself has disappeared and most of his deep-space units appear presently to be out of communication and their whereabouts are presently unknown. This development has apparently sparked outbreaks of violence on most of the civilized worlds, in some cases amounting to open revolt against the established governments. The warring factions seem split by a fear of the open markets on the part of the general populaces, and a belief that the charges against Graeme are an attempt to remove what safeguards on the rights of the individual still remain in effect.

"As far as this office has been informed, fighting is going on on the present worlds—Venus, Mars, Cassida, New Earth, Freiland, Association, Harmony, and Ste. Marie; and the governments of the following worlds are known to be deposed, or in hiding—Cassida, New Earth, and Freiland. No outbreaks are reported on Old Earth, Dunnin's World, Mara, Kultis, or Ceta. And there is no present violence here on Coby at all. Prince William has offered the use of his leased troops as a police force to end the disturbances; and levies of Cetan troops are either on, or en route to, all trouble spots at the present time. William has announced that his troops will be used to put down trouble wherever they find it, without respect to what faction this leaves in power. 'Our job is not to take sides,' he is reported as stating, 'but to bring some kind of order out of the present chaos and put out the flames of self-destruction.'

"A late signal received from Old Earth reports that a number of the insurgent factions are agitating for the appointment of William as World's Regent, with universal authority and strong-man powers to deal with the present emergency. A somewhat similar movement puts forward the name of Graeme, the missing Com Chief, for a similar position."

"That's all for now," concluded the man at the desk, "watch for our next signal in fifteen minutes."

"Good," said Donal, and gestured to El Man to shut off the receiver, which the scarred Dorsai captain did. "How long until planetfall?"

"A couple of hours," replied El Man. "We're a bit ahead of schedule. That was the last phase shift. We're on our way in on straight drive now. Do you have co-ordinates on our landing point?"

Donal nodded; and stood up.

"I'll come up to control," he said.

The process of bringing the N4J into the spot on the surface of Coby, corresponding to the co-ordinates indicated by Donal, was a time-consuming but simple procedure—only mildly complicated by Donal's wish to make their visit undetected. Coby had nothing to defend in the sense a terraformed world might have; and they settled down without incident on its airless surface, directly over the freight lock to one of the subsurface transportation tunnels.

"All right," said Donal, five minutes later, to the armed contingent of men assembled in the lounge. "This is an entirely volunteer mission, and I'll give any of you one more chance to withdraw without prejudice if you want to." He waited. Nobody stirred. "Understand," said Donal, "I want nobody with me simply because he was shamed into volunteering, or because he didn't want to hesitate when his shipmates volunteered." Again he waited. There were no withdrawals. "Right, then. Here's what we'll be doing. You'll follow me down that freight lock and into a receiving room with a door into a tunnel. However, we won't be taking the door, but burning directly through one of the walls to the service section of an adjoining residence. You've all seen a drawing of our route. You're to follow me, or whoever remains in command; and anyone who can't keep up gets left behind. Everybody understand?" He looked around their faces.

"All right," he said. "Let's go."

He led out down the passageway of the ship, out through their lock and down into the freight lock into the receiving room. This turned out to be a large, gloomy chamber with fused rock walls. Donal measured off a section of one wall and set his torchmen to work. Three minutes later they were in the service section of a Coby residence.

The area in which they found themselves was a network of small tunnels wide enough for only one man at a time, and interspersed with little niches and crannies holding technical devices necessary to the maintenance and appearance of the residence. The walls were coated with a permanent illuminating layer; and, in this cold white light, they filed along one of the tunnels and emerged into a garden.

The cycle of the residence's system was apparently now set on night. Darkness held the garden and a fine imitation of the starry heavens glittered overhead. Ahead and to their right was the clump of main rooms, soft-lit with interior light.

"Two men to hold this exit," whispered Donal. "The rest of you follow me."

He led the way at a low crouching run through the garden

and to the foot of some wide stairs. At their top, a solitary figure
could be seen pacing back and forth on a terrace before an open
wall.

"Captain—" said Donal. El Man slipped away into the bushes
below the terrace. There was a little wait in the artificial night
and then his dark shadow was seen to rise suddenly upon the
terrace behind the pacing figure. They melted together, sagged,
and only the shadow of El Man was left. He beckoned them up.

"Three men to hold this terrace," whispered Donal, as they
all came together at the head of the stairs. El Man told off the
necessary number of the assault party; and they continued on
into the lighted interior of the house.

For several rooms it seemed almost as if they would achieve
their objective without meeting anyone other than the man
they had come to seek. Then, without anything in the way of
warning at all, they were suddenly in the middle of a pitched
battle.

As they emerged into the main hall, hand weapons opened up
on them from three converging rooms at once. The shipmen,
automatically responding to training, dropped to the floor, took
cover and returned the fire. They were pinned down.

They were, but not the three Dorsai. Donal, Ian, and El Man,
reacting in that particular way that was a product of genes, reflexes and their own special training, and that made the Dorsai
so particularly valuable as professional soldiers—these three had
responded automatically and in unison a split-second before the
fire opened up on them. It was almost as if some small element
of precognition had entered the picture. At any rate, with a
reaction too quick for thought, these three swung about and
rushed one of the enemy doorways, reached it and closed with
their opponents within before that opposition could bring their

fire to bear. The three found themselves in a darkened room and fighting hand to hand.

Here again, the particular character of the Dorsai soldier paid off. There were eight men in ambush within this particular room and they were all veteran soldiers. But no two of them were a match at hand-to-hand fighting with any single Dorsai; and in addition the Dorsai had the advantage of being able, almost by instinct, to recognize each other in the dark and the melee, and to join forces for a sudden common effort without the need for discussion. The total effect of these advantages made it almost a case of three men who could see fighting eight who were blind.

In Donal's case, he plunged into the dark room right on the heels of El Man and to El Man's left, with Ian right behind *him*. Their charge split the defenders within into two groups and also carried them farther back into obscurity—a movement which the Dorsai, by common silent consent, improved on for the purpose of further separating the enemy. Donal found himself pushing back four men. Abandoning three of these to Ian behind him under the simple common-sense precept that you fight best when you fight only one man at a time, he dove in almost at the level of his opponent's knees, tackled him, and they went down and rolled over together, Donal taking advantage of the opportunity to break the other soldier's back in the process.

He continued his roll and came up, pivoting and instinctively side-stepping. A dark body flung past him—but that instinct spoken of before warned him that it was El Man, flinging himself clear across the room to aid the general confusion. Donal reversed his field and went back the way from which El Man had come. He came up against an opponent plunging forward with a knife held low, slipped the knife, chopped at the man's neck with the calloused edge of his hand—but missed a clean killing stroke and only broke the man's collar bone. Leaving that opponent however in the interests of keeping on the move, Donal spun off to the right, cornered another man against the wall and crushed this one's windpipe with a stiff-fingered jab. Rebounding from the wall and spinning back into the center of the room, his ears told him that El Man was finishing off one opponent and Ian was engaged with the remaining two. Going to help him, Donal caught one of Ian's men from behind and paralyzed him with a kidney punch. Ian, surprisingly enough, was still engaged with the remaining enemy. Donal went forward and found out why. Ian had caught himself another Dorsai.

Donal closed with both men and they went down in a two-on-one pin, the opponent in a stretcher that held him helpless between Donal and his uncle.

"Shai Dorsai!" gasped Donal. "Surrender!"

"Who to?" grunted the other.

"Donal and Ian Graeme," said Ian. "Foralie."

"Honored," said the strange Dorsai. "Heard of you. Hord Vlaminck, Snelbrich Canton. All right then, let me up. My right arm's broken, anyway."

Donal and Ian let go and assisted Vlaminck to his feet. El Man had finished off what else remained, and now came up to them.

"Hord Vlaminck—Coruna El Man," said Donal.

"Honored," said El Man.

"Honor's mine," replied Vlaminck. "I'm your prisoner, gentlemen. Want my parole?"

"I'd appreciate it," said Donal. "We've got work to do here yet. What kind of contract are you under?"

"Straight duty. No loyalty clause. Why?"

"Any reason why I can't hire you on a prisoner's basis?" asked Donal.

"Not from this job." Vlaminck sounded disgusted. "I've been sold twice on the open market because of a typo in my last contract. Besides," he added, "as I say, I've heard of you."

"You're hired, then. We're looking for the man you're guarding here. Can you tell us where we'll find him?"

"Follow me," said Vlaminck; and led the way back through the darkness; and opened a door. They stepped through into a short corridor that led them up a ramp and to another door.

"Locked," said Vlaminck. "The alarm's gone off." He looked at them. Further than this he could not in honor go, even on a hired prisoner's basis.

"Burn it down," said Donal.

He and Ian and El Man opened up on the door, which glowed stubbornly to a white heat, but finally melted. Ian threw a concussion bolt at it and knocked it open.

Within, a large man with a black hood over his head was crouched against the far wall of the room, a miner's heavy-duty ion gun in his hand pointing a little unsteadily at them and shifting from one to the other.

"Don't be a fool," said Ian. "We are all Dorsai."

The gun sagged in the hand of the hooded man. A choked, bitter exclamation came from behind the mask.

"Come on," Donal gestured him out. He dropped the gun and came, shoulders bowed. They headed back through the house.

The fire fight in the hall was still going on as they retraced their footsteps; but died out as they reached the center hall. Two of the five men they had left behind there were able to navigate on their own power and another one could make it back to the ship with assistance. The other two were dead. They returned swiftly to the terrace, through the garden, and back into the tunnel, picking up the rest of their complement as they went. Fifteen minutes later, they were all aboard and the N4J was falling into deep space.

In the lounge, Donal was standing before the hooded man, who sat slumped on a float.

"Gentlemen," said Donal, "take a look at William's social technician."

Ian and El Man, who were present, looked sharply over at Donal—not so much at the words as at the tone in which he had said them. He had spoken in a voice that was, for him, unexpectedly bitter.

"Here's the man who sowed the whirlwind the civilized worlds are reaping at this moment," went on Donal. He stretched out his hand to the black hood. The man shrank from him, but Donal caught the hood and jerked it off. A slow exhalation of breath slipped out between Donal's lips.

"So you sold out," he said.

The man before them was ArDell Montor.

Commander in Chief II

ArDell looked back at him out of a white face, but with eyes that did not bend before Donal's bleak glance.

"I had to have work," he said. "I was killing myself. I don't apologize."

"Was that all the reason?" asked Donal, ironically.

At that, ArDell's face did turn aside.

"No—" he said. Donal said nothing. "It was her," ArDell whispered. "He promised me her."

"*Her!*" The note in Donal's voice made the other two Dorsai take an instinctive step toward him. But Donal held himself without moving, under control. "Anea?"

"She might have taken pity on me—" ArDell whispered to the floor of the lounge. "You don't understand . . . living close to her all those years . . . and I was so miserable, and she . . . I couldn't help loving her—"

"No," said Donal. Slowly, the sudden lightning of his tension leaked out of him. "You couldn't help it." He turned away. "You fool," he said, with his back to ArDell. "Didn't you know him well enough to know when he was lying to you? He had her in mind for himself."

"William? *No!*" ArDell was suddenly on his feet. "Not him— with her! It can't be . . . such a thing!"

"It won't," said Donal, wearily. "But not because it depends on people like you to stop him." He turned back to face ArDell. "Lock him up, will you, captain." El Man's hard hand closed on ArDell's shoulder and turned him toward the entrance to the lounge. "Oh . . . and captain—"

"Sir?" said El Man, turning to face him.

"We rendezvous with all units under Fleet Commander Llu-drow as soon as possible."

"Yes, sir." El Man half-pushed, half-carried ArDell Montor out of the room; and, as if symbolically, out of the main current of the history of mankind which he had attempted to influence with his science for William, Prince of Ceta.

The N4J set out to make contact with Lludrow. It was not a thing to be quickly or easily accomplished. Even when it is known where it should be, it is far from easy to track down and pinpoint as small a thing as a fleet of human ships in the in-conceivable vastnesses of interstellar space. For the very good reasons that there is always the chance of human error, that a safety margin must always be maintained—better to fall short of your target than to come out too close to it—and that there is, for practical purposes, no such thing as standing still in the universe. The N4J made a phase shift from where it calculated it was, to where it calculated the fleet to be, sent out a call signal and got no answer. It calculated again, signaled again—and so continued until it got first, a very faint signal in response, then a stronger one, and finally, one which permitted commu-nication. Calculations were then matched between the flagship of the fleet and the N4J—and at last a meeting was effected.

By that time, better than three more days of the alloted week of incommunicado had passed. Donal went aboard the flagship with Ian, and took command.

"You've got the news?" was his first question of Lludrow when the two of them were together again.

"I have," said the Fleet commander. "I've had a ship secretly in shuttle constantly between here and Dunnin's World. We're right up to date."

Donal nodded. This was a different problem from the N4J's

of finding Lludrow. A shuttle between a planet whose position and direction of movement was well known, and a fleet which knew its own position and drift, could hop to within receiving distance of that same planet in one jump, and return as easily, provided the distance was not too great—as it sometimes was between the various planets themselves—for precise calculation.

"Want to see a digest—or shall I just brief you?" asked Lludrow.

"Brief me," said Donal.

Lludrow did. The hysteria that had followed on the charges of the Commission against Donal and Donal's disappearance had caused the existing governments, already shaky and torn by the open-market dissension, to crumble on all the worlds but those of the Exotics, the Dorsai, Old Earth, and the two small planets of Coby and Dunnin's World. Into the perfect power vacuum that remained, William and the armed units of Ceta had moved swiftly and surely. Pro-tem governments in the name of the general populace, but operating directly under William's orders, had taken over New Earth, Freiland, Newton, Cassida, Venus, Mars, Harmony and Association and held them now in the iron grip of martial law. As William had cornered less sentient materials in the past, he had just prior to this cornered the field troops of the civilized world. Under the guise of training, reassignment, lease, stand-by—and a dozen other paper maneuvers—William had had under Cetan contract actual armies on each of the worlds that had fallen into disorder. All that had been necessary for him was the landing of small contingents, plus officers for the units already present, with the proper orders.

"Staff meeting," said Donal.

His staff congregated in the executive room of the flagship. Lludrow, Fleet Commander, Ian, Field Commander—and half a dozen senior officers under each.

*   *   *

"Gentlemen," said Donal, when they were seated around the table. "I'm sure all of you know the situation. Any suggestions?"

There was a pause. Donal ran his eye around the table.

"Contact Freiland, New Earth—or some place where we have support," said Ian. "Land a small contingent and start a counteraction against the Cetan command." He looked at his nephew. "They know your name—the professionals on all sides. We might even pick up support out of the enemy forces."

"No good," said Lludrow, from the other side of the table. "It's too slow. Once we were committed to a certain planet, William could concentrate his forces there." He turned to Donal. "Ship for ship, we overmatch him—but his ships would have ground support from whatever world we were fighting on; and our ground forces would have their hands full trying to establish themselves."

"True enough," Donal said. "What's your suggestion, then?"

"Withdraw to one of the untouched worlds—the Exotics, Coby, Dunnin's World. Or even the Dorsai, if they'll take us. We'll be safe there, in a position of strength, and we can take our time then about looking for a chance to strike back."

Ian shook his head.

"Every day—every hour," he said, "William grows stronger on those worlds he's taken over. The longer we wait, the greater the odds against us. And finally, he'll have the strength to come after us—and take us."

"Well, what do you want us to do, then?" demanded Lludrow. "A fleet without a home base is no striking weapon. And how many of our men will want to stick their necks out with us? These are professional soldiers, man—not patriots fighting on their home ground!"

"You use your field troops now or never!" said Ian shaking

his head. "We've got forty thousand battle-ready men aboard these ships. They're my responsibility and I know them. Set them down on some backwater planet and they'll fall apart in two months."

"I still say—"

"All right. All right!" Donal was rapping with his knuckles on the table to call them back to order. Lludrow and Ian sat back on their floats again; and they all turned to look at Donal.

"I wanted you all to have a chance to speak up," he said, "because I wanted you to feel that we had explored every possibility. The truth of the matter is that both you gentlemen are right in your objections—just as there is some merit in each of your plans. However, both your plans are gambles; long gambles—desperate gambles."

He paused to look around the table.

"I would like to remind you right now that when you fight a man hand-to-hand, the last place you hit him is where he expects to be hit. The essence of successful combat is to catch your enemy unawares in an unprotected spot—one where he is not expecting to be caught."

Donal stood up at the head of the table.

"William," he said, "has for the last few years put his emphasis on the training of ground troops—field troops. I have been doing the same thing, but for an entirely different purpose."

He placed his finger over a stud on the table before him and half-turned to the large wall behind him.

"No doubt all you gentlemen have heard the military truism that goes—you can't conquer a civilized planet. This happens to be one of the ancient saws I personally have found very irritating; since it ought to be obvious to any thinking person that in theory you can conquer anything—given the necessary wherewithal. The case for conquering a civilized world becomes then a thing of perfect possibility. The only problem is to provide that which is necessary to the action."

They were all listening to him—some a little puzzled, others doubtfully, as if they expected all of what he was saying to turn suddenly into some joke to relieve the tension. Only Ian was phlegmatic and absorbing.

"Over the past few years, this force, which we officer, has developed the wherewithal—some of it carried over from previous forces, some of recent development. Your men know the techniques, although they have never been told in what way they were going to apply them. Ian, here, has produced through rigorous training the highly specialized small unit of the field forces—the Group, which under ordinary battle conditions numbers fifty men, but which we have streamlined to a number of thirty men. These Groups have been trained to take entirely independent action and survive by themselves for considerable periods of time. This same streamlining has gone up through the ranks—extending even to your fleet exercises, which have also been ordered, with a particular sort of action in mind."

He paused.

"What all this boils down to, gentlemen," he said, "is that we are all about to prove that old truism wrong—and take a civilized world, lock, stock, and barrel. We will do it with the men and ships we have at hand right here, and who have been picked and trained for this specific job—as the planet we are about to take has been picked and thoroughly intelligenced." He smiled at them. They were all sitting on the edges of their floats now.

"That world,"—he pressed the stud that had been under his finger all this time; the wall behind him vanished to reveal the three-dimensional representation of a large, green planet—"is the heart of our enemy's power and strength. His home base—Ceta!"

It was too much—even for senior officers. A babble of voices burst out around the table all at once. Donal paid no attention. He had opened a drawer at his end of the table and produced a thick sheaf of documents, which he tossed on the table before him.

"We will take over Ceta, gentlemen," he said. "By, in a twenty-four hour period, replacing *all* her local troops, *all* her police, *all* her garrisons and militia and law enforcement bodies and arms, with our own men."

He pointed to the sheaf of documents.

"We will take them over piecemeal, independently, and simultaneously. So that when the populace wakes up the following morning they will find themselves guarded, policed and held, not by their own authorities, but by us. The details as to targets and assignments are in this stack, gentlemen. Shall we go to work?"

They went to work. Ceta, large, low-gravity planet that it was, had huge virgin areas. Its civilized part could be broken down into thirty-eight major cities, and intervening agricultural and residential areas. There were so many military installations, so many police stations, so many armories, so many garrisons of troops—the details fell apart like the parts of a well-engineered mechanism, and were fitted together again with corresponding units of the military force under Donal's command. It was a masterpiece of combat preplanning.

"Now," said Donal, when they were done. "Go out and brief your troops."

He watched them all leave the conference room—all, with the exception of Ian, whom he had detained; and Lee, for whom he had just rung. When the others were gone, he turned to the two still with him.

"Lee," he said, "in six hours every man in the fleet will know what we intend to do. I want you to go out and find a man—

not one of the officers—who doesn't think it'll work. Ian"—he looked over at his uncle—"when Lee finds such a man and reports to you, I want you to see that the man is sent up to see me, right away. Is that clear?"

The other two nodded; and went out, to do each his own job in his own fashion. So it was that a disgruntled Groupman from a particular landing force had a surprising meeting and surprisingly cordial chat with his commander in chief, and that they went out together, half an hour later, arm-in-arm, to the control room of the flagship, where Donal requested, and got, a voice-and-picture hookup to all ships.

"All of you," Donal said, smiling at them out of their screens after he had been connected, "have by this time been informed about the impending action. It's the result of a number of years of top-level planning and the best intelligence service we have been lucky enough to have. However, one of you has come to me with the natural fear that we may be biting off more than we can chew. Therefore, since this is an entirely new type of operation and because I believe firmly in the rights of the individual professional soldier not to be mishandled, I'm taking the unprecedented step of putting the coming assault on Ceta to a vote. You will vote as ships, and the results will be forwarded by your captain, as for or against, to the Flagship here. Gentlemen"—Donal reached out an arm and brought the man Lee had discovered into the screen area with him—"I want you to meet Groupman Theiss, who had the courage to stand up like a free man and ask questions."

Caught unawares, and dazzled by the sudden limelight into which he had been thrust, the Groupman licked his lips and grinned a little foolishly.

"I leave the decision to all of you," added Donal, and signaled for the viewing eyes to be cut off.

*   *   *

Three hours later, Groupman Theiss was back on his own ship, astounding his fellow soldiers with an account of what had happened to him; and the votes were in.

"Almost unanimous," reported Lludrow, "in favor of the attack. Only three ships—none of the first line, and none troop carriers—voting against."

"I want those three ships held out of the attack," said Donal. "And a note made of their names and captains. Remind me about that after this is over. All right." He got up from the float where he had been sitting in the Flagship Lounge. "Give the necessary orders, commander. We're going in."

They went in. Ceta had never taken the thought of enemy attack too seriously. Isolated in her position as the single inhabitable planet, as yet largely unexplored and unexploited, that circled her G_8 type sun of Tau Ceti; and secure in the midst of an interstellar maze of commitments that made every other planetary government to some extent dependent upon her good will, she had only a few ships in permanent defensive orbit about her.

These ships, their position and movement fully scouted by Donal's intelligence service, were boxed and destroyed by Donal's emerging fleet almost before they could give warning. And what warning they did give fell on flabbergasted and hardly-believing ears.

But by that time the asault troops were falling planetward, dropping down on city and military installation and police station behind the curtain of night as it swung around the big, but swiftly-turning world.

They came down in most cases almost on top of their targets, for the ships that had sowed them in the sky above had not been hampered in that action by enemy harassment. And the reaction of those on the ground was largely what might have been expected, when veteran troops, fully armed and armored, move in on local police, untried soldiers in training, and men relaxed in garrison. Here and there, there was sharp and bitter fighting where an assault unit found itself opposed to leased troops as trained in war as they. But in that case, reinforcements were speedily brought in to end the action.

Donal himself went down with the fourth wave; and when the sun rose the following morning large and yellow on the horizon, the planet was secured. Two hours later, an orderly brought him word that William himself had been located—in his own residence outside the city of Whitetown, some fifteen hundred kilometers distant.

"I'll go there," said Donal. He glanced around him. His officers were busy, and Ian was off somewhere with an arm of his field troops. He turned to Lee. "Come on, Lee," he said.

They took a four-man platform and made the trip, with the orderly as guide. Coming down in the garden of the residence, Donal left the orderly with the platform, motioned Lee to accompany him, and entered the house.

He walked through silent rooms, inhabited only by furniture. All the residents of the house seemed to have vanished. After some little time, he began to think that perhaps the report had been in error; and that William was gone, too. And then he passed through an archway into a little anteroom and found himself facing Anea.

She met his gaze with a pale but composed face.

"Where is he?" asked Donal.

She turned and indicated a door on the far side of the room. "It's locked," she said. "He was in there when your men started to land; and he's never come out. Nobody else would stay here with him. I . . . I couldn't leave."

"Yes," said Donal, somberly. He examined the locked door from across the room. "It wouldn't have been easy—for him."

"You care about him?" Her voice brought his head up sharply. He looked at her, seeking some note of mockery in her expression. But there was none. She was honestly questioning.

"I care somewhat for every man," he said. He walked across the room to the door and laid his hand upon it on a sudden impulse, he put his thumb into the finger-lock—and the door swung open.

A sudden coldness blossomed inside him.

"Stay with her," he threw over his shoulder to Lee. He pushed open the door, found himself faced by another, heavier door—but one which also opened to his touch—and went in.

At the end of a long room William sat behind a desk occupied by a mass of papers. He stood up as Donal entered.

"So you're finally here," he said, calmly. "Well, well."

Going closer, Donal examined the man's face and eyes. There was nothing there to evoke such a notion; but Donal had the sudden suspicion that William was not as he should be.

"It was a very good landing. Very good," said William tiredly. "It was a clever trick. I acknowledge the fact, you see. I underestimated you from the first day I met you. I freely admit it. I'm quite conquered—am I not?"

Donal approached to the other side of the desk. He looked into William's calm exhausted face.

"Ceta is in my control," said Donal. "Your expeditionary forces on the other worlds are cut off—and their contracts aren't worth the paper they're written on. Without you to give the orders, it's all over with."

"Yes . . . yes, I thought as much," said William, with the hint of a sigh. "You're my doom, you know—my weird. I should have recognized it earlier. A force like mine among men must be balanced. I thought it would be balanced with numbers; but it wasn't." He looked at Donal with such a strange, searching expression that Donal's eyes narrowed.

"You're not well," said Donal.

"No, I'm not well." William rubbed his eyes, wearily. "I've been working too hard lately—and to no purpose. Montor's calculations were foolproof; but the more perfect my plan, the more perfectly it always went awry. I hate you, you know," said William, emotionlessly, dropping his hand and looking up at Donal again. "No one in all the history of man has ever hated the way I hate you."

"Come along," said Donal, going around the desk toward him. "I'll take you to someone who can help you—"

"No. Wait—" William held up his hand and backed away from Donal. Donal stopped. "I've got something to show you first. I saw the end the minute I got reports your men were landing. I've been waiting nearly ten hours now." He shivered, suddenly. "A long wait. I had to have something to keep myself occupied." He turned about and walked briskly back to a set of double doors set in a far wall. "Have a look," he invited; and pressed a button.

The doors slid back.

Donal looked. Hanging in the little close area revealed there was something only barely recognizable by what was left of its face. It was, or had been, his brother Mor.

Secretary for Defense

Flashes of clarity began to return.

For some time, now and again, they had been calling him from the dark corridors down which he walked. But he had been busy, too busy to respond until now. But now—slowly—he let himself listen to the voices, which were sometimes those of Anea, and Sayona, and Ian, and sometimes the voices of those he did not know.

He rose to them reluctantly, slow to abandon the halls of darkness where he traveled. Here was the great ocean he had always hesitated to enter; but now that he was in it, it held him warm, and would have possessed him except for their little voices calling him back to petty things. Yet, duty lay to them, and not to it—that duty that had been impressed on him from his earliest years. The things undone, the things ill-done—and what he had done to William.

"Donal?" said the voice of Sayona.

"I'm here," he said. He opened his eyes; and they took in a white hospital room and the bed in which he lay, with Sayona and Anea and Galt standing beside it—along with a short man with a mustache in the long pink jacket of one of the Exotic psychiatric physicians.

Donal swung his legs over the edge of the bed and stood up. His body was weak from long idleness, but he put the weakness aside the way a man puts aside any irritating, but small and unimportant thing.

"You should rest," said the physician.

Donal looked at him casually. The physician looked away; and Donal smiled, to ease the man.

"Thanks for curing me, doctor," he said.

"I didn't cure you," said the physician, a little bitterly, his head still averted.

Donal turned his glance on the other three; and a sadness touched him. In themselves, they had not changed, and the hospital room was like similar rooms had always been. But yet, in some way, all had dwindled—the people and the place. Now there was something small and drab about them, something tawdry and limited. And yet, it was not their fault.

"Donal" began Sayona, on a strangely eager, questioning note. Donal looked at the older man; and he, like the physician, looked automatically away. Donal shifted his glance to Galt, who also dropped his eyes. Only Anea, when he gazed at her, returned his glance with a child's pure stare.

"Not now, Sayona," said Donal. "We'll talk about it later. Where's William?"

"One floor down . . . Donal—" the words broke suddenly from Sayona's lips in a rush. "What did you do to him?"

"I told him to suffer," said Donal, simply. "I was wrong. Take me to him."

They went slowly—and, on Donal's part, a little unsteadily—out the door and down to a room on the floor below. A man there lay rigid on a bed like the one Donal had occupied—and it was hard to recognize that man as William. For all the asepsis of the hospital, a faint animal smell pervaded the room; and the face of the man was stretched into a shape of inhumanity by all known pain. The skin of the face was tautened over the flesh and bones like cloth of thinnest transparency over a mask of clay, and the eyes recognized no one.

"William—" said Donal, approaching the bed. The glazed eyes moved toward the sound of his voice. "Mor's trouble is over."

A little understanding flickered behind the Pavlovian focus-ing of the eyes. The rigid jaws parted and a hoarse sound came from the straining throat. Donal put his hand on the drum-tight brow.

"It'll be all right," he said. "It'll be all right, now."

Slowly, like invisible bonds melting away, the rigidity began to melt out of the man before them. Gradually he softened back into the shape of humanity again. His eyes, now comprehend-ing, went to Donal as if Donal's tall form was one light in a cavern of lightlessness.

"There'll be work for you to do," said Donal. "Good work. All you ever wanted to do. I promise you."

William sighed deeply. Donal took his hand from the brow. The eyes dropped closed; and William slept.

"Not your fault," said Donal, absently, looking down at him. "Not your fault, but your nature. I should have known." He turned a little unsteadily, to the others who were staring at him with new eyes. "He'll be all right. Now, I want to get to my headquarters on Cassida. I can rest on the way. There's a great deal to do."

The trip from the Maran hospital where both Donal and Wil-liam had been under observation, to Tomblecity on Cassida, passed like a dream for Donal. Waking or dreaming, he was still half in that ocean into which at Mor's death he had finally stepped, and the dark waters of which would never entirely leave him now. It was to become finally a matter of living with it—this sea of understanding along the margin of which he had wandered all the young years of his life, and which no other human mind would be able to comprehend, no matter how long his explanation. He understood now why he understood—this much had the shock of Mor's death brought him. He had been like any young animal, hesitant on the edge of the unknown,

before his own uncertain desires and the sharp nudge of circumstance combined to tumble him headlong into it.

He had had to learn first to admit, then to live with, and
finally to embrace his difference.

It had been necessary that what was uniquely Donal be
threatened—first by the psychic shocks of the phase shifts during the attack on Newton; and second by the manner of Mor's
dying, for which only he knew how truly he was responsible—
in order that he be forced to fight for survival; and fighting,
discover fang and use of claw. In that final battle he had seen
himself at last, full-imaged in the unplumbed depths; and recognized himself at last for what he was—a recognition no one
else would ever be able to make. Anea, alone, would know
without needing to understand, what he was; it is Woman's
ancient heritage to appreciate without the need to know. Sayona, William, and a few such would half-recognize, but never
understand. The rest of the race would never know.

And he—he himself, knowing and understanding, was like
a man who could read, lifting the first small book from a library
the shelves of which stretched off and away to infinity. A child
in a taller land.

Anea, Sayona, Galt and the others came with him back to
Tomblecity. He did not have to ask them to come with him.
Now, they followed instinctively.

Donal

The man was different.

Already, a few people were beginning to say it. And in this fact lay the seeds of a possible difficulty. It was necessary, considered Donal, that a means be taken to lightning-rod such a recognition, and render it harmless.

He stood in that position which was becoming very common with him of late, alone on a balcony of his residence outside Tomblecity, hands clasped behind his back like a soldier at parade rest, gazing out toward the Milky Way and the unknown stars. He heard Anea come up behind him.

"Sayona's here," she said.

He did not turn. And after a moment she spoke again.

"Do you want me to talk to him by myself?" she asked.

"For a little while," answered Donal, still without moving. He heard her footsteps move away from him into the bigness of the lounge behind him. He lost himself in the stars again; and, after a moment, there was the sound of a man's voice and a murmur of conversation between it and Anea's. At this distance, their words were indistinguishable; but Donal did not have to hear the words to know what they were saying.

Eight months had gone by since he had opened his eyes onto the full universe that was exposed to his view alone. *Eight months*, thought Donal to himself. And in that short time, order had been returned to the civilized worlds. A parliament of peoples had been formed with an interiorly elected council of thirty-two Senior Representatives, two for each world. Today,

here on Cassida, that parliament had voted on its choice for a
permanent Secretary for Defense—

Donal's mind reached out and enclosed the problem of what
Sayona would, this moment, be saying to Anea.

". . . And then he went around the room, a little before the
voting." Sayona's voice was now murmuring in the lounge behind him. "He said a word here, and a word there—nothing
important. But when he was done, he had them in the palm of
his hand. It was just as it was last month when he mingled with
the delegates to the full parliament."

"Yes," replied Anea. "I can see it how it was."

"Do you understand?" asked Sayona, looking at her keenly.

"No," she said, serenely. "But I've seen it. He blazes—*blazes*—
like an atomic flare among a field full of little campfires. Their
small lights fade when they get too close to him. And he hoods
his light, when he's amongst them, to keep from blinding them."

"Then you're not sorry—?"

"Sorry!" Her happy laugh tore his question to foolish ribbons.

"I know," said Sayona, soberly, "what effect he has on men.
And I can guess his effect on other women. Are you sure you've
got no regrets?"

"How could I?" But she looked at him suddenly, question-
ingly. "What do you mean?"

"That's why I've come tonight," said Sayona. "I've got something to tell you . . . if I can ask you a question after I'm
through?"

"What kind of question?" she queried sharply.

"Let me tell you first," he said. "Then you can answer or not,
whichever you like. It's nothing that can touch you—now. Only
I should have told you before. I'm afraid I've put it off, until . . .
well, until there was no more putting off possible. What do you
know about your own gene history, Anea?"

"Why," she looked at him, "I know all about it."

"Not this part," said Sayona. "You know you were bred for

certain things—" He put one old, slim hand on the edge of her float in a gesture that begged for understanding.

"Yes. Mind and body," she answered, watching him.

"And more," said Sayona. "It's hard to explain in a moment. But you know what was behind Montor's science, don't you? It treated the human race as a whole, as a single social entity, self-repairing in the sense that as its individual components die off they are replaced by the birth of new components. Such an entity is manipulable under statistical pressures, in somewhat the same manner that a human being may be manipulated by physical and emotional pressures. Increase the temperature of a room in which a man stands, and he will take off his jacket. This was William's key to power."

"But—" she stared at him. "*I'm* an individual—"

"No, no. Wait," Sayona held up his hand. "That was *Montor's* science. Ours on the Exotics had somewhat the same basis, but a differing viewpoint. We regarded the race as manipulable through its individuals, as an entity in a constant state of growth and evolution by reason of the birth of improved individuals among the mass that constituted it. Gene-selection, we believed, was the key to this—both natural or accidental, and controlled."

"But it is!" said Anea.

"No," Sayona shook his head slowly. "We were wrong. Manipulation by that approach is not truly possible; only analysis and explanation. It is adequate for an historian, for the meditative philosopher. And such, Anea, have we of the Exotics been, wherefore it seemed not only valid, but complete, to us.

"But manipulation by that means is possible only in small measure—very small. The race is not controllable from within the race; such gene-selection as we did could use only those characteristics which we *already* knew and understood. And it repelled us from those genes which we detected, and could not understand, and, of course, we could not work with ones we did not know existed, or could exist.

"We were, without seeing the fact, crippled both at the beginning and the end; we had only the middle. We could not conceive of characteristics to breed toward—goals—which were not already presented to us, and already understood by us. That was the proper end, however—truly new characteristics. And the beginning was, necessarily, truly new genes, and gene-combinations.

"The problem was stated long ago; we deceived ourselves that the statement was not meaningful. Simply, it is this; could a congress of gorillas, gathered to plan the breeding of the super-gorilla, plan a human being? Discard the line of development of mightier muscles, stronger and longer teeth, greater specialization to master their tropical environment?

"Manipulation of the race from within the race is a circular process. What we can do, the valuable thing we can do, is to stabilize, conserve, and spread the valuable genetic gifts that come to us from outside our own domain.

"William—and you must have known this better than any one else, Anea—belongs to that small and select group of men who have been the conquerors of history. There's a name, you know, for this rare and freakish individual—but a name means nothing by itself. It's only a tag hung on something we never completely understood. Such men are unopposable—they can do great good. But also, usually, an equally great deal of harm, because they are uncontrolled. I'm trying to make you understand something rather complex. We, on the Exotics, spotted William for what he was when he was still in his early twenties. At that time the decision was taken to select the genes that would result in you."

"*Me!*" She stiffened suddenly, staring at him.

"You." Sayona bent his head to her briefly. "Didn't you ever wonder that you were so instinctively opposed to William in everything he did? Or why he was so perversely insistent on possessing your contract? Or why we, back on Kultis, allowed such an apparently unhappy relationship to continue?"

Anea shook her head slowly. "I . . . I must have. But I don't remember—"

"You were intended as William's complement, in a psychological sense." Sayona sighed. "Where his instincts were for control for the sake of controlling, yours were towards goals, purposes, and you did not care who controlled so long as the control was directed toward that purpose. Your eventual marriage—which we aimed for—would have, we hoped, blended the two natures. You would have acted as the governor William's personality needed. The result would have been beneficial . . . we thought."

She shuddered.

"I'd never have married him."

"Yes," said Sayona with a sigh, "you would have. You were designed—if you'll forgive the harsh word—to react at full maturity to whatever man in the galaxy stood out above all others." A little of Sayona's gravity lifted for a moment, and a twinkle crept into his eyes. "That, my dear, was by no means difficult to provide for; it would have been near impossible to prevent it! Surely you see that the oldest and greatest of the female instincts is to find and conserve the strength of the strongest male she can discover. And the ultimate conservation is to bear his children."

"But—there was Donal!" she said, her face lighting up.

"Quite so," Sayona chuckled. "If the strongest male in the galaxy were wrongly directed, misusing his great strength—still, for the sake of the great value of that strength, you would have sought him out. Strength, abilities, are tools; these are important. How they are used is a separate matter.

"But with Donal on the scene . . . Well, he was the ruin of all our theories, all our plans. The product of one of those natural accidents, outside our domain, a chance combining of genes even superior to William's. The blending of a truly great line of thinkers, with an equally great line of doers.

"I failed to realize this, even when we tested him." Sayona shook his head as though to clear it. "Or . . . perhaps our tests were just not capable of measuring the really important characteristics in him. We . . . well, we don't know. It's that that worries me. If we've failed to discover a true mutation—someone with a great new talent that could benefit the race, then we have failed badly."

"Why, what would it have to do with you?" she asked.

"It would be in the area where we are supposed to have knowledge. If a cyberneticist fails to recognize that his companion has a broken bone, he is not culpable; if a physician makes the same mistake, he merits severe punishment.

"It would be our duty to recognize the new talent, isolate it, and understand it, we on the Exotics. It may be that Donal has something he does not recognize himself." He looked at her. "And that is the question I must ask you. You are closer to him than anyone else; do *you* think Donal may have something— something markedly different about him? I don't mean simply his superior genius; that would be simply more of the same kind of thing other men have had; I mean some true ability over and above that of the normal human."

Anea became very still for a long moment, looking beyond rather than at Sayona. Then she looked at Sayona again, and said, "Do you want me to guess? Why don't you ask him?"

It was not that she did not know the answer; she did not know how, or what she knew, nor did she know how to convey it, nor whether it was wise to convey it. But the knowing within her was quietly and completely certain that Donal knew, and would know what should and should not be said.

Sayona shrugged wryly. "I am a fool; I do not believe what all my own knowledge assures me. It was perfectly certain that the Select of Kultis would make such an answer. I am afraid to ask him; knowing that makes the fear no less. But you are right, my dear. I . . . will ask him."

She lifted her hand.

"Donal!" she called.

Out on the balcony he heard her voice. He did not move his eyes from the stars.

"Yes," he answered.

There were footsteps behind him, and then the voice of Sayona.

"Donal—"

"You'll have to forgive me," said Donal, without turning. "I didn't mean to make you wait. But I had something on my mind."

"Quite all right," said Sayona. "I hate to disturb you—I know how busy you've been lately. But there was a question I wanted to ask."

"Am I a superman?" asked Donal.

"Yes, that's essentially it," Sayona chuckled. "Has somebody else been asking you the same question?"

"No," Donal was smiling himself. "But I imagine there's some would like to."

"Well, you mustn't blame them," said Sayona, seriously. "In a certain sense, you actually are, you know."

"In a sense?"

"Oh," Sayona made a little dismissing gesture with his hand. "In your general abilities, compared to the ordinary man. But that wasn't my question—"

"I believe you have said that a name is without meaning in itself. What do you mean by 'Superman'? Can your question be answered, if that tag has no meaning, no definition?

"And who would want to be a Superman?" asked Donal in a tone halfway between irony and sadness, his eyes going to the depth beyond depth of starspace. "What man would want twenty billion children to raise? What man would cope with so many? How would he like to make the necessitous choices between them, when he loved them all equally? Think of the responsibility involved in refusing them candy when they shouldn't—but could—have it, and seeing that they went to the dentist against their wills! And if 'Superman' means a unique individual—think of having twenty billion children to raise, and no friend to relax with, complain to, to blow off steam to, so that the next day's chores would be more bearable.

"And if your 'Superman' were so super, who could force him to spend his energies wiping twenty billion noses, and cleaning up the messes twenty billion petulant bratlings made? Surely a Superman could find some more satisfying use for his great talents?"

"Yes, yes," said Sayona. "But of course, I wasn't thinking of anything so far-fetched." He looked at Donal's back with mild annoyance. "We know enough about genetics now to realize that we could not have, suddenly, a completely new version of the human being. Any change would have to come in the shape of one new, experimental talent at a time."

"But what if it were an undiscoverable talent?"

"Undiscoverable?"

"Suppose," said Donal, "I have the ability to see a strange new color? How would I describe it to you—who cannot see it?"

"Oh, we'd locate it all right," replied Sayona. "We'd try all possible forms of radiation until we found one you could identify as the color you were seeing."

"But still you wouldn't be able to see it, yourselves."

"Well, no," said Sayona. "But that would be hardly important, if we knew what it was."

*   *   *

"Are you sure?" persisted Donal, not turning. "Suppose there was someone with a new way of thinking, someone who in childhood forced himself to do his thinking within the framework of logic—because that was the only way those around him thought. Gradually, however, as he grows older he discovers that there are relationships for him that do not exist for other minds. He knows, for example, that if I cut down that tree just below us out here in my garden, some years in time, and some light-years in distance away, another man's life will be changed. But in logical terms he cannot explain his knowledge. What good would it do you then, to know what his talent *was?*"

"No good at all, of course," said Sayona, good-humoredly, "but on the other hand it would do him no good at all, either, since he lives in, and is part of, a logical society. In fact, it would do him so little good, he would undoubtedly never discover his talent at all; and the mutation, being a failure, would die aborning."

"I disagree with you," said Donal. "Because I, myself, am an intuitional superman. I have a conscious intuitive process. I use intuition consciously, as you use logic, to reach a conclusion. I can cross-check, one intuition against the other, to find out which is correct; and I can build an intuitive structure to an intuitive conclusion. This is one, single talent—but it multiplies the meaning and the power of all the old, while adding things of its own."

Sayona burst out laughing.

"And since, according to my own argument, this ability would do you so little good that you wouldn't even be able to discover it, it therefore stands that you wouldn't be able to answer my question about being a superman in the affirmative, when I ask it! Very good, Donal. It's been so long since I've had the Socratic method used in argument against me I didn't even recognize it when I came face to face with it."

"Or perhaps you instinctively would prefer not to recognize my talent," said Donal.

"No, no. That's enough," said Sayona, still laughing. "You win, Donal. Anyway, thank you for setting my mind at rest. If we had overlooked a real possibility, I would have held myself personally responsible. They would have taken *my* word for it and—I would have been negligent." He smiled. "Care to tell me what the real secret of your success has been, if it's not a wild talent?"

"I *am* intuitive," said Donal.

"Indeed you are," said Sayona. "Indeed you are. But to be merely intuitive—" he chuckled. "Well, thank you, Donal. You don't know how you've relieved my mind on this particular score. I won't keep you any longer." He hesitated, but Donal did not turn around. "Good night."

"Good night," said Donal. He heard the older man's footsteps turn and move away from him.

"Good night," came Sayona's voice from the lounge behind him.

"Good night," answered Anea.

Sayona's steps moved off into silence. Still Donal did not turn. He was aware of the presence of Anea in the room behind him, waiting.

"Merely intuitive," he echoed to himself, in a whisper. "*Merely*—"

He lifted his face once more to the unknown stars, the way a man lifts his face from the still heat of the valley to the coolness of the hills, in the early part of the long work day when the evening's freedom is yet far off. And the look on his face was one which no living person—not even Anea—had seen. Slowly, he lowered his eyes, and slowly turned; and, as he

turned, the expression faded from him. As Anea had said, carefully he hooded the brilliance of his light that he might not
blind them; and, turning full around at last, entered once more,
and for a little while again, into the habitation of Man.

THE SPIRIT OF
> > DORSAI < <

This book is dedicated to my grandmother,
Mary Elizabeth Ford
and to my great-grandmother,
Margaret Minteer

Prologue

She was tall, slim, and so blonde as to be almost white-haired. There was an erectness to her body that no man could have possessed without stiffness. As she sat cross-legged, her gray eyes gazing down into the valley on the Dorsai that held Fal Morgan and the surrounding homesteads, her face had the quality of a profile stamped on a silver coin.

"Amanda . . ." said Hal Mayne, gently.

Lost in her thoughts, she did not hear him; and the moment was so close to perfection that he was reluctant to disturb it. The part of him that was a poet, which had survived the months of being a hunted guerrilla on Harmony and even the sickness and the brutalities of the prison there before his escape, stirred again, watching her. Here, on the roof of a warriors' world, under a clean and cloudless sky in a time when the human race was everywhere submitting to the chains of a new slavery, she wore an armor of sunlight, unconquerable. Beside her, in his much taller, wide-shouldered but gaunt, body, pared thin by privation and suffering, he felt like some great dark bird of earth-bound flesh and bone, bending above an entity of pure spirit.

As he waited, her eyes lost their abstraction. As if they had been separated so far that his voice, speaking her name, had had to stretch across time and space to only now reach her, she turned finally back to him.

"Did you say something?" she asked.

"I was going to say how much you resemble that picture of her—of the first Amanda Morgan," he said. "It could be a picture of you."

She smiled a little.

"Yes," she said, "both the second Amanda to bear the name, and I look very much like her. It happens."

"It's still a strange thing, with only three of you of that name in your family in two hundred years," he said. "Does it just happen she had her picture printed at the same age you are now?" he said.

"No." She shook her head. "It wasn't."

"It wasn't?"

"No. That picture you saw in our hall was made when she was much older than I am now."

He frowned.

"It's true," she said. "We age very slowly, we Morgans—and she was something special."

"Not as special as you," he said. "She couldn't be. You're Dorsai—end-result Dorsai. She lived before people like you were what you are now."

"That's not true," the third Amanda said. "She was Dorsai before there was a Dorsai world. What she was, was the material out of which our people and our culture here were made."

He shook his head, slowly.

"How can you be so sure about what she was—two hundred standard years ago?"

"How can I?" She looked at him for a moment. "In many ways, I am her."

He watched her.

"A reincarnation?"

"No," she answered. "Not really. But something . . . more as if time didn't matter. As if it's all the same thing; her, there in the beginning of our world, and I here, at . . ."

"The end of it," he suggested.

"No." She looked at him steadily with those gray eyes. "The end won't be until the last Dorsai is dead. In fact, not even then. The end will only be when the last human is dead—because what makes us Dorsai is something that's a part of all humans; that part the first Amanda had when she was born, back on Earth."

Something—the shadow of a swooping bird, perhaps—shuttered the sunlight from his eyes for a split second.

"*You think so much of her,*" he said, thoughtfully. "*But it's Cletus Grahame and his textbooks on the military art he wrote two hundred years ago—it's Donal Graeme and the way he brought the inhabited worlds together, one hundred years ago—that other worlds think of when they use the word 'Dorsai'.*"

"*We've had Graemes for our next neighbor since Cletus,*" she replied. "*What's thought of them, they earned. But the first Amanda was here before either of them. She founded our family. She cleared the outlaws from these mountains before Cletus came; and when she was ninety-three, she held Foralie district against Dow deCastries' veteran troops whom they invaded, thinking they'd have no trouble with the children, the women, the sick and the old that were all that were left here, then.*"

"*You mean,*" Hal said, "*that time deCastries tried to take over the Dorsai, at the very end of Cletus' struggle with him?*"

"*With him and all the power of Earth behind him, in a time when everyone thought Earth was more powerful than all the other inhabited worlds combined.*"

"*But wasn't it Cletus who gave directions for the defense of Dorsai, that time?*"

"*Cletus wasn't here. He left two of his officers, Arvid Johnson and Bill Athyer to coordinate the defense and give the districts a general survey of the strategical and tactical situations involved. But their job was only a matter of laying out the military physics of the situation, with Cletus' theories and principles as guidelines. It was up to each district individually after that, to draw up its own plan for dealing with the invaders. That's what Foralie did—knowing it would be under the gun more than any other district, since Foralie homestead was here, and Cletus would be expected to return to it as soon as he heard the Dorsai had been invaded.*"

"*And it was the first Amanda who was given charge of Foralie district, by the people in the district, then?*" he asked. "*Why her? She hadn't been a soldier.*"

"*I told you,*" she said. "*During the Outlaw Years, she'd led the way in clearing out the lawless mercenaries. After she did that—and other things—with just the women, the cripples, old men and children to help her, the rest of the districts followed her example and law came to all the Dorsai. She was the best person to command."*

"How did they do it, then?"

"Clean out the outlaws?" the third Amanda asked.

"No—though I want to hear that sometime, too. What I meant was, how did Amanda and Foralie district defeat first-line troops? Most military scholars seem to think that the invaders defeated themselves, that they had to defeat themselves; because there was no way a gaggle of women, children and old people could possibly have done it."

"In a way you could say the troops did defeat themselves—did you ever read Cletus' Tactics of Mistake?" she answered. "But actually what happened was a case of putting our strengths against the weaknesses of the invaders."

"Weaknesses? What weaknesses did first-line troops have?"

She looked at him again with those level eyes.

"They weren't willing to die unless they had to."

"That?" Hal looked at her curiously. "That's a weakness?"

"Comparatively. Because we were."

"Willing to die?" he studied her. "Noncombatants? Old people, mothers—"

"And children. Yes." The armor of sunlight around her seemed to invest her words with a quality of truth greater than he had ever known from anyone else. "The Dorsai was formed by people who were willing to pay with their lives in others' battles, in order to buy freedom for their homes. Not only the men who went off to fight, but those at home had that same image of freedom and were willing to live and die for it."

"But simply being willing to die—"

"You don't understand, not being born here," she said. "It was a matter of their being able to make harder choices than people less willing. Amanda and the others in the district best qualified to decide

sat down and considered a number of plans. They all entailed casualties—and the casualties could include the people who were considering the plans. They chose the one that gave the district the greatest effectiveness against the enemy for the least number of deaths; and, having chosen it, they were all ready to be among those who would die, if necessary. The invading soldiers had no such plan—and no such courage."

He shook his head.

"I don't understand," he said.

"That's because you're not Dorsai. And because you don't understand someone like the first Amanda."

"No," he said. "That's true. I don't."

He looked at her.

"How did it happen?" he asked. "How did she—how did they do it? I have to know."

"You do?" Her gaze was unmoving on him.

"Yes," he said. There were so many things he had not been able to explain, things he had not admitted to her yet. There was the matter of his visit to Foralie, and the particular moment in which he had stepped into the doorway which some of the towering Graeme men, such as Ian and Kensie, the twin uncles of Donal Graeme, had been said to fill from sill to lintel and from side to side. As it had been with them, Hal's unshod feet had rested on the sill and the top of his head brushed the lintel. But unlike them, his shoulder-points had not touched the frame on either side.

It might be that with recovered health and some years of growth yet, that, too, could happen. But it did not matter. What mattered—and what he could not yet bring himself to talk about—was the sudden, poignant, feeling in him of kinship with the Graemes, unexpected as a blow, that had come on him without warning, as he stood in the doorway.

"I need to know," he said again.

"All right," she said. "I'll tell you just how it was."

Amanda Morgan

Stone are my walls, and my roof is of timber;
But the hands of my builder are stronger by far.
The roof may be burned and my stones may be scattered.
Never her light be defeated in war . . .
Song of the house named Fal Morgan

Amanda Morgan woke suddenly in darkness, her finger automatically on the firing button of the heavy energy handgun. She had heard—or dreamed she heard—the cry of a child. Rousing further, she remembered Betta in the next room and faced the impossibility of her great-granddaughter giving birth without calling her. It had been part of her dream, then.

Still, for a few seconds more, she lay, feeling the ghosts of old enemies still around her and the sleeping house. The cry had merged with the dream she had been having. In her dream, she had been reliving the long-ago swoop on her skimmer, handgun in fist, down into the first of the outlaw camps. It had been when Dorsai was new; and the camps, back in the mountains, had been bases for the out-of-work mercenaries. She had finally led the women of Foralie district against these men who had raided their homes for so long, in the intervals when the professional soldiers of their own households were away fighting on other worlds.

The last thing the outlaws had expected from a bunch of women had been a frontal assault in full daylight. Therefore, it had been that she had given them. In her dream she had been recalling the fierce bolts from the handgun slicing through makeshift walls and the bodies beyond, setting fire to dried wood and oily rags.

By the time she had been in among the huts, some of the outlaws were already armed and out of their structures; and the rest of the fight had disintegrated into a mixed blur of bodies and weapons. The outlaws were all veterans—but so, in their own way, were the women from the households. There were good shots on both sides; and in her younger strength, then, she was a match for any out-of-condition mercenary. Also, she was carried along in a rage they could not match . . .

She blinked, pushing the images of the dream from her. The outlaws were gone now—as were the Eversills who had tried to steal her land, and other enemies. They were all gone, now, making way for new foes. She listened a moment longer, but about her the house of Fal Morgan was still.

After a moment she got up anyway, stepping for a second into the chill bath of night air as she reached for a robe from the chair by her bed. Strong moonlight, filtering through sheer curtains, gave back her ghost in dim image from the tall armoire mirror. A ghost from sixty years past. For a second before the robe settled about her, the lean and still-erect shape in the mirror invented the illusion of a young, full-fleshed body. She went out.

Twenty steps down the long panelled corridor, with the familiar silent cone rifles and other combat arms standing like sentries in their racks on either wall, she became conscious of the fact that habit still had the energy handgun in her grasp. She shelved it in the rack and went on to her great-granddaughter's door. She opened it and stepped in.

The moonlight shone through the curtains even more brightly on this side of the house. Betta still slept, breathing heavily, her swollen middle rising like a promise under the covering blankets. The concern about this child-to-be, which had occupied Amanda all these past months, came back on her with fresh urgency. She touched the rough, heavy cloth over the unborn life briefly and lightly with her fingertips. Then she turned and went back out. Down the corridor and around the corner, the Earth-built clock in the living room chimed the first quarter of an hour past four A.M.

She was fully awake now, and her mind moved purposefully. The birth was due at any time now; and Betta was insistent about wanting to use the name Amanda if it was a girl. Was she wrong in withholding it, again? Her decision could not be put off much longer. In the kitchen she made herself tea. Sitting at the table by the window, she drank it, gazing down over the green tops of the conifers, the pines and spruce on the slope that fell away from the side of the house, then rose again to the close horizon of the ridge in that direction, and the mountain peaks beyond, overlooking Foralie Town and Fal Morgan alike, together with a dozen similar homesteads.

She could not put off any longer the making up of her mind. As soon as the baby was born, Betta would want to name her. On the surface, it did not seem such an important matter. Why should one name be particularly sacred? Except that Betta did not realize, none of them in the family seemed to realize, how much the name Amanda had come to be a talisman for them all.

The trouble was, time had caught up with her. There was no guarantee that she could wait around for more children to be born. With the trouble that was probably coming, the odds were against her being lucky enough to still be here for the official naming of Betta's child, when that took place. But there had been a strong reason behind her refusal to let her name be given to one of the younger generations, all these years. True, it was not an easy reason to explain or defend. Its roots were in something as deep as a superstition—the feeling in her that Fal Morgan would only stand as long as that name in the family could stand like a pillar to which they could all anchor. And how could she tell ahead of time how a baby would turn out?

Once more she had worn a new groove around the full circle of the problem. For a few moments, while she drank her tea, she let her thoughts slide off to the conifers below, which she had stretched herself to buy as seedlings when the Earth stock had finally been imported here to this world they called the Dorsai. They had grown until now they blocked the field of fire from the house in that direction. During the Outlaw Years, she would never have let them grow so high.

With what might be now coming in the way of trouble from Earth, they should probably be cut down completely—though the thought of it went against something deep in her. This house, this land, all of it, was what she had built for herself, her children and their children. It was the greatest of her dreams, made real; and there was no part of it, once won, that she could give up easily.

Still seated by the window, slowly drinking the hot tea, her mind went off entirely from the threats of the present to her earliest dreams, back to Caernarvon and the Wales of her childhood, to her small room on a top floor with the ceiling all angles.

She remembered that, now, as she sat in this house with only two lives presently stirring between its walls. No—three, with the child waiting to be born, who would be having dreams of her own, before long. How old had she herself been when she had first dreamed of running the wind?

That had been a very early dream of hers, a waking dream—also invoked as she was falling asleep. So that with luck, sometimes, it became a real dream. She had imagined herself being able to run at great speed along the breast of the rolling wind, above city and countryside. In her imagination she had run barefoot, and she had been able to feel the texture of the flowing air under her feet, that was like a soft, moving mattress. She had been very young. But it had been a powerful thing, that running.

In her imagination she had run from Caernarvon and Cardiff clear to France and back again; not above great banks of solar collectors or clumps of manufactories, but over open fields and mountains and cattle, and over flowers in fields where green things grew and where people were happy. She had gotten finally so that she could run, in her imagination, farther and faster than anyone.

None was so fleet as she. She ran to Spain and Norway. She ran across Europe as far as Russia, she ran south to the end of Africa and beyond that to the Antarctic and saw the great whales still alive. She ran west over America and south over South America. She saw the cowboys and gauchos as they once had been, and she saw the strange people at the tip of South America where it was quite cold.

She ran west over the Pacific, over all the south Pacific and over the north Pacific. She ran over the volcanos of the Hawaiian Islands, over Japan and China and Indo-China. She ran south over Australia and saw deserts, and the great herds of sheep and the wild kangaroos hopping.

Then she went west once more and saw the steppes and the Ukraine and the Black Sea and Constantinople that was, and Turkey, and all the plains where Alexander marched his army to the east, and then back to Africa. She saw strange ships with lug sails on the sea east of Africa, and she ran across the Mediterranean where she saw Italy. She looked down on Rome, with all its history, and on the Swiss alps where people yodeled and climbed mountains when they were not working very hard; and all in all she saw many things, until she finally ran home and fell asleep on the breast of the wind and on her own bed. Remembering it all, now that she was ninety-two years old— which was a figure that meant nothing to her—she sat here, light years from it all, on the Dorsai, thinking of it all and drinking tea in the last of the moonlight, looking down at her conifers.

She stirred, pushed the empty cup from her and rose. Time to begin the day—her control bracelet chimed with the note of an incoming call.

She thumbed the bracelet's com button. The cover over the phone screen on the kitchen wall slid back and the screen itself lit up with the heavy face of Piers von Linden. That face looked out and down at her, the lines that time had cut into it deeper than she had ever seen them. A sound of wheezing whistled and sang behind the labor of his speaking.

"Sorry, Amanda," his voice was hoarse and slow with both age and illness. "Woke you, didn't I?"

"Woke me?" She felt a tension in him and was suddenly alert. "Piers, it's almost daybreak. You know me better than that. What is it?"

"Bad news, I'm afraid . . ." his breathing, like the faint distant music of war-pipes, sounded between words. "The invasion from Earth is on its way. Word just came. Coalition first-line troops— to reach the planet here in thirty-two hours."

"Well, Cletus told us it would happen. Do you want me down in town?"

"No," he said.

Her voice took on an edge in spite of her best intentions.

"Don't be foolish, Piers," she said. "If they can take away the freedom we have here, then the Dorsai ceases to exist—except for a name. We're all expendable."

"Yes," he said, wheezing, "but you're far down on the list. Don't be foolish, yourself, Amanda. You know what you're worth to us."

"Piers, what do you want me to do?"

He looked at her with a face carved by the same years that had touched her so lightly.

"Cletus just sent word to Eachan Khan to hold himself out from any resistance action here. That leaves us back where we were to begin with in a choice for a Commander for the district. I know, Betta's about due—"

"That's not it." She broke in. "You know what it is. You ought to. I'm not that young any more. Does the district want someone who might fold up on them?"

"They want you, at any cost. You know that," Piers said, heavily. "Even Eachan only accepted because you asked someone else to take it. There's no one in the district, no matter what their age or name, who won't jump when you speak. No one else can say that. What do you think they care about the fact you aren't what you were, physically? They want you."

Amanda took a deep breath. She had had a feeling in her bones about this. He was going on.

"I've already passed the word to Arvid Johnson and Bill Athyer—those two Cletus left behind to organize the planet's defense. With Betta as she is, we wouldn't have called on you if there was any other choice—but there isn't, now—"

"All right," said Amanda. There was no point in trying to dodge what had to be. Fal Morgan would have to be left empty and unprotected against the invaders. That was simply the way of it. No point, either, in railing against Piers. His exhaustion under the extended asthmatic attack was plain. "I'll be glad to if I'm really needed, you know that. You've already told Johnson and Athyer I'll do it?"

"I just said I'd ask you."

"No need for that. You should know you can count on me. Shall I call and tell them it's settled?"

"I think . . . they'll be contacting you."

Amanda glanced at her bracelet. Sure enough, the tiny red phone light on it was blinking—signalling another call in waiting. It could have begun that blinking any time in the last minute or so; but she should have noticed it before this.

"I think they're on line now," she said. "I'll sign off. And I'll take care of things, Piers. Try and get some sleep."

"I'll sleep . . . soon," he said. "Thanks, Amanda."

"Nonsense." She broke the connection and touched the bracelet for the second call. The contrast was characteristic of this Dorsai world of theirs—sophisticated com equipment built into a house constructed by hand, of native timber and stone. The screen grayed and then came back into color to show an office room all but hidden by the largeboned face of a blond-haired man in his middle twenties. The single barred star of a vice-marshall glinted on the collar of his gray field uniform. Above it was a face that might have been boyish once, but now had a stillness to it, a quiet and waiting that made it old before its time.

"Amanda ap Morgan?"

"Yes," said Amanda. "You're Arvid Johnson?"

"That's right," he answered. "Piers suggested we ask you to take on the duty of Commander of Foralie District."

"Yes, he just called."

"We understand," Arvid's eyes in the screen were steady on her, "your great-granddaughter's pregnant—"

"I've already told Piers I'd do it." Amanda examined Arvid minutely. He was one of the two people on which they must all depend—with Cletus Grahame gone. "If you know this district, you know there's no one else for the job. Eachan Khan could do it, but apparently that son-in-law of his just told him to keep himself available for other things."

"We know about Cletus asking him to stay out of things," said Arvid. "I'm sorry it has to be you—"

"Don't be sorry," said Amanda. "I'm not doing it for you. We're all doing it for ourselves."

"Well, thanks anyway." He smiled, a little wearily.

"As I say, it's not a matter for thanks."

"Whatever you like."

Amanda continued to examine him closely, across the gulf

of the years separating them. What she was seeing, she decided, was that new certainty that was beginning to be noticeable in the Dorsai around Cletus. There was something about Arvid that was as immovable as a mountain.

"What do you want me to do first?" she asked.

"There's to be a meeting of all district commanders of this island at South Point, at 0900 this morning. We'd like you here. Also, since Foralie's the place Cletus is going to come back to— if he comes back—you can expect some special attention; and Bill and I would like to talk to you about that. We can arrange pickup for you from the Foralie Town airpad, if you'll be waiting there in an hour."

Amanda thought swiftly.

"Make it two hours. I've got things to do first."

"All right. Two hours, then, Foralie Town airpad."

"Don't concern yourself," said Amanda. "I'll remember."

She broke the connection. For a brief moment more she sat, turning things over in her mind. Then she rang Foralie home-stead, home of Cletus and Melissa Grahame.

There was a short delay, then the narrowboned face of Mel-issa—Eachan Khan's daughter, now Cletus' wife—took shape under tousled hair on the screen. Melissa's eyelids were still heavy with sleep.

"Who—oh, Amanda," she said.

"I've just been asked to take over district command, from Piers," Amanda said. "The invasion's on its way and I've got to leave Fal Morgan in an hour for a meeting at South Point. I don't know when or if I'll be back. Can you take Betta?"

"Of course." Melissa's voice and face were coming awake as she spoke. "How close is she?"

"Any time."

"She can ride?"

"Not horseback. Just about anything else."

Melissa nodded.

"I'll be over in the skimmer in forty minutes." She looked out of the screen at Amanda. "I know—you'd rather I moved in with her there. But I can't leave Foralie, now. I promised Cletus."

"I understand," said Amanda. "Do you know yet when Cletus will be back?"

"No. Any time—like Betta." Her voice thinned a little. "I'm never sure."

"No. Nor he, either, I suppose." Amanda watched the younger woman for a second. "I'll have Betta ready when you get here. Goodby."

"Goodby."

Amanda broke contact and set about getting Betta up and packed. This done, there was the house to be organized for a period of perhaps some days without inhabitants. Betta sat bundled in a chair in the kitchen, waiting, as Amanda finished programming the automatic controls of the house for the interval.

"You can call me from time to time at Foralie," Betta said.

"When possible," said Amanda.

She glanced over and saw the normally open, friendly face of her great-granddaughter, now looking puffy and pale above the red cardigan sweater enveloping her. Betta was more than capable in ordinary times; it was only in emergencies like this that she had a tendency to founder. Amanda checked her own critical frame of mind. It was not easy for Betta, about to have a child with her husband, father and brother all off-planet, in combat, and—the nature of war being what it was—the possibility existing that none of them might come back to her. There were only three men at the moment, left in the house of ap Morgan, and only two women; and now one of those two, Amanda, herself, was going off on a duty that could end in a hangman's rope or a firing squad. For she did not delude herself that the Earth-bred Alliance and Coalition military would fight with the same restraint toward civilians the soldiers of the younger worlds showed.

But it would not help to fuss over Betta now. It would help none of them—there was an approaching humming noise outside the house that crescendoed to a peak just beyond the kitchen door, and stopped.

"Melissa," said Betta.

"Come on," Amanda said.

She led the way outside. Betta followed, a little clumsily, and Melissa with Amanda helped her into the open cockpit of the ducted fan skimmer.

"I'll check up on you when I have time," Amanda said, kissing her great-granddaughter briefly. Betta's arms tightened fiercely around her.

"*Mandy!*" The diminutive of her name which only the young children normally used and the sudden desperate appeal in Betta's voice sent a surge of empathy arcing between them. Over Betta's shoulder, Amanda saw the face of Melissa, calm and waiting. Unlike Betta, Melissa came into her own in a crisis— it was in ordinary times that the daughter of Eachan Khan fumbled and lost her way.

"Never mind me," said Amanda, "I'll be all right. Take care of your own duties."

With strength, she freed herself and waved them off. For a second more she stood, watching their skimmer hum off down the slope. Betta's farewell had just woken a grimness in her that was still there. Melissa and Betta. Either way, being a woman who was useful half the time was no good. Life required you to be operative at all hours and seasons.

That was the problem with a talisman-name like her own. She who would own it must be operative in just that way, at all times. When someone of that capability should be born into the family, she could release the name of Amanda, which she had so far refused to every female child in the line. As she refused it to Betta for this child. And yet . . . and yet, it was not right to lock up the name forever. As each generation moved farther away from her own time, it and the happenings connected with it would then become more and more legendary, more and more unreal . . .

She put the matter for the thousandth time from her mind and turned back to buttoning up Fal Morgan. Passing down the long hall, she let her fingers trail for a second on its dark wainscotting. Almost, she could feel a living warmth in the wood, the heart of the house beating. But there was nothing more she could do to protect it now. In the days to come, it, too, must take its chances.

Fifteen minutes later, she was on her own skimmer, headed downslope toward Foralie Town. At her back was an overnight bag, considerably smaller than the one they had packed for Betta. Under her belt was a heavy energy pistol on full charge and in perfect order. In the long-arm boot of the skimmer was an ancient blunderbus of a pellet shotgun, its clean and decent barrel replaced minutes before by one that was rusted and old, but workable. As she reached the foot of the slope and started the rise to the ridge, her face was filled by the mountains and Fal Morgan moved for the moment into the back of her mind.

The skimmer hummed upslope, only a few feet above the ground. Out from under the spruce and pine, the highland sun was brilliant. The thin earth cover, broken by outcroppings of granite and quartz was brown, sparsely covered by tough green grasses. The air was cold and light, yet unwarmed by the sun. She felt it deep in her lungs when she breathed. *The wine of the morning*, her own mother had called air like this, nearly a century ago.

She mounted to the crest of the ridge and the mountains stood up around her on all sides, shoulder to shoulder like friendly giants, as she topped the ridge and headed down the further slope to Foralie, now visible, distant and small by the river bend, far below. The sky was brilliantly clear with the new day. Only a small, stray cloud, here and there, graced its perfection. The mountains stood, looking down. There were people here who were put off by their bare rock, their remote and icy summits, but she herself found them honest—secure, strong and holding, brothers to her soul.

A deep feeling moved in her, even after all these years. Even more than for the home she had raised, she had found in herself a love for this world. She loved it as she loved her children, her children's children and her three husbands—each different, each unmatchable in its own way.

She had loved it, not more, but as much as she had loved her first-born, Jimmy, all the days of his life. But why should she love the Dorsai so much? There had been mountains in Wales— fine mountains. But when she had first come here after her second husband's death, something about this land, this planet, had spoken to her and claimed her with a voice different from any she had ever heard before. She and it had strangely become joined, beyond separation. A strange, powerful, almost aching affection had come to bind her to it. Why should just a world, a place of ordinary water and land and wind and sky, be something to touch her so deeply?

But she was sliding swiftly now, down the gentler, longer curve of the slope that led to Foralie Town. She could see the brown track of the river road, now, following the snake of blue water that wound away to the east and out between a fold in the mountains, and in its other direction from the town, west and up until it disappeared in the rocky folds above, where its source lay in the water of permanent ice sheets at seventeen thousand feet. Small clumps of the native softwood trees moved and passed like shutters between her and sight of the town below as she descended. But at this hour she saw no other traffic about.

Twenty minutes later, she came to the road and the river below the town, and turned left, upstream toward the buildings that were now close.

She passed out from behind a clump of small softwoods and slid past the town manufactory and the town dump, which now separated her from the river and the wharf that let river traffic unload directly to the manufactory. The manufactory itself was silent and inactive, at this early hour. The early sun winked on the rubble of refuse, broken metal and discarded material of all kinds, in the little hollow below the exhaust vent of the manufactory's power unit.

The Dorsai was a poor world in terms of arable land and most natural resources; but it did supply petroleum products from the drowned shorelines of the many islands that took the place of continents on the watery planet. So crude oil had been the fuel chosen for the power generator at the manufactory, which had been imported at great cost from Earth. The tools driven by that generator were as sophisticated as any found on Earth, while the dump was as primitive as any that pioneer towns had ever had. Like her Fal Morgan and the communications equipment within its wall.

She stopped the skimmer and got off, walking a dozen feet or so back into the brush across the road from the dump. She took the heavy energy handgun from her belt and hung it low on the branch of a sapling, where the green leaves all about would hide it from anyone not standing within arm's reach of it. She made no further effort to protect it. The broad arrow stamped on its grip, mark of the ap Morgans, would identify it to anyone native to this world who might stumble across it.

She returned to the skimmer, just as a metal door in the side of the manufactory slid back with a rattle and a bang. Jhanis Bins came out, wheeling a dump carrier loaded with silvery drifts of fine metallic dust.

Amanda walked over to him as he wheeled the carrier to the

dump and tilted its contents onto the rubble inches below the exhaust vent. He jerked the carrier back on to the roadway and winked at Amanda. Age and illness had wasted him to a near skeleton, but there was still strength in his body, if little endurance. Above the old knife-scar laying all the way across his eyes held a sardonic humor.

"Nickel grindings?" asked Amanda, nodding at what Jhanis had just dumped.

"Right," he said. There was grim humor in his voice as well as his eyes. "You're up early."

"So are you," she said.

"Lots to be done." He offered a hand. "Amanda."

She took it.

"Jhanis."

He let go and grinned again.

"Well, back to work. Luck, Commander, ma'am."

He turned the carrier back toward the manufactory.

"News travels fast," she said.

"How else?" he replied, over his shoulder, and went inside. The metal door rolled on its tracks, slamming shut behind him.

Amanda remounted the skimmer and slide it on into town. As she came to a street of houses just off the main street, she saw Bhaktabahadur Rais, sweeping the path between the flowers in front of his house, holding the broom awkwardly but firmly in the clawed arthritic fingers of the one hand remaining to him. The empty sleeve of the other arm was pinned up neatly just below the shoulder joint. The small brown man smiled warmly as the skimmer settled to the ground when Amanda stopped its motors opposite him. He was no bigger than a twelve-year boy, but in spite of having almost as many years as Amanda, he moved as lightly as a child.

He carried the broom to the skimmer, leaned it against his shoulder and saluted. There was an impish sparkle about him.

"All right, Bhak," said Amanda. "I'm just doing what I'm

asked. Did the young ones and their Ancients get out of town?"

He sobered.

"Piers sent them out two days ago," he said. "You didn't know?"

Amanda shook her head.

"I've been busy with Betta. Why two days ago?"

"Evidence they were out before we heard any Earth troops were coming." He shifted his broom back into his hand. "If nothing had happened it would have been easy to have called them back after a few days. If you need me for anything, Amanda—"

"I'll ask, don't worry," she said. It would be easier at any time for Bhak to fight, than wait. The kukri in its curved sheath still lay on his mantelpiece. "I've got to get on to the town hall."

She lifted the skimmer on the thrust of its fans. Their humming was loud in the quiet street.

"Where's Betta?" Bhak raised his voice.

"Foralie."

He smiled again.

"Good. Any news of Cletus?"

She shook her head and set the skimmer off down the street. Turning on to the main street, past the last house around the corner, she checked suddenly and went back. A heavy-bodied girl with long brown hair and a round somewhat bunched-up face was sitting on her front step. Amanda stopped the skimmer, got out and went up to the steps. The girl looked up at her.

"Marte," said Amanda, "what are you doing here? Why didn't you go out with the other boys and girls?"

Marte's face took on a slightly sullen look.

"I'm staying with Grandma."

"But you wanted to go with one of the teams," said Amanda gently. "You told me so just last week."

Marte did not answer. She merely stared hard at the concrete of the walk between her feet. Amanda went up the steps past her and into the house.

"Berthe?" she called, as the door closed behind her.

"Amanda? I'm in the library." The voice that came back was deep enough to be male, but when Amanda followed it into a room off to her right, the old friend she found among the crowded bookshelves there, seated at a desk, writing on a sheet of paper, was a woman with even more years than herself.

"Hello, Amanda," Berthe Haugsrud said. "I'm just writing some instructions."

"Marte's still here," Amanda said.

Berthe pushed back in her chair and sighed.

"It's her choice. She wants to stay. I can't bring myself to force her to go if she doesn't want to."

"What have you told her?" Amanda heard the tone of her voice, sharper than she had intended.

"Nothing." Berthe looked at her. "You can't hide things from her, Amanda. She's as sensitive as . . . anyone. She picked it up—from the air, from the other young ones. Even if she doesn't understand details, she knows what's likely to happen."

"She's young," said Amanda. "What is she—not seventeen yet?"

"But she's got no one but me," said Berthe. Her eyes were black and direct under the wrinkled lids. "Without me, she'd have nobody. Oh, I know everyone in town would look after her, as long as they could. But it wouldn't be the same. Here, in this house, with just the two of us, she can forget she's different. She can pretend she's just as bright as anyone. With that gone . . ."

They looked at each other for a moment.

"Well, it's your decision," said Amanda, turning away.

"And hers, Amanda. And hers."

"Yes. All right. Goodby, Berthe."

"Goodby, Amanda. Good luck."

"The same to you," said Amanda, soberly. "The same to you."

She went out, touching Marte softly on the girl's bowed head as she went by. Marte did not stir or respond. Amanda remounted the skimmer and drove it around the further corner, down the main street to the square concrete box that was the town hall.

"Hello, Jenna," she said, stepping into the outer office. "I'm here to be sworn in."

Jenna Chalk looked up from her desk behind the counter that bisected the front office. She was a pleasant, rusty-haired woman, small and in her mid-sixties, looking like anything in the universe but the ex-mercenary she once had been.

"Good," she said. "Piers has been waiting. I'll bring the papers and we'll go back—"

"Still here?" said Amanda. "What's he doing waiting around?"

"He wanted to see you." Jenna slid her hands into the two wrist-crutches leaning against her desk, and levered herself to her feet. Leaning on one crutch, she picked up the folder before her on her desk and turned, leading the way down the corridor behind the counter that led toward the back of the building and the other offices there. Amanda let herself through the swinging gate in the counter and caught up.

"How is he?" Amanda asked.

"Worn out—a little easier since the sun came up," said Jenna, hobbling along. Her bones, over the years, had become so fragile that they shattered at a touch, and her legs had broken so many times now that it was almost a miracle that she could walk at all. "I think he'll let himself risk some medication, after he sees you take over."

"He didn't need to wait for me," said Amanda. "That was foolish."

"It's his way," said Jenna. "The habits of seventy years don't change."

She stopped and pushed open the door they had come up against. Together they entered and found the massive, ancient shape of Piers propped up in a highbacked chair behind the wide desk of his office.

"Piers," said Amanda. "You didn't need to wait. Go home."

"I want to witness your signing-in," said Piers. Talking was still difficult for him, but Amanda noted that his breathing did seem to have eased slightly with the sunrise, in common asthmatic fashion. "Just in case the troops they drop here decide to check records."

"All right," said Amanda.

Jenna was already switching on the recording camera eye in the wall. They went through the ritual of signing papers and administering an oath to Amanda that gave her the official title of Mayor of Foralie Town, which would be a cover for her secret rank of district commander.

"Now, for God's sake, go home!" said Amanda to Piers when they were done. "Take some of that medicine of yours and sleep."

"I will," said Piers. "Thank you for this, Amanda. And good luck. My skimmer's out back. Could you help me to it?"

Amanda put one hand under the heavy old man's right elbow and helped him to his feet. The years had taken much of her physical strength, but she still knew how to concentrate what she had at the point needed. She piloted Piers out the back way and helped him into the seat of his skimmer.

"Can you get down, and take care of yourself by yourself, when you get home?" she asked.

"No trouble," Piers grunted at her. He put the skimmer's power on and it lifted. He glanced at her once more.

"Amanda."

"Piers." She laid a hand for a second on his shoulder.

"It's a good world, Amanda."

"I know. I think so, too."

"Goodby."

"Goodby," said Amanda; and watched the skimmer take him away.

She turned back into the town hall.

"Marte's still here," she said to Jenna. "I guess, we'll just have to let her stay, if that's what she wants."

"It is," said Jenna.

"Are there any others still around I don't know about?"

"No, the young ones are all gone—and their Ancients."

"Have you got a map for me?"

Jenna reached into her folder and came out with a map of the country about Foralie Town, up into the mountains surrounding. Initials in red were scattered about it.

"Each team under the initials of its Ancient," Jenna said.

Amanda studied it.

"They're all out in position, now, then?"

Jenna nodded.

"And they're all armed?"

"With the best we had to give them," Jenna said. She shook her head. "I can't help it, Amanda. It's bad enough for us at our age, but to give our young people hand weapons and ask them to stop—"

"Do you know an alternative?" said Amanda.

Jenna shook her head again, silently.

"An aircraft's due to pick me up from the pad here in three-quarters of an hour," Amanda said. "I'll be checking the situation out around the town otherwise, between now and then. Just in case I don't get back here before we're hit, are you going to have any trouble convincing the invaders that I'm a Mayor and nothing more?"

Jenna snorted.

"I've been clerk in this town hall nine years—"

"All right," said Amanda. "I just wanted to put it in words. If the troops they send in won't billet in town, try and get them to camp close in on the upriver side."

"Of course," said Jenna. "I know. You don't have to tell me, Amanda. Anyway, there shouldn't be much trouble getting them there. It's a natural bivouac area."

"Yes. All right, then," Amanda said. "Take care of yourself, too, Jenna."

"We both better take care of ourselves," said Jenna. "Luck, Amanda."

Amanda went out.

She was on the airpad, waiting, when a light, four-place gravity aircraft dropped suddenly out of the blue above and touched down lightly on the pad. A door swung open. She went forward, carrying her single piece of luggage, and climbed in. The craft took off. Amanda found herself seated next to Geoff Harbor, district commander of North Point.

"You both know each other, don't you?" asked the pilot, looking back over his shoulder.

"For sixteen years," said Geoff. "Hello, Amanda."

"Geoff," she said. "They bringing you in for this meeting, too? Are you all ready, up there at North Point?"

"Yes. All set," he answered both questions, looking at her curiously above his narrow nose and wedge-shaped chin. He was only in his forties, but twenty years of living with the aftereffects of massive battle injuries had given his skin a waxy look. "I was expecting Eachan."

"Eachan was asked by Cletus Grahame to hold himself ready for something else," said Amanda. "Piers took charge and I just replaced him this morning."

"Asthma getting him?"

"The pressure of all this thing pushed him into an attack, I think," said Amanda. "Have you met this Arvid Johnson, or the other one—Bill Athyer?"

"I've met Arvid," said Geoff. "He's what Cletus Grahame's now calling a 'battle op'—a field tactician. Athyer's a strategist and they work as a team—but you must have heard all this."

"Yes," said Amanda. "But what I want to know is some first-hand opinions on what they're like."

"Arvid struck me as being damn capable," said Geoff. "If they work well together, then Bill Athyer can't be much less. And if Cletus put them in charge of the defense here . . . but you know Cletus, of course?"

"He's a neighbor," said Amanda. "I've met him a few times."

"And you've got doubts about him, too?"

"No," said Amanda. "But we're trying to make bricks without straw. A handful of adults with a force of half-grown teenagers to knock down an assault force of first-line troops. Miracles are going to have to be routine, and nothing's so good we shouldn't worry about whether it's good enough."

Geoff nodded.

A short while later they set down on the airpad outside the island government center at South Point. A lean, brown-skinned soldier wearing the collar tabs that showed Groupman's rank—one of the staff of a dozen or so combat-qualified Dorsai that Arvid Johnson and Bill Athyer had been allowed to keep for their defense of the planet—was waiting for them as they stepped out of the aircraft. He led them to a briefing room already half-full of district commanders from all over the island, then turned to the room at large.

"If you'll take seats—" he announced. The district commanders sorted themselves out on the folding chairs facing a platform at one end of the room. A minute or so later, two men came in and stepped up on the platform. One was Arvid Johnson. Seen at full-length he was a tower of a man, with blond hair that in this artificial light looked so pale it seemed almost invisible. The unconquerability of him radiated to the rest of them in the room. The man beside him was of about the same age, but small, with a heavy beak of a nose—what Amanda had learned to call a "Norman nose," when she had been a little girl. His eyes swept the room like gun muzzles.

The small man, Amanda thought, must be Bill Athyer, the strategist. At first glance, Bill might have appeared not only unimpressive, but sour—but Amanda's swift and experienced perceptions picked up something vibrant and brilliant in him. Literally, without loosing whatever painful and inhibiting self-consciousness and self-doubt he had been born with, he must somewhere have picked up the inner fire that now shone through his unremarkable exterior. He was all flame within— and that flame made him a strange contrast to the cool, almost remote competence of Arvid.

"Sorry to spring this on you," Arvid said, when both men were standing on the platform and facing the audience. "But it seems, after all, we can't wait for the district commanders who aren't here yet. We've just had word that whoever's navigating the invasion ships is either extremely lucky or very good. He's brought them out of their last phase shift right on top of the planet. They're in orbit overhead now and already dropping troops on our population centers."

He paused and looked around the room.

"The rest of the Dorsai's been notified, of course," he said. "Bill Athyer and myself, with the few line soldiers we've got, are going to have to start moving—and keep moving. Don't try to find us—we'll find you. Communication will be known-person to known-person. In short, if the word you get from us doesn't come through somebody you trust implicitly, disregard it."

"This is one of our strengths," said Bill Athyer, so swiftly, it was almost as if he interrupted. His voice was harsh, but crackled with something like high excitement. "Just as we know the terrain, we know each other. These two things let us dispense with a lot the invader has to have. But be warned—our advantages are going to be of most use only during the first few days. As they get to know us, they'll begin to be able to guess what we can do. Now, you've each submitted operational plans for the defense of your particular district within the general guidelines Arvid and I drew up. We've reviewed these plans, and by now you've all seen our recommendations for amendations and additions. If, in any case, there's more to be said, we'll get in touch with you as necessary. So you'd probably all better head back to your districts as quickly as possible. We've enough aircraft waiting to get you all back—hopefully before the invasion forces hit your districts. Get moving—is Amanda Morgan here?"

"Here!" called Amanda.

"Would you step up here, please?"

With Bill Athyer's last words, all the seated commanders had gotten to their feet, and she was hidden in the swarm of bodies. She pushed her way forward to the platform and looked up into the faces of the unusual pair standing there.

"I'm Amanda Morgan," she said.

"A word with you before you leave," said Bill. "Will you come along?"

He led the way out of the briefing room. Arvid and Amanda followed. They stepped into a small office and Arvid shut the door behind them on the noise in the hall, as the other commanders moved to their waiting aircraft.

"You took command of the Foralie District just this morning," Bill said. "Have you had any chance to look at the plans handed in by the man you replaced?"

"Piers von Linden checked with several of us when he drafted them," Amanda said. "But in any case, anyone in Foralie District over the age of nine knows how we're going to deal with whoever they send against us."

"All right," said Bill. Arvid nodded.

"You understand," Bill went on. "In Foralie, there, you'll be at the pick-point for whatever's going to happen. You can probably expect, if our information's right, to see Dow deCastries himself, as well as extra troops and a rank-heavier staff of enemy officers than any of the other districts. They'll be zeroing in on Foralie homestead."

The thought of Betta and the unborn child there was a sudden twinge in Amanda's chest.

"There's no one at Foralie but Melissa Grahame and Eachan Khan, right now," she said. "Nobody to speak of."

"There's going to be. Cletus will be on his way back as soon as the information we're invaded hits the Exotics—and I think you know the Exotics get news faster than anyone else. He may be on his way right now. Dow deCastries will be expecting this. So you can also expect your district to be one of the first, if not the first, hit. Odds are good that you, at least, aren't going to get home before the first troops touch down in your district. But we'll do our best for you. We've got our fastest aircraft holding for you now. Any last questions, or needs?"

Amanda looked at them both. Young men both of them.

"Not now," she said. "In any case, we know what we have to do."

"Good." It was Arvid speaking again. "You'd better get going, then."

The craft they were holding for her turned out to be a small, two-place high altitude gravity flyer, which rocketed to the ten-kilometer altitude, then back down toward Foralie on a flight path like the trajectory of a fired mortar shell. They were less than half an hour in the air. Nonetheless, as they plunged toward Foralie Town airpad, the com system inside the craft crackled.

"*Identify yourself. Identify yourself. This is Outpost Four-nine-three, Alliance-Coalition Expeditionary Force to the Dorsai. You are under our weapons. Identify yourself.*"

The pilot glanced briefly at Amanda and touched the transmit button on his control wheel.

"What'd you say?" he asked. "This is Mike Amery, on a taxi run from South Point just to bring the Foralie Town Mayor home. Who did you say you were?"

"Outpost Four-nine-three, Alliance-Coalition Expeditionary Force to the Dorsai. Identify the person you call the Mayor of Foralie Town."

"Amanda Morgan," said Amanda, clearly, to the com equipment, "of the household ap Morgan, Foralie District."

"Hold. Do not attempt to land until we check your identification. Repeat. Hold. Do not attempt to land until given permission."

The speaker was abruptly silent again. The pilot checked the landing pattern for the craft. They waited. After several minutes the order came to bring themselves in.

Two transport-pale, obviously Earth-native, privates in Coalition uniforms were covering the aircraft hatch with cone rifles, as Amanda preceded the pilot out on to the pad. A thin, serious-faced young Coalition lieutenant motioned the two of them to a staff car.

"Where do you think you're taking us?" Amanda demanded. "Who are you? What're you doing here, anyway?"

"It'll all be explained at your town hall, ma'am," said the lieutenant. "I'm sorry, but I'm not permitted to answer questions."

He got into the staff car with them and tapped the driver on the shoulder. They drove to town, through streets empty of any human figures not in uniforms. With the emptiness of the streets was a stillness. On the north edge of the town, on the upslope of the meadow which Amanda had mentioned to Jenna, Amanda could glimpse beehive-shaped cantonment-huts of bubble plastic being blown into existence in orderly rows—and from this area alone came a sound, distant but real, of voices and activities. Amanda felt the prevailing wind from the south on the back of her neck, and scented the faint odors of the fresh riverwater and the dump, carried by it, although the manufactory itself was silent.

The staff car reached the town hall. The pilot was left in the outer office, but Amanda was ushered in past guards to the office that had been Piers', and was now hers. There, a large map of the district had been imaged on one wall and several officers of grades between major and brigadier general were standing about in a discussion that seemed very close to argument. Only one person in the room wore civilian clothing, and this was a tall, slim man seated at Amanda's desk, tilted back in its chair, apparently absorbed in studying the map that was imaged.

He seemed oddly remote from the rest, isolated by position or authority and willing to concentrate on the map, leaving the officers to their talk. The expression on his face was thoughtful, abstract. Few men Amanda had met in her long life could have legitimately been called handsome, but this man was. His features were so regular as to approach unnaturalness. His dark hair was touched with gray only at the temples, and his high forehead seemed to shadow deep-set eyes, so dark that they appeared inherently unreadable. If it had not been for those eyes and an air of power that seemed to wrap him like light from some invisible source, he might have looked too pretty to be someone to reckon with. Watching him now, however, Amanda had few doubts as to his ability, or his identity.

"Sir—" began the lieutenant who had brought Amanda in; but the brigadier to whom he spoke, glancing up, interrupted him, speaking directly to Amanda.

"You're the Mayor, here? What were you doing away from the town? Where are all your townspeople—"

"General," Amanda spoke slowly. She did not have to invent the anger behind her words. "Don't ask me questions. I'll do the asking. Who're you? What made you think you could walk into this office without my permission? Where'd you come from? And what're you doing here, under arms, without getting authority, first—from the island authorities at South Point, and from us?"

"I think you understand all right—" began the General.

"I think I don't," said Amanda. "You're here illegally and I'm still waiting for an explanation—and an apology for pushing yourself into my office without leave."

The brigadier's mouth tightened, and the skin wrinkled and puffed around his eyes.

"Foralie District's been occupied by the Coalition-Alliance authorities," he said. "That's all you need to know. Now, I want some answers—"

"I'll need a lot more of an explanation than that," broke in Amanda. "Neither the Alliance nor the Coalition, nor any Coalition-Alliance troops have any right I know of to be below parking orbit. I want your authority for being here. I want to talk to your superior—and I want both those things now!"

"What kind of a farce do you think you're playing?" The words burst out of the brigadier. "You're under occupation—"

"General," said a voice from the desk, and every head in the room turned to the man who sat there. "Perhaps I ought to talk to the Mayor."

"Yes sir," muttered the brigadier. The skin around his eyes was still puffy, his face darkened now with blood-gorged capillaries. "Amanda Morgan, this is Dow deCastries, Supreme Commander of Alliance-Coalition forces."

"I didn't imagine he could be anyone else," said Amanda. She took a step that brought her to the outer edge of her desk, and looked across it at Dow.

"You're sitting in my chair," she said.

Dow rose easily to his feet and stepped back, gesturing to the now empty seat.

"Please . . ." he said.

"Just stay on your feet. That'll be good enough for now," said Amanda. She made no move to sit down herself. "You're responsible for this?"

"Yes, you could say I am." Dow looked at her thoughtfully. "General Amorine—" he spoke without looking away from Amanda—"the Mayor and I probably had better talk things over privately."

"Yes sir, if that's what you want."

"It is. It is, indeed." Now Dow did look at the brigadier, who stepped back.

"Of course, sir," Amorine turned on the lieutenant who had brought Amanda in. "You checked her for weapons, of course?"

"Sir . . . I—" The lieutenant was flustered. His stiff embarrassment pleaded that you did not expect a woman Amanda's age to go armed.

"I don't think we need worry about that, General." Dow's voice was still relaxed; but his eyes were steady on the brigadier.

"Of course, sir." Amorine herded his officers out. The door closed behind them, leaving Amanda and Dow standing face to face.

"You're sure you won't sit down?" asked Dow.

"This isn't a social occasion," said Amanda.

"No," said Dow. "Unfortunately, no it isn't. It's a serious situation, in which your whole planet has been placed under Alliance-Coalition control. Effectively, what you call the Dorsai no longer exists."

"Hardly," said Amanda.

"You have trouble believing that?" said Dow. "I assure you—"

"I've no intention of believing it, now, or later," Amanda said. "The Dorsai isn't this town. It isn't any number of towns just like it. It's not even the islands and the sea—it's the people."

"Exactly," said Dow, "and the people are now under control

of the Alliance-Coalition. You brought it on yourselves, you know. You've squandered your ordinary defensive force on a dozen other worlds, and you've got nothing but non-combatants left here. In short, you're helpless. But that's not my concern. I'm not interested in your planet, or your people, as people. It's just necessary we make sure they aren't led astray again by another dangerous madman like Cletus Grahame."

"Madman?" echoed Amanda, dryly.

Dow raised his eyebrows.

"Don't you think he was mad in thinking he could succeed against the two richest powers on the most powerful human world in existence?" He shook his head. "But there's not much point in our arguing politics, is there? All I want is your cooperation."

"Or else what?"

"I wasn't threatening," Dow said mildly.

"Of course you were," said Amanda. She held his eyes with her own for a long second. "Do you know your Shakespeare?"

"I did once."

"Near the end of *Macbeth*, when Macbeth himself hears a cry in the night that signals the death of Lady Macbeth," Amanda said, "he says *'there was a time my senses would have cool'd to hear a night-shriek . . .'* remember it? Well, that time passes for all of us, with the years. You'll probably have a few to go yet to find that out for yourself; but if and when you do you'll discover that eventually you outlive fear, just as you outlive a lot of other things. You can't bully me, you can't scare me—or anyone else in Foralie District with enough seniority to take my place."

It was his turn now to consider her for a long moment without speaking.

"All right," he said. "I'll believe you. My only interest, as I say, is in arresting Cletus Grahame and taking him back to Earth with me."

"You occupy a whole world just to arrest one man?" Amanda said.

"Please." He held up one long hand. "I thought we were going to talk straightforwardly with each other. I want Cletus. Is he on the Dorsai?"

"Not as far as I know."

"Then I'll go to his home and wait for him to come to me," said Dow. He glanced at the map. "That'll be Foralie—the homestead marked there near your own Fal Morgan?"

"That's right."

"Then I'll move up there, now. Meanwhile I want to know what the situation is here, clearly. Your able fighting men are all off planet. All right. But there's no one in this town who isn't crippled, sick, or over sixty. Where are all your healthy young women, your teenagers below military age, and anyone else who's effective?"

"Gone off out of town," said Amanda.

Dow's black eyes seemed to deepen.

"That hardly seems normal. I assume you had warnings of us, at least as soon as we were in orbit. I'd be very surprised if it wasn't news of our being in orbit that brought you back here in that aircraft just now. You wouldn't have messaged ahead, telling your children and able-bodied adults to scatter and hide?"

"No," said Amanda. "I didn't; and no one here gave any such direction."

"Then maybe you'll explain why they're all gone?"

"Do you want a few hundred reasons?" Amanda said. "It's the end of summer. The men are gone. This town is just a supply and government center. Who's young and wants to hang around here all day? The younger women living in town are up visiting at the various homesteads where they've got friends and there's some social life. The babies and younger children went with their mothers. The older children are off on team exercises."

"Team exercises?"

"Military team exercises," said Amanda, bluntly and with grim humor, watching him. "Otherwise known as 'creeping and crawling.' This is a world where the main occupation, once you're grown, is being a mercenary soldier. So this is our version of field trips. It's good exercise, the youngsters get some academic credit for it when they go back to school in a few weeks, and it's a chance for them to get away from adult supervision and move around on their own, camping out."

Dow frowned.

"No adult supervision?"

"Not a lot," said Amanda. "There's one adult—called an 'Ancient'—with each team, in case of emergencies; but in most cases the team makes its own decision about what kind of games it'll play with other teams in the same area, where it'll set up camp, and so forth."

"These children," Dow was still frowning, "are they armed?"

"With real weapons? They never have been."

"Are they likely to get any wild notions about doing something to our occupying forces—"

"Commander," said Amanda, "Dorsai children don't get wild notions about military operations. Not if they expect to stay Dorsai as adults."

"I see," said Dow. He smiled slowly at her. "All the same, I think we better get them and the ablebodied adults back into town here, where we can explain to them what the situation is and what they should or shouldn't do. Also, there's a few of your other people who're conspicuous by their absence. For example, where are your medical people?"

"We've got one physician and three meds, here in Foralie District," said Amanda. "They all ride circuit most of the time. You'll find them scattered out at various homesteads, right now."

"I see," said Dow again. "Well, I think you better call them in as well, along with any other adult from the homesteads who's physically able to come."

"No," said Amanda.

He looked at her. His eyebrows raised.

"Courage, Amanda Morgan," he said, "is one thing. Stupidity, something else."

"And nonsense is nonsense wherever you find it," said Amanda. "I told you, you couldn't bully me—or anyone else you'll find in this town. And you'll need one of us who's here to deal with the people of the district for you. I can bring the youngsters back in if necessary, and with them such adults from the homesteads who don't need to stay where they are. If the medical people are free to come in, I can get them, too. But in return, I'll want some things from you."

"I don't think you're in a position to bargain."

"Of course I am," said Amanda. "Let's not play games. It's much easier for you if you can get civilian cooperation—it's much faster. Difficulty with the populace means expense, when you're carrying the cost of enough troops to nail down a planet—even as sparsely settled a planet as this one. And you yourself said once you get Cletus you'll be taking off without another thought for the rest of us."

"That's not exactly what I said," Dow replied.

Amanda snorted.

"All right," he said, "what was it you had in mind?"

"First, get your troops out of our town unless you were thinking of billeting them in our homes, here?"

"I think you saw camp being set up just beyond the houses a street or two over."

"All right," Amanda said. "Then I want them to stay out of town unless they've got actual business here. When they do come in, they're to come in as visitors, remembering their manners. I don't want any of your officers, like that brigadier just now, trying to throw their weight around. Our people are to be free of any authority from yours, so we can get back to business as usual—and that includes putting the manufactory back into operation, immediately. I noticed you'd had the power shut off. Don't you realize we've got contracts to fill—contracts for manufactured items, so that we can trade with the rest of Dorsai for the fish, the grain and other things we have to have to live?"

"All right," said Dow. "I suppose we can agree to those things."

"I'm not finished," Amanda said, swiftly. "Also, you and all the rest of your forces are to stay put, in your encampment. I don't want you upsetting and alarming the district while I go find the teams and get people back here from the homesteads. It'll take me a week, anyway—"

"No," said Dow. "We'll be putting out patrols immediately; and I myself'll be leaving with an escort for Foralie homestead in a few hours."

"In that case—" Amanda was beginning, but this time it was Dow who cut her short.

"In that case—" his voice was level, "you'll force me to take the more difficult and time-consuming way with your people. I didn't bargain with you on any of the other things you asked for. I'm not bargaining now. Go ahead and take back your town, start up your manufactory, and round up only those you feel can come in safely. But our patrols go out as soon as we're ready to send them; and I leave, today, just as I said. Now, do we have an agreement?"

Amanda nodded, slowly.

"We have," she said. "All right, you'd better get those officers of yours back in here. I'm going to have to move to cover the district personally, even in a week. I'll go right now, but I want to hear that manufactory operating before I'm out of earshot of town. I suppose you've got Jhanis Bins closed up in his house, like everyone else."

"Whoever he is," said Dow. "He'd be under house quarantine, yes."

"All right, I'll call him," said Amanda. "But I want your General Amorine to send an officer to get him and take him safely to the manufactory, just in case some of your enlisted men may not have heard word of this agreement by that time."

"Fair enough," said Dow. He stepped to the desk and keyed the com system there. "General, will you and your staff step back into the office, here?"

"Yes, Mr. deCastries." The voice from the wall came promptly.

Twenty minutes later, Amanda reached the airpad in the same staff car that had brought her in from it. Under the eye of the two enlisted men on duty there, her skimmer stood waiting for her.

"Thanks," she said to the young lieutenant who had brought her in. She climbed out of the staff car, walked across the pad and got into her skimmer.

"Just a minute," called the lieutenant.

She looked back to see him standing up in his staff car. There was a shine to his forehead that told of perspiration.

"You've got a weapon there, ma'am," he said. "Just a minute. Soldier—you!" He pointed to one of the enlisted men guarding the pad. "Get that piece and bring it over to me."

"Lieutenant," said Amanda, "this is still a young planet and we had lawless people roaming around our mountains as recently as just a few years back. We all carry guns here."

"Sorry, ma'am. I have to examine it. Soldier . . ."

The enlisted man came over to the skimmer, pulled the pellet shotgun from the scabbard beside her and winked at her.

"Got to watch you dangerous outworlders," he said, under his breath. He glanced over the pellet gun, turned it up to squint down its barrel and chuckled, again under his breath.

He carried the weapon to the lieutenant, and said something

Amanda could not catch. The lieutenant also tilted the pellet gun up to look briefly into its barrel, then handed it back.

"Take it to her," he ordered. He lifted his head and called across to Amanda. "Be careful with it, ma'am."

"I will be," said Amanda.

She received the ancient weapon, powered up the skimmer and slid off through the fringe of trees around the pad.

She took her way toward the downriver side of town. As she went, the sudden throb of the engines in the manufactory erupted on her ear. She smiled, but she was suddenly conscious of the prevailing wind in her face. Sweating, she asked herself, at your age? She turned her scorn inward. Where was all that talk of yours to deCastries about having outlived fear?

She swung through town and around by the river road past the dump. The manufactory stood, noisily operating. There was no Coalition uniform in sight outside the building and the side looking in her direction was blank of windows. She stopped her skimmer long enough to walk back into the brush and retrieve the energy handgun she had hung on the tree. Then she remounted her skimmer and headed upslope, out of town.

Her mind was racing. Dow had intimated he would head out to Foralie homestead yet this afternoon. Which meant Amanda herself would have to go directly there to get there before him. She had hoped to come in there with evening, and perhaps even stay overnight to see how Betta was doing. Now it would have to be a case of getting in and out in an hour at most. And, almost more important, either before or after she reached there, she had to reach the team which was holding the territory through which Dow and his escort would pass.

Who was Ancient for that team? So many things had happened so far this day that she had to search her memory for a moment before it came up with the name of Ramon Dye. Good. Ramon was one of the best of the Ancients; and, aside from the fact that he was legless, strong as a bull.

Thinking deeply, she slid the skimmer along under maximum power. She was burning up a month's normal expenditure of energy in a few days, with her present spendthrift use of the vehicle; but there was a time for thriftiness and a time to spend. Of her two choices, it would have to be a decision to contact Ramon's team first, before going to Foralie. Ramon's team would have to send runners to the other teams, since even visual signals would be too risky, with the Coalition troops at Foralie town probably loaded with the latest in surveillance equipment. The more time she could give the runners, the better.

It was a stroke of bad luck, Dow's determination to send out patrols and go so immediately to Foralie himself. Bad on two counts. Patrols out meant some of the troops away from the immediate area of the town, at all times. It would have been much better to have them all concentrated there. Also, patrols out meant that sooner or later some of them would have to be taken care of by the teams—and that, while it would have to be faced if and when it came, was something not good to think about until then. There would be a heavy load thrown on the youngsters—not only to do what had to be done, but to do it with the coolheadedness and calculation of adults, without which they could not succeed, and their lives would be thrown away for nothing.

She reminded herself that up through medieval times, twelve- and fourteen-year-olds had been commonly found in armies. Ship's boys had been taken for granted in the navies of the eighteenth and nineteenth centuries. But these historical facts brought no comfort. The children who would be going up against Earth-made weapons here would be children she had known since their birth.

But she must not allow them to guess how she felt. Their faith in their seniors, well-placed or misplaced, was something they would need to hang on to as long as possible for their own sakes.

She came at last to a mountain meadow a full meter high with fall grass. The meadow was separated by just one ridge from Foralie homestead. Amanda turned her skimmer into the shade of a clump of native softwoods on the upslope edge of the meadow, below the ridge. On the relatively open ground beneath those trees she put the vehicle down and waited.

It was all of twenty minutes before her ear picked up—not exactly a sound that should not have been there, but a sound that was misplaced in the rhythm of natural noises surrounding her. She lifted her voice.

"All right!" she called. "I'm in a hurry. Come on in!"

Heads emerged above the grasstops, as close as half a dozen meters from her and as far out as halfway across the meadow. Figures stood up; tanned, slim figures in flexible shoes, twill slacks strapped tight at the ankle and long-sleeved, tight-wristed shirts, all of neutral color. One of the tallest, a girl about fifteen, put two fingers in her mouth and whistled.

A skimmer came over the ridge and hummed down toward Amanda until it sank to a stop beside her on the ground. The team members, ranging in age from eight years of age to sixteen, were already gathering around the two of them.

Amanda waited until they were all there, then nodded to the man on the other skimmer and looked around the closed arc of sun-browned faces, sun-bleached hair.

"The invaders are here, in Foralie town," she said. "Coalition first-line troops under a brigadier and staff, with Dow de-Castries."

The faces looked back at her in silence. Adults would have reacted with voice and feature. These looked at her with the same expressions they had shown before; but Amanda, knowing them all, could feel the impact of the news on them.

"Everyone's out?" the man on the other skimmer asked.

Amanda turned again to the Ancient. Perched on his skimmer the way he was, Ramon Dye might have forced a stranger to look twice before discovering that there were no legs below Ramon's hips. Strapped openly in the boot of his vehicle, behind him, were the two artificial legs he normally used in town; but out here, like the team members, he was stripped to essentials. His square, quiet face under its straight brown hair looked at her with concern.

"Everybody's out but those who're supposed to be there," said Amanda. "Except for Marte Haugsrud. She decided to stay with her grandmother."

Still, there was that utter silence from the circle of faces, although more than half a dozen of them had grown up within a few doors of Berthe. It was not that they did not feel, Amanda reminded herself; it was that by instinct, like small animals, they were dumb under the whiplash of fate.

"But we've other things to talk about," she said—and felt the emotion she had evoked in them with her news, relax under the pressure of her need for their attention. "DeCastries is taking an armed escort with him to Foralie to wait for Cletus; and he's also going to start sending out patrols, immediately."

She looked about at them all.

"I want you to get runners out to the nearest other teams— nothing but runners, mind you, those troops will be watching for any recordable signalling—and tell them to pass other runners on to spread the word. Until you get further word from me, all patrols are to be left alone; completely alone, no matter what they do. Watch them, learn everything you can about them, but stay out of sight. Pass that word on to the homesteads, as well as to the other teams."

She paused, looking around, waiting for questions. None came.

"I've made an agreement with deCastries that I'll bring all the teams and all the able adults in from the homesteads to

Foralie Town, to be told the rules of the occupation. I've told him it'll take me at least a week to round everyone up. So we've got that much time, anyway."

"What if Cletus doesn't come home in a week?" asked the girl who had whistled for Ramon.

"Cross that bridge when we come to it," said Amanda. "But I think he'll be here. Whether he is or not, though, we've still got the district to defend. Word or orders from Arvid Johnson and Bill Athyer is to be trusted only if it comes through someone you trust personally—pass that along to the other teams and homesteads, too. Now, I'm going on up to Foralie to brief them on Dow's coming. Any questions or comments, so far?"

"Betta hasn't had her baby yet," said a young voice.

"Thanks for telling me," said Amanda. She searched the circle with her eyes, but she was not able to identify the one who had just spoken. "Let's stick to business for the moment, though. I've got a special job for your best infiltrator—unless one of the neighboring teams has someone better than you have. Have they?"

Several voices told her immediately that the others had not.

"Who've you got, then?"

"Lexy—" the voices answered.

An almost white-haired twelve-year old girl was pushed forward, scowling a little. Amanda looked at her—Alexandra Andrea, from Tormai homestead. Lexy, like the others, was slim by right of youth; but a squareness of shoulder and a sturdiness of frame were already evident. For no particular reason, Amanda suddenly remembered how her own hair, as a child, had been so blond as to be almost white.

The memory of her young self brought another concern to mind. She looked searchingly at Lexy. What she knew about Lexy included indications of a certain amount of independence and a flair for risk-taking. Even now, obviously uncomfortable at being shoved forward this way, Lexy was still broadcasting an impression of truculence and self-acknowledged ability. Character traits, Amanda thought, remembering her own childhood again, that could lead to a disregard of orders and to chance-taking.

"I need someone to go in close to the cantonments the occupation troops have set up at Foralie Town," she said aloud. "Someone who can listen, pick up information, and get back with it safely. Note—I said safely."

She locked eyes with Lexy.

"Do you take chances, Lexy?" she asked. "Can I trust you to get in and get out without taking risks?"

There was a sudden outbreak of hoots and laughter from the team.

"Send Tim with her!"

Lexy flushed. A slight boy, Lexy's age or possibly as much as a year or two younger, was pushed forward. Beside Lexy, he looked like a feather beside a rock.

"Timothy Royce," Amanda said, looking at him. "How good are you, Tim?"

"He's good," said Lexy. "That is, he's better than the rest of these elephants."

"Lexy won't take chances with Tim along," said the girl who had whistled. Amanda was vainly searching her memory for this one's name. Sometimes when they shot up suddenly, she lost track of who they were; and the tall girl was already effectively an adult.

"How about it, Tim?" Amanda asked the boy. Tim hesitated.

"He gets scared," a very young voice volunteered.

"No, he doesn't!" Lexy turned on the crowd. "He's cautious, that's all."

"No," said Tim, unexpectedly. "I do get scared. But with Lexy I can do anything you want."

He looked openly at Amanda.

Amanda looked at Ramon.

"I can't add anything," he said, shaking his head. "Lexy's good, and Tim's pretty good—and they work well together."

His eyes settled on Amanda's suddenly.

"But do you have to have someone from one of the teams?"

"Who else is there?"

"One of the older ones, then . . ." his voice trailed off. Amanda looked back at the faces ringed about.

"Team?" she asked.

There was a moment of almost awkward silence and then the girl who had whistled—Fran Abo, the name suddenly leaped into existence in Amanda's mind—spoke.

"Any of us'll go," she said. "But Lexy's the best."

"That's it, then," said Amanda. She put the power to her skimmer, and lifted it off the ground. "Lexy, Tim—I'll meet you after dark tonight, just behind the closest ridge above the meadow north of town. All of you—be careful. Don't let the patrols see you. And get those runners out as fast as you can."

She left them, the circle parted and she hummed up and over the ridge. Foralie homestead lay on a small level space a couple of hundred meters beyond her, on a rise that commanded a clear view in all directions as far as the town itself.

Behind the long, low, timbered house there, she could see the oversize jungle gym that Cletus had caused to be constructed before his marriage to Melissa. It had been a device to help him build himself back physically after his knee operation, and there was no reason for it to evoke any particular feeling in her. But now, seeing its spidery and intricate structure casting its shadow on the roof of the long, plain-timbered house beneath it, she suddenly felt—almost as if she touched the cold metal of it with her hand—the hard, intricately woven realities that would be bringing Dow and Cletus to their final meeting beneath that shadow.

She slid the skimmer down to the house. Melissa, with the tall, gray-mustached figure of Eachan Khan beside her, came out of the front door; and they were standing, waiting for her as she brought the skimmer up to them and dropped it to the ground.

"Betta's fine, Amanda," said Melissa. "Still waiting. What's going on?"

"The occupation troops are down in Foralie Town."

"We know," said Eachan Khan, in his brief, clipped British-accented speech. "Watched them drop in, using the scope on our roof."

"They've got Dow deCastries with them," Amanda said, getting down from the skimmer. "He's after Cletus, of course. He plans to come up here to Foralie right away. He may be right behind me—"

The ground under her feet seemed to rock suddenly. She found Eachan Khan holding her up.

"Amanda!" said Melissa, supporting her on the other side. "When did you eat last?"

"I don't rememb . . ." she found the words had difficulty coming out. Her knees trembled, and she felt close to fainting. A distant fury filled her. This was the aspect of her age that she resented most deeply. Rested and nourished, she could face down a deCastries. But let any unusual time pass without food and rest and she became just another frail oldster.

Her next awareness was of being propped up on a couch in the Foralie sitting room, with a pillow behind her back. Melissa was helping her sip hot, sweet tea with the fiery taste of Dorsai whisky in it. Her head began to clear. By the time the cup was empty, there was a plate of neatly cut sandwiches made by Eachan Khan, on the coffee table beside her. She had forgotten how delicious sandwiches could be.

"What's the rest of the news, then?" Eachan asked, when she had eaten. "What happened to you today?"

She told them.

". . . I must admit, Eachan," she said, as she wound up, looking at the stiff-backed ex-general, "I wasn't too pleased about Cletus asking you to sit on your hands, here—and even less pleased with you for agreeing. But I think I understand it better since I met deCastries, himself. If any one of them's likely to suspect how we might defend ourselves, it'll be him, not those officers with him. And the one thing that'll go farther to keep him from starting to suspect anything, will be finding you puttering around here, keeping house right under his nose while he waits for Cletus. He knows your military reputation."

"Wouldn't call it puttering," said Eachan. "But you're right. Cletus does have a tendency to think around corners."

"Let alone the fact—" Amanda held his eye with her own, "that if something happens to me, you'll still be here to take over."

"Depends on circumstance."

"Nonetheless," said Amanda.

"Of course," Eachan said. "Naturally, if I'm free—and needed—I'd be available."

"Yes—" Amanda broke off suddenly. "But I've got to get out of here!"

She sat up abruptly on the couch, swinging her feet to the floor.

"DeCastries and his escort are probably right behind me. I'd just planned to drop by and brief you—"

She got to her feet, but lightheadedness took her again at the sudden movement and she sat down again, unexpectedly.

"Amanda, be sensible. You can't go anywhere until you've rested for a few hours," said Melissa.

"I tell you, deCastries—"

"Said he'd be up here yet today? I don't think so," said Eachan.

She turned, almost to glare at him.

"What makes you so sure?"

"Because he's no soldier. Bright of course—Lord yes, he's

bright. But he's not a soldier. That means he's in the hands of those officers of his. Earth-bound types, still thinking in terms of large-unit movements. They might get patrols out, late in the day, but they won't get Dow off."

"What if he simply orders them to get him off?" Amanda demanded.

"They'll promise him, of course, but somehow everybody won't be together, the vehicles won't be set, with everything harnessed up and ready to go, before sundown; and even Dow'll see the sense of not striking out into unfamiliar territory with night coming on."

"How can you be that sure?" Melissa asked her father.

"That brigadier's got his own future to think of. Better to have Dow down on him over not getting off on time than to send someone like Dow out and turn out to be the officer who lost him. The day's more than half over. If Dow and his escort get bogged down for even a few hours by some hair-brained locals fighting back—that's the way the brigadier'll be thinking—they could end up being caught out, unable to move, in the open at dark. Strange country, nighttime, and an open perimeter's chancy with a prize political package like Dow. No, no—he won't be here until tomorrow at the earliest."

Eachan cocked an eye on Amanda.

"But if you like," he said, "Melly and I'll take turns on the scope up on the roof. If anything moves out of Foralie we can see it; and by the time we're sure it's definitely moving in this direction, we'll still have two hours before it can get here at column speed. Take a nap, Amanda. We'll call you if you need to move."

Amanda gave in. Stretched out on a large bed in one of the wide, airy bedrooms of Foralie, the curtains drawn against the sunlight, she fell into a heavy sleep from which she roused, it seemed, within minutes. But, blinking the numbness of slumber from her vision, she saw that beyond the closed curtains there was now darkness, and the room around her was plunged in a deeper gloom than that of curtained daylight.

"What time is it?" she called out, throwing back the single blanket with which she had been covered. No answer came. She sat on the edge of the bed, summoning herself to awareness, then got to her feet and let herself out into the hall, where artificial lights were lit.

"What time is it?" she repeated, coming into the kitchen. Both Eachan Khan and Melissa looked up from the table there, and Melissa got to her feet.

"Two hours after sunset," she answered. But Amanda had already focused on the wall clock across the room, which displayed the figure 21:10. "Sit down, Amanda. You'll want some tea."

"No," said Amanda. "I was supposed to meet two of the youngsters from the local team just above Foralie Town before sunset—"

"We know," said Eachan. "We had a runner from that team when they saw you didn't leave here. The two you're talking about went, and Ramon went with them. He knows what you want in the way of information."

"I've got to get down there, to meet them."

"Amanda—sit!" said Melissa from the kitchen unit. "Tea'll be ready for you in a second."

"I don't want any tea," said Amanda.

"Of course you do," said Melissa.

Of course, she did. It was another of her weaknesses of age. She could almost taste the tea in anticipation, and her sleep-heavy body yearned for the internal warmth that would help it wake up. She sat down at the table opposite Eachan.

"Fine watch you keep," she said to him.

"Nothing came from Foralie Town in this direction before

sunset," he said. "They're not starting out with Dow in the dark, as I said. So I came back inside, of course. You could stay the night, if you want."

"No, I've got to get there; and I've a lot of ground to cover—" she broke off as Melissa placed a steaming cup before her. "Thanks, Melissa."

"But why don't you stay the night?" Melissa asked, sitting back down at the table, herself. "Betta's already asleep, but you could see her in the morning—"

"No. I've got to go."

Melissa looked at her father.

"Dad?"

"No," said Eachan, "I think perhaps she's right. But will you come back for the night, afterwards, Amanda?"

"No. I don't know where I'll light."

"If you change your mind," said Melissa. "Just come to the door and ring. But I don't have to tell you that."

Amanda left Foralie homestead half an hour later. The moon, which had been full the night before, was just past full, but scattered clouds cut down the brilliant night illumination she had woken to early that morning. She made good time on the skimmer toward the ridge where she had arranged to meet Lexy and Tim. A hundred meters or so behind it, she found Ramon's skimmer, empty, and dropped her own beside it. No one was in sight. Ramon could not walk upright without his prosthetics, but he could creep-and-crawl as well as any other adult. Amanda was about to work her way up to the ridge, herself, staying low so that any instruments in the cantonment below would not discover her, when a rustle in the shadows warned her of people returning. A few moments later, Ramon, Lexy and Tim all rose from the ground at arms-length from her.

"Sorry," said Amanda, "I should have been here earlier."

"It wasn't necessary," said Ramon. His powerful arms hauled

him up on to his own skimmer and he sat upright there.

"Yes, it was," said Amanda. "You didn't let these two go in until things were shut down—"

"They didn't go down until full dark," said Ramon. "Not until the last of the patrols had left and the manufactory was shut down. The townsfolk were all inside and the troops were all in their cantonment area. Tim stayed beyond the perimeter there and Lexy went up to just outside the outer line of huts, close enough so she could hear them talking, but with plenty of room to leave if she needed to."

Amanda transferred her attention to Lexy.

"What were they talking about?"

"Usual stuff," said Lexy. "The officers, and the equipment, how long they'd be here before they'd ship off again. Regular soldier off-duty talk."

"Did they talk about when deCastries would be leaving for Foralie?"

"First thing in the morning. They'd stalled about getting ready so he couldn't get off today," said Lexy. "They don't think much of those of our people who're left here; but still none of them I heard talking felt much like starting out with night coming on."

"What do they think of their officers?"

"Nothing great. There's a major they all like, but he's not on the general's staff. They really draw the line between enlisted and officer."

"Now, you see for yourself, how that is with Old World troops," commented Ramon to the two young ones.

"It's a pretty stupid way for them to be, all the same, out here in hostile territory," said Lexy. "But they've got a good pool of light vehicles. No armor. Vehicle-mounted light weapons and handweapons. I could have brought you one of their cone rifles—"

"Oh, could you?"

There was a little silence in the darkness, that betrayed Lexy's recognition of her slip of the tongue.

"The whole line of huts was empty. All I did was look in the last one in the line," said Lexy. "These Earth troops—they're worse than elephants. I could have gone in and picked their pockets and got out without their knowing about it."

The moon came from behind a cloud that had been hiding it, and in the pale light Amanda could see Lexy's face . . . tight-mouthed.

"Ramon," said Amanda. "Didn't you tell them specifically not to go into the cantonment area?"

"I'm sorry, Amanda," said Ramon. "I didn't. Not specifically."

"Lexy, under no conditions, now or in the future, do you or anyone else go beyond the outer line of huts." Exasperation took her suddenly. "And don't bristle! If you have to resent an order, try to keep the fact to yourself."

Another cloud obscured the moon. Lexy's voice came unexpectedly out of the darkness.

"Why?"

"For one reason, because an hour later you may wish you had. For another, learn never to challenge automatically. No one's that good. Sit on your impulse until you know everything that's likely to happen when you act on it."

Silence out of the darkness. Amanda wondered whether Lexy was filing the information she had just received in the automatic discard file of her mind, or—just possibly—tucking it away for future reference.

"Now," Amanda said. "Anything else? Any talk of plans? Any talk of Cletus being on the way here?"

"No," said Lexy. "They did talk about relocation, after Cletus is tried back on earth. And they even said something about changing the name of our planet. That doesn't make sense."

Amanda breathed deeply.

"I'm afraid it does," she said.

"Amanda?" It was Ramon asking. "I'm not sure I follow you."

"DeCastries tried to give me the impression that this whole invasion was designed only to arrest Cletus and take him back to Earth to stand trial. I let him think I went along with that. But of course they've got a lot more than that in mind, with the expense they've gone to here. What they really want to do is bury the Dorsai—and everyone in uniform wearing that name. Obviously what they've planned is to use Cletus' trial as a means to whip up Earth sentiment. Then, with a lot of public backing, they can raise the funds they'd need to spread our people out on other worlds, and give this world a new name and a new breed of settler."

Amanda thought for a moment, while the moon continued to play peekaboo with the clouds.

"I'd better go back to Foralie tonight, after all," she said. "Eachan will have to know this, in case he has to take over. Lexy—anything else?"

"Nothing, Amanda, really. Just off-duty talk."

"All right. I want this listening to go on—only at night, though, after the town and the cantonment's settled down. Ramon, will you stay on top of that? And also make sure neither Lexy or anyone else goes into the cantonment area. Past the outer line sentries is all right, if they know what they're doing. But not, repeat not, into the cantonment streets; and never into the huts, themselves. There's more here than just your personal risk to think about, Lexy. It's our whole world, and all of us, at stake."

Silence.

"All right, Amanda, we'll take care of it," said Ramon. "And we'll get word to you if anything breaks."

"The necessary thing," said Amanda, "is letting me know if there's any word of Cletus getting here. All right. I'll see you tomorrow evening."

She lifted her skimmer on minimum power to keep the sound

of its motors down and swung away in the direction of Foralie. Had she been unfairly hard on Lexy? The thought walked through her mind, unbidden. It was not an unfamiliar thought, nowadays; Betta, Melissa, Lexy . . . a number of them evoked it in her. How far was she justified in expecting them to react as she, herself, would? To what extent was it right of her to expect a future Amanda to react as she would?

No easy answer came to her. On the surface it was unfair. She was unfair. On the other hand there were the inescapable facts. There was the need that someone, at least, react as she did; and the reality that what she required of them was what experience had taught her life required of them all. Forcibly, she put the unresolved problem once again from her; and made herself concentrate on the imperatives of the moment.

Mid-morning of the following day she lay in tall grass, high on a slope, and watched the train that was the escort of Dow deCastries, winding up through the folds of the hills toward Foralie. Around her were the members of Ramon's team. The train consisted of what looked like two platoons of enlisted men, under four officers and Dow himself, all sliding over the ground in air-cushion staff cars, with a heavy energy rifle deck-mounted on every car but the one occupied by Dow. The vehicles moved with the slowness of prudence, and there were flankers out on skimmers, as well as two skimmers at point.

"They'll reach Foralie in another twenty minutes or so," Ramon said in Amanda's ear. "What should we do about getting runners in to Eachan and Melissa?"

"Don't send anyone in," Amanda said. "Eachan will come out to you if he wants contact. Or maybe Melissa will. At any rate, let them set it up. Tell them I've gone to look at the situation generally throughout the district. I need to know what the other patrols sent out are doing."

She waited until the train had disappeared over the ridge toward which it had been heading, then slid back down into the small slope behind her, where her skimmer was hidden.

"You're fully powered?" asked Ramon, looking at the skimmer.

"Enough for non-stop operation for a week," said Amanda. "I'll see you this evening, down above the cantonments."

The rest of that day she was continually on the move. It was quite true, as she had told Dow, that it would take her a week to fully cover the homesteads of the Foralie district. But it was not necessary for what she had in mind to call at every homestead, since she had a communications network involving the teams and the people in the homesteads themselves. She needed only to call at those few homesteads where she needed personal contact with such as the medical personnel or such as Tosca Aras, invalided home and anchored in his house by age and a broken leg. Tosca, like Eachan, was an experienced tactical mind to whom the rest could turn in case anything took her out of action.

In any case, her main interest was in the patrols Dow had sent out. Eachan, watching with the scope on the Foralie rooftop, reported two had gone out the evening before and this morning another four had taken their way on different bearings, out into the district. In each case they seemed to be following a route taking them to the homesteads of a certain area of the district on a swing that looked like it might last twenty-four hours, and at the end of that time bring them back to Foralie Town and their cantonments.

"They don't seem to be out looking for trouble," Myron Lee, Ancient for one of the other teams, said to Amanda as they stood behind a thicket, looking down on one of these patrols. Myron, lean to the point of emaciation and in his fifties, was hardly any stronger physically than Amanda, but radiated an impression of unconquerable energy.

"On the other hand," he went on, "they didn't exactly come out unprepared for trouble, either."

The patrol they were watching, like all the others Amanda had checked, was a single platoon under a single commissioned officer. But its personnel were mounted on staff cars and skimmers, as the escort for Dow had been; and in this case, every staff car mounted a heavy energy rifle, while the soldiers riding both these and the skimmers carried both issue cone rifles and sidearms.

"What have they been doing when they reach a homestead?" Amanda asked.

"They take the names and images of the people there, and take images of the homestead, itself. Census work, of a sort," said Myron.

Amanda nodded. She had been given the same description whenever she had asked that question about other patrols. It was not unusual military procedure to gather data about the people and structures in any area where a force was stationed— but the method of the particular survey seemed to imply that the people and buildings surveyed might need to be taken by force, at some time in the future.

By evening she was back behind the ridge overlooking the meadow holding the cantonments. Lexy, Tim and Ramon had been waiting when she got there. They waited a little longer together, while twilight gave way to full dark. The clouds were even thicker this night; and when the last of the light was gone, they could not see each other, even at arm's length.

"Go ahead," Amanda said to the two youngsters. "Remember, word of Cletus, or any word of what's going on in town, are the two things I particularly want to hear about."

There was the faintest rustle of grass, and she was alone with Ramon.

A little over an hour later the two team members were back.

"Nothing much of anything going on," Lexy reported. "Nothing about Cletus coming. They'd like some news themselves about how long they're going to be here and what they're going to do. All they say about the town is that it's dull—they say what good would it be if they could go in there? There's no place to drink or anything else going on. They did mention an old lady being sick, but they didn't say which one."

"Berthe Haugsrud's the oldest," said Ramon's voice, out of the darkness.

Amanda snorted.

"At their age," she said, "anyone over thirty's old. All right, we'll meet here again and try it once more, tomorrow night."

She left them and swung east to the Aras homestead, to see if the district's single physician, Dr. Ekram Bayar, who had been reported there, had heard word of any sick in Foralie Town.

"He's gone over to Foralie," Tosca Aras' diminutive daughter Mene told her. "Melissa phoned to say Betta was going into labor. Ekram said he didn't expect any problems, but since he was closer than any of the medicians, he went himself. But he's coming back here. Do you want to phone over there, now?"

Amanda hesitated.

"No," she said. "I've been staying off the air so that whatever listening devices they've got down in the troop area can't be sure where I am. I'll wait a bit, here. Then, if he doesn't come soon, you could call for me and find out how things are."

"You could take a nap," said Mene.

"No, I've got things to do," said Amanda.

But she ended up taking the nap. Mene called her awake on the intercom at what turned out to be an hour and a half later and she came into the Aras sitting room to find Tosca himself up, with his broken leg stretched out stiffly on a couch, and both Mene and Ekram with the old general, having a drink before dinner.

"Amanda!" Mene said. "It was a false alarm about Betta."

"Uh!" Amanda found a chair and dropped heavily into it. "The pains stopped?"

"Before Ekram even got there."

Amanda looked across at the physician, a sturdy, brown-faced thirty-year-old with a shock of black, straight hair and a bushy black mustache.

"She probably doesn't need me at all," he said to Amanda. "I'd guess, she'll have one of the easier births on record around here."

"You don't know that," said Amanda.

"Of course I don't know," he said. "I'm just giving you my opinion."

It came to her suddenly that Ekram, like herself and everyone else, had been under an emotional strain since the invasion became a reality. She became aware suddenly of Tosca stretching out an arm in her direction.

"Here," he said. He was handing her a glass.

"What's this? Whisky? Tosca, I can't—"

"You aren't going any place else tonight," he said. "Drink it."

She became conscious that the others all had glasses in their hands.

"And then you can have dinner," said Tosca.

"All right." She took the glass and sipped cautiously at it. Tosca had diluted the pure liquor with enough water so that it was the sort of mixture she could drink with some comfort. She looked over the rim of her glass at the physician.

"Ekram," she said. "I had some of the team children listening outside the cantonments. They reported the soldiers had been mentioning someone—an old woman, they said—was sick in town . . ."

"Berthe." He put down his glass on the coffee table before the couch on which he sat, his face a little grim. "I should go down there."

"No," said Tosca.

"If you get in there, they may not let you out again," said Amanda. "They'll have military medicians."

"Yes. A full physician, a lieutenant colonel—there for the

benefit of this Dow deCastries more than for the troops, I'd
guess," Ekram said. "I've talked to him over ihe air. Something
of a political appointee, I gather. Primarily a surgeon, but he
seemed capable, and he said he'd take care of anyone in town
when I wasn't there. He expects me to be available most of the
time, of course."

"You told him you had your hands full up here?"

"Oh, yes," Ekram gnawed a corner of his mustache, something he almost never did. "I explained that with most of the
mothers of young children being upcountry right now . . ."

He trailed off.

"He accepted that, all right?"

"Accepted it? Of course, he accepted it. I hope you realize,
Amanda—" he stared hard at her, "it's not my job to ignore
people."

"Who're you ignoring? Berthe? You told the truth. You've got
patients needing you all over the place, up here."

"Yes," he said.

But his gaze was stony. It went off from her to the unlit, wide
stone fireplace across the room and he drank sparsely from his
glass, in silence.

"I'll have dinner in a few minutes," said Mene, leaving them.

With dinner, Ekram became more cheerful. But by the following morning the phone began to ring with calls from other
households relaying word they had heard in conversations with
people still in the town, of now two or three of the older people
there being ill.

"Not one of the ones who're supposed to be sick has called,"
Mene pointed out over the breakfast table.

"They wouldn't, of course. Noble—yes, damned noble, all of
them! All of you. I'm sorry, Amanda—" he turned stiffly to
Amanda. "I'm going down."

"All right," said Amanda.

She had meant to leave early; but she had stayed around,

fearing just such a decision from Ekram. They would have to give, somewhat. But they need not give everything.

"All right," she said again. "But not until this evening. Not until things are shut down for the day."

"No," said Ekram, "I'm going now."

"Ekram," said Amanda. "Your duty's to everyone. Not just to those in the town. The real need for you may be yet to come. You're our only physician; and we may get to the equivalent of a field hospital before this is over."

"She's right," said Tosca.

"Damn it!" said Ekram. He got up from the table, slammed his chair back into place and walked out of the kitchen. "Damn this whole business!"

"It's hard for him, of course," said Tosca. "But you needn't worry, Amanda."

"All right," Amanda said. "Then I'll get going."

She spent the day out, tracking the patrols. In one or two instances, where the sweep was the third through a particular area, the majority at least of the soldiers in a particular patrol were those who had been out on the first sweep—not only to her eyes but the sharper observation of the team members who had been keeping track of those patrols. She watched them closely through a scope, trying to see if there were any signs of sloppiness or inattention evident in the way they performed their duties; but she was unable to convince herself that she saw any.

She had a good deal more success, with the help of the team members, in identifying patterns of behavior that were developing in the way they made their sweeps. Their approach to a household, for one thing, had already begun to settle down to a routine. That was the best clue that the line soldiers had yet given as to their opinion of the dangerousness of those still left in Foralie district. She found herself wondering, briefly, how all the other districts in all the other cantons of the Dorsai were doing with their defense plans and their particular invaders. Some would have more success against the Earth troops, some less—that was inherent in the situation and the nature of things.

She sent word to the households themselves, to the effect that the people in them should, whenever possible, do and say the same thing each time to the patrols so as to build a tendency in these contacts toward custom and predictability.

It was mid-afternoon when a runner caught up with her with a message that had been passed by phone from homestead to homestead for her, in the guise of neighborly gossip.

"Ekram's left the upcountry for town," she was told. The runner, a fourteen-year-old boy, looked at her with the steady blue eyes of the D'Aurois family.

"Why?" Amanda asked. "Did whoever passed the message say why?"

"He was at the Kiempii homestead, and he got a call from the military doctor," the boy said. "The other doctor's worried about identifying whatever's making people sick in town."

"That's all?"

"That's all Reiko Kiempii passed on, Amanda."

"Thank you," she said.

"—Except that she said the latest word is nothing's happened yet with Betta."

"Thanks," Amanda said.

She was a good hour of skimmer time from the Kiempii homestead, it was not far out of her way on her route to meet Lexy, Tim and Ramon once more above the meadow with the cantonment huts. She left her checking on the patrols and headed out.

When she got there, Reiko was outside, waiting, having heard Amanda was on the way. Amanda slid the skimmer to a stop and spoke eye to eye with the calm, tall, bronzed young woman, without getting out of the vehicle.

"The call went to Foralie first," Reiko told her, "but Ekram had already moved on. It finally caught up with him here, about two hours ago."

"Then you don't know what the military doctor told him?"

"No, all Ekram said was that he had to go down, that he couldn't leave it all to the other physician any longer."

Amanda looked at Maru Kiempii's daughter, bleakly.

"Three hours until dark," she said, "before I can get Lexy down to listen to what they're talking about in the cantonments."

"Eat something. Rest," said Reiko.

"I suppose so."

Amanda had never had less appetite or felt less like resting in her life. She could feel events building inexorably toward an explosion, as she had felt the long rollers of the Atlantic surf on the harsh seashores of her childhood, building to the one great wave that would drive spray clear to the high rocks on which she stood watching.

But it was common sense to eat and rest, with much of a long day behind her and possibly a long night ahead.

Just before sunset, she left the Kiempii homestead, and arrived at the meeting place with Lexy, Tim and Ramon before full dark. The clouds were thick and the air that wrapped about them was heavy with the dampness of the impending weather.

"Ekram still in town?" she asked.

"Yes," said Ramon. "We've got a cordon circling the whole area, outside the picket line the troops set up around the town. No one's gone out all day but patrols. If Ekram does, we'll get word as soon as he leaves."

"Good," said Amanda. "Lexy, Tim, be especially careful. A night like this their sentries could be in a mood to shoot first and check afterward. And the same thing applies to the soldiers in the cantonment area, itself."

"All right," said Lexy.

They went off. Amanda did not offer to talk and Ramon did not intrude questions upon her. Now that she was at the scene of some actual action, she began to feel the fatigue of the day in spite of her rest up at Kiempii homestead and she dozed lightly, sitting on her skimmer.

She roused at a touch on her arm.

"They're coming back," said Ramon's voice in her ear.

She sat up creakily and tried to blink the heavy obscurity out of her eyes. But it was almost solid around her. The only thing visible was the line of the ridge-crest, some thirty meters off, silhouetted against the lighter dark of the clouded sky. The clouds were low enough to reflect a faint glow from the lights of the town and the cantonment beyond the ridge.

"Amanda, we heard about Cletus—" It was Lexy's voice, right at her feet. She could see nothing of either youngster.

"What did you hear?"

"Well, not about Cletus, himself, exactly—" put in Tim.

"Practically, it was," said Lexy. "They've got word from one of their transport ships, in orbit. It picked up the signal of a ship phasing in, just outside our star system. They think it's Cletus, coming. If it is, they figure that in a couple more short phase shifts he ought to be in orbit here; and he ought to be down on the ground at Foralie by early afternoon tomorrow, at the latest."

"Did they say anything about their transport trying to arrest him in orbit?"

"No," said Lexy.

"Did you expect them to, Amanda?" Ramon asked.

"No," said Amanda. "He's coming of his own choice and it makes sense to let anything you want all the way into a trap before you close it. Once in orbit, his ship wouldn't be able to get away without being destroyed by theirs, anyway. But mainly, they want to be sure to get him alive for that full-dress trial back on Earth, so they can arrange to have the rest of us deported and scattered. So, I wouldn't expect they'll do anything until he's grounded. But there's always orders that get misunderstood, and commanders who jump the gun."

"Tomorrow afternoon," said Ramon musingly. "That's it, then."

"That's it," said Amanda, grimly. "Lexy, what else?"

"Lots of people in town are sick—" Lexy's voice was unaccustomedly hushed, as if it had finally come home to her what this situation was leading to, with people she had known all her life. "Both docs are working."

"How about the soldiers? Any of them sick?"

"Yes, lots," said Lexy. "Just this evening, a whole long line of them went on sick call."

Amanda turned in the direction of Ramon's flitter and spoke to the invisible Ancient.

"Ramon," she said, "how many hours was Ekram in town in the afternoon?"

"Not more than two."

"We've got to get him out of there . . ." But her tone of voice betrayed the fact that she was talking to herself, rather than to the other three, and no one answered.

"I want to know the minute he leaves," Amanda said. "If he isn't gone by morning . . . I'd better stay here tonight."

"If you want to move back beyond the next ridge, we can build you a shelter," Ramon said. "We can build it up over you and your skimmer and you can tap heat off the skimmer. That way you can be comfortable and maybe get some sleep."

Amanda nodded, then remembered they could not see her.

"Fine," she said.

In the shelter, with the back of her driver's seat laid down and the other seat cushions arranged to make a bed, Amanda lay, thinking. Around her, a circle of cut and stripped saplings had been driven into the earth and bent together at their tops to make the frame. This sagged gently over her head under the weight of the leafy branches that interwove the saplings, the

whole crowned and made waterproof by the groundsheet from
the boot of the skimmer. In spite of the soft warmth filling the
shelter from the skimmer, humming on minimum power to its
heater unit, the slight weight of her old down jacket, spread
over her shoulders, gave her comfort.

She felt a strange sadness and a loneliness. Present concerns
slid off and were lost in personal memories. She found herself
thinking once more of Jimmy, her first-born—Betta's grandfather—whom she had loved more than any of her other children,
though none of them had known it. Jimmy, whom she had cared
for as a child and adult through his own long life and all three
of her own marriages, and brought at last with her here to the
Dorsai to found a household. He was the Morgan from which
all the ap Morgans since were named. He had lived sixty-four
years, and ended up a good man and a good father—but all
those years she had held the reins tight upon him.

Not his fault. As a six-month-old baby he had been taken—
legally stolen from her by her in-laws, after his father's death,
and the less than a short year and a half of their marriage. She
had fought for four years after that, fought literally and legally,
until finally she had worn her father and mother-in-law down
to where they were forced to allow her visiting rights; and then
she had stolen him back. Stolen him, and fled off-Earth to the
technologically-oriented new world of Newton; where she had
married again, to give the boy a home and a father.

But when she had finally got him back, he had been damaged.
Lying now, in this shelter in the Dorsai hills, she once more
faced the fact that it might not have been her in-laws' handling
of him alone that had been to blame. It could also have been
something genetic in their ancestry and her first husband's. But
whatever it was, she had lost a healthy, happy baby, and re-
gained a boy given to sudden near-psychotic outbursts of fury
and ill-judgment.

But she had encompassed him, guarded him, controlled

him—keeping him always with her and bringing him through the years to a successful life and a quiet death. Only—at a great cost. For she had never been free in all that time to let him know how much she loved him. Her sternness, her unyielding authority, had made up the emotional control he had required, to supply the lack of it in himself. When he lay dying at last, in the large bedroom at Fal Morgan, she had been torn by the desire to let him know how she had always felt. But a knowledge of the selfishness of that desire had sustained her in silence. To put into plain words the role she had played for him all his life would have taken away what pride he had in the way he had lived, would have underlined the fact that without her he could never have stood alone.

So, she had let him go, playing her part to the last. At the very end he had tried to say something to her. He had almost spoken; and a small corner of her mind clung to the thought that there, in the last moment, he had been about to say that he understood, that he had always understood, that he knew how she loved him.

Now, lying in the darkness of the shelter, Amanda came as close as she ever had in her existence to crying out against whatever ruled the universe. Why had life always called upon her to be its disciplinarian, its executioner, as it was doing now, once again? Cheek pressed against the tough, smooth-worn leather of the skimmer seat cushion, she heard the answer in her own mind—it had been because she would do the job and others would not.

She was too old for tears. She drifted off into sleep without feeling the tide that took her out, dry-eyed.

A rustle, the sound of the branches that completely enclosed her being pulled apart, brought her instantly awake. Gray daylight was leaking through the cover below the cap of the groundsheet, and there was the sound of a gust of rain pattering on the groundsheet itself.

"Amanda—" said Ramon, and crawled into the shelter. There was barely room for him to squat beside her skimmer. His face, under a rain-slick poncho hood, was on a level with hers.

She sat up.

"What time is it?"

"Nine hundred hours. It's been daylight for nearly three hours. Ekram's still in town. I thought you'd want to be wakened."

"Thanks."

"General Amorine—that brigadier in charge of the troops— has been phoning around the homesteads. He wants you to come in and talk to him."

"He can do without. Twelve hours," said Amanda. "How could I sleep twelve hours? Are the patrols out? How did the troops on them look?"

"A little sloppy in execution. Everybody hunched up—under rain gear of course. But they didn't look too happy, even aside from that. Some were coughing, the team members said."

"Any news from the homesteads—any news they've heard over the air, by phone from town?"

"Ekram and the military doc were up all night."

"We've got to get him out of there—" Amanda checked and corrected herself. "I've got to get him out of there. What's the weather for the rest of today?"

"Should clear by noon. Then cold, windy and bright."

"By the time Cletus is here we should have good visibility?"

"We should, Amanda."

"Good. Pass the word. I want those patrols observed all the time. Let me know if you can how many of the men on them become unusually sick or fall out. Also check with Dow's escort troops, at Foralie. Chances are they're all in good shape, but it won't hurt to check. The minute Cletus arrives, pass the word for the four other teams closest to Foralie to move in and join

up with your team. Ring Foralie completely with the teams—
what's that?"

Ramon had just put a thermos jug and a small metal box on
the deck of her skimmer.

"Tea and some food," Ramon said. "Mene sent it down."

"I'm not an invalid."

"No, Amanda," said Ramon, backing out through the opening in the shelter on hands and knees. Outside, he pushed the
branches back into place to seal the gap he had made entering.
Left to herself, her mind busy, Amanda drank the hot tea and
ate the equally hot stew and biscuits she found in the metal box.

Finished, she got up and donned her own poncho, dismantled
the shelter and put the ground cloth back in the boot, the seat-
back and cushions back in place. Outside, the wind was gusty
and cold with occasional rain. She lifted her skimmer and slid
it down to just behind the lower ridge, where the ponchoed
figure of Ramon sat keeping a scope trained on the cantonments
and town below.

"I've changed my mind about that commanding officer,"
Amanda told him. "I'm going in to talk to him—"

A gust of wind and rain made her duck her head.

"Amanda?" Ramon was frowning up at her. "What if he won't
let you out again?"

"He'll let me out," Amanda said. "But whether I'm there or
not, the teams are going to have to be ready to move against
deCastries' escort and any troops they send up with Cletus, once
Cletus gets to Foralie. Just as they want Cletus for trial, we want
Cletus safe, and we want deCastries, alive—not dead. If most
of the rest of the districts can't break loose, we want something
to bargain with. Cletus'll know how to use deCastries that way."

"If you're not available and it's time to attack them should
we wait for Eachan to come out and take over?"

"If you think there's time—you and the other Ancients. If

time looks tight, don't hesitate. Move on your own."

Ramon nodded.

"I'll look for you here when I come back," Amanda said; and lifted her skimmer, sending it off at a slant behind the cover of the ridge to approach the town from the opposite, down-river side.

She paused behind a ridge to drop off her handgun and then came up along the river road, where she encountered a Coalition-Alliance sentry in rain gear, about five hundred meters out behind the manufactory. She slid the skimmer directly at him and set it down, half a dozen meters from him. He held his cone rifle pointed toward her as he walked forward.

"Take that gun out of its scabbard, ma'am," he said, nodding at the pellet shotgun, "and hand it to me—butt first."

She obeyed.

He cradled the cone rifle in one arm to take the heavy weight of the pellet gun in both hands. He glanced at it, held it up to look into the barrel and handed it back to her.

"Not much of a weapon, ma'am."

"No?" Amanda, holding the recovered pellet gun in the crook of her arm, swung it around horizontally until its muzzle rested against the deckface between her and the boot, the deckface over the power unit. "What if I decide to pull the trigger right now?"

She saw his face go still, caught between shock and disbelief.

"You hadn't thought of that?" said Amanda. "The pellets from this weapon could add enough kinetic energy to the power core to blow it, you, and me to bits. In your motor pool I could set off a chain explosion that would wipe out your full complement of vehicles. Had you thought of that?"

He stared at her for a second longer, then his face moved.

"Maybe you think you better impound it, after all?"

"No," he said. "I don't think you're about to commit suicide, even if they'd let you anywhere near our motor pool—which they wouldn't."

He coughed.

"What's your business in town, ma'am?"

"I'm Amanda Morgan, Mayor of Foralie Town," she said. "That's my business. And for that matter, your commanding officer's been asking to see me. Don't tell me they didn't give you an image and a description of me?"

"Yes," he said. He coughed, lowered his rifle, and wiped from his cheek some of the moisture that had just dripped from the edge of his rain hood. He had a narrow young face. "You're to go right on in."

"Then why all this nonsense?"

He sighed a little.

"Orders, ma'am."

"Orders!" She peered at him. "You don't look too well."

He shook his head.

"Nothing important, ma'am. Go ahead."

She lifted her skimmer and went past him. The sound of the manufactory grew on her ear. She checked the skimmer outside its sliding door, strongly tempted to look inside and see if Jhanis Bins was still at the control board. The town dump looked even less attractive than it ordinarily did. The nickel grindings, which Jhanis had dumped just the other day, had slumped into pockets and hollows; and now these were partially filled with liquid that in the gray day looked to have a yellowish tinge. She changed her mind about going in to look for Jhanis. Time was too tight. She touched the power control bar of the skimmer and headed on into town, feeling the wet, rain-studded wind on the back of her neck.

The streets were empty. Down a side alley she saw a skimmer that she recognized as Ekram's, behind the house of Marie Du-reaux. She went on, past the city hall and up to the edge of the cantonment area, where she was again stopped, this time by two sentries.

"Your general wanted to see me," she said, after identifying herself.

"If you'll wait a moment while we call in, ma'am . . ."

A moment later she was waved through, and directed to a command building four times the size of the ordinary cantonment huts but made of the same blown bubble plastic. Once again she was checked by sentries and ushered, eventually, into an office with a desk, a chair behind it, and one less-comfortable chair facing it.

"If you'll have a seat here," said the sergeant who brought her in.

She sat and waited for some ten or twelve minutes. At the end of that time a major came in, carrying a folder of record films, which he slipped into the desk viewer, punching up the first one.

"Amanda Morgan?" he said, looking over the top of the viewer, which was slanted toward him, hiding the film on display from her.

"That's right," said Amanda. "And you're Major—"

He hesitated.

"Major Suel," he said, after a second. "Now, about the situation here in town and in the district—"

"Just a second, Major," said Amanda. "I came in to talk to your general."

"He's busy. You can talk to me. Now, about the situation—"

He broke off. Amanda was already on her feet.

"You can tell the general for me, I don't have time to waste. Next time he can come and find me." Amanda turned toward the door.

"Just a minute—" There was the sound of the major's chair being pushed back. "Just a minute!"

"No minute," said Amanda. "I was asked to come in to talk to General Amorine. If he's not available, I've got my hands too full to wait around."

She reached for the door. It did not open for her.

"Major," she said, looking back over her shoulder. "Open this door."

"Come back and sit down," he said, standing behind his desk. "You can leave after we've talked. This is a military base—"

He broke off again. Amanda had come back to the desk and walked around it to face the desk viewer. She reached out to press his phone button and the document on the viewer vanished to show the face of the sergeant who had let her in here.

"Sir—" the sergeant broke off in confusion, seeing Amanda.

"Sergeant," said Amanda, "connect me with Dow deCastries up at Foralie Homestead, right away."

"Cancel that!" said the major. "Sergeant—cancel that."

He punched off the phone and walked to the door.

"Wait!" he threw back at Amanda and went out.

Amanda followed him to the door, but found it once more locked to her touch. She went back and sat down. Less than five minutes later, the major returned with the skin taut over the bones of his face. He avoided looking directly at her.

"This way, if you will," he said, holding the door open.

"Thank you, Major."

He brought her to a much larger and more comfortable office, with a tall window against which the rain was now gusting. There was a desk in the corner, but the rest of the furniture consisted of padded armchairs, with the single exception of a single armless straight-backed chair facing the desk. It was to this chair that Amanda was taken.

General Amorine, who had been standing by the window, walked over to seat himself behind the desk.

"I've been trying to get you for two days," he said.

Amanda, who had not been invited to sit, did so anyway.

"And I've been busy doing what I promised Dow deCastries I'd do," she said. "I still am busy at it; and this trip in to see you is delaying it."

He looked at her, stiff-faced. A cough took him by the throat.

"Mayor," he said, when the coughing was done, "you're in no position to push."

"General, I'm not pushing. You are."

"I'm the commanding officer of the occupying force here," he said. "It's my job to push when things don't work."

He checked, as if he would cough again, but did not. A gust of rain rattled loudly against the office window in the brief moment of silence between them. Amanda waited.

"I say," he repeated. "It's my job to push when things don't work."

"I heard you," said Amanda.

"They aren't working now," Amorine said. "They aren't working to my satisfaction. We want a census of this district and all pertinent data—and we want it without delay."

"There hasn't been any delay."

"I think there has."

Amanda sat, looking at him.

"I know there has," Amorine said.

"For example?"

He looked at her for several seconds without saying anything.

"How long," he said, "has it been since you were on Earth?"

"Seventy years, or so," said Amanda.

"I thought so," he said. "I thought it had been something like that long. Out here on the new worlds, you've forgotten just what Earth is like. Here, on wild planets with lots of space and only handfuls of people even in your largest population centers, you tend to forget."

"The mess and the overcrowding?"

"The people and the power!" he said, harshly—and broke off to cough again. He wiped his mouth. "When you think in terms of people out here, you think in terms of thousands—millions, at the most, when your thinking is planet-wide. But on Earth those same figures are billions. *You* think in terms of a few hundred thousand square meters of floor space given over to manufactory on a whole world. On Earth that space is measured in trillions of square meters. You talk about using a few million kilowatt-hours of energy. Do you know how kilowatt-hours of used energy are counted on Earth?"

"So?" said Amanda.

"So—" he coughed. "So, you forget the differences. Out here for seventy years, you forget what Earth really is, in terms of wealth and strength; and you begin to think that you can stand up against her. The greatest power the human race has ever known looms over you like a giant, and you let yourself dream that you can fight that power."

"Come into our backyard, and we can fight you," said Amanda. "You're a long way from your millions and trillions now, General."

"No," said Amorine, and he said it without coughing or heat. "That's your self-delusion, only. Earth's got the power to wipe clean every other humanly-settled world whenever she wants to. When Earth moves, when she decides to move, you'll vanish. And you people here are indeed going to vanish. I want you to believe that—for your own sake. You'll save yourself and all the people you love a great deal of pain if you can wake yourself up to an understanding of what the facts are."

He looked at her. She looked back.

"You are all, all of you, already gone," he said. "For the moment you've still got your town, and your homes, and your own name, but all those things are going to go. You, yourself, in your old age, are going to be moved to another place, a place you don't know, to die among strangers—all this because you've been foolish enough to forget what Earth is."

He paused. She still sat, not speaking.

"There's no reprieve, no choice," he said. "What I'm telling you is for your own information only. Our politicians haven't announced it yet—but the Dorsai is already a forgotten world; and everyone on it will soon be scattered individually through all the other inhabited planets. For you—for you, only—I've got an offer, that for you, only, will make things easier."

He waited, but still she gave him no assistance.

"You're being non-cooperative with our occupation, here," he said. "I don't care what Mr. deCastries' opinion of you is. I *know*. I know non-cooperation when I run into it. I'd be a failure in my job if I didn't. Bear in mind, we don't have to have your cooperation, but it'd help. It'd save paperwork, effort, and explanations. So, what I'm offering you is, cooperate and I'll promise this much for you: I'll ensure that whatever few years you have left can be lived here, on your own world. You'll have to watch everyone else being shipped off; but you, at least, won't have to end your days among strangers."

He paused.

"But you'll have to take me up on this, now," he said, "or you'll lose the chance, for good. Say yes now, and follow through, or the chance is gone. Well?"

"General," said Amanda. "I've listened to you. Now, you listen to me. You're the one who's dreaming. It's not us who are already dead and gone—it's you and your men. You're already defeated. You just don't know it."

"Mrs. Morgan," said Amorine, heavily, "you're a fool. There's no way you can defeat Earth."

"Yes," said Amanda, bleakly. Another gust of rain came and rattled against the window, like the tapping of the fingers of dead children. "Believe me, there is."

He stood up.

"All right," he said. "I tried. We'll do it our own way from now on. You can go."

Amanda also stood up.

"One thing, however," she said. "I want to see Cletus when he lands."

"Cletus? Cletus Grahame, you mean?" Amorine stared at her. "What makes you think he's going to land?"

"Don't talk nonsense, General," Amanda said. "You know as well as I do, he's due in by early afternoon."

"Who told you that?"

"Everyone knows it."

He stared at her.

"Damn!" he said, softly. "No, you cannot see Grahame—now or in the future."

"I've got to be able to report to the local people that he's well and agreeable to being in your custody," Amanda said. "Or do you want the district to rise in arms spontaneously?"

He stared at her balefully. Staring, he began to cough again. When the fit was over, he nodded.

"He'll be down in a little over an hour. Shall we find you a place to wait?"

"If it's an hour, I'll go into town and get some things done. Will you leave word at the airpad, so I can get past your soldiers?"

He nodded.

"Ask for Lieutenant Estrange," he said.

She went out.

Back in town she found Ekram's skimmer still parked behind the house of Marie Dureaux. She parked her own skimmer beside his and let herself in the back door, into the kitchen.

Ekram was there, washing his hands at the sink. He looked back over his shoulder at her at the sound of her entrance.

"Marie?" Amanda said.

"Marie's dead." He turned his head back to the sink.

"And you're still in town here."

He finished washing and turned to face her, wiping his hands on a dishtowel.

"Berthe Haugsrud's dead," he said. "Bhaktabahadur Rais is dead. Fifteen more are dying. Young Marte Haugsrud's sick. There's five dead soldiers in the cantonments, thirty more dying, and most of the rest sick."

"So you leave," she said.

"Leave? How can I leave? Their medical officer knows something's going on. There's just nothing he can do about it. He'd be an absolute, incompetent idiot not to know that something's going on, particularly since they've been getting word from other occupation units—not from many, but even a few's enough—where the same thing's happening. All that's kept them blind this long is the fact it started hitting our people first. If I run, now—"

He broke off. His face was lean with weariness, stubbled with beard.

"You go," Amanda said. "That's an order."

"To hell with orders!"

"Cletus is due to land in an hour. You've had three hours in town here during daylight hours. In three more hours we're going to have open war. Get out of here, get up in those hills and get ready to handle casualties."

"The kids . . ." he swayed a little on his feet. "Kids, kids and guns . . ."

"Will you go?"

"Yes." His voice was dull. He walked stiff-jointedly past her and out the back door. Following him, she saw him climb, still with the awkwardness of exhaustion, on to his skimmer, lift it, and head it out of town.

Amanda went back inside to see whether there was anything she could do for the remains of Marie. But there was nothing. She left and went to the Haugsrud house to see if Marte could be brought to leave town with her, now that Berthe was dead. But the doors were locked and Marte refused to answer, though Amanda could see her through a window, sitting on the living room couch. Amanda tried several ways to force her way in, but time began to grow short. She turned away at last and headed toward the airpad.

She was almost late getting there. By the time she had made contact with Lieutenant Estrange and been allowed to the airpad itself, a shuttleboat, bearing the inlaid sunburst emblem of the Exotics, was landed; and Cletus was stepping out on to the pad. A line of vehicles and an armed escort was already waiting for him.

He was wearing a sidearm, which was taken from him, and led toward the second of the waiting staff cars.

"I've got to speak to him!" said Amanda fiercely to Estrange. "Weren't you given orders I was to be able to speak to him?"

"Yes. Please—wait a minute. Wait here."

The lieutenant went forward and spoke to the colonel in charge of operation. After some little discussion, Estrange came back and got Amanda.

"If you'll come with me?" He brought her to Cletus, who was already seated in the staff car.

"Amanda!" Cletus looked out over the edge of the open window of the staff car. "Is everyone all right?"

"Fine," said Amanda. "I've taken over the post of Mayor from Piers."

"Good," said Cletus, urgently. His cheerful, lean face was a little thinner than when she had seen it last, marked a little more deeply by lines of tension. "I'm glad it's you. Will you tell everyone they must keep calm about all this? I don't want anyone getting excited and trying to do things. These occupying soldiers have behaved themselves, haven't they?"

"Oh, yes," said Amanda.

"Good. I thought they would. I'll leave matters in your hands, then. They're taking me up to Grahame House—to Foralie, I mean. Apparently Dow deCastries is already there, and I'm sure once I've had a talk with him we can straighten this all out. So all anyone needs to do is just sit tight for a day or two, and everything will be all right. Will you see the district understands that?"

Out of the corners of her eyes, Amanda could see the almost-wondering contempt growing on the faces of the Coalition officers and men within hearing.

"I'll take care of it, Cletus."

"I know you will. Oh—how's Betta?"

"You'll see her when you get to Foralie," said Amanda. "She's due to have her baby any time now."

"Good. Good. Tell her I saw her brother David just a few days ago, and he's fine. No—wait. I'll tell her myself, since I'll be seeing her first. Talk to you shortly, Amanda."

"Yes, Cletus," said Amanda, stepping back from the staff car. The convoy got underway and moved out.

"And that's this military genius of theirs?" she heard one of the enlisted men muttering to another, as she turned away with Estrange.

Five minutes later she was on her way past the cordon of sentries enclosing the town and twelve minutes after that, having stopped only to pick up her handgun, she stood beside Ramon, on his skimmer, looking down from cover on the more slowly-moving convoy as it headed in the direction of Foralie.

"We'll want all the available teams in position around Foralie before they get there," she said. "But when they show up, let them through. We'll want them together with Dow's escort before we hit them."

"Most of the men in that convoy are sick," said Ramon.

"Yes," said Amanda, half to herself. "But the ones who've been up there with Dow all this time are going to be perfectly healthy. And they're front line troops. If we don't get them in the first few minutes, it's going to cost us—"

"Maybe not," said Ramon. She looked at him.

"What do you mean?"

"I mean, not all of them up at Foralie may be healthy. I haven't had a chance to tell you, but a patrol came up there early today and stayed for about two hours. They could have switched personnel."

"Not likely." Amanda frowned. "Dow's their prize package. Why would they take the healthy troops they have protecting him; and replace them with cripples, just to get more of their able-bodied down at town?"

"They might have some reason we don't know about."

Amanda shook her head.

"I don't believe it," she said. "In fact, until I hear positively there's been a change of personnel at Foralie, I won't believe it. We'll continue on the assumption that they're all healthy troops there, and the only advantage we've got is surprise. Cletus, bless him, helped us with that, as much as he could. He did everything possible to put their suspicions to sleep, down in town."

"He did?" Ramon stared at her. "What did he do?"

Amanda told him what Cletus had said from the staff car in the hearing of the convoy soldiery.

Ramon's face lengthened.

"But maybe he really means we shouldn't do anything until . . ."

His voice failed at the look on Amanda's face.

"If a rooster came up to you and quacked," said Amanda, sharply, "would you ignore everything else about it and decide it'd turned into a drake?"

She looked down her nose at him.

"Even if Cletus actually had taken leave of his senses, that wouldn't alter the situation for the rest of us," she went on. "We've still got to move in, rescue him, and take deCastries when he reaches Foralie. It's the one chance we've got. But don't concern yourself. Cletus understands the situation here."

She nodded at his skimmer.

"You go get the teams into position. I'll meet you at Foralie before they get there."

"Where will you be?" Ramon's face was a little pale.

"I'll be rounding up any adults capable of using a weapon—except the women with young children—from the near households. We'll need anyone we can get."

"What about the other patrols?"

"Once we've got deCastries, we shouldn't have much opposition from anyone else who's been in Foralie Town. A good half of them are going to be dead in a week, and the most of the rest won't be able to fight."

"They might fight even if they're not able."

"How can they—" she broke off, suddenly seeing the white look in Ramon's eyes. "What's the matter with you? You ought to know that."

"I didn't want to know," he said. "I didn't listen when they told us."

"Didn't you?" said Amanda. "Well, you'd better listen now, then. Carbon monoxide passed over finely divided nickel gives you a liquid—nickel carbonyl, a volatile liquid that melts at twenty-five degrees Centigrade, boils at forty-three degrees and evaporates at normal temperatures in the open. One part in a million of the vapors can be enough to cause allergic dermatitis and edema of the lungs—irreversible."

His face was stark. His mouth was open as if he gasped for breath.

"I don't mind the fighting," he said thickly. "It's just the thought of the casualties among the soldiers. If this war could only be stopped now, before it starts—"

"Casualties? Before it starts?" Amanda held him with her eyes. "What do you think Berthe Haugsrud and Bhak and the others have been, down in town?"

He did not answer.

"They're our casualties," she said, "already counted. The war you want to stop before it starts has been going for two days. Did you think it would all take place with no cost at all?"

"No, I . . ." He swayed a little on his skimmer; and the momentary gust of anger he had sparked off in her went away, suddenly.

"I know," she said. "There's things that aren't easy for you to think about. They aren't easy for Ekram. Nor for me, nor any of us. Nor was it easy for those people like Berthe, down in town, who stayed there knowing what was going to happen to them. But do you have any more of it to face or live with than they did, or the boys and girls on the teams will?"

"No," he said. "But I can't help how I feel."

"No," she said. "No, of course you can't. Well, do the best you can, anyway."

He nodded numbly and reached for the power bar of his skimmer. Amanda watched him lift and slide away, gazing for a long moment after his powerful shoulders, now slumped and weary. Then she mounted her own skimmer and took off at right angles to his route.

She reproached herself as she went for her outburst at him. He was still young and had not seen what people could do to people. He had no basis of experience from which to imagine what would happen to the dispossessed Dorsai, once they were scattered thinly among the populations of other worlds who had been educated to hold them in detestation and contempt. He could still cling to a hope that somehow an enemy could be defeated with such cleverness that neither friend nor foe need suffer.

She headed toward the Aras homestead to pick up Mene as the first of her adult recruits for the assault on Foralie.

Travelling there, even now, she found the mountains calming her spirit. The rain had stopped, according to the weather predictions Ramon had given her, and a swift wind was tearing the cloud cover to tatters. The sky revealed was a high, hard blue; and the air, on the wings of a stiff breeze, piping with an invigorating cold. She felt stilled, concentrated and clear of mind.

For better or for worse, they must now move into literal combat. There was no more time to worry whether individuals would measure up. There was no time for her cataloguing of the sort of lacks she had noted in Betta, in Melissa, in Lexy and just now in Ramon. Time had run out on her decision of the name for Betta's child. She must leave word with others before the actual assault on Foralie about what she had decided, one way or another, so that it could be passed on to Betta if necessary. She would do just that. At the last minute she would make up her mind one way or another and have done with it.

Forty-five minutes later, she swung her skimmer up to a fold in the hills, carrying Mene Aras with her. As she topped the rise and dipped down into the hidden hollow beyond, she saw the Ancients of five teams; together with a dozen or so of the team-leaders and runners from them, plus Jer Walker leaning on both his walking canes and a half-rifle slung from the shoulders of his frail, ninety-year-old body. Nine of the other women, most of them young, and also armed, were already there. But most welcome of all was the sight of the unusual pair that were Arvid Johnson and Bill Athyer, together with six of the Dorsai they had been able to keep as staff.

Amanda slid her skimmer to a stop, stepped off and walked up to Arvid and Bill.

"I was deliberately not counting on you," she said, "but I thought you might be here in time."

"You'll need us," Arvid said. "I take it you knew Swahili is now the officer in charge of Dow's escort? He came up here with replacement troops this morning."

"Swahili?" Amanda frowned, for the name had a familiar ring but eluded identification.

"He's a major with these Coalition troops. But he was one of Eachan Khan's officers," Bill said. "A Dorsai, once—but probably you've never seen him. He didn't like any place where there wasn't any fighting going on. He joined Eachan some years ago, out on one of the off-world contracts and I think he was only here in this district briefly, once or twice. The only things that usually brought him to the Dorsai were short visits to that new training center Cletus set up on the other side of the world."

"The point is, though, he literally is a Dorsai—or was. One of the best we ever had, in fact," said Arvid. "If anyone's going to catch us moving in before we want them to know we're there, it'll be him."

There was a strange, almost sad note in Arvid's voice.

"Yes, he's that good. Some of us—" Bill glanced for a second at his tall companion, "thought he was the best we had . . . in some ways. At any rate, that's why Arvid and I'll be going in first, to secure the house."

"You're taking charge, then?" said Amanda.

"We hadn't planned on it," said Arvid, swiftly. "It's your district, of course—"

"Don't talk nonsense," said Amanda. "We'll do anything that works. Did you really think I'd be prickly about my authority?"

"No," said Arvid. "Not really. But I do think you should stay in overall command. These local people know you, not me. Just give us four minutes head start, then move in. We'll take the house. That'll leave you the compound area that was set up for the escort troops, beside the house. How do you plan to handle that?"

"The only way we can," said Amanda. "I'll go in first, with the other adults behind me—openly, like neighbors coming to visit—and I'll try to disarm the sentry. Then we'll take the compound—we adults—building by building. Meanwhile, the teams will lie out around with their weapons and try to see that,

whatever happens, none of the soldiers break out of the compound area after we've gone in."

Arvid nodded.

"All right," he said. "Our word is that all the men in the
convoy bringing Cletus in are pretty well sick and useless. I
suppose you also have the information that most of the well
troops that came up originally with Dow were traded back to
town for the personnel of the patrol that came up with Swahili—a patrol of sick that were sent up this morning? That
should make things easier for you."

Amanda scowled.

"I heard that from Ramon—one of my team Ancients," she
said. "I don't believe it. Why trade good fighting men for bad
around someone as important as Dow?"

"It checks out, all the same," said Arvid. "We hear Dow was
called by their military physician late last night. He was the one
who ordered the change."

"You monitored that call?"

"No. Just got a report on it, passed out through Foralie town."

Amanda shook her head stubbornly.

"One further piece of evidence," said Arvid. "On the basis of
the report, I had a couple of my staff check the patrol that went
out and the patrol that came back. It was a completely different
set of faces that returned."

Amanda sighed.

"All right. If that's right . . ." she swung away from him.
"Take off any time you're ready."

"We're ready now," said Arvid. "Four minutes."

"Good luck," she said, and went over to her own group, the
assorted gang of women, Jer, the five Ancients and the young
team-members, carrying their cone and energy rifles in the crook
of their arms, muzzle down, like hunting weapons.

"All right," she said to them all. "You know what you're supposed to do and you heard me talking just now with Arvid and Bill . . ."

She hesitated, finding herself strangely, uncharacteristically, at a loss for words. There was something that needed to be said; something that she had been working toward for a very long time, that she needed to tell them before they went where they were going. But whatever it was, it would not define itself for her. A skimmer topped the ridge opposite the one that overlooked Foralie and came sliding down to them under full power, carrying Reiko Kiempii, armed. Amanda saw the tall young woman's eyes slip past her for a second to Arvid. Then Reiko had reached the rest of them and jumped off her skimmer.

"I got word over the phone just before I left home," she said to Amanda. "Betta's in labor—the real thing, this time."

"Thanks," said Amanda, hardly knowing she spoke.

Suddenly, as if a switch had been pulled, the words she had been looking for were ready to her tongue. With this news everything abruptly fell into order—her silent lifelong love for Jimmy and for Fal Morgan, the years of struggling to survive back when the outlaw mercenaries had prowled the new Dorsai settlements, the sending out of the men in each generation to be killed, to earn the necessary credits that alone would let them all continue to survive—just as they were, and wished to be.

As they were.

Those were the magic words. They had a right to be as they were; and it was a right worth all it cost. This harsh world had been one that no one else had wanted. But they had taken it, she and the others like her. They had built it with their own hands and blood. It was theirs. *You love*, she thought suddenly, *what you give to—and in proportion as you give.*

That was all she had wanted to say. But now, looking around her at the adolescent faces of the young team members, at the other adult women, at old Jer Walker, she realized there had never been any need to tell the rest of them that. From the youngest to the oldest, they already knew it. It was in their bones and blood, as it was in hers. Perhaps not all of them had yet put it into words in their minds, as she had just done in hers—but they knew.

She looked at them. Mixed in among their living figures she thought she saw the presence of ghosts—of Berthe Haugsrud, of Bhaktabahadur Rais, of Jimmy himself and all those from other households who had died for the Dorsai, both here and on other worlds. Like the mountains, these stood up all around them, patiently waiting.

It came to her then like a revelation that none of it mattered—their individual weaknesses, the things that they seemed to lack that she herself either had innately, or time had taught her. She had been guilty of Amandamorphism—thinking only someone exactly like herself could earn even passing marks to qualify for the role she had played here so long. But that idea was nonsense. The fact that no two people were exactly alike had nothing to do with the fact that two people could be equally useful.

There came a time when anyone had to face the leaving of ultimate decisions to others, and to time itself. A time when faith proved to either have been placed, or misplaced, but when it was too late to do anything more about it. It was not up to her to leave Betta a last decision about the use of the Amanda name for Betta's child. Betta herself was the one to decide that, as Amanda had made necessary decisions in her own time, and all generations to come would have to make their own decisions in their time.

"What are you smiling at, Amanda?" said Reiko, looming beside and over her.

"Nothing," said Amanda. "Nothing at all."

She turned to the rest of them.

"I'll go in first," she said, "as soon as Arvid and Bill with their team have had their four minute lead. The rest of you, follow me, coming two to a skimmer, from different directions. We'll use Betta as an excuse for gathering at Foralie, as long as that's conveniently turned up. Actually, the excuse won't matter . . ."

She looked around at their faces.

"Myself, first. Then Mene and Reiko. The rest team up as you wish. Team members, stay close and fire as needed; but don't move in to the compound unless or until you're called in by one of us who've gone ahead. That includes Ancients. Ancients, stay with your teams. In case everything falls apart here, it'll be up to each of you to pull your team off, get it back into the mountains, and keep it alive. Everybody understand?"

They nodded or murmured their understanding.

"All right—" She was interrupted by a flicker of red, a cloth being waved briefly from just behind the crest of the ridge overlooking Foralie. "All right. Convoy in sight. It'll take it another five minutes or so to reach the house. Everybody up behind the ridge, ready to go."

Lying with the others, just behind the crest of the ridge, she looked through a screen of grass at the convoy. Even to her eye, its vehicle column seemed to move somewhat sluggishly. Evidently that part of Arvid's information—about the convoy troops all being sick—was correct. She crossed her fingers mentally upon the hope that the rest of what he had told her was also reliable—but with misgivings. Counting the team members, the Dorsai would outnumber the troops of the convoy and those already at Foralie nearly five to one—but children against experienced soldiers made that figure one of mockery. Experienced soldiers against civilians was bad enough.

The convoy was almost to the house. She pushed herself backwards and got to her feet below the crest of the ridge. Looking over, she saw the last of the Dorsai soldiers belonging to Bill and Arvid already disappearing—they would be crawling forward through the tall grass now, to get as close as they could come to the house before making their move. She checked her watch, counting off the minutes. When four were gone, she waved to the other civilians, mounted her skimmer and took it up over the ridge, directly down upon the single sentry standing in front of the compound of bubble plastic structures at the far end of the house. The convoy had pulled out of sight into the compound just moments before she reached him; and his head was still turned, looking after it. She had set the skimmer down before he belatedly turned to the sound of her power unit. His cone rifle swung up hastily, to cover her.

"Stay right there—" he was beginning, when she interrupted him.

"Oh, stop that nonsense! My great-granddaughter's having a baby. Where is she?"

"Where? She . . . oh, the house, of course, ma'am."

"All right, you go tell her I'll be right there. I've got to speak to whoever's in charge of that convoy—"

"I can't leave my post. I'm sorry, but—"

"What do you mean, you can't leave your post? Don't you recognize me? I'm the Mayor of Foralie Town. You must have been shown an image of me as part of your briefing. Now, you get in there—"

"I'm sorry. I really can't—"

"Don't tell me can't—"

They argued, the sentry forgetting his weapon to the point where its barrel sagged off to one side. A new humming announced another skimmer that slid down upon them with Reiko and Mene aboard.

"Halt—" said the soldier, swinging his rifle to command these new arrivals.

"Now what're you doing?" said Amanda, exasperatedly. Out of the corner of her eye, she saw Cletus being escorted into the house. The majority of the soldiers of the convoy should now be out of their vehicles and moving inside one or another of the cantonment buildings. There was still no sign of Arvid, Bill and their team.

"Don't you understand that neighbors come calling when there's a birth?" she said sharply, interrupting another argument that was developing between the sentry and Reiko. "I know these neighbors well. I'll vouch for them . . ."

"In a second, ma'am . . ." the sentry threw over his shoulder at her and turned back to Reiko.

"No second," said Amanda.

The difference in the tone of her voice brought him around. He froze at the sight of Amanda's heavy handgun pointed at his middle. Ineffective as they were at ordinary rifle distance, the energy handguns were devastating at point-blank range like this. Even if Amanda's aim should be bad—and she held the gun too steadily to suggest bad aim—any pressure on its trigger would mean his being cut almost in two.

"Just keep talking," said Amanda softly. She held the gun low, so that the sentry's own body shielded any view of it from the compound or the house. "You and I are just going on with our conversation. Wave these two to the compound as if you were referring them to someone there. There'll be other skimmers coming—"

"Yes . . . two more. On the way now," Mene's voice almost hissed, close by her ear.

"—and after each one stops here for a moment, you'll wave them to the compound, too. Do you understand?" Amanda said.

"Yes . . ." His eyes were on the steady muzzle of her handgun.

"Good. Mene, Reiko, go ahead. Wait until enough others catch up with you before you make a move, though."

"Leave it to us," said Reiko. Their skimmer lifted and hummed toward the compound.

"Just stand relaxed," Amanda told the sentry. "Don't move your rifle."

She sat. The sentry's face showed the pallor of what was perhaps illness, now overlaid with a mute desperation. He did not move. He was not as youthful as some of the other soldiers, but from the relative standpoint of Amanda's years they were all young. Other skimmers came and moved on to the compound, until all the adults had gone by her.

"Stand still," Amanda said to the sentry.

Off to one side, a movement caught her eye. It was a figure slipping around the corner of the house and entering the door. Then another. Arvid and Bill with their men—at last.

She turned her head slightly to look. Five . . . six figures flickered around the corner of the house and in through the door. Out of the other corner of her eyes she caught movement close to her. Looking back, she saw the sentry bringing up the barrel of his rifle to knock the energy weapon out of her hand. Twenty, even ten years before, she would have been able to move the handgun out of the way in time, but age had slowed her too much.

She felt the shock against her wrist as metal met metal and the energy gun was sent flying. But she was already stooping to the scabbard with the pellet shotgun as the sentry's cone rifle swung back to point at her. The stream of cones whistled over her bent head, then lowered. She felt a single heavy shock in the area of her left shoulder, but then the shotgun had, in its turn, batted the light frame of the cone rifle aside and the sentry was looking into the wide muzzle of the heavier gun.

"Drop it," said Amanda.

Her own words sounded distant in her own ears. There was a strange feeling all through her. The impact had been high enough so that possibly the single cone that struck her had not made a fatal wound; but shock was swift with missiles from that weapon.

The cone rifle dropped to the ground.

"Now lie down, face down . . ." said Amanda. She was still hearing her voice as if from a long distance away, and the world about her had an unreal quality to it. "No, out of arm's reach of the rifle . . ."

The sentry obeyed. She touched the power bar of her skimmer, lifted it and lowered it carefully on the lower half of his body. Then she killed the power, and got off. Pinned down by the weight upon him, the sentry lay helpless.

"If you call or struggle, you'll get shot," she told him.

"I won't," said the sentry.

There was the whistling of cone rifle fire from the direction of the cantonment. She turned in that direction, but there was no one to be seen outside the buildings she faced. The vehicle park was behind them, however, screened by them from her sight.

She bent to pick up the handgun, then thought better of it. The pellet shotgun was operable in spite of the rust in its barrel, and uncertain as she was now, she was probably better off with a weapon having a wide shot pattern. She began to walk unsteadily toward the compound. Every step took an unbelievable effort and her balance was not good, so that she wavered as she went. She reached the first building and opened its door. A supply room—empty. She went on to the next and opened the door, too wobbly to take ordinary precautions in entering. The thick air of a sickroom took her nostrils as she entered. Tina Alchenso, one of the other women, stood with an energy rifle, covering a barracks-like interior in which all the soldiers there seemed sick or dying. The air seemed heavy as well with the scentless odor of resignation and defeat. Those who were able had evidently been ordered out of their beds. They lay face down on the floor in the central aisle, hands stretched out beyond their heads.

"Where's everybody?" Amanda asked.

"They went on to the other buildings," Tina said.

Amanda let herself out again and went on, trying doors as she went. She found two more buildings where one of the adults

stood guard over ill soldiers. She was almost back to the vehicle
parking area, when she saw a huddled figure against the outside
wall of a building.

"Reiko!" she said, and knelt clumsily beside the other woman.

"Stop Mene," Reiko barely whispered. She was bleeding
heavily just above the belt of her jumper. "Mene's out of her
head."

"All right," said Amanda. "You lie quiet."

With an effort, she rose and went on. There was the next
building before her. She opened the door and found Mene holding her energy rifle on yet another room of sick and dying soldiers. Mene's face was white and wiped clean of expression. Her
eyes stared, fixed, and her finger quivered on the firing button
of the weapon. The gaze of all the men in the room were on
her face; and there was not even the sound of breathing.

"Mene," said Amanda, gently. Mene's gaze jerked around to
focus on Amanda for a brief moment before returning to the
soldiers.

"Mene . . ." said Amanda, softly. "It's almost over. Don't hurt
anyone, now. It's just about over. Just hold them a while longer.
That's all, just hold them."

Mene said nothing.

"Do you hear me?"

Mene nodded jerkily, keeping her eyes on the men before
her.

"I'll be back soon," said Amanda.

She went out. The world was even more unreal about her
and she felt as if she was walking on numb legs. But that was
unimportant. Something large was wrong with the overall situation.

Something was very wrong. There were only two more huts
shielding her from the vehicle park where the convoy had just
unloaded. Those two buildings could not possibly hold all the
rest of the original escort, plus the troops of the convoy. Nor

should just those two huts be holding two or three of her adults. It did not matter what Arvid had told her. Something had gone astray—she could feel it like a cold weight in her chest below the weakness and unreality brought on by her wound.

She tried to think with a dulled mind. She could gamble that Arvid and Bill's team had already subdued the house; and go back there now, without checking further, to get help . . . her mind cleared a little. A move like that would be the height of foolishness. Even if Arvid and Bill had men to spare to come back here with her, going for assistance would waste time when there might be no time to waste.

She took a good grip on her pellet gun, which was becoming an intolerable weight in her hands, and started around the curved wall on one of the huts.

Possibly the sense of unreality that held her was largely to blame—but it seemed to her that there was no warning at all. Suddenly she found herself in the midst of a tight phalanx of vehicles, the front ones already loaded with weaponed and alert-looking soldiers, and the rear ones with other such climbing into them. But, if her appearance among them had seemed sudden to her, it had apparently seemed the same to them.

She was abruptly conscious that all movement around her had ceased. Soldiers were poised, half-in, half-out of their vehicles. Their eyes were on her.

Plainly, her fears had been justified. The apparent replacement of well soldiers by sick ones had been a trap; and these she faced now were about to move in for a counterattack. She felt the last of her energy and will slipping away, took one step forward, and jammed the muzzle of her pellet shotgun against the side panel shielding the power unit in the closest vehicle.

"Get down," she said to the officers and men facing her.

They stared at her as if she was a ghost risen out of the ground before them.

"I'll blow every one of you up if I have to—and be glad to," she said. "Get out. Lie down, face down, all of you!"

For a second more they merely sat frozen, staring. Then understanding seemed to go through them in an invisible wave. They began to move out of their seats.

"Hurry . . ." said Amanda, for her strength was going fast. "On the ground . . ."

They obeyed. Dreamily, remotely, she saw them climbing from the vehicles and prostrating themselves on the ground.

Now what do I do? Amanda thought. She had only a minute or two of strength left.

The answer came from the back of her head—the only answer. *Press the firing button of the pellet gun, after all, and make sure no one gets away—*

Unexpectedly, there was the sound of running feet behind her. She started to glance back over her shoulder; and found herself caught and upheld. She was surrounded by the field uniforms of four of the Dorsai staff members who had been with Arvid and Bill.

"Easy . . ." said the one holding her—almost carrying her, in fact. "We've got it. It's all over."

There succeeded a sort of blur, and then a large space of nothing at all. At last things cleared somewhat—but only somewhat—and she found herself lying under covers, in one of the Foralie bedrooms. Like someone in a high fever, she was conscious of people moving all around her at what seemed like ungracious speed, and talking words she could not quite catch. Her shoulder ached. Small bits and phrases of dialogue came clear from moment to moment.

". . . *shai Dorsai!*"

What was that? That ridiculous phrase that the children had made up only a few years back, and which was now beginning to be picked up by their elders as a high compliment? It was supposed to mean "real, *actual* Dorsai." Nonsense.

It occurred to her, as some minor statistic might, that she was dying; and she was vaguely annoyed with herself for not having realized this earlier. There were things she should think about, if that was the case. If Betta had been in labor before the attack began, she might well have her child by now.

If so, it was important she tell Betta what she had decided just before they moved in on the troops, that the use of the Amanda name was her responsibility now, and the responsibility of succeeding generations . . .

"Well," said a voice just above her, and she looked up into the face of Ekram. He stank of sweat and anesthetic. "Coming out of it, are you?"

"How long . . ." it was incredibly hard to speak.

"Oh, about two days," he answered with abominable cheerfulness.

She thought of her need to tell Betta of her decision.

"Betta . . ." she said. It was becoming a little easier to talk; but the effort was still massive. She had intended to ask specifically for news of Betta and the child.

"Betta's fine. She's got a baby boy, all parts in good working order. Three point seven three kilograms."

Boy! A shock went through her.

Of course. But why shouldn't the child be a boy? No reason—except that, deluded by her own aging desires, she had fallen into the comfortable thought that it would not be anything but a girl.

A boy. That made the matter of names beside the point entirely.

For a moment, however, she teetered on the edge of self-pity. After all she had known, after all these years, why couldn't it have been a girl—under happier circumstances when she could have lived to know it, and find that it was a child who could safely take up her name?

She hauled herself back to common sense. What was all this foolishness about names, anyway? The Dorsai had won, had kept itself independent. That was her reward, as well as the reward to all of them—not just the sentimental business of passing her name on to a descendent. But she should still tell Betta of her earlier decision, if Ekram would only let them bring the girl to her. It would be just like the physician to decide that her dying might be hurried by such an effort, and refuse to let Betta come. She would have to make sure he understood this was not a decision for him to make. A deathbed wish was sacred and he must understand that was what this was . . .

"Ekram," she managed to say faintly. "I'm dying . . ."

"Not unless you want to," said Ekram.

She stared at him aghast. This was outrageous. This was too much. After all she had been through . . . then the import of his words trickled through the sense of unreality wrapping her.

"Bring Betta here! At once!" she said; and her voice was almost strong.

"Later," said Ekram.

"Then I'll have to go to her," she said, grimly.

She was only able to move one of her arms feebly sideways on top of her covers, in token of starting to get up from the bed. But it was enough.

"All right. All right!" said Ekram. "In just a minute."

She relaxed, feeling strangely luxurious. It was all right. The name of the game was survival, not how you did it. A boy! Almost she laughed. Well, that sort of thing happened, from time to time. In a few more years it could also happen that this boy could have a sister. It was worth waiting around to see. She would still have to die someday, of course—but in her own good time.

Interlude

The voice of the third Amanda ceased. In the still mountain afternoon there were no other sounds but the hum of some nearby insects. A little breeze sprang up, and was gone again.

With her words still echoing in his mind, Hal thought of the struggle she had been speaking of, that early Dorsai fight to stay free of Dow deCastries; and its likeness to the present fight on all the worlds, to resist the loss of human freedom to the Other Men and Women— those cross-breeds from human splinter cultures such as that on the Dorsai itself . . . This present fight in which he and the third Amanda were both caught up.

"What happened inside Foralie?" he asked. "Inside the house, I mean, after Arvid Johnson and Bill Athyer with their men went inside? What happened with Cletus and Dow—or were they just able to take over with no trouble?"

"Something more than no trouble," she said. "Swahili was there, remember, and Swahili had been a Dorsai. But Eachan Khan killed Swahili when Swahili let himself be distracted for a second and Arvid and Bill were able to control the situation. Dow had a sleeve gun of his own, it turned out. He hurt Cletus, but didn't manage to kill him. In the end it was Dow who was shipped back to Earth as a prisoner."

"I see," said Hal. But his first question had immediately raised another one in his mind.

"How was that other business worked?" he asked. "That Coalition trick of having a contingent of well soldiers up there at Foralie after they'd seemed to have been rotated down into the area of town?

Where did they come from, the soldiers Amanda found waiting, and ready to fight, in the vehicle park?"

"*You remember the military physician had phoned Dow deCastries the night before,*" Hal's Amanda said. "*He was a political appointee himself and he knew General Amorine was another. Besides, Amorine was sick himself from the nickel carbonyl vapors. The military physician knew that taking his suspicions to Amorine would simply have meant Amorine arresting Ekram and trying to force some kind of answer out of him—and the military doctor was only too aware of what it would be like for him to face alone a situation where everybody was dying. So, he went directly to Dow, instead.*"

"*I don't understand what that would have to do with it . . .*" Hal frowned.

"*Dow had been getting the reports from other areas. A thousand different things were going wrong in a thousand different places with his occupation forces; and, next to Cletus, he had the best mind on the planet.*" She paused to look at him. "*Don't underestimate what Dow was.*"

"*I didn't intend to.*"

"*What he saw,*" Amanda said, "*was that, for all practical purposes, his occupation of the Dorsai had failed. But he could still, with some luck, grab Cletus and take him off-planet as a prisoner—or at the worst, get away himself. This, if he had military control in this one district alone.*"

"*And he figured out that as soon as Cletus reached Foralie, Foralie would be attacked by the local people in a try to rescue him?*"

"*Of course,*" Amanda shrugged. "*It was obvious—as the first Amanda essentially said, to Ramon, when Ramon wondered if Cletus hadn't really meant what he said at the airpad—that they should do nothing against the soldiers. One way or another the district had to attack, then. So he sent up the patrol that morning with only sick soldiers; and it brought back well soldiers, all right; but those same well soldiers—only now pretending to be sick—went back up as the troops in the convoy that escorted Cletus to Foralie.*"

"Ah," said Hal, nodding. "How long did the first Amanda actually live?"

"She lived to be a hundred and eight."

"And saw a second Amanda?"

Hal's Amanda shook her head.

"No. It was nearly a hundred years before there was a second Amanda," she said.

Hal smiled.

"Who had the wisdom to name the second one Amanda?"

"No one," Amanda said. "She was named Elaine; but by the time she was six years old everyone was already calling her the second Amanda. You might say, she named herself."

Once more, in the back of his mind, Hal felt an obscure alerting to attention of that part of him which recognized the existence of The Purpose.

"Tell me something about the second Amanda," he said.

The third Amanda hesitated for a brief moment.

"For one thing," she said, "the second Amanda was the one both Kensie and Ian Graeme were in love with."

"Kensie and Ian?" Hal felt a strange coldness move through him. "But Kensie never married and Ian . . ."

"That's right," Amanda said. "Ian's wife, the mother of his children, was named Leah. But it was the second Amanda both twins fell in love with in the first place."

"How did it happen?"

The third Amanda looked down toward Fal Morgan.

"The second Amanda grew up with Kensie and Ian," she said. "How could it be any other way when the two households were practically side by side, here? She grew up with them; and by the time they were nearly grown, if she loved either of them, it was probably Kensie, with that brightness and warmth that was such a natural part of him."

"She loved Kensie?"

"I said—if she loved either of them . . . then. She was young, *they were young. She had had them around all her life. What was there about them to make her suddenly fall seriously in love with either one of them? But then they graduated from the Academy and went off to the wars; and when they came back, it was all different."*

She paused.

"Different? How?" Hal said gently, to get her going again.

She sighed once more.

"It's not easy to describe," she said. "It's something that happens often, with the situation we have here on the Dorsai. You grow up, knowing the boys of your district, and those from a lot of others. And when they finally sign contracts and go off-planet, that's all they are, still—just tall boys. But then, perhaps it's a year, or several, before they come home; and when they do you find they're . . . different."

"You mean, they've become men."

"Not only men," she said, "but men you never thought might come from the boys you knew. Some things you hardly noticed about them have moved forward in them and taken over. Other things you thought were the most important part of what made them, have gone way back in them, or been lost forever. They've grown up in ways you didn't expect. Suddenly, it's as if you never had known them. They can be anybody . . . strangers."

Her voice had sunk so low that she seemed to be speaking more to herself than him; and her gaze was on nothing.

"You sit and talk with them, after they come home," she went on, "and you realize you're talking to someone who's gone away from what was common to both of you and now has something that has nothing to do with you, that you've never known and maybe never will know . . ."

She looked at him. Her eyes were brilliant.

"And then you discover that the same thing that happened to them has happened to you. You were a girl they grew up with when they left; but that girl is gone, gone forever. With you, too, some things have come forward, other things have gone back or been lost forever. Now they sit talking to a woman they don't know, that now they

maybe never will know. And so, everything changes."

"I see," he said. "And it changed that much for the second Amanda and for Kensie and Ian?"

"Yes," she said soberly. "They came back, two strangers, and fell in love with a stranger they had once grown up with. With any other three people that would have been problem enough—but those twins were half and half of each other, and Amanda knew it."

"What happened?"

The third Amanda, Hal's Amanda, did not answer. She had drawn her knees up to her chin, and hugged them. Now she rested her chin upon her knees, staring down into the valley.

"What happened?" Hal asked again.

"Everybody had simply assumed that Kensie and Amanda would end up together," she said, at last, "including Ian. When Ian found he was in love with Amanda himself, it was unthinkable to him that he should interfere in any way with his twin brother. So he married Leah, who had wanted him for a long time. Married her simply and quickly."

"And took himself out of the picture."

"No," Amanda shook her head. "Because he had made a mistake. After the two of them had come home, different, it wasn't Kensie, but Ian, that the second Amanda had fallen in love with. Only with Ian being the kind of person he was, there was no chance that, having once married Leah, that situation could ever be changed."

"But you say . . ." began Hal puzzled, then checked himself. "But, if she had any love for Kensie at all, what was to keep her from ending up with him? Certainly that would have been better than the two of them—"

"The way they were." Amanda turned her head to look at Hal. "Kensie and Ian were too close not to know each other's feelings; and Kensie loved Amanda as completely as Amanda loved Ian. Knowing how she loved Ian, Kensie could not take the place he would have filled in her life if things had been otherwise. He went back to the wars as if . . . he was too much a Dorsai to deliberately put himself in the way of getting killed. But for all his brightness, he lived in the shadow of death for years after that; and it seemed as if death was perversely avoiding him."

She looked away from him, down to the valley again.

"The Exotics say," she went on, "that there are ontogenetic laws which explain why someone like Kensie could lead a charmed life under such conditions."

"Yes," said Hal. He had not realized how strangely he had said the word until he looked up and saw her gazing at him.

"You know something about ontogenetics?" she asked. "Something that applies to the second Amanda, and Ian and Kensie?"

"To Ian and Kensie, maybe," he said. The part of him that concerned itself with what he called The Purpose—that half-seen thing he must do with his life—was working powerfully, now; and he heard his own words almost as if someone else was speaking them. "Ontogenetics merely says nothing happens by chance or accident. Everything is interrelated. Stop and think. When Donal Graeme was moving toward his goal of bringing all the inhabited worlds under one order, his enemy was William of Ceta, just as Dow deCastries was the special opponent of Cletus Grahame."

"Yes," Amanda frowned. "But what of it?"

"To defeat William, who had unlimited power and wealth, Donal needed to defeat all possible military opponents. To do that he needed a military force larger than had ever been seen on the inhabited worlds. Only one other man could train that force as Donal needed it trained—and the rule in the Graeme household was that no two of their men served in the same place at the same time; for the same reason that a father and mother of young children may travel by different spacecraft, so that in case a phase shift accident should take one of them, the other would still be there to take care of the children."

"But it was different with Ian and Kensie," Amanda said. "They were allowed to serve in the same force, together."

"Until Kensie's death. Then the rule was broken once more by Eachan Khan Graeme, who you'll remember was the family head,

Donal's father and Ian's older brother." The Purpose-oriented part of Hal's mind was in complete control of him, now. He went on, not noticing the sudden intensity with which she was regarding him. "He asked Donal to find work with him for Ian, as the only means of rousing Ian after his twin's death."

She was watching him closely.

"You know a good deal about the Graemes," she said.

Suddenly aware of her attention, he grew flustered.

"I . . . don't," he said. "I only know something about ontogenetics."

"What you're saying adds up to the fact that Donal had Kensie killed to free Ian for his own use."

"No, no . . ." he protested. "Only Donal's need for Ian, acting on the network of cause and effect—"

"No!" she said. "Do you think any such forces could combine to kill Kensie, and Ian wouldn't be aware of it? They were one person, those twins!"

"But you said yourself that Kensie had been searching for death, ever since he had lost Amanda," he protested. "Maybe Ian simply, at last, let him go. You remember Kensie was assassinated. Dorsai aren't easy to assassinate, unless they don't care any more—"

"No!" the third Amanda said, again, almost violently. "That wasn't the way it was, at all. You don't know . . . did you know that Tomas Velt, the Blauvain chief of police, wrote Eachan Khan Graeme afterwards, telling him the whole story? Velt was there and saw it all. Do you know what he saw?"

"No," said Hal. The part of him concerned with The Purpose drew close to the front of his mind and spoke through his lips almost against his will, as if it, not he, controlled them. "But I want to know."

"I'll tell you, then," said Amanda, "I'll tell it all to you, just as I read it when I was young—just as Velt wrote it to Eachan Khan Graeme after Kensie's body had been shipped home here for burial . . ."

Brothers

Physically, he was big, very big. The professional soldiers of several generations from that small, harsh world called the Dorsai, are normally larger than men from other worlds; but the Graemes are large even among the Dorsai. At the same time, like his twin brother, Ian, Commander Kensie Graeme was so well-proportioned in spite of his size that it was only at moments like this, when I saw him standing next to a fellow Dorsai like his executive officer, Colonel Charley ap Morgan, that I could realize how big he actually was. He had the black, curly hair of the Graemes, the heavy-boned face and brilliant gray-green eyes of his family; also, that utter stillness at rest and that startling swiftness in motion that was characteristic of the several-generations Dorsai.

So, too, had Ian, back in Blauvain; for physically the twins were the image of each other. But otherwise, temperamentally, their difference was striking. Everybody loved Kensie. He was like some golden god of the sunshine. While Ian was dark and solitary as the black ice of a glacier in a land where it was always night.

". . . Blood," Pel Sinjin had said to me on our drive out here to the field encampment of the Expedition. "You know what they say, Tom. Blood and ice water, half-and-half in his veins, is what makes a Dorsai. But something must have gone wrong with those two when their mother was carrying them. Kensie got all the blood. Ian . . ."

He had let the sentence finish itself. Like Kensie's own soldiers, Pel had come to idolize the man, and downgrade Ian in proportion. I had let the matter slide.

Now, Kensie was smiling at us, as if there was some joke we were not yet in on.

"A welcoming committee?" he said. "Is that what you are?"

"Not exactly," I said. "We came out to talk about letting your men into Blauvain city for rest and relaxation; now that you've got those invading soldiers from the Friendly Worlds all rounded up, disarmed, and ready for shipment home—what's the joke?"

"Just," said Charley ap Morgan, "that we were on our way into Blauvain to see you. We just got a repeater message that you and other planetary officials here on Ste. Marie are giving Ian and Kensie, with their staffs, a surprise victory dinner in Blauvain this evening."

"Hells Bells!" I said.

"You hadn't been told?" Kensie asked.

"Not a damn word," I said.

It was typical of the fumbling of the so-called government-of-mayors we had here on our little world of Ste. Marie. Here was I, Superintendent of Police in Blauvain—our capital city—and here was Pel, commanding general of our planetary militia which had been in the field with the Exotic Expedition sent to rescue us from the invading puritan fanatics from the Friendly Worlds; and no one had bothered to tell either one of us about a dinner for the two Commanders of that Expedition.

"You're going in, then?" Pel asked Kensie. Kensie nodded. "I've got to call my HQ."

Pel went out. Kensie laughed.

"Well," he said, "this gives us a chance to kill two birds at once. We'll ride back with you and talk on the way. Is there some difficulty about Blauvain absorbing our men on leave?"

"Not that way," I said. "But even though the Friendlies have all been rounded up, the Blue Front is still with us in the shape of a good number of political outlaws and terrorists that want to pull down our present government. They lost the gamble they took when they invited in the Friendly troops; but now they may take advantage of any trouble that can be stirred up around your soldiers while they're on their own in the city."

"There shouldn't be any," Kensie reached for a dress gunbelt of black leather and began to put it on over the white dress uniform he was already wearing. "But we can talk about it, if you like.—You'd better be doing some dressing yourself, Charley."

"On my way," said Charley ap Morgan; and went out.

So, fifteen minutes later, Pel and I found ourselves headed back the way we had come, this time with three passengers. I was still at the controls of the police car as we slid on its air cushion across the rich grass of our Ste. Marie summer toward Blauvain; but Kensie rode with me in front, making me feel small beside him—and I am considered a large man among our own people on Ste. Marie. Beside Kensie, I must have looked like a fifteen year old boy in relative comparison. Pel was equally small in back between Charley and a Dorsai Senior Commandant named Chu Van Moy—a heavy-bodied, black Mongol, if you can imagine such a man, from the Dorsai South Continent.

". . . No real problem," Kensie was saying as we left the grass at last for the vitreous road surface leading us in among the streets and roads of the city—in particular the road curving in between the high office buildings of Blauvain's West Industrial Park, now just half a kilometer ahead, "we'll turn the men loose in small groups if you say. But there shouldn't be any need to worry. They're mercenaries, and a mercenary knows that civilians pay his wages. He's not going to make any trouble which would give his profession a bad name."

"I don't worry about your men," I said. "It's the Blue Front fabricating some trouble in the vicinity of some of your men and then trying to pin the blame on them, that worries me. The only way to guard against that is to have your troops in small enough numbers so that my policemen can keep an eye on the civilians around them."

"Fair enough," said Kensie. He smiled down at me. "I hope, though, you don't plan on having your men holding our men's hands all through their evenings in town—"

Just then we passed between the first of the tall office buildings. A shadow from the late morning sun fell across the car, and the high walls around us gave Kensie's last words a flat echo. Right on the heels of those words—in fact, mixed with them— came a faint sound as of multiple whistlings about us; and Kensie fell forward, no longer speaking, until his forehead against the front windscreen stopped him from movement.

The next thing I knew I was flying through the air, literally. Charley ap Morgan had left the police car on the right side, dragging me along with a hand like a steel clamp on my arm, until we ended up against the front of the building on our right. We crouched there, Charley with his dress handgun in his fist and looking up at the windows of the building opposite. Across the narrow way, I could see Chu Van Moy with Pel beside him, a dress gun also in Chu's fist. I reached for my own police belt-gun, and remembered I was not wearing it.

About us there was utter silence. The narrow little projectiles from one or more sliver rifles, that had fluted about us, did not come again. For the first time I realized there was no one on the streets and no movement to be seen behind the windows about us.

"We've got to get him to a hospital," said Pel, on the other side of the street. His voice was strained and tight. He was staring fixedly at the still figure of Kensie, still slumped against the windscreen.

"A hospital," he said again. His face was as pale as a sick man's.

Neither Charley or Chu paid any attention. Silently they were continuing to scan the windows of the building opposite them.

"A hospital!" shouted Pel, suddenly.

Abruptly, Charley got to his feet and slid his weapon back into its holster. Across the street, Chu also was rising. Charley looked at the other Dorsai.

"Yes," said Charley, "where is the nearest hospital?"

But Pel was already behind the controls of the police car. The rest of us had to move or be left behind. He swung the car toward Blauvain's Medical Receiving, West, only three minutes away.

He drove the streets like a madman, switching on the warning lights and siren as he went. Screaming, the vehicle careened through traffic and signals alike, to jerk to a stop behind the ambulance entrance at Medical West. Pel jumped from the car.

"I'll get a life support system—a medician—" he said, and ran inside.

I got out; and then Charley and Chu got out, more slowly. The two Dorsais were on opposite sides of the car.

"Find a room," Charley said. Chu nodded and went after Pel through the ambulance entrance.

Charley turned to the car. Gently, he picked up Kensie in his arms, the way you pick up a sleeping child, gently, holding Kensie to his chest so that Kensie's head fell in to rest on Charley's left shoulder. Carrying his Field Commander, Charley turned and went into the medical establishment. I followed.

Inside, there was a long corridor with hospital personnel milling about. Chu stood by a doorway a few meters down the hall to the left, half a head taller than the people between us. With Kensie in his arms, Charley went toward the other Commandant.

Chu stood aside as Charley came up. The door swung back automatically, and Charley led the way into a room with surgical equipment in sterile cases along both its sides, and an operating table in its center. Charley laid Kensie softly on the table, which was almost too short for his tall body. He put the long legs together, picked up the arms and laid their hands on the upper thighs. There was a line of small, red stains across the front of his jacket, high up, but no other marks. Kensie's face, with its eyes closed, looked blindly to the white ceiling overhead.

"All right," said Charley. He led the way back out into the hall. Chu came last and turned to click the lock on the door into place, drawing his handgun.

"What's this?" somebody shouted at my elbow, pushing toward Chu. "That's an emergency room. You can't do that—"

Chu was using his handgun on low aperture to slag the lock of the door. A crude but effective way to make sure that the room would not be opened by anyone with anything short of an industrial, heavy-duty torch. The man who was talking was middle-aged, with a gray mustache and the short green jacket of a senior surgeon. I intercepted him and held him back from Chu.

"Yes, he can," I said, as he turned to stare furiously in my direction. "Do you recognize me? I'm Tomas Velt, the Superintendent of Police."

He hesitated, and then calmed slightly—but only slightly.

"I still say—" he began.

"By the authority of my office," I said, "I do now deputize you as a temporary Police Assistant.—That puts you under my orders. You'll see that no one in this hospital tries to open that door or get into that room until Police authorization is given. I make you responsible. Do you understand?"

He blinked at me. But before he could say anything, there was a new outburst of sound and action; and Pel broke into our group, literally dragging along another man in a senior surgeon's jacket.

"Here!" Pel was shouting. "Right in here. Bring the life support—"

He broke off, catching sight of Chu.

"What?" he said. "What's going on? Is Kensie in there? We don't want the door sealed—"

"Pel," I said. I put my hand on his shoulder. "Pel!"

He finally felt and heard me. He turned a furious face in my direction.

"Pel," I said quietly, but slowly and clearly to him. "He's dead. Kensie. Kensie is dead."

Pel stared at me.

"No," he said irritably, trying to pull away from me. I held him. "No!"

"Dead," I said, looking him squarely in the eyes. "Dead, Pel."

His eyes stared back at me, then seemed to loose their focus and stare off at something else. After a little they focused back on mine again and I let go of him.

"Dead?" he repeated. It was hardly more than a whisper.

He walked over and leaned against one of the white-painted corridor walls. A nurse moved toward him and I signalled her to stop.

"Just leave him alone for a moment," I said. I turned back to the two Dorsai officers who were now testing the door to see if it was truly sealed.

"If you'll come to Police Headquarters," I said, "we can get the hunt going for whoever did it."

Charley looked at me briefly. There was no more friendly humor in his face now; but neither did it show any kind of shock, or fury. The expression it showed was only a businesslike one.

"No," he said briefly. "We have to report."

He went out, followed by Chu, moving so rapidly that I had to run to keep up with their long strides. Outside the door, they climbed back into the police car, Charley taking the controls. I scrambled in behind them and felt someone behind me. It was Pel.

"Pel," I said. "You'd better stay—"

"No. Too late," he said.

And it was too late. Charley already had the police car in motion. He drove no less swiftly than Pel had driven, but without madness. For all that, though, I made most of the trip with my fingers tight on the edge of my seat; for with the faster speed of Dorsai reflexes he went through available spaces and openings in traffic where I would have sworn we could not get through.

We pulled up before the office building attached to the Exotic Embassy as space for Expeditionary Base Headquarters. Charley led the way in past a guard, whose routine challenge broke off in mid-sentence as he recognized the two of them.

"We have to talk to the Base Commander," Charley said to him. "Where's Commander Graeme?"

"With the Blauvain Mayor, and the Outbond." The guard, who was no Dorsai, stammered a little. Charley turned on his heel. "Wait—sir, I mean the Outbond's with *him*, here in the Commander's office."

Charley turned again.

"We'll go on in. Call ahead," Charley said.

He led the way, without waiting to watch the guard obey, down a corridor and up an escalator ramp to an outer office where a young Force-Leader stood up behind his desk at the sight of us.

"Sir—" The Force-Leader said to Charley, "the Outbond and the Mayor will only be with the Commander another few minutes—"

Charley brushed past him, and the Force-Leader spun around to punch at his desk phone. Heels clicking on the polished stone floor, Charley led us toward a further door and opened it, stepping into the office beyond. We followed him there—into a large, square room with windows overlooking the city and our own broad-shouldered Mayor, Moro Spence, standing there with a white-haired, calm-faced, hazel-eyed man in a blue robe

both facing a desk at which sat the mirror image of Kensie that
was his twin brother, Ian Graeme.

Ian spoke to his desk as we came in.

"It's all right," he said. He punched a button and looked up
at Charley, who went forward with Chu beside him, to the very
edge of the desk, and then both saluted.

"What is it?" asked Ian.

"Kensie," said Charley. His voice became formal. "Field Commander Kensie Graeme has just been killed, sir, as we were on
our way into the city."

For perhaps a second—no longer—Ian sat without speaking.
But his face—so like Kensie's and yet so different—did not
change expression.

"How?" he asked, then.

"By assassins we couldn't see," Charley answered. "Civilians
we think. They got away."

Moro Spence swore.

"The Blue Front!" he said. "Ian . . . Ian, listen . . ."

No one paid any attention to him. Charley was briefly re-
counting what had happened from the time the message about
the invitation had reached the encampment—

"But there wasn't any celebration like that planned!" protested Moro Spence, to the deaf ears around him. Ian sat quietly,
his harsh, powerful face half in shadow from the sunlight coming
in the high window behind him, listening as he might have
listened to a thousand other reports. There was still no change
visible in him; except perhaps that he, who had always been
remote from everyone else, seemed even more remote now. His
heavy forearms lay on the desktop, and the massive hands that
were trained to be deadly weapons in their own right lay open
and still on the papers beneath them. Almost, he seemed to be
more legendary character than ordinary man; and that impression was not mine alone, because behind me I heard Pel hiss on
a breath of sick fury indrawn between his teeth; and I remem-

bered how he had talked of Ian being only ice and water, Kensie only blood.

The white-haired man in the blue robe, who was the Exotic, Padma, Outbond to Ste. Marie for the period of the Expedition, was also watching Ian steadily. When Charley was through with his account, Padma spoke.

"Ian," he said; and his calm, light baritone seemed to linger and reecho strangely on the ear, "I think this is something best handled by the local authorities."

Ian glanced at him.

"No," he answered. He looked at Charley. "Who's Duty Officer?"

"Ng'kok," said Charley.

Ian punched the phone button on his desk.

"Get me Colonel Waru Ng'kok, Encampment HQ," he said to the desk.

" 'No?' " echoed Moro. "I don't understand Commander. We can handle it. It's the Blue Front, you see. They're an outlawed political—"

I came up behind him and put my hand on his shoulder. He broke off, turning around.

"Oh, Tom!" he said, on a note of relief. "I didn't see you before. I'm glad you're here—"

I put my finger to my lips. He was politician enough to recognize that there are times to shut up. He shut up now; and we both looked back at Ian.

". . . Waru? This is Base Commander Ian Graeme," Ian was saying to his phone. "Activate our four best Hunter Teams; and take three Forces from your on-duty troops to surround Blauvain. Seal all entrances to the city. No one allowed in or out without our authority. Tell the involved troops briefing on these actions will be forthcoming."

As professional, free-lance soldiers, under the pattern of the Dorsai contract—which the Exotic employers honored for all their military employees—the mercenaries were entitled to know the aim and purpose of any general orders for military action they were given. By a ninety-six per cent vote among the enlisted men concerned, they could refuse to obey the order. In fact, by a hundred per cent vote, they could force their officers to use them in an action they themselves demanded. But a hundred per cent vote was almost unheard of. The phone grid in Ian's desk top said something I could not catch.

"No," replied Ian, "that's all."

He clicked off the phone and reached down to open a drawer in his desk. He took out a gunbelt—a working, earth-colored gunbelt unlike the dress one Kensie had put on earlier—with sidearm already in its holster; and, standing up, began to strap it on. On his feet, he dominated the room, towering over us all.

"Tom," he said, looking at me, "put your police to work, finding out what they can. Tell them all to be prepared to obey orders by any one of our soldiers, no matter what his rank."

"I don't know if I've got the authority to tell them that," I said.

"I've just given you the authority," he answered calmly. "As of this moment, Blauvain is under martial law."

Moro cleared his throat; but I jerked a hand at him to keep him quiet. There was no one in this room with the power to deal with Ian's authority now, except the gentle-faced man in the blue robe. I looked appealingly at Padma, and he turned from me to Ian.

"Naturally, Ian, measures will have to be taken, for the satisfaction of the soldiers who knew Kensie," Padma said softly, "but perhaps finding the guilty men would be better done by the civilian police without military assistance?"

"I'm afraid we can't leave it to them," said Ian briefly. He turned to the other two Dorsai officers. "Chu, take command of the Forces I've just ordered to cordon the city. Charley, you'll take over as Acting Field Commander. Have all the officers and men in the encampment held there, and gather back any who are off post. You can use the office next to this one. We'll brief the troops in the encampment, this afternoon. Chu can brief his forces as he posts them around the city."

The two turned and headed toward the door.

"Just a minute, gentlemen!"

Padma's voice was raised only slightly. But the pair of officers paused and turned for a moment.

"Colonel ap Morgan, Commandant Moy," said Padma, "as the official representative of the Exotic Government, which is your employer, I relieve you from the requirement of following any further orders of Commander Ian Graeme."

Charley and Chu looked past the Exotic, to Ian.

"Go ahead," said Ian. They went. Ian turned back to Padma. "Our contracts provide that officers and men are not subject to civilian authority while on active duty, engaged with an enemy."

"But the war—the war with the Friendly invaders—is over," said Moro.

"One of our soldiers has just been killed," said Ian. "Until the identity of the killers is established, I'm going to assume we're still engaged with an enemy."

He looked again at me.

"Tom," he said. "You can contact your Police Headquarters from this desk. As soon as you've done that, report to me in the office next door, where I sent Charley."

He came around the desk and went out. Padma followed him. I went to the desk and put in a phone call to my own office.

"For God's sake, Tom!" said Moro to me, as I punched phone buttons for the number of my office, and started to get the police machinery rolling. "What's going on, here?"

I was too busy to answer him. Someone else was not.

"He's going to make them pay for killing his brother," said Pel savagely, from across the room. "That's what's going on!"

I had nearly forgotten Pel. Moro must have forgotten him absolutely; because he turned around to him now as if Pel had suddenly appeared on the scene in a cloud of fire and brimstone-odorous smoke.

"Pel?" he said. "Oh, Pel—get your militia together and under arms, right away. This is an emergency—"

"Go to hell!" Pel answered him. "I'm not going to lift a finger to keep Ian from hunting down those assassins. And no one else in the militia who knew Kensie Graeme is going to lift a finger, either."

"But this could bring down the government!" Moro was close to the idea of tears, if not to the actual article. "This could throw Ste. Marie back into anarchy; and the Blue Front will take over by default!"

"That's what the planet deserves," said Pel, "when it lets men like Kensie be shot down like dogs—men who came here to risk their lives to save our government!"

"You're crazier than these mercenaries are!" said Moro, staring at him. Then a touch of hope lifted Moro's drawn features. "Actually, Ian seems calm enough. Maybe he won't—"

"He'll take this city apart if he has to," said Pel, savagely. "Don't blind yourself."

I had finished my phoning. I punched off, and straightened up, looking at Pel.

"I thought you told me there was nothing but ice and water to Ian?" I said.

"There isn't," Pel answered. "But Kensie's his twin brother. That's the one thing he can't sit back from and shuffle off. You'll see."

"I hope and pray I don't," I said; and I left the office for the one next door where Ian was waiting for me. Pel and Moro followed; but when we came to the doorway of the other office, there was a soldier there who would let only me through.

". . . We'll want a guard on that hospital room, and a Force guarding the hospital itself," Ian was saying slowly and deliberately to Charley ap Morgan as I came in. He was standing over Charley, who was seated at a desk. Back against a wall stood the silent figure in a blue robe that was Padma. Ian turned to face me.

"The troops at the encampment are being paraded in one hour," he said. "Charley will be going out to brief them on what's happened. I'd like you to go with him and be on the stand with him during the briefing."

I looked back at him, up at him. I had not gone along with Pel's ice-and-water assessment of the man. But now for the first time I began to doubt myself and began to believe Pel. If ever there had been two brothers who had seemed to be opposite halves of a single egg, Kensie and Ian had been those two. But here was Ian with Kensie dead—perhaps the only living person on the human-inhabited worlds among the stars who had loved or understood him—and Ian had so far shown no more emotion at his brother's death than he might have on discovering an incorrect Order of the Day.

It occurred to me then that perhaps he was in emotional shock—and this was the cause of his unnatural calmness. But the man I looked at now had none of the signs of a person in shock. I found myself wondering if any man's love for his brother could be hidden so deep that not even that brother's violent death could cause a crack in the frozen surface of the one who went on living.

If Ian was repressing emotion that was due to explode sometime soon, then we were all in trouble. My Blauvain police and the planetary militia together were toy soldiers compared to these professionals. Without the Exotic control to govern them, the whole planet was at their mercy. But there was no point in admitting that—even to ourselves—while even the shadow of independence was left to us.

"Commander," I said. "General Pel Sinjin's planetary militia were closely involved with your brother's forces. He would like to be at any such briefing. Also, Moro Spence, Blauvain's Mayor and protem President of the Ste. Marie Planetary Government, would want to be there. Both these men, Commander, have as deep a stake in this situation as your troops."

Ian looked at me.

"General Sinjin," he said, after a moment. "Of course. But we don't need mayors."

"Ste. Marie needs them," I said. "That's all our Ste. Marie World Council is, actually—a collection of mayors from our largest cities. Show that Moro and the rest mean nothing, and what little authority they have will be gone in ten minutes. Does Ste. Marie deserve that from you?"

He could have answered that Ste. Marie had been the death of his brother—and it deserved anything he wished to give it. But he did not. I would have felt safer with him if he had. Instead, he looked at me as if from a long, long distance for several seconds, then over at Padma.

"You'd favor that?" he asked.

"Yes," said Padma. Ian looked back at me.

"Both Moro and General Sinjin can go with you, then," he said. "Charley will be leaving from here by air in about forty minutes. I'll let you get back to your own responsibilities until then. You'd Letter appoint someone as liaison from your police, to stand by here in this office."

"Thanks," I said. "I will."

I turned and went out. As I left, I heard Ian behind me, dictating.

". . . All travel by the inhabitants of the city of Blauvain will be restricted to that which is absolutely essential. Military passes must be obtained for such travel. Inhabitants are to stay off the streets. Anyone involved in any gathering will be subject to investigation and arrest. The City of Blauvain is to recognize the fact that it is now under martial, not civil, law . . ."

The door closed behind me. I saw Pel and Moro waiting in the corridor.

"It's all right," I told them, "you haven't been shut out of things—yet."

We took off from the top of that building, forty minutes later, Charley and myself up in the control seats of a military eight-man liaison craft with Pel and Moro sitting back among the passenger seats.

"Charley," I asked him, in the privacy of our isolation together up front in the craft, once we were airborne. "What's going to happen?"

He was looking ahead through the forward vision screen and he did not answer for a moment. When he did, it was without turning his head.

"Kensie and I," he said softly, almost absently, "grew up together. Most of our lives we've been in the same place, working for the same employers."

I had thought I knew Charley ap Morgan. In his cheerfulness, he had seemed more human, less of a half-god of war than other Dorsai like Kensie or Ian—or even lesser Dorsai officers like Chu. But now he had moved off with the rest. His words took him out of my reach, into some cold, high, distant country where only Dorsai lived. It was a land I could not enter, the rules of which I would never understand. But I tried again, anyway.

"Charley," I said, after a moment of silence, "that doesn't answer what I asked you."

He looked at me then, briefly.

"I don't know what's going to happen," he said.

He turned his attention back to the controls. We flew the rest of the way to the encampment without talking.

When we landed, we found the entire Expedition drawn up in formation. They were grouped by Forces into Battalion and

Arm Groups; and their dun-colored battle dress showed glints of light in the late afternoon sunlight. It was not until we mounted the stand facing them that I recognized the glitter for what it was. They had come to the formation under arms, all of them—although that had not been in Ian's orders. Word of Kensie had preceded us. I looked at Charley; but he was paying no attention to the weapons.

The sun struck at us from the southwest at a lowered angle. The troops were in formation, with their backs to the old factory, and when Charley spoke, the amplifiers caught up his voice and carried it out over their heads.

"Troops of the Exotic Expeditionary Force in relief of Sainte Marie," he said. "By order of Commander Ian Graeme, this briefing is ordered for the hundred and eighty-seventh day of the Expedition on Ste. Marie soil."

The brick walls slapped his words back with a flat echo over the still men in uniform. I stood a little behind him, in the shadow of his shoulders, listening. Pel and Moro were behind me.

"I regret to inform you," Charley said, "that sniper activity within the City of Blauvain, this day, about thirteen hundred hours, cost us the life of Commander Kensie Graeme."

There was no sound from the men.

"The snipers have not yet been captured or killed. Since they remain unidentified, Commander Ian Graeme has ordered that the condition of hostilities, which was earlier assumed to have ended, is still in effect. Blauvain has been placed under martial law, sufficient force has been sent to seal the city against any exit or ingress, and all persons under Exotic contract to the Expedition have been recalled to this encampment . . ."

I felt the heat of a breath on my ear and Pel's voice whispered to me.

"Look at them!" he said. "They're ready to march on Blauvain right now. Do you think they'll let Kensie be killed on some stinking little world like this of ours, and not see that somebody pays for it?"

"Shut up, Pel," I murmured out of the corner of my mouth at him. But he went on.

"Look at them!" he said. "It's the order to march they're waiting for—the order to march on Blauvain. And if Charley doesn't end up giving it, there'll be hell to pay. You see how they've all come armed?"

"That's right, Pel, Blauvain's not your city!" It was a bitter whisper from Moro. "If it was Castelmane they were itching to march on, would you feel the same way about it?"

"Yes!" hissed Pel, fiercely. "If men come here to risk their lives for us, and we can't do any better than let them be gunned down in the streets, what do we deserve? What does anyone deserve?"

"Stop making a court case out of it!" whispered Moro harshly. "It's Kensie you're thinking of—that's all. Just like it's only Kensie they're thinking of, out there . . ."

I tried again to quiet them, then realized that actually it did not make any difference. For all practical purposes, the three of us were invisible there behind Charley. The attention of the armed men ranked before us was all on Charley, and only on him. As Pel had said, they were waiting for one certain order; and only that order mattered to them.

It was like standing facing some great, dun-colored, wounded beast which must charge at any second now, if only because in action there would be relief from the pain it was suffering. Charley's expressionless voice went on, each word coming back like a slapping of dry boards together, in the echo from the factory wall. He was issuing a long list of commands having to do with the order of the camp, and its transition back to a condition of battle-alert.

I could feel the tension rising as he approached the end of

his list of orders without one which might indicate action by
the Expedition against the city in which Kensie had died. Then,
suddenly, the list was at an end.

". . . That concludes," said Charley, in the same unvarying
tones, "the present orders dealing with the situation. I would
remind the personnel of this Expedition that at present the
identity of the assassins of Commander Graeme is unknown.
The civilian police are exerting every effort to investigate the
matter; and it is the opinion of your officers that nothing else
can be done for the moment but to give them our complete
cooperation. A suspicion exists that a native, outlawed political
party, known as The Blue Front, may have been responsible for
the assassination. If this should be so, we must be careful to
distinguish between those of this world who are actually guilty
of Commander Graeme's death and the great majority of innocent bystanders."

He stopped speaking.

There was not a sound from the thousands of men ranked
before him.

"All right, Brigade-Major," said Charley, looking down from
the stand at the ranking officer in the formation. "Dismiss your
troops."

The Brigade-Major, who had been standing like all the rest
facing the stand, wheeled about.

"Atten-shun!" he snapped, and the amplifier sensors of the
stand picked his voice up and threw it out over the men in
formation as they had projected Charley's voice. "Dis-miss!"

The formation did not disperse. Here and there, a slight wavering in the ranks showed itself, and then the lines of standing
figures were motionless again. For a long second, it seemed that
nothing more was going to happen, that Charley and the mercenary soldiers before him would stand facing each other until
the day of Judgment . . . and then somewhere among the ranks,
a solitary and off-key bass voice began to sing.

"They little knew of brotherhood . . ."

Other voices rapidly picked it up.

". . . The faith of fighting men—
"Who once to prove their lie was good
"Hanged Colonel Jacques Chrétien . . ."

—And suddenly they were all singing in the ranks facing us. It was a song of the young Colonel who had been put to death one hundred years before, when the Dorsai were just in their beginning. A New Earth city had employed a force of Dorsai with the secret intention of using them against an enemy force so superior as to surely destroy them utterly—so rendering payment for their services unnecessary while at the same time doing considerable damage to the enemy. Then the Dorsai had defeated the enemy, instead, and the city faced the necessity of paying, after all. To avoid this, the city authorities came up with the idea of charging the Dorsai commanding officer with dealing with the enemy, taking a bribe to claim victory for a battle never fought at all. It was the technique of the big lie; and it might even have worked if they had not made the mistake of arresting the commanding officer, to back up their story.

It was not a song to which I would have had any objection, ordinarily. But now—suddenly—I found it directed at me. It was at Pel, Moro, myself, that the soldiers of the Expedition were all singing it. Before, I had felt almost invisible on the stand behind Charley ap Morgan. Now, we three civilians were the focus of every pair of eyes on the field—we civilians who were like the civilians that had hanged Jacques Chrétien; we who were Ste. Marians, like whoever had shot Kensie Graeme. It was like facing into the roaring maw of some great beast ready to swallow us up. We stood facing it, frozen.

Nor did Charley ap Morgan interfere.

He stood silent himself, waiting while they went through all
the verses of the song to its end:—

> . . . One fourth of Rochmont's fighting strength—
> One battalion of Dorsai—
> Were sent by Rochmont forth alone,
> To bleed Helmuth, and die.
>
> But look, look down from Rochmont's heights
> Upon the Helmuth plain.
> At all of Helmuth's armored force
> By Dorsai checked, or slain.
>
> Look down, look down, on Rochmont's shame
> To hide the wrong she'd done,
> Made claim Helmuth had bribed Dorsai—
> No battle had been won.
>
> To prove that lie, the Rochmont Lords
> Arrested Jacques Chrétien,
> On charge he dealt with Helmuth's Chiefs
> For payment to his men.
>
> Commandant Arp Van Din sent word:
> "You may not judge Dorsai,
> "Return our Colonel by the dawn,
> "Or Rochmont town will die."
>
> Strong-held behind her walls, Rochmont
> Scorned to answer them,
> Condemned, and at the daybreak, hanged,
> Young Colonel Jacques Chrétien.

Bright, bright, the sun that morning rose
Upon each weaponed wall.
But when the sun set in the west,
Those walls were leveled all.

Then soft and white the moon arose
On streets and roofs unstained,
But when that moon was down once more
No street nor roof remained.

No more is there a Rochmont town
No more are Rochmont's men.
But stands a Dorsai monument
To Colonel Jacques Chrétien.

So pass the word from world to world,
Alone still stands Dorsai.
But while she lives, no one of hers,
By foreign wrong shall die.

They little knew of brotherhood
—The faith of fighting men—
Who once to prove their lie was good
Hanged Colonel Jacques Chrétien!

It ended. Once more they were silent—utterly silent. On the platform Charley moved. He took half a step forward and the sensors picked up his voice once more and threw it out over the heads of the waiting men.

"Officers! Front and Center. Face your men!"

From the end of each rank figures moved. The commissioned and non-commissioned officers stepped forward, turned and marched to a point opposite the middle of the rank they had headed, turned once more and stood at attention.

"Prepare to fire."

The weapons in the hands of the officers came up to waist level, their muzzles pointing at the men directly before them. The breath in my chest was suddenly a solid thing. I could not have inhaled or exhaled if I had tried. I had heard of something like this but I had never believed it, let alone dreamed that I would be there to see it happen. Out of the corner of my eye I could see the angle of Charley ap Morgan's face, and it was a Dorsai face in all respects now. He spoke again.

"The command to dismiss has been given," Charley's voice rang and reechoed over the silent men, "and not obeyed. The command will be repeated under the stricture of the Third Article of the Professional Soldier's Covenant. Officers will open fire on any refusing to obey."

There was something like a small sigh that ran through all the standing men, followed by the faint rattle of safeties being released on the weapons of the men in ranks. They stood facing their officers and non-commissioned officers now—fellow soldiers and old friends. But they were all professionals. They would not simply stand and be executed if it came to the final point. The breath in my chest was now so solid it hurt, like something jagged and heavy pressing against my ribs. In ten seconds we could all be dead.

"Brigade-Major," said the level voice of Charley. "Dismiss your troops."

The Brigade-Major, who had turned once more to face Charley, when Charley spoke to him, turned back again to the parade ground of men.

"Dis—" No more than in Charley's voice was there perceptible change in the Brigade-Major's command from the time it had been given before, "—miss!"

The formations dissolved. All at once the ranks were breaking up, the men in them turning away, the officers and noncoms lowering the weapons they had lifted to ready position at

Charley's earlier command. The long-held breath tore itself out of my lungs so roughly it ripped at my throat. I turned to Charley but he was halfway down the steps from the platform, as expressionless as he had been all through the last few minutes. I had to half-run to catch up to him.

"Charley!" I said, reaching him.

He turned to look at me as he walked along. Suddenly I felt how pale and sweat dampened I was. I tried to laugh.

"Thank God that's over," I said.

"Over?" He shook his head. "It's not over, Tom. The enlisted men will be voting now. It's their right."

"Vote?" The world made no sense to me, for a second. Then suddenly it made too much sense. "You mean—they might vote to march on Blauvain, or something like that?"

"Perhaps—something like that," he said.

I stared at him.

"And then?" I said. "You wouldn't . . . if their vote should be to march on Blauvain—what would you do?"

He looked at me almost coldly.

"Lead my troops," he said.

I stopped. Standing there, I watched him walk away from me. A hand tugged at my elbow; and I turned around to see that Pel and Moro had caught up to me. It was Moro who had his hand on my arm.

"Tom," said Moro, "what do we do, now?"

"See Padma," I said. "If he can't do something, I don't know anybody who can."

Charley was not flying directly back to Blauvain. He was already in a staff meeting with his fellow officers, who were barred from the voting of the enlisted men by the Covenant. We three civilians had to borrow a land car from the encampment motor pool.

It was a silent ride, most of the way back into town. Once again I was at the controls, with Pel beside me. Sitting behind us, just before we reached the west area of the city, Moro leaned forward to put his head between us.

"Tom," he said. "You'll have to put your police on special duty. Pel, you've got to mobilize the militia—right now."

"Moro," I answered—and I suddenly felt dog-tired, weary to the point of exhaustion. "I've got less than three hundred men, ninety-nine per cent of them without anything more exciting in the way of experience than filling out reports or taking charge at a fire, an accident or a family quarrel. They wouldn't face those mercenaries even if I ordered them to."

"Pel," he said, turning away from me, "your men are soldiers. They've been in the field with these mercenaries—"

Pel laughed at him.

"Over a hundred years ago, a battalion of Dorsai took a fortified city—Rochmont—with nothing heavier than light field pieces. This is a *brigade*—six battalions—armed with the best weapons the Exotics can buy them—facing a city with no natural or artificial defenses at all. And you want my two thousand militiamen to try to stop them? There's no force on Ste. Marie that could stop those professional soldiers."

"At Rochmont they were all Dorsai—" Moro began.

"For God's sake!" cried Pel. "These are Dorsai-officered, the best mercenaries you can find. Elite troops—the Exotics don't hire anything else for fear they might have to touch a weapon themselves and damage their enlightenment—or whatever the hell it is! Face it, Moro! If Kensie's troops want to chew us up, they will. And there's nothing you or I can do about it!"

Moro said nothing for a long moment. Pel's last words had hit a near-hysterical note. When the Mayor of Blauvain did speak again, it was softly.

"I just wish to God I knew why you want just that to happen, so badly," he said.

"Go to hell!" said Pel. "Just go—"

I slammed the car into retro and we skidded to a halt, thumping down on the grass as the air-cushion quit. I looked at Pel.

"That's something I'd like to know, too," I said. "All right, you liked Kensie. So did I. But what we're facing is anything from the leveling of a city to a possible massacre of a couple of hundred thousand people. All that for the death of just one man?"

Pel's face looked bitter and sick.

"We're no good, we Ste. Marians," he said, thickly. "We're a fat little farm world that's never done anything since it was first settled but yell for help to the Exotics every time we got into trouble. And the Exotics have bailed us out every time, only because we're in the same solar system with them. What're we worth? Nothing! At least the Dorsai and the Exotics have got some value—some use!"

He turned away from Moro and myself; and we could not get another word out of him.

We drove on into the city; where, to my great relief, I finally got rid of Pel and Moro both; and was able to get to Police Headquarters and take charge of things.

As I had expected, things badly needed taking care of there. As I should also have expected, I had very much underestimated how badly they needed it. I had planned to spend two or three hours getting the situation under control, and then be free to seek out Padma. But, as it ended up, it took me nearly seven straight hours to damp down the panic, straighten out the confusion, and put some purpose and order back into the operations of all my people, off-duty and otherwise, who had reported for emergency service. Actually, it was little enough we were required to do—merely patrol the streets and see that the town's citizens stayed off the streets and out of the way of the mercenaries. Still, that took seven hours to put into smooth operation; and at the end of that time I was still not free to go hunting for Padma, but had to respond to a series of calls for my presence by the detective crew assigned to work with the mercenaries in tracking down the assassins.

I drove through the empty nighttime streets slowly, with my emergency lights on and the official emblem on my police car clearly illuminated. Three times, however, I was stopped and checked by teams of three to five mercenaries, in battle dress and fully weaponed, that appeared unexpectedly. The third time, the Groupman—a non-commissioned officer—in command of the team stopping me, joined me in the car. When twice after that we encountered military teams, he leaned out the right window to show himself; and we were waved through.

We came at last to a block of warehouses on the north side of the city; and to one warehouse in particular. Within, the large, echoing structure was empty except for a few hundred square feet of crated harvesting machinery on the first of its three floors. I found my men on the second floor in the transparent cubicles that were the building's offices, apparently doing nothing.

"What's the matter?" I said, when I saw them. They were not only idle, but they looked unhappy.

"There's nothing we can do, Superintendent," said the senior detective lieutenant present—Lee Hall, a man I'd known for sixteen years. "We can't keep up with them, even if they'd let us."

"Keep up?" I asked.

"Yes sir," Lee said. "Come on, I'll show you. They let us watch, anyway."

He led me out of the offices up to the top floor of the warehouse, a great, bare space with a few empty crates scattered between piles of unused packing materials. At one end, portable floodlights were illuminating an area with a merciless blue-white light that made the shadows cast by men and things look solid enough to stub your toe on. He led me toward the light until a Groupman stepped forward to bar our way.

"Close enough, Lieutenant," he said to Lee. He looked at me. "This is Tomas Velt, Blauvain superintendent of police."

"Honored to meet you, sir," said the Groupman to me. "But you and the Lieutenant will have to stand back here if you want to see what's going on."

"What is going on?" I asked.

"Reconstruction," said the Groupman. "That's one of our Hunter Teams."

I turned to watch. In the white glare of the light were four of the mercenaries. At first glance they seemed engaged in some odd ballet or mime acting. They were at little distances from one another; and first one, then another of them would move a short distance—perhaps as if he had gotten up from a non-existent chair and walked across to an equally non-existent table, then turned to face the others. Following which another man would move in and apparently do something at the same invisible table with him.

"The men of our Hunter Teams are essentially trackers, Superintendent," said the Groupman quietly in my ear. "But some teams are better in certain surroundings than others. These are men of a team that works well in interiors."

"But what are they doing?" I said.

"Reconstructing what the assassins did when they were here," said the Groupman. "Each of three men on the team takes the track of one of the assassins, and the fourth man watches them all as coordinator."

I looked at him. He wore the sleeve emblem of a Dorsai, but he was as ordinary-looking as myself or one of my detectives. Plainly, a first-generation immigrant to that world; which explained why he was wearing the patches of a non-commissioned, rather than a commissioned officer along with that emblem.

"But what kind of signs are they tracking?" I asked.

"Little things, mostly." He smiled. "Tiny things—some things you or I wouldn't be able to see if they were pointed out to us.

Sometimes there's nothing and they have to go on guess—that's where the coordinator helps." He sobered. "Looks like black magic, doesn't it? It does, even to me, sometimes, and I've been a Dorsai for fourteen years."

I stared at the moving figures.

"You said—three," I said.

"That's right," answered the Groupman. "There were three snipers. We've tracked them from the office in the building they fired from, to here. This was their headquarters—the place they moved from, to the office, just before the killing. There's sign they were here a couple of days, at least, waiting."

"Waiting?" I asked. "How do you know there were three and they were waiting?"

"Lots of repetitive sign. Habitual actions. Signs of camping beds set up. Food signs for a number of meals. Metal lubricant signs showing weapons had been disassembled and worked over here. Signs of a portable, private phone—they must have waited for a phone call from someone telling them the Commander was on his way in from the encampment."

"But how do you know there were only three?"

"There's sign for only three," he said. "Three—all big for your world, all under thirty. The biggest man had black hair and a full beard. He was the one who hadn't changed clothes for a week—" The Groupman sniffed the air. "Smell him?"

I sniffed hard and long.

"I don't smell a thing," I said.

"Hmm," the Groupman looked grimly pleased. "Maybe those fourteen years have done me some good, after all. The stink of him's in the air, all right. It's one of the things our Hunter Teams followed to this place."

I looked aside at Lee Hall, then back at the soldier.

"You don't need my detectives at all, do you?" I said.

"No sir," he looked me in the face. "But we assume you'd want them to stay with us. That's all right."

"Yes," I said. And I left there. If my men were not needed, neither was I; and I had no time to stand around being useless. There was still Padma to talk to.

But it was not easy to locate the Outbond. The Exotic Embassy either could not or would not tell me where he was; and the Expedition Headquarters in Blauvain also claimed not to know. As a matter of ordinary police work, my own department kept track of important outworlders like the Graeme brothers and the Outbond, as they moved around our city. But in this case, there was no record of Padma ever leaving the room in which I had last seen him with Ian Graeme, early in the day. I finally took my determination in both hands and called Ian himself to ask if Padma was with him.

The answer was a blunt "no." That settled it. If Padma was with him, a Dorsai like Ian would have refused to answer rather than lied outright. I gave up. I was lightheaded with fatigue and I told myself I would go home, get at least a few hours sleep, and then try again.

So, with one of the professional soldiers in my police car to vouch for me at roadblocks, I returned to my own dark apartment; and when, alone at last, I came into the living room and turned on the light, there was Padma waiting for me in one of my own chair-floats.

The jar of finding him there was solid—more like an emotional explosion than I would have thought. It was like seeing a ghost in reality, the ghost of someone from whose funeral you have just returned. I stood staring at him.

"Sorry to startle you, Tom," he said. "I know, you were going to have a drink and forget about everything for a few hours. Why don't you have the drink, anyway?"

He nodded toward the bar built into a corner of the apartment living room. I never used the thing unless there were guests on hand; but it was always stocked—that was part of the maintenance agreement in the lease. I went over and punched the buttons for a single brandy and water. I knew there was no use offering Padma alcohol.

"How did you get in here?" I said, with back to him.

"I told your supervisor you were looking for me," Padma said. "He let me in. We Exotics aren't so common on your world here that he didn't recognize me."

I swallowed half the glass at a gulp, carried the drink back, and sat down in a chair opposite him. The background lighting in the apartment had gone on automatically when night darkened the windows. It was a soft light, pouring from the corners of the ceiling and from little random apertures and niches in the walls. Under it, in his blue robe, with this ageless face, Padma looked like the image of a buddha, beyond all the human and ordinary storms of life.

"What are you doing here?" I asked. "I've been looking all over for you."

"That's why I'm here," Padma said. "The situation being what it is, you would want to appeal to me to help you with it. So I wanted to see you away from any place where you might blame my refusal to help on outside pressures."

"Refusal?" I said. It was probably my imagination; but the brandy and water I had swallowed seemed to have gone to my head already. I felt lightminded and unreal. "You aren't even going to listen to me first before saying no?"

"My hope," said Padma, "is that you'll listen to me, first, Tom, before rejecting what I've got to tell you. You're thinking that I could bring pressure to bear on Ian Graeme to move his soldiers half a world away from Blauvain, or otherwise take the situation out of its critical present phase. But the truth is I could not; and even if I could, I would not."

"Would not," I echoed, muzzily.

"Yes. Would not. But not just because of personal choice. For four centuries now, Tom, we students of the Exotic Sciences have been telling other men and women that our human race was committed to a future, to the workings of history as it is. It's true we Exotics have a calculative technique now, called ontogenetics, that helps us to resolve any present or predicted moment into its larger historical factors. We've made no secret of having such techniques. But that doesn't mean we can control what will happen, particularly while other men still tend to reject the very thing we work with—the concept of a large, shifting pattern of events that involves all of us and our lives."

"I'm a Catholic," I said. "I don't believe in predestination."

"Neither do we on Mara and Kultis," said Padma. "But we do believe in a physics of human action and interaction, which we believe works in a certain direction, toward a certain goal which we now think is less than a hundred years off—if, in fact, we haven't already reached it. Movement toward that goal has been building up for at least the last thousand years; and by now the momentum of its forces is massive. No single individual or group of individuals at the present time have the mass to oppose or turn that movement from its path. Only something greater than a human being as we know a human being might do that."

"Sure," I said. The glass in my hand was empty. I did not remember drinking the rest of its contents; but the alcohol was bringing me a certain easing of weariness and tension. I got up, went back to the bar, and came back with a full glass, while Padma waited silently. "Sure, I understand. You think you've spotted a historical trend here; and you don't want to interfere for fear of spoiling it. A fancy excuse to do nothing."

"Not an excuse, Tom," Padma said; and there was something different, like a deep gong-note in his voice, that blew the fumes of the brandy clear from my wits for a second and made me look at him. "I'm not telling you I won't do anything about the situation. I'm telling you that I can't do anything about it. Even if I tried to do something, it would be no use. It's not for you alone that the situation is too massive; it's that way for everyone."

"How do you know if you don't try?" I said. "Let me see you try, and it not work. Then maybe I'd believe you."

"Tom," he said, "can you lift me out of this chair?"

I blinked at him. I am no Dorsai, as I think I have said, but I am large for my world, which meant in this case that I was a head taller than Padma and perhaps a quarter again the weight. Also I was undoubtedly younger; and I had worked all my life to stay in good physical condition. I could have lifted someone my own weight out of that chair with no trouble, and Padma was less than that.

"Unless you're tied down," I said.

"I'm not." He stood up briefly, and then sat again. "Try and lift me, Tom."

I put my glass down, stepped over to his float and stood behind him. I wrapped my arms around his body under his armpits, and lifted—at first easily, then with all my strength.

But not only could I not lift him, I could not budge him. If he had been a lifesized statue of stone I would have expected to feel more reaction and movement in response to my efforts.

I gave up finally, panting, and stood back from him.

"What do you weigh?" I demanded.

"No more than you think. Sit down again, Tom—" I did. "Don't let it bother you. It's a trick, of course. No, not a mechanical trick, a physiological one—but a trick just the same, that's been shown on stage at times, at least during the last four hundred years."

"Stand up," I said. "Let me try again."

He did. I did. He was still immovable.

"Now," he said, when I had given up a second time. "Try once more; and you'll find you can lift me."

I wiped my forehead, put my arms around him, and heaved upward with all my strength. I almost threw him against the ceiling overhead. Numbly I set him down again.

"You see?" he said, reseating himself. "Just as I knew you could not lift me until I let you, I know that there is nothing I can do to alter present events here on Ste. Marie from their present direction. But you can."

"*I* can?" I stared at him, then exploded. "Then for God's sake tell me how?"

He shook his head, slowly.

"I'm sorry, Tom," he said. "But that's just what I can't do. I only know that, resolved to ontogenetic terms, the situation here shows you as a pivotal character. On you, as a point, the bundle of human forces that were concentrated here and bent toward destruction by another such pivotal character, may be redirected back into the general historical pattern with a minimum of harm. I tell you this so that being aware of it, you can be watching for opportunities to redirect. That's all I can do."

Incredibly, with those words, he got up and went toward the door of the apartment.

"Hold on!" I said, and he stopped, turning back momentarily. "This other pivotal character. Who's he?"

Padma shook his head again.

"It would do you no good to know," he said. "I give you my word he is now far away from the situation and will not be coming back to it. He is not even on the planet."

"One of the assassins of Kensie!" I said. "And they've gotten away, off-planet!"

"No," said Padma. "No. The men who assassinated Kensie are only tools of events. If none of them had existed, three others would have been there in their place. Forget this other pivotal character, Tom. He was no more in charge of the situation he created than you are in charge of the situation here and now. He was simply, like you, in a position that gave him freedom of choice. Good night."

With those last words, he was suddenly out the door and gone. To this day I cannot remember if he moved particularly swiftly; or whether for some reason I now can't remember I simply let him go. Just—all at once I was alone.

Fatigue rolled over me like the heavy waves of some ocean of mercury. I stumbled into the bedroom, fell on my sleeping float, and that was all I remembered until—only a second later, it seemed—I woke to the hammering of my telephone's chimes on my ears.

I reached out, fumbled at the bedside table and pushed the *on* button.

"Velt here," I said, thickly.

"Tom—this is Moro. Tom? Is that you, Tom?"

I licked my lips, swallowed and spoke more understandably.

"It's me," I said. "What's the call for?"

"Where've you been?"

"Sleeping," I said. "What's the call for?"

"I've got to talk to you. Can you come—"

"You come here," I said. "I've got to get up and dress and get some coffee in me before I go anyplace. You can talk to me while I'm doing it."

I punched off. He was still saying something at the other end of the line but just then I did not care what it was.

I pushed my dead-heavy body out of bed and began to move. I was dressed and at the coffee when he came.

"Have a cup." I pushed it at him as he sat down at the porch table with me. He took it automatically.

"Tom—" he said. The cup trembled in his hand as he lifted it and he sipped hastily from it before putting it down again. "Tom, you were in the Blue Front once, weren't you?"

"Weren't we all?" I said. "Back when we and it were young together; and it was an idealistic outfit aimed at putting some order and system into our world government."

"Yes, yes, of course," Moro said. "But what I mean is, if you were a member once, maybe you know who to contact now—"

I began to laugh. I laughed so hard I had to put my cup down to avoid spilling it.

"Moro, don't you know better than that?" I said. "If I knew who the present leaders of the Blue Front were, they'd be in jail. The Blauvain police commissioner—the head law enforcement man of our capital city—is the last man the Blue Front would be in touch with nowadays. They'd come to you, first. You were a member once, too, back in college days, remember?"

"Yes," he said miserably. "But I don't know anything now, just as you're saying. I thought you might have informers, or suspicions you couldn't prove, or—"

"None of them," I said. "All right. Why do you want to know who's running the Blue Front, now?"

"I thought I'd make an appeal to them, to give up the assassins of Kensie Graeme—to save the Blauvain people. Tom—" he stared directly at me. "Just an hour ago the enlisted men of the mercenaries took a vote on whether to demand their officers lead them on the city. They voted over ninety-four per cent, in favor. And Pel . . . Pel's finally mobilized his militia; but I don't think he means to help *us*. He's been trying to get in to talk to Ian all day."

"All day?" I glanced at the time on my wrist unit. "4:25—it's not 4:25 P.M., *now?*"

"Yes," said Moro, staring at me. "I thought you knew."

"I didn't mean to sleep like this!" I came out of the chair, moving toward the door. "Pel's trying to see Ian? The sooner we get down and see him ourselves, the better."

So we went. But we were too late. By the time we got to Expedition Headquarters and past the junior officers to the door of the office where Ian was, Pel was already with Ian. I brushed aside the Force-Leader barring our way and walked in, followed by Moro. Pel was standing facing Ian, who sat at a desk surrounded by stacks of filmprints. He got to his feet as Moro and I appeared.

"That'll be all right, Force-Leader," he said to the officer be-hind us. "Tom, I'm glad you're here. Mr. Mayor, though, if you don't mind waiting outside, I'll see you in a few minutes."

Moro had little choice but to go out again. The door shut behind him, Ian waved me to a chair beside Pel, and sat down again himself.

"Go ahead, General," he said to Pel. "Repeat what you'd started to tell me, for the benefit of Tom, here."

Pel glanced savagely at me for a second out of the edge of his eyes before answering.

"This doesn't have anything to do with the Police Commis-sioner of Blauvain," he said, "or anyone else of Ste. Marie."

"Repeat," said Ian again. He did not raise his voice. The word was simply an iron door dropped in Pel's way, forcing him to turn back. Pel glanced once more, grimly at me.

"I was just saying," he said, "if Commander Graeme would go to the encampment and speak to the enlisted men there, he could probably get them to vote unanimously."

"Vote unanimously for what?" I asked.

"For a house-to-house search of the Blauvain area," Ian an-swered.

"The city's been cordoned," Pel said quickly. "A search like that would turn up the assassins in a matter of hours, with the whole expeditionary force searching."

"Sure," I said, "and with the actual assassins, there'd be a few hundred suspected assassins, or people who fought or ran for the wrong reason, killed or wounded by the searchers. Even if the Blue Front didn't take advantage of the opportunity—which they certainly would—to start gunfights with the soldiers in the city streets."

"What of it?" said Pel, talking to Ian rather than to me. "Your troops can handle any Blue Front people. And you'd be doing Ste. Marie a favor to wipe them out."

"If the whole thing didn't develop into a wiping-out of the whole civilian population of the city," I said.

"You're implying, Tom," said Pel, "that the Exotic troops can't be controlled by—"

Ian cut him short.

"Your suggestion, General," he said, "is the same one I've been getting from other quarters. Someone else is here with it right now. I'll let you listen to the answer I give him."

He turned toward his desk annunciator.

"Send in Groupman Whallo," he said.

He straightened up and turned back to us as the door to his office opened and in came the mercenary noncom I had brushed past out there. In the light, I saw it was the immigrant Dorsai of the Hunter Team I had encountered—the man who had been a Dorsai fourteen years.

"Sir!" he said, stopping a few steps before Ian and saluting. Uncovered himself, Ian did not return the salute.

"You've got a message for me?" Ian said. "Go ahead. I want these gentlemen to hear it, and my answer."

"Yes sir," said Whallo. I could see him glance at and recognize me out of the corner of his eyes. "As representative of the enlisted men of the Expedition, I have been sent to convey to you the results of our latest vote on orders. By unanimous vote, the enlisted men of this command have concurred in the need for a single operation."

"Which is?"

"That a house-to-house search of the Blauvain city area be made for the assassins of Field Commander Graeme," said Whallo. He nodded at Ian's desk and for the first time I saw solidigraphs there—artists' impressions, undoubtedly, but looking remarkably lifelike of three men in civilian clothes. "There's no danger we won't recognize them when we find them."

Whallo's formal and artificial delivery was at odds with the way I had heard him speak when I had run into him at the

Hunter Team site. There was, it occurred to me suddenly, probably a military protocol even to matters like this—even to the matter of a man's death and the possible death of a city. It came as a little shock to realize it and for the first time I began to feel something of what Padma had meant in saying that the momentum of forces involved here was massive. For a second it was almost as if I could feel those forces like great winds, blowing on the present moment.—But Ian was already answering him.

"Any house-to-house search involves possible military errors and danger to the civilian population," he was saying. "The military record of my brother is not to be marred after his death by any intemperate order from me."

"Yes sir," said Whallo. "I'm sorry sir; but the enlisted men of the expedition had hoped that the action would be ordered by you. Their decision calls for six hours in which you may consider the matter before our Enlisted Men's Council takes the responsibility for the action upon itself. Meanwhile, the Hunter Teams will be withdrawn—this is part of the voted decision."

"That, too?" said Ian.

"I'm sorry, sir. But you know," said Whallo, "they've been at a dead end for some hours now. The trail was lost in traffic; and the men might be anywhere in the central part of the city."

"Yes," said Ian. "Well, thank you for your message, Groupman."

"Sir!" said Whallo. He saluted again and went out.

As the door closed behind him, Ian's head turned back to face Pel and myself.

"You heard, gentlemen," he said. "Now, I've got work to do."

Pel and I left. In the corridor outside, Whallo was already gone and the young Force-Leader was absent. Only Moro stood waiting for us. Pel turned on me, furiously.

"Who asked you to show up here?" he demanded.

"Moro," I answered. "And a good thing, too. Pel, what's got into you? You act as if you had some personal axe to grind in seeing the Exotic mercenaries level Blauvain—"

He spun away from me.

"Excuse me!" he snapped. "I've got things to do. I've got to phone my Headquarters."

Puzzled, I watched him take a couple of long strides away from me and out of the outer office. Suddenly, it was as if the winds of those massive forces I had felt for a moment just past in Ian's office had blown my head strangely clean, clear and empty, so that the slightest sound echoed with importance. All at once, I was hearing the echo of Pel saying those identical words as Kensie was preparing to leave the mercenary encampment for the non-existent victory dinner; and a half-recognized but long-held suspicion in me flared into a raging certainty.

I took three long strides after him and caught him. I whirled him around and rammed him up against a wall.

"It was you!" I said. "You called from the Encampment to the city just before we drove in. It was you who told the assassins we were on the way and to move into position to snipe at our car. You're Blue Front, Pel; and you set Kensie up to be murdered!"

My hands were on his throat and he could not have answered if he had wanted to. But he did not need to. Then I heard the click of bootheels on the floor of the polished stone corridor flagging outside the office, and let go of him, slipping my hand under my uniform jacket to my beltgun.

"Say a word," I whispered to him, "or try anything . . . and I'll kill you before you can get the first syllable out. You're coming along with us!"

The Force-Leader entered. He glanced at the three of us curiously.

"Something I can do for you gentlemen?" he asked.

"No," I said. "No, we're just leaving."

With one arm through Pel's and the hand of my other arm under my jacket on the butt of my beltgun, we went out as close as the old friends we had always been, Moro bringing up the rear. Out in the corridor, with the office door behind us, Moro caught up with me on the opposite side from Pel.

"What are you going to do?" Moro whispered. Pel had still said nothing; but his eyes were like the black shadows of meteor craters on the gray face of an airless moon.

"Take him downstairs and out to a locked room in the nearest police post," I said. "He's a walking stick of high explosive if any of the mercenaries find out what he did. Someone of his rank involved in Kensie's killing is all the excuse they need to run our streets red in the gutters."

We got Pel to a private back room in Post Ninety-six, a local police center less than three minutes drive from the building where Ian had his office.

"But how can you be sure, he—" Moro hesitated at putting it into words, once we were safe in the room. He stood staring at Pel, who sat huddled in a chair, still without speaking.

"I'm sure," I said. "The Exotic, Padma—" I cut myself off as much as Moro had done. "Never mind. The main thing is he's Blue Front, he's involved—and what do we do about it?"

Pel stirred and spoke for the first time since I had almost strangled him. He looked up at Moro and myself out of his gray-dead face.

"I did it for Ste. Marie!" he said, hoarsely. "But I didn't know they were going to kill him! I didn't know that. They said it was just to be shooting around the car—for an incident—"

"You hear?" I jerked my head at Moro. "Do you want more proof than that?"

"What'll we do?" Moro was staring in fascinated horror at Pel.

"That was my question," I reminded him. He stood there looking hardly in better case than Pel. "But it doesn't look like you're going to be much help in answering it." I laughed, but not happily. "Padma said the choice was up to me."

"Who? What're you talking about? What choice?" asked Moro.

"Pel here—" I nodded at him, "knows where the assassins are hiding."

"No," said Pel.

"Well, you know enough so that we can find them," I said. "It makes no difference. And outside of this room, there's only two people in Ste. Marie we can trust with that information."

"You think I'd tell you anything?" Pel said. His face was still gray, but it had firmed up now. "Do you think even if I knew anything I'd tell you? Ste. Marie needs a strong government to survive and only the Blue Front can give it to her. I was ready to give my life for that, yesterday. I'm still willing. I won't tell you anything—and you can't make me. Not in six hours."

"What two people?" Moro asked me.

"Padma," I said, "and Ian."

"Ian!" said Pel. "You think he'll help you? He doesn't give a damn for Ste. Marie, either way. Did you believe that talk of his about his brother's military record? He's got no feelings. It's his own military record he's concerned with; and he doesn't care if the mercenaries tear Blauvain up by the roots, as long as it's done over his own objection. He's just as happy as any of the other mercenaries with that vote. He's just going to sit out his six hours and let things happen."

"And I suppose Padma doesn't care either?" Moro was beginning to sound a little ugly himself. "It was the Exotics sent us help against the Friendlies in the first place!"

"Who knows what Exotics want?" Pel retorted. "They pretend to go about doing nothing but helping other people, and never dirtying their hands with violence and so on; and somehow with all that they keep on getting richer and more powerful all the time. Sure, trust Padma, why don't you? Trust Padma and see what happens!"

Moro looked at me uncomfortably.

"What if he's right?" Moro said.

"What if he's right?" I snarled at him. "Moro can't you see this is what Ste. Marie's trouble has always been? Here's the troublemaker we always have around—someone like Pel—whispering that the devil's in the chimney and you—like the rest of our people always do—starting to shake at the knees and wanting to sell him the house at any price! Stay here both of you; and don't try to leave the room."

I went out, locking the door behind me. They were in one of a number of rooms set up behind the duty officer's desk and I went up to the night sergeant on duty. He was a man I'd known back when I had been in detective training on the Blauvain force, an old-line policeman named Jaker Reales.

"Jaker," I said, "I've got a couple of valuable items locked up in that back room. I hope to be back in an hour or so to collect them; but if I don't, make sure they don't get out and nobody gets in to them, or knows they're there. I don't care what kind of noises may seem to come out of there, it's all in the imagination of anyone who thinks he hears them, for twenty-four hours at least, if I don't come back."

"Got you, Tom," said Jaker. "Leave it up to me, sir."

"Thanks, Jaker," I said.

I went out and back to Expedition Headquarters. It had not occurred to me to wonder what Ian would do now that his Hunter Teams had been taken from him. I found Expedition Headquarters now quietly aswarm with officers—officers who clearly were most of them Dorsai. No enlisted men were to be seen.

I was braced to argue my way into seeing Ian; but the men on duty surprised me. I had to wait only four or five minutes outside the door of Ian's private office before six Senior Commandants, Charley ap Morgan among them, filed out.

"Good," said Charley, nodding as he saw me; and then went on without any further explanation of what he meant. I had no time even to look after him. Ian was waiting.

I went in. Ian sat massively behind his desk, waiting for me, and waved me to a chair facing him as I came in. I sat down. He was only a few feet from me, but again I had the feeling of a vast distance separating us. Even here and now, under the soft lights of this nighttime office, he conveyed, more strongly than any Dorsai I had ever seen, a sense of difference. Generations of men bred to war had made him; and I could not warm to him as Pel and others had warmed to Kensie. Far from kindling any affection in me, as he sat there, a cold wind like that off some icy and barren mountaintop seemed to blow from him to me, chilling me. I could believe Pel, that Ian was all ice and no blood; and there was no reason for me to do anything for him— except that as a man whose brother had been killed, he deserved whatever help any other decent, law-abiding man could give him.

But I owed something to myself, too, and to the fact that we were not all villains, like Pel, on Ste. Marie.

"I've got something to tell you," I said. "It's about General Sinjin."

He nodded, slowly.

"I've been waiting for you to come to me with that," he said.

I stared at him.

"You knew about Pel?" I said.

"We knew someone from the Ste. Marie authorities had to be involved in what happened," he said. "Normally, a Dorsai officer is alert to any potentially dangerous situation. But there was the false dinner invitation; and then the matter of the assassins happening to be in just the right place at the right time, with just the right weapons. Also, our Hunter Teams found clear evidence the encounter was no accident. As I say, an officer like Field Commander Graeme is not ordinarily killed that easily."

It was odd to sit there and hear him speak Kensie's name that way. Title and name rang on my ears with the strangeness one feels when somebody speaks of himself in the third person.

"But Pel?" I said.

"We didn't know it was General Sinjin who was involved," Ian said. "You identified him yourself by coming to me about him just now."

"He's Blue Front," I said.

"Yes," said Ian, nodding.

"I've known him all my life," I said, carefully. "I believe he's suffered some sort of nervous breakdown over the death of your brother. You know, he admired your brother very much. But he's still the man I grew up with; and that man can't be easily made to do something he doesn't want to do. Pel says he won't tell us anything that'll help us find the assassins; and he doesn't think we can make him tell us inside of the six hours left before your soldiers move in to search Blauvain. Knowing him, I'm afraid he's right."

I stopped talking. Ian sat where he was, behind the desk, looking at me, merely waiting.

"Don't you understand?" I said. "Pel can help us, but I don't know of any way to make him do it."

Still Ian said nothing.

"What do you want from me?" I almost shouted it at him, at last.

"Whatever," Ian said, "you have to give."

For a moment it seemed to me that there was something like a crack in the granite mountain that he seemed to be. For a moment I could have sworn that I saw into him. But if this was true, the crack closed up immediately, the minute I glimpsed it. He sat remote, icy, waiting, there behind his desk.

"I've got nothing," I said, "unless you know of some way to make Pel talk."

"I have no way consistent with my brother's reputation as a Dorsai officer," said Ian, remotely.

"You're concerned with reputations?" I said. "I'm concerned with the people who'll die and be hurt in Blauvain if your mercenaries come in to hunt door-to-door for those assassins. Which is more important, the reputation of a dead man, or the lives of living ones?"

"The people are rightly your concern, Commissioner," said Ian, still remotely, "the professional reputation of Kensie Graeme is rightly mine."

"What will happen to that reputation if those troops move into Blauvain in less than six hours from now?" I demanded.

"Something not good," Ian said. "That doesn't change my personal responsibilities. I can't do what I shouldn't do and I must do what I ought to do."

I stood up.

"There's no answer to the situation, then," I said. Suddenly, the utter tiredness I had felt before was on me again. I was tired of the fanatic Friendlies who had come out of another solar system to exercise a purely theoretical claim to our revenues and world surface as an excuse to assault Ste. Marie. I was tired of the Blue Front and people like Pel. I was tired of off-world people of all kinds, including Exotics and Dorsais. I was tired, tired . . . It came to me then that I could walk out. I could refuse to make the decision that Padma had said I would make and the whole matter would be out of my hands. I told myself to do that, to get up and walk out; but my feet did not budge. In picking on me, events had chosen the right idiot as a pivot point. Like Ian, I could not do what I should not do, and I must do what I ought to do.

"All right," I said, "Padma might be able to do something with him."

"The Exotics," said Ian, "force nobody." But he stood up.

"Maybe I can talk him into it," I said, exhaustedly. "At least, I can try."

Once more, I would have had no idea where to find Padma in a hurry. But Ian located him in a research enclosure, a carrel in the stacks of the Blauvain library; which like many libraries on all the eleven inhabited worlds, had been Exotic-endowed. In the small space of the carrel Ian and I faced him; the two of us standing, Padma seated in the serenity of his blue robe and unchanging facial expression. I told him what we needed with Pel, and he shook his head.

"Tom," he said, "you must already know that we who study the Exotic sciences never force anyone or anything. Not for moral reasons alone; but because using force would damage our ability to do the sensitive work we've dedicated our lives to doing. That's why we hire mercenaries to fight for us, and Cetan lawyers to handle our off-world business contracts. I am the last person on this world to make Pel talk."

"Don't you feel any responsibility to the innocent people of this city?" I said. "To the lives that will be lost if he doesn't?"

"Emotionally, yes," Padma said, softly. "But there are practical limits to the responsibility of personal inaction. If I were to concern myself with all possible pain consequent upon the least, single action of mine, I would have to spend my life like a statue. I was not responsible for Kensie's death; and I am not responsible for finding his killers. Without such a responsibility I can't violate the most basic prohibition of my life's rules."

"You knew Kensie," I said. "Don't you owe anything to him? And don't you owe anything to the same Ste. Marie people you sent an armed expedition to help?"

"We make it a point to give, rather than take," Padma said, "just to avoid debts like that which could force us into doing what we shouldn't do. No, Tom. The Exotics and I have no obligation to your people, or even to Kensie."

"—And to the Dorsai?" asked Ian, behind me.

I had almost forgotten he was there, I had been concentrating so hard on Padma. Certainly, I had not expected Ian to speak. The sound of his deep voice was like a heavy bell tolling in the small room; and for the first time Padma's face changed.

"The Dorsai . . ." he echoed. "Yes, the time is coming when there will be neither Exotics nor Dorsai, in the end when the final development is achieved. But we Exotics have always counted on our work as a step on the way to that end; and the Dorsai helped us up our step. Possibly, if things had gone otherwise, the Dorsai might have never been; and we would still be where we are now. But things went as they have; and our thread has been tangled with the Dorsai thread from the time your many-times removed grandfather Cletus Grahame first freed all the younger worlds from the politics of Earth. . . ."

He stood up.

"I'll force no one," he said. "But I will offer Pel my help to find peace with himself, if he can; and if he finds such peace, then maybe he will want to tell you willingly what you want to know."

Padma, Ian and I went back to the police station where I had left Pel and Moro locked up. We let Moro out, and closed the door upon the three of us with Pel. He sat in a chair, looking at us, pale, pinch-faced and composed.

"So you brought the Exotic, did you, Tom?" he said to me. "What's it going to be? Some kind of hypnosis?"

"No, Pel," said Padma softly, pacing across the room to him as Ian and I sat down to wait. "I would not deal in hypnosis, particularly without the consent of the one to be hypnotized."

"Well, you sure as hell haven't got my consent!" said Pel.

Padma had reached him now and was standing over him. Pel looked up into the calm face above the blue robe.

"But try if you like." Pel said, "I don't hypnotize easily."

"No," said Padma. "I've said I would not hypnotize anyone;

but in any case, neither your nor anyone else can be hypnotized without his or her innate consent. All things between individuals are done by consent. The prisoner consents to his captivity as the patient consents to his surgery—the difference is only in degree and pattern. The great, blind mass that is humanity in general is like an amoebic animal. It exists by internal laws that cohere its body and its actions. Those internal laws are based upon conscious and unconscious, mutual consents of its atoms—ourselves—to work with each other and cooperate. Peace and satisfaction come to each of us in proportion to our success in such cooperation, in the forward-searching movement of the humanity-creature as a whole. Nonconsent and noncooperation work against the grain. Pain and self-hate result from friction when we fight against our natural desire to cooperate . . ."

His voice went on. Gently but compellingly he said a great deal more, and I understood all at the time; but beyond what I have quoted so far—and those first few sentences stay printed-clear in my memory—I do not recall another specific word. I do not know to this day what happened. Perhaps I half-dozed without realizing I was dozing. At any rate, time passed; and when I reached a point where the memory record took up again, he was leaving and Pel had altered.

"I can talk to you some more, can't I?" Pel said as the Outbond rose to leave. Pel's voice had become clear-toned and strangely young-sounding. "I don't mean now. I mean, there'll be other times?"

"I'm afraid not," Padma said. "I'll have to leave Ste. Marie shortly. My work takes me back to my own world and then on to one of the Friendly planets to meet someone and wind up what began here. But you don't need me to talk to. You created your own insights as we talked, and you can go on doing that by yourself. Goodby, Pel."

"Goodby," said Pel. He watched Padma leave. When he

looked at me again his face, like his voice, was clear and younger than I had seen it in years. "Did you hear all that, Tom?"

"I think so . . ." I said; because already the memory was beginning to slip away from me. I could feel the import of what Padma had said to Pel, but without being able to give it exact shape, it was as if I had intercepted a message that had turned out to be not for me, and so my mental machinery had already begun to cancel it out. I got up and went over to Pel. "You'll help us find those assassins, now?"

"Yes," he said. "Of course I will."

He was able to give us a list of five places that were possible hiding places for the three we hunted. He provided exact directions for finding each one.

"Now," I said to Ian, when Pel was through, "we need those Hunter Teams of yours that were pulled off."

"We have Hunters," said Ian. "Those officers who are Dorsai are still with us; and there are Hunters among them."

He stepped to the phone unit on the desk in the room and put a call in to Charley ap Morgan, at Expeditionary Headquarters. When Charley answered, Ian gave him the five locations Pel had supplied us.

"Now," he said to me as he turned away from the phone. "We'll go back to my office."

"I want to come," said Pel. Ian looked at him for a long moment, then nodded, without changing expression.

"You can come," he said.

When we got back to the Expeditionary Headquarters building, the rooms and corridors there seemed even more aswarm with officers. As Ian had said, they were mostly Dorsai. But I saw some among them who might not have been. Apparently Ian commanded his own loyalty, or perhaps it was the Dorsai concept that commanded its own loyalty to whoever was commanding officer. We went to his office; and, sitting there, waited while the reports began to come in.

The first three locations to be checked out by the officer Hunter Teams drew blanks. The fourth showed evidence of having been used within the last twenty-four hours, although it was empty now. The last location to be checked also drew blank.

The Hunter Teams concentrated on the fourth location and began to work outward from it, hoping to cross sign of a trail away from it. I checked the clock figures on my wrist unit. It was now nearing one A.M. in the morning, local time; and the six hour deadline of the enlisted mercenaries was due to expire in forty-seven minutes. In the office where I waited with Ian, Pel, Charley ap Morgan, and another senior Dorsai officer, the air was thick with the tension of waiting. Ian and the two other Dorsai sat still; even Pel sat still. I was the one who fidgeted and paced, as the time continued to run out.

The phone on Ian's desk flashed its visual signal light. Ian reached out to punch it on.

"Yes?" he said.

"Hunter Team Three," said a voice from the desk. "We have clear sign and are following now. Suggest you join us, sir."

"Thank you. Coming," said Ian.

We went, Ian, Charley, Pel and myself, in an Expedition Command Car. It was an eerie ride through the patrolled and deserted streets of my city. Ian's Hunter Team Three was ahead of us and led us to an apartment hotel on the upper north side of the city, in the oldest section.

The building had been built of poured cement faced with Castlemane granite. Inside, the corridors were old-fashionedly narrow and close-feeling, with dark, thick carpeting and metal walls in imitation oak woodgrain. The soundproofing was good, however. We mounted to the seventh story and moved down the hall to suite number 415 without hearing any sound other than those we made, ourselves.

"Here," finally said the leader of the Hunter Team, a lean,

gnarled Dorsai Senior Commandant in his late fifties. He gestured to the door of 415. "All three of them."

"Ian," said Charley ap Morgan, glancing at his wrist unit.
"The enlisted men start moving into the city in six minutes.
You could go meet them to say we've found the assassins. The
others and I—"

"No," said Ian. "We can't say we've found them until we see
them and identify them positively." He stepped up to one side
of the door; and, reaching out an arm, touched the door annunciator stud.

There was no response. Above the door, the half-meter
square annunciator screen stayed brown and blank.

Ian pressed the button again.

Again we waited, and there was no response.

Ian pressed the stud. Holding it down, so that his voice would
go with the sound of its announcing chimes to the ears of those
within, he spoke.

"This is Commander Ian Graeme," he said. "Blauvain is now
under martial law; and you are under arrest in connection with
the assassination of Field Commander Kensie Graeme. If necessary, we can cut our way in to you. However, I'm concerned
that Field Commander Graeme's reputation be kept free of crit-
icism in the matter of determining responsibility for his death.
So I'm offering you the chance to come and surrender."

He released the stud and stopped talking. There was a long
pause. Then a voice spoke from the annunciator grille below
the screen, although the screen itself remained blank.

"Go to hell, Graeme," said the voice. "We got your brother;
and if you try to blast your way in here, we'll get you, too."

"My advice to you," said Ian—his voice was cold, distant,
and impersonal, as if this was something he did every day, "is
to surrender."

"You guarantee our safety if we do?"

"No," said Ian. "I only guarantee that I will see that Field

Commander Graeme's reputation is not adversely affected by the way you're handled."

There was no immediate answer from the screen. Behind Ian, Charley looked again at his wrist unit.

"They're playing for time," he said. "But why? What good will that do them?"

"They're fanatics," said Pel, softly. "Just as much fanatics as the Friendly soldiers were, only for the Blue Front instead of for some puritan form of religion. Those three in there don't expect to get out of this alive. They're only trying to set a higher price on their own deaths—get something more for their dying."

Charley ap Morgan's wrist unit chimed.

"Time's up," he said to Ian. "The enlisted men are moving into the suburbs of Blauvain now, to begin their search."

Ian reached out and pushed the annunciator stud again, holding it down as he spoke to the men inside.

"Are you coming out?"

"Why should we?" answered the voice that had spoken the first time. "Give us a reason."

"I'll come in and talk to you if you like," said Ian.

"No—" began Pel out loud. I gripped his arm, and he turned on me, whispering. "Tom, tell him not to go in! That's what they want."

"Stay here," I said.

I pushed forward until Charley ap Morgan put out an arm to stop me. I spoke across that arm to Ian.

"Ian," I said, in a voice safely low enough so that the door annunciator would not pick it up. "Pel says—"

"Maybe that's a good idea," said the voice from the annunciator. "That's right, why don't you come on in, Graeme? Leave your weapons outside."

"Tom," said Ian, without looking either at me or Charley ap Morgan, "Stay back. Keep him back, Charley."

"Yes sir," said Charley. He looked into my face, eye to eye with me. "Stay out of this, Tom. Back up."

Ian stepped forward to stand square in front of the door, where a beam coming through it could go through him as well. He was taking off his sidearm as he went. He dropped it to the floor, in full sight of the screen, through the blankness of which those inside would be looking out.

"I'm unarmed," he said.

"Of that sidepiece, you are," said the annunciator. "Do you think we're going to take your word for the rest of you? Strip."

Without hesitation, Ian unsealed his uniform jacket and began to take off his clothes. In a moment or two, he stood naked in the hallway; but if the men in the suite had thought to gain some sort of moral advantage over him because of that, they were disappointed.

Stripped, he looked—like an athlete—larger and more impressive than he had, clothed. He towered over us all in the hall, even over the other Dorsai there; and with his darkly tanned skin under the lights he seemed like a massive figure carved in oak.

"I'm waiting," he said, after a moment, calmly.

"All right," said the voice from the annunciator. "Come on in."

He moved forward. The door unlatched and slid aside before him. He passed through and it closed behind him. For a moment we were left with no sound or word from him or the suite; then, unexpectedly, the screen lit up. We found ourselves looking over and past Ian's bare shoulders at a room in which three men, each armed with a rifle and a pair of sidearms, sat facing him. They gave no sign of knowing that he had turned on the annunciator screen, the controls of which would be hidden behind him, now that he stood inside the door, facing the room.

The center one of the three seated men laughed. He was the big, black-bearded man I had found vaguely familiar when I saw

the solidigraphs of the three of them in Ian's office; and I recognized him now. He was a professional wrestler. He had been
arraigned on assault charges four years ago, but lack of testimony
against him had caused the charges to be dismissed. He was not
as tall as Ian, but much heavier of body; and it was his voice we
had been hearing, because now we heard it again as his lips
moved on the screen.

"Well, well, Commander," he said. "Just what we needed—
a visit from you. Now we can rack up a score of two Dorsai
Commanders before your soldiers carry what's left of us off to
the morgue; and Ste. Marie can see that even you people can
be handled by the Blue Front."

We could not see Ian's face; but he said nothing and apparently his lack of reaction was irritating to the big assassin, because he dropped his cheerful tone and leaned forward in his
chair.

"Don't you understand, Graeme?" he said. "We've lived and
died for the Blue Front, all three of us—for the one political
party with the strength and guts to save our world. We're dead
men no matter what we do. Did you think we don't know that?
You think we don't know what would happen to us if we were
idiots enough to surrender the way you said? Your men would
tear us apart; and if there was anything left of us after that, the
government's law would try us and then shoot us. We only let
you in here so that we could lay you out like your twin brother,
before we were laid out ourselves. Don't you follow me, man?
You walked into our hands here like a fly into a trap, never
realizing."

"I realized," said Ian.

The big man scowled at him and the muzzle of the heat rifle
he held in one thick hand, came up.

"What do you mean?" he demanded. "Whatever you think
you've got up your sleeve isn't going to save you. Why would
you come in here, knowing what we'd do?"

"The Dorsai are professional soldiers," said Ian's voice, calmly. "We live and survive by our reputation. Without that reputation none of us could earn our living. And the reputation of the Dorsai in general is that sum of the reputations of its individual men and women. So Field Commander Kensie Graeme's professional reputation is a thing of value, to be guarded even after his death. I came in for that reason."

The big man's eyes narrowed. He was doing all the talking and his two companions seemed content to leave it that way.

"A reputation's worth dying for?" he said.

"I've been ready to die for mine for eighteen years," said Ian's voice, quietly. "Today's no different than yesterday."

"And you came in here—" the big man's voice broke off on a snort. "I don't believe it. Watch him, you two!"

"Believe or not," said Ian. "I came in here, just as I told you, to see that the professional reputation of Field Commander Graeme was protected from events which might tarnish it. You'll notice—" his head moved slightly as if indicating something behind him and out of our sight, "I've turned on your annunciator screen, so that outside the door they can see what's going on in here."

The eyes of the three men jerked upwards to stare at the screen inside the suite, somewhere over Ian's head. There was a blur of motion that was Ian's tanned body flying through the air, a sound of something smashing and the screen went blank again.

We outside were left blind once more, standing in the hall-way, staring at the unresponsive screen and door. Pel, who had stepped up next to me, moved toward the door itself.

"Stay!" snapped Charley.

The single sharp tone was like a command given to some domestic beast. Pel flinched at the tone, but stopped—and in that moment the door before us disintegrated to the roar of an explosion in the room.

"Come on!" I yelled, and flung myself through the now-open doorway.

It was like diving into a centrifuge filled with whirling bodies. I ducked to avoid the flying form of one of the men I had seen in the screen, but his leg slammed my head, and I went reeling, half-dazed and disoriented, into the very heart of the tumult. It was all a blur of action. I had a scrambled impression of explosions, of fire-beams lancing around me—and somehow in the midst of it all, the towering, brown body of Ian moving with the certainty and deadliness of a panther. All those he touched went down; and all who went down, stayed down.

Then it was over. I steadied myself with one hand against a half-burned wall and realized that only Ian and myself were on our feet in that room. Not one of the other Dorsai had followed me in. On the floor, the three assassins lay still. One had his neck broken. Across the room a second man lay obviously dead, but with no obvious sign of the damage that had ended his life. The big man, the ex-wrestler, had the right side of his forehead crushed in, as if by a club.

Looking up from the three bodies, I saw I was now alone in the room. I turned back into the corridor, and found there only Pel and Charley. Ian and the other Dorsai were already gone.

"Where's Ian?" I asked Charley. My voice came out thickly, like the voice of a slightly drunken man.

"Leave him alone," said Charley. "You don't need him, now. Those are the assassins there; and the enlisted men have already been notified and pulled back from their search of Blauvain. What more is needed?"

I pulled myself together; and remembered I was a policeman.

"I've got to know exactly what happened," I said. "I've got to know if it was self-defense, or . . ."

The words died on my tongue. To accuse a naked man of anything else in the death of three heavily armed individuals who had threatened his life, as I had just heard them do over the annunciator, was ridiculous.

"No," said Charley. "This was done during a period of martial law in Blauvain. Your office will receive a report from our command about it; but actually it's not even something within your authority."

Some of the tension that had been in him earlier seemed to leak out of him, then. He half-smiled and became more like the friendly officer I had known before Kensie's death.

"But that martial law is about to be withdrawn," he said. "Maybe you'll want to get on the phone and start getting your own people out here to tidy up the details."

—And he stood aside to let me go.

One day later, and the professional soldiers of the Exotic Expeditionary Force showed their affection for Kensie in a different fashion.

His body had been laid in state for a public review in the open, main floor lobby of the Blauvain City Government building. Beginning in the gray dawn and through the cloudless day—the sort of hard, bright day that seems impatient with those who will not bury their dead and get on to further things—the mercenaries filed past the casket holding Kensie, visible at full length in dress uniform under the transparent cover. Each one as he passed touched the casket lightly with his fingertips, or said a word to the dead man, or both. There were over ten thousand soldiers passing one at a time. They were unarmed, in field uniforms and their line seemed endless.

But that was not the end of it. The civilians of Blauvain had formed along either side of the street down which the line of troops wound on its way to the place where Kensie lay waiting for them. The civilians had formed in the face of strict police orders against doing any such thing; and my men could not drive them away. The situation could not have offered a better opportunity for the Blue Front to cause trouble. One heat grenade tossed into that line of slowly moving, unarmed soldiers, for example . . . But nothing happened.

By the time noon came and went without incident, I was ready to make a guess why not. It was because there was something in the mood of the civilian crowd itself that forbade terrorism, here and now. Any Blue Front activists trying such a thing would have been smothered by the very civilians around them in whose name they were doing it.

Something of awe and pity, and almost of envy, seemed to be stirring the souls of the Blauvain people; those same people of mine who had huddled in their houses twenty hours before, in undiluted fear of the very men now lined up before them and moving slowly to the City Government building. Once more, as I stood on a balcony above the lobby holding the casket, I felt those winds of vast movement I had sensed first for a moment in Ian's office, the winds of those forces of which Padma had spoken to me. The Blauvain people were different today and showed the difference. Kensie's death had changed them.

Then, something more happened. As the last of the soldiers passed, Blauvain civilians began to fall in behind them, extending the line. By mid-afternoon, the last soldier had gone by and the first figure in civilian clothes passed the casket, neither touching it nor speaking to it, but pausing to look with an unusual, almost shy curiosity upon the face of the body inside, in the name of which so much might have happened.

Already, behind that one man, the line of civilians was half again as long as the line of soldiers had been.

It was nearly midnight, long past the time when it had been planned to shut the gates of the lobby, when the last of the civilians had gone and the casket could be transferred to a room at Expeditionary Headquarters from which it would be shipped back to Dorsai. This business of shipping a body home happened seldom, even in the case of mercenaries of the highest rank; but there had never been any doubt that it would happen in the case of Kensie. The enlisted men and officers of his command had contributed the extra funds necessary for the shipment.—Ian, when his time came, would undoubtedly be buried in the earth of whatever world on which he fell. Only if he happened to be at home when the time came, would that earth be soil of the Dorsai. But Kensie had been—Kensie.

"Do you know what's been suggested to me?" asked Moro, as he, Pel and I, along with several of the Expedition's senior officers—Charley ap Morgan among them—stood watching Kensie's casket being brought into the room at Expedition HQ. "There's a proposal to get the city government to put up a statue of him, here in Blauvain. A statue of Kensie."

Neither Pel nor I answered. We stood watching the placing of the casket. For all its massive appearance, four men handled it and the body within easily. The apparently thick metal of its sides were actually hollow to reduce shipping weight. The soldiers settled it, took off the transparent weather cover and carried it out. The body of Kensie lay alone, uncovered; the profile of his face, seen from where we stood, quiet and still against the light pink cloth of the casket's lining. The senior officers who were with us and who had not been in the line of soldiers filing through the lobby, now began to go into the room, one at a time to stand for a second at the casket before coming out again.

"It's what we never had on Ste. Marie," said Pel, after a long moment. He was a different man since Padma had talked to him. "A leader. Someone to love and follow. Now that our people have seen there is such a thing, they want something like it for themselves."

He looked up at Charley ap Morgan, who was just coming back out of the room.

"You Dorsai changed us," Pel said.

"Did we?" said Charley, stopping. "How do you feel about Ian now, Pel?"

"Ian?" Pel frowned. "We're talking about Kensie. Ian's just—what he always was."

"What you all never understood," said Charley, looking from one to the other of us.

"Ian's a good man," said Pel. "I don't argue with that. But there'll never be another Kensie."

"There'll never be another Ian," said Charley. "He and Kensie made up one person. That's what none of you ever understood. Now half of Ian is gone, into the grave."

Pel shook his head slowly.

"I'm sorry," he said. "I can't believe that. I can't believe Ian ever needed anyone—even Kensie. He's never risked anything, so how could he lose anything? After Kensie's death he did nothing but sit on his spine here insisting that he couldn't risk Kensie's reputation by doing anything—until events forced his hand. That's not the action of a man who's lost the better half of himself."

"I didn't say better half," said Charley. "I only said half—and just half is enough. Stop and try to feel for a moment what it would be like. Stop for a second and feel how it would be if you were amputated down the middle—if the life that was closest to you was wrenched away, shot down in the street by a handful of self-deluded, crackpot revolutionaries from a world you'd come to rescue. Suppose it was like that for you, how would you feel?"

Pel had gone a little pale as Charley talked. When he answered his voice had a slight echo of the difference and youngness it had had after Padma had talked to him.

"I guess . . ." he said very slowly, and ran off into silence.

"Yes?" said Charley. "Now you're beginning to understand, to feel as Ian feels. Suppose you feel like this and just outside the city where the assassins of your brother are hiding there are six battalions of seasoned soldiers who can turn that same city—

who can hardly be held back from turning that city—into an-other Rochmont, at one word from you. Tell me, is it easy, or is it hard, not to say that one word that will turn them loose?"

"It would be . . ." the words seemed dragged from Pel, "hard . . ."

"Yes," said Charley, grimly, "as it was hard for Ian."

"Then why did he do it?" demanded Pel.

"He told you why," said Charley. "He did it to protect his brother's military reputation, so that not even after his death should Kensie Graeme's name be an excuse for anything but the highest and best of military conduct."

"But Kensie was dead. He couldn't hurt his own reputation!"

"His troops could," said Charley. "His troops wanted someone to pay for Kensie's death. They wanted to leave a monument to Kensie and their grief for him, as long-lasting a monument as Rochmont has been to Jacques Chrétian. There was only one way to satisfy them, and that was if Ian himself acted for them— as their agent—in dealing with the assassins. Because nobody could deny that Kensie's brother had the greatest right of all to represent all those who had lost with Kensie's death."

"You're talking about the fact that Ian killed the men, per-sonally," said Moro. "But there was no way he could know he'd come face to face—"

He stopped, halted by the thin, faint smile on Charley's face.

"Ian was our Battle Op, our strategist," said Charley. "Just as Kensie was Field Commander, our tactician. Do you think that a strategist of Ian's ability couldn't lay a plan that would bring him face to face, alone, with the assassins once they were lo-cated?"

"What if they hadn't been located?" I asked. "What if I hadn't found out about Pel, and Pel hadn't told us what he knew?"

Charley shook his head.

"I don't know," he said. "Somehow Ian must have known this way would work—or he would have done it differently. For some reason he counted on help from you, Tom."

"Me!" I said. "What makes you say that?"

"He told me so." Charley looked at me strangely. "You know, many people thought that because they didn't understand Ian, that Ian didn't understand them. Actually, he understands other people unusually well. I think he saw something in you, Tom, he could rely on. And he was right, wasn't he?"

Once more, the winds I had felt—of the forces of which Padma had spoken, blew through me, chilling and enlightening me. Ian had felt those winds as well as I had—and understood them better. I could see the inevitability of it now. There had been only one pull on the many threads entangled in the fabric of events here; and that pull had been through me to Ian.

"When he went to that suite where the assassins were holed up," said Charley, "he intended to go in to them alone, and unarmed. And when he killed them with his bare hands, he did what every man in the Expeditionary force wanted to do. So, when that was done, the anger of the troops was lightning-rodded. Through Ian, they all had their revenge; and then they were free. Free just to mourn for Kensie as they're doing today. So Blauvain escaped; and the Dorsai reputation has escaped stain, and the state of affairs between the inhabited worlds hasn't been upset by an incident here on Ste. Marie that could make enemie. out of worlds, like the Exotic and the Dorsai, and Ste. Marie, who should all be friends."

He stopped talking. It had been a long speech for Charley; and none of us could think of anything to say. The last of the senior officers, all except Ian, had gone past us now, in and out of the room, and the casket was alone. Then Pel spoke.

"I'm sorry," he said, and he sounded sorry. "But even if what you say is all true, it only proves what I always said about Ian. Kensie had two mens' feelings, but Ian hasn't any. He's ice and water with no blood in him. He couldn't bleed if he wanted to. Don't tell me any man torn apart emotionally by his twin brother's death could sit down and plan to handle a situation so cold-bloodedly and efficiently."

"People don't always bleed on the outside where you can see—" Charley broke off, turning his head.

We looked where he was looking, down the corridor behind us, and saw Ian coming, tall and alone. He strode up to us, nodded briefly at us, and went past into the room. We saw him walk to the side of the casket.

He did not speak to Kensie, or touch the casket gently as the soldiers passing through the lobby had done. Instead he closed his big hands, those hands that had killed three armed men, almost casually on the edge of it, and looked down into the face of his dead brother.

Twin face gazed to twin face, the living and the dead. Under the lights of the room, with the motionless towering figure of Ian, it was as if both were living, or both were dead—so little difference there was to be seen between them. Only, Kensie's eyes were closed and Ian's opened; Kensie slept while Ian waked. And the oneness of the two of them was so solid and evident a thing, there in that room, that it stopped the breath in my chest.

For perhaps a minute or two Ian stood without moving. His face did not change. Then he lifted his gaze, let go of the casket and turned about. He came walking toward us, out of the room, his hands at his sides, the fingers curled into his palms.

"Gentlemen," he said, nodding to us as he passed, and went down the corridor until a turn in it took him out of sight.

Charley left us and went softly back into the room. He stood a moment there, then turned and called to us.

"Pel," he said, "come here."

Pel came; and the rest of us after him.

"I told you," Charley said to Pel, "some people don't bleed on the outside where you can see it."

He moved away from the casket and we looked at it. On its edge were the two areas where Ian had laid hold of it with his hands while he stood looking down at his dead brother. There was no mistaking the places, for at both of them, the hollow metal side had been bent in on itself and crushed with the strength of a grip that was hard to imagine. Below the crushed area, the cloth lining of the casket was also crumpled and rent; and where each fingertip had pressed, the fabric was torn and marked with a dark stain of blood.

Epilogue

". . . So," said the third Amanda, at last, "you see how it really was."

Hal Mayne nodded. He lifted his head suddenly to see her staring penetratingly at him.

"Or," she said, "do you see something more than I see, even in this?"

He opened his mouth to deny that, and found he could not.

"Maybe," he said. Loneliness and a need to explain himself swept through him without warning, like a heavy tide. "You've got to understand I'm a poet. I . . . I handle things all the time I don't understand. I'm almost like someone in total darkness, feeling things, sensing things, but never seeing shapes I can describe to other people."

She breathed slowly, in and out.

"So," she said, "there was something more to this interest of yours in the ap Morgans and the Graemes, all along."

"Yes . . . no!" he said, almost explosively. "You still don't understand. I ca..'t prove anything, but I can feel . . . connections."

His hands moved, reached out almost as if by their own wills, to grasp at the empty air in front of him.

"Connections," he said, "between the past and the present. Between Cletus and Donal and many others, not related at all. Connections between you and the other two Amandas, and between the ap Morgans and the Graemes—and between all these things and the movement of the Splinter Culture cross-breeds—the Others, as they're calling themselves now—and the rest of the human race on all the worlds. I'm fumbling in the dark, but I'm getting there . . . I can feel myself getting there!"

She had relaxed. She still watched him, but no longer accusingly.

"So that's why you have to head back now, to Earth and the Final Encyclopedia," she said.

"Yes." He looked at her starkly. "I had to leave to save my life. But now, I have to go back. Everything on Coby, on Harmony, even everything here, keeps pointing me back there."

He reached for her hand. She let him take it, but without returning the pressure of his fingers.

"Amanda," he said urgently. "Come back with me. I don't mean just because I want you with me. I mean because that's where all things are finally coming together. That's where it all ends—or starts. You should be there—just as I have to be there. Amanda, come with me."

She sat still for a moment, then her eyes went past him. Gently, she withdrew her hand from his.

"If you're right, then I will come," she said. "But not now, Hal. Not now. In my own good time."